C000258082

Rivers Run Red
Book One of the Morhudrim Cycle
by A D Green
1st Edition - October 2019
Release Version 1v10 10th August 2022

ASIN : 1700420550
ISBN: 9781700420558

Cover artwork by A D Green/MidJourney

Cover design by vikncharlie

Map artwork by A D Green

Edited by M. C. Green, BSc and Graduate Diploma in Arts (English)

For Jordan Green
Who inspired me to start writing and telling my stories – Thank you

Contents

Map of The Rivers Region

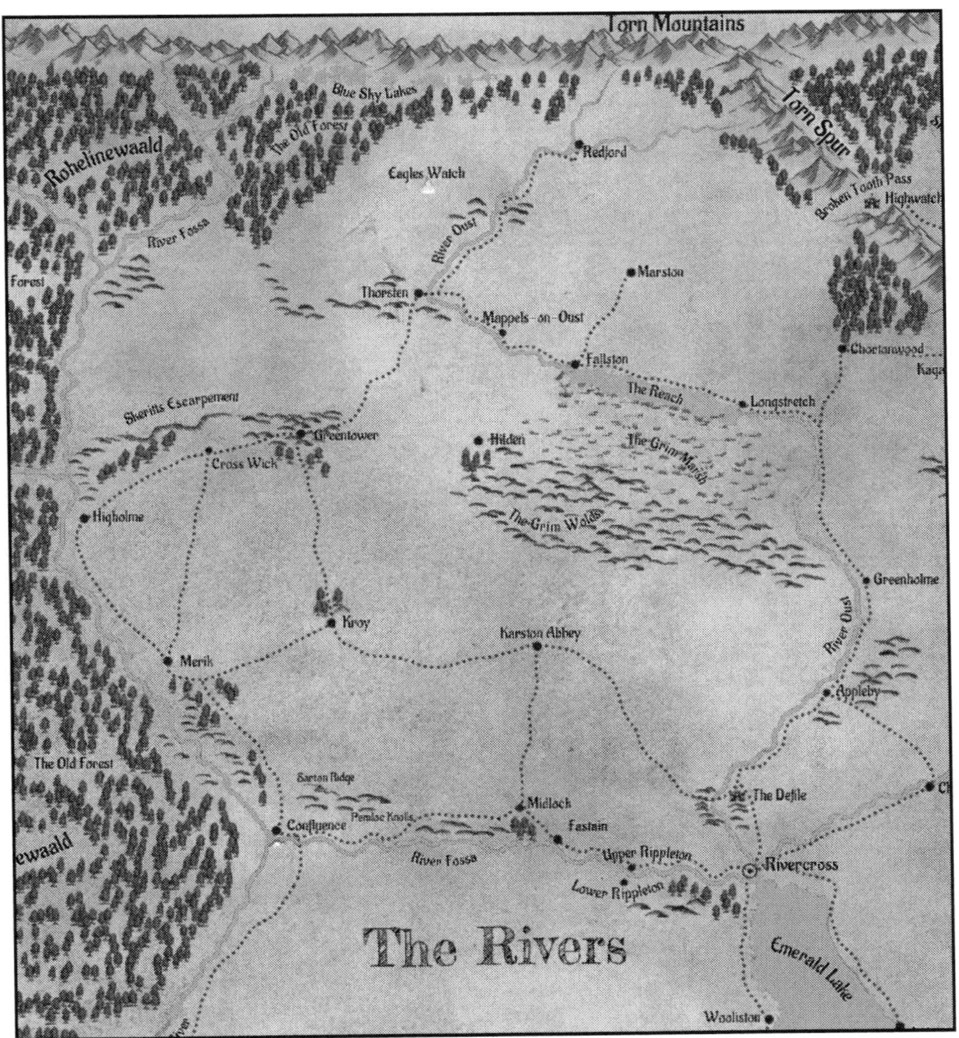

When the Forgotten One returns, then shall the rivers run red and the shadows fall. And where the darkness resides there too shall chaos reign and all shall end, lest the light that was lost be found again.

Excerpt from the Gnarhlson Prophecies

Prologue

1006 cycle of the 4th Age
3rd Cycle of Ankor (The Wane - Autumn)
Ick-Báal Mountains, Norde-Targkish

The Traveller became motionless as he crested the rise, his hooded eyes scouring the way ahead. A hard wind beat against him, tearing at his cloak and sending ice crystals whipping and scratching at his face in warning.

Before him, loomed the Ick-Báal Mountains, immense and timeless. He traced their jagged peaks until he found the cropped giant, Furous then tracked lower, past the mountain's slopes and the grey mantle of trees gathered about its ankles. His squinted gaze settled over his destination; the fractured outline of a city, its broken spires, all but one, stretching skeletal fingers to the sky.

Tal'Draysil.

The name resonated. Like a low struck chord it hummed through his body. A glance at the enlarged sun told him that he'd reach the ruins before nightfall. His eyes travelled to the silver disk, hanging in miniature counterpoint to the sun, reflecting its light. It was the smallest of Nu's tri-moons and it set his mind wandering.

'The three eyes' the urak named the moons; celestial bodies from which their many gods watched over them from the void. Whilst to the humans they were 'the Trinity', home to each of their three deities. Only through them could their souls pass and reach the One.

With a flicker of a smile, the Traveller took a swig from his waterskin. The taste was sharp and fresh in his mouth. Then his dark eyes returned once again to their study of the ruined city. It had been many years since his last visit but Tal'Draysil looked just as he remembered it. He shivered as an uneasiness settled over him that had little to do with the cold. Stoppering the water skin, he pulled his cloak tight and set off once more, pale footprints trudging out behind him in the snow.

As the sun fled west, dragging the daylight with it, the Traveller reached the decaying walls of Tal'Draysil and he set up camp outside its bounds. What needed doing was best done in the hard light of day and he was unwilling to accept the relative shelter the ancient city offered. It held too many ghosts and no comfort for him.

* * *

Morning's first light arrived casting Tal'Draysil in half shadows. Entering the ruins through a cracked and broken gatehouse, the Traveller wandered streets that had seen no life in a millennium. Only their kind came to this place now and only to check its prison lay undisturbed and its warding held strong.

The Traveller stopped. He was stood at the ruin's centre, in a large square surrounded by walls of broken stone. And at its heart, a slim tower, stark in its completeness, rising like a spear.

Reaching up, the Traveller lowered his hood to reveal the sleek head of an ilf. Red and gold leaf skin, edged in blue, moulded smoothly to the contours of his humanlike face. Thick vine-like tresses sprang from his crown and were gathered and tied at his nape to fall down his back. The dark orbs of his eyes surveyed the square. Something was off. His memory picked out the change. The scattered remains of a beast, little more than a lump, hardly distinguishable in the hard frost from the surrounding debris.

Closing his eyes, he centred himself and focused on the subtle shifting of energies around him. Life was everywhere, from hardy lichen on the walls to moss lying in the damp sunless corners of the ruins. But it was the energy surrounding the tower that he sought. It was strong, standing like a beacon against the pale backdrop of surrounding life.

And it was changed.

The weavings, cast so long ago, swirled and eddied still, but they were different. Like a thread picked and unravelled from a garment, there was a hole in the weave; a scar that breached the swirling ward.

Walking to the tower, the ilf examined it. The hole was subtle, the energy around it cunningly reworked so that the warding appeared at first glance to be whole. How it was done intrigued him. It should have been impossible to rework a living ward without collapsing the entire construct. This was precise and surgical in its execution. It fascinated his intellect. This was beyond his art.

The intervention, the reworking of part of the ward was impressive too for its audacity. Had it been removed incorrectly, or broken, the ward would have collapsed and the subsequent cascading release of energy would have been catastrophic. No trace of Tal'Draysil would have remained and what lay within the tower would have been no more.

That Tal'Draysil and the tower still stood spoke for itself. Closer inspection of the breach offered no further clue. It was so well worked he couldn't discern where the weaves had been changed or whether it was wrought from inside or outside the warding.

The shadows were short and the sun was at its zenith. He'd been stood long in contemplation. How it was done would have to wait. Of more import was what lay within. He already knew the answer but he sat anyway. With a thought, he conjured a ball of light in his hand and sent it through the breach.

Inside, the tower was dark and empty but for a staircase that spiralled up the interior wall. The ball of light rose until eventually, it reached a platform. It was bathed in light that streamed in from a doorway. The door itself lay smashed and broken on the floor, its frame charred black. The ball hovered momentarily, the ilf taking in the scene before moving through the entrance to the room beyond.

There were no windows yet, through some artifice, light flooded the room emanating from the ceiling above. Its stone floor was etched in gold runes which surrounded four iron posts that seemed to grow from the floor. Blackened chains hung broken from the posts. Although expected the ilf still found the scene disturbing. The Tainted was gone. Da'Mari and the other Nu'Rakauma would need to know. It was too soon.

The ball of light vanished with a blink.

The ilf stood, worry lining his face. It was a long journey back to Da'Mari and time was of the essence. Weighing his need, and deciding it was great enough, he started etching a rune onto the frosted cobbles of the square with his staff. It was a long, laborious process. The sun had about vanished behind the western mountains by the time he'd finished.

He felt a rippling of energy in the aether and, alarmed, turned to face the tower. A shadow detached itself from its girth. Its energies had been hidden by the tower's warding, else he would have sensed it as soon as he entered Tal'Draysil.

The shadow was large, eight feet or more in height, and vaguely humanoid in shape. Bathed in a dark, swirling mist that clung to its frame, it was indistinct in form but hinted at long limbs and an elongated, spiked head, beneath its black tendrils. Morhudrim. Fear pervaded, even as a weight clouded his mind, pressing in on him. The pressure grew, forcing him to his knees as the shadow glided forward. Dark fingers of smoke snaked out from the Tainted, reaching.

Incanting, he whispered a mantra and the pressure against his mind eased enough that he could regain his feet. Stepping onto the rune, he thumped his staff down in its centre and, with a thought, triggered sigils etched along its length. Energy flared as the rune on the ground blazed into life, even as the shadow fingers reached him. Latching onto his face, they sought egress through mouth and eyes. Pain ripped through him, like nails driven into flesh. His mantra almost failed but he held it, just. Convulsing, gasping for breath, as the dark tendrils choked him, a light suddenly flared. It forced the shadow back, screeching.

With a tearing sound, the air inside the rune parted. With his last conscious effort, the ilf tipped forward, collapsing through the portal, which zipped shut behind him before disappearing with a snap.

The Morhudrim screamed its rage, the sound echoing in the amphitheatre of broken stone.

Chapter 1 : The Hunt

1017 cycle of the 4th Age
3rd Cycle of Ankor (The Wane - Autumn)
The Old Forest, The Rivers

Nihm hunted.

Crouching low, she examined the forest floor. The crush of leaf and moss was an arcane language, signs decipherable with study. It told Nihm she was close. Drawing up, she was moving again, feet gliding silently.

The wind rustled the trees and weak shafts of sunlight broke through in places, relieving the dusky gloom. Nihm felt the familiar surge in her veins. She knew the hunt, its dangers as well as the thrill. She had to stay focused. Her quarry was near.

The ground rose gently, shrubs lining its crest where an old kaorak tree had fallen leaving a break in the canopy. Moving up the slope, she smelt the air and listened to the life of the forest. A White-crown warbled high in the treetops and was answered.

Nihm scanned ahead, tracking, following the tell-tale up the rise; there wasn't much, just bent leaf and bruised moss to show the way. Nearing the top, she slid into the shadow of the fallen giant. Peeking over the kaorak's trunk into the dell below, Nihm glimpsed a figure, dark hooded and cloaked. He sat on a stump, silent and unmoving, with a large black wolfdog at his feet. Nihm was downwind but even so, the wolfdog's head came up, ears erect.

Ducking back down, Nihm unlimbered her bow, smoothly fitting an arrow, a puncher with a blunt head. It didn't fly well and was only accurate over a short distance but the man was no use to her dead. She glanced again over the trunk before standing, bracing and drawing her bowstring back against her cheek, all in one smooth practised motion. As Nihm sighted down the shaft, she took a breath and held it before releasing arrow and breath together.

The arrow flew true. With a thump, it smacked solidly into the man's back. It bounced, falling away and the figure toppled forward with a loud clatter onto the ground. Too loud, the noise was off. Nihm stared into the hollow. The wolfdog looked over at the fallen man but otherwise didn't move. Something was wrong.

Leaning against the dead tree, she considered the scene. In a heartbeat, a hand shot up, gripped Nihm's tunic, and yanked her unceremoniously over the fallen giant. Crying out, she was launched into the air and over, her back crushing a small shrub as she landed heavily. Lying winded, a black-bearded face loomed above her.

"Dead!" said the face before disappearing from view.

Groaning, Nihm rolled off the shrub and onto her hands and knees. She glanced at the retreating back of her father, Darion, as he ambled into the dell. Her Da was a big man but despite this moved with an easy grace and sureness.

"Didn't have ta throw me so hard Da," Nihm moaned rising gingerly. Hands-on hips, she stretched her aching back out. A line of fire seared her lower back where the shrub had crushed her pack against her. Something hard inside had scored her through her leather vest.

"Stop ya whining girl. I gave ya a soft landing didn' I?" Darion chuckled, then turned and caught her scowling face. "More an you deserve lass," he strolled up to the prone figure on the ground, the wolfdog watching him all the way, tongue lolling.

"Good girl, Bindu." He ruffled the wolfdog's ears. Bindu nudged a nose under his hand. "Go on away with you," he growled and Bindu raced off towards Nihm, tail wagging.

Darion deftly removed the cloak and overcoat from the fallen man, revealing a bunch of bound sticks cleverly tied to give a frame for the hanging. He bent and rummaged among the bundle and pulled a flat pan out. He ran a finger over its base and felt the tiny knuckle where the flathead had struck. He smiled briefly before painting a frown on his face and turning to Nihm.

"Fetch my pack." He nodded behind her at the old tree. Then sat on the stump and stared off into the forest waiting.

Nihm was angry. She'd failed. She glared at Darion's back. If look was an arrow she'd be going home alone, yet it was herself she was mad at. Then Bindu was there demanding attention. Hunkering down, Nihm threw arms around her neck breathing in her scent. Nihm loved the old dog and felt calmed.

"A lotta use you were you old rascal. Ya coulda warned me." She scratched behind Bindu's ears.

"I can't hear ya moving lass. Stop your mooning."

Scowling, Nihm let Bindu go and went to recover her bow from the forest floor. It was autumn and she brushed fallen leaves off its curved length, checking it quickly for damage. A little damp; she'd have to wipe it down before it set in and ruined her string, or worse yet her bow. Nihm walked the few paces back to the kaorak trunk and hefted her Da's pack, grunting as she hitched it over a shoulder. Picking her way carefully down to the clearing, she slung it at Darion's feet before easing off her own and laying her bow upon it.

Crouching opposite her Da, Nihm watched as he pulled tinder and flint from a pouch. She could see, as he knelt over the bundle of sticks, that it was already packed with dried leaves.

Darion mumbled as he struck the flint and a small puff of smoke trickled out of the kindling. He blew gently on it and a small flame licked out and suddenly it was a fire.

Nihm marvelled at his skill. It sometimes took her half an hour or more to get a fire started but her Da never needed more than one attempt. *"One of these turns I'll tell ya the secret to it."* He'd told her once. She was still waiting.

"We'll overnight here. Set up camp and I'll get supper," Darion said rising, "Bindu, stay."

Nihm fetched loose branches from the undergrowth, feeding the little fire to stop it guttering out. The sun had about run its course and a dusky gloom had settled by the time enough firewood had been gathered. Bindu slept near the flames, enjoying its warmth.

After unpacking the bedrolls and laying them out, Nihm took a cloth and rubbed her bow down. Satisfied, she leant on its tines and straining, deftly removed the bowstring and placed it in her belt pouch.

"Ho."

Nihm turned and watched as her Da strolled into camp. Darion settled down next to his pack, placing a neatly gutted trout and water skin on the ground. Bindu looked interested but didn't bother to get up.

That night, they dined well on fish and arrowroot and afterwards settled on their bedrolls.

"Did I do so bad? You've said nothing about my test," Nihm said.

"Test? There's no test. Only life and doin," Darion said, lying flat and closing his eyes.

"What! You told me to track and tag you," Nihm exploded. "Said you thought I was ready. How is that not a test?"

"Calm lass. Ya temper illustrates ya ill-discipline. That's why you're dead and I'm not."

"You're such an ass sometimes. Can't you just explain like a normal person?"

"Mind ya tongue, lest my mood fail me." Darion snapped, then in a more measured tone. "'Stead of venting ya bad temper see if'n ya can explain your own failing. Now, what did I ask of you?"

Nihm huffed, then considered, thinking back to earlier that morning. "Okay lass," she mimicked in a deep voice, "ya've tracked deer and hunted boar. See if'n ya can track me? Give an hour and see if ya can tag us by sunset."

There was a grunt from the bedroll. "Continue."

"Continue what? I tracked you. It was easy. I found and tagged you too if you hadn't tricked me at the end there… I'm still sore now." Nihm rubbed her back at the memory.

Darion sat up and stared at his daughter. "Ya disappoint me. There's life and doin'. Ya want me to explain?"

Nihm was silent, her anger gone as quick as it came. That one sentence cut deep. Da had never been disappointed in her before. Finally, sullenly, she muttered. "Yes."

Darion settled back down, tucked his hands behind his head and began.

"I asked ya to track me. Tagging made ya think it a game and it was and it wasnae," he said. "Life isn't just for you lass, there are no rules. If ya hunt deer and the deer smells you, it runs away. If ya hunt boar and the boar smells you maybe it runs or maybe not, maybe the boar charges. Do ya understand now?"

Nihm didn't answer but lay back on her roll and looked at the night sky through the broken canopy. It was clear and bursting with stars. One of the moons was visible, her own, Nihmrodel, taken for her naming. It was the smallest of the tri-moons. She breathed deeply, feeling the familiar connection to the moon because of it. It always calmed her. More reflective, she thought on the hunt and her Da's words.

He'd taught her in the ways of the forest for as long as she could remember. He never offered much praise, it was not his way, but she knew he thought well of her. Glimpsed his pride, even as he sought to hide it. Thinking about it now, she had thought it a game.

"I think I understand."

Darion smiled. "Good Lass, let's hear what ya think."

"I think you're not a deer and definitely not a boar," Nihm said. "It was not a test you gave or a challenge really but a lesson."

"And the lesson?"

"Hunting man is dangerous," Nihm replied.

"Good. Continue."

"A man is devious," Nihm said and Darion chuckled. "Hunting a man is difficult, unpredictable. A man lays a trail like any beast. But, if the man knows he is hunted then he knows the path the hunter follows and suddenly the man is the hunter, if he chooses. So the lesson is, know your quarry," Nihm said.

"Just so. Consider the hunted, what they are, what they have, what they could do, and prepare accordingly. A careful hunter would do well to always consider these things. Now, what mistakes did ya make?"

Nihm had already thought on her failings and was quick to answer.

"I tracked easily but… well… I wasn't tracking you so much as you were leading me," she said. "I was too quick when I found you, and careless. I should have observed rather than reacted. Then, I would see that your stick man wasn't moving. I saw your cloak and hood and Bindu lying there and saw what I wanted. I should've seen the trap or felt it."

"Why did ya not?"

"I guess I was too eager to put an arrow in your back," Nihm smirked.

"Yes, that woulda smarted by the way. Did ya think I would sit in the open and wait for ya to plink me with a puncher? At my age? Ya're excellent with the bow Nihm, but a puncher to the back of the head can kill just the same. Ya should've been suspicious." Darion lectured.

"Thinking about it now, that was a bad mistake. So did I fail my lesson?" Her Da was silent a while. Nihm was just starting to wonder if he'd reply when he did.

"Well, ya died. But no lass, as long as ya learnt the lesson it's not wasted. Just try not to learn it again in the real. As annoying as ya are I'd miss ya fierce-like."

With that, he rolled over. "Bindu guard," he growled. The wolfdog got up from the fire and padded off into the night.

* * *

It was still dark when they broke camp the next day. They chewed hardtack and ate nuts for breakfast. Nihm scavenged some ommi berries, tart at this time of year. Her Da accepted some.

"Not too many lass or ya stomach will not thank ya for them." He warned, popping a couple in his mouth with a few nuts.

They talked little as they trekked home, following old deer runs with Bindu ranging ahead. The woods were alive with bird song and once they saw deer and another time heard, in the distance, the rumbling call of a forest bear. The forest lightened as the day drew in. It wasn't long after, that they heard the soft tumble of water and, excited, Nihm raced ahead.

The mighty Fossa, thought Nihm, bursting through to a clearing on the edge of the river. Although the Fossa didn't look so mighty here, she could just about throw a stone to its far bank. Thought was enough and leaning her pack and bow against a tree, Nihm scrambled on the ground for a suitable candidate. Finding a nice smooth stone on the river's edge that fit her hand nicely, she backed up and prepared to launch it.

"No lass, that's nae a good idea," Darion said, as he broke through the undergrowth and saw Nihm gathering herself. "Ilf land, let not the touch of man sully it." He quoted the old saying.

But Nihm was committed, or so she told herself, skipping forward, arm back for the throw. Darion mumbled under his breath and, distracted, Nihm's left foot clipped her right as she planted it and her skip turned to a stumble. Suddenly, arms flailing, she fell, headfirst into the shallows at the river's edge.

Nihm's face slapped the surface and kissed the river bed. It was bitterly cold and she leapt up with a splutter, choking out water. Blood dribbling from her nose, she waded back to the side, her clothes sopping wet.

The shock of the cold water had left her gasping and embarrassed. But that turned immediately to anger at hearing her Da's laughter. She pulled her cloak off, balled it, and threw it at his face. He caught it easily but not without getting a spray of water for his trouble, which set him off even more. It was an infectious laugh and Nihm couldn't help but grin before joining in.

Stepping behind a bush, Nihm wrung her clothes out before donning them again. It was going to be a cold and wet walk home but at least it wasn't far, a couple of hours at most. The Fossa marked the western border of their land. From here the woodland thinned out changing to grassland.

Darion whistled for Bindu and Nihm wondered suddenly where the wolfdog had gone. She should've come when Nihm fell in the river, or at their laughing afterwards. Nihm quickly wrapped her cloak about her shoulders as her Da whistled again, a different tone, lower. Nihm knew it for the recall and this time, heard a deep bark as Bindu responded.

Stepping out from the bushes, Nihm moved to Darion's side. He'd gathered their packs and held her bow out. Taking it, Nihm saw he'd strung it with one of his dry strings. His own bow was set and the tie on his long knife had been slipped. Nihm did the same, just as Bindu bounded from the bushes.

The wolfdog sat in front of Darion, an excited tension to her. Kneeling he ruffled her neck.

"What is it old girl?"

At this, Bindu was up and back at the undergrowth she'd come from. Turning her head, Bindu looked back at them.

"Okay, show us what ya found."

Bindu disappeared into the bush, Nihm and Darion trailing behind. As Nihm had been taught and taking Darion's lead, she sniffed the air, eyes ranging, listening for any sounds that didn't belong.

Bindu didn't lead them far. It was downwind of their spot by the river or Nihm was sure they would have smelt it.

A massive forest bear, dead and stinking, lay in a dried pool of blood. A thick shaft stood out from its flank and a deep wound was hacked into its neck. It must have cut an artery, as blood, dried black, painted a path on the forest floor and coated the leaves of the undergrowth.

"Bindu guard," Darion murmured, bending to examine the bear, disturbing a horde of flies.

Nihm watched him work, saw him spend some time over the front paws. The bear's head was bloody and her Da looked grim as he examined the red-raw mass where its ears should have been.

Darion moved to the arrow and pried it loose with his knife. He gave it a cursory glance, before carefully wrapping and placing it in his pack. He searched the area around the bear, probing with eyes and fingers.

"Best hurry home," he muttered, standing abruptly, brow creased.

"Who killed the bear? Was it ilf?" Nihm had never seen an ilf but she knew all the land to the west of the Fossa was theirs.

"Nay, the ilfanum don't kill like this. This was urak." He spat this last. Nihm, about to speak was stayed by his look.

"Now's not the time, Nihm. Need to check on your Ma and the homestead." Darion gathered his pack and held his bow ready with an arrow on the string. He whistled at Bindu as he set off, leaving Nihm to trail behind.

They soon cleared the forest and followed an overgrown path through the grasslands, moving quickly. The sun had passed its zenith when they crested the rise above their home. Darion hunkered down in the tall grass and Nihm followed his lead.

A lazy ribbon of smoke rose from the large stone and timber house. Four large dogs were in the yard; two laid in the shade of the smokehouse and two sprang about playing and nipping at each other, one dark, the other a dirty white. Nihm grinned at the sight.

A woman emerged from the smokehouse and walked towards the homestead before stopping, turning then staring up the small rise. She squinted, shielding her eyes before cupping her mouth and shouting.

"Stop gawping like a young boy Darion. You're late."

"How does she do that?" Nihm said, standing up in the tall grass. The woman waved and she waved back, smiling. All four dogs were up and barking. The two that were playing, stopped their game and raced towards her.

"Aye, it's a talent alright," Darion muttered, rising and strolling down the slope, "Comin' Marron."

Nihm skipped ahead, laughing as the young dogs reached her. They jumped and brushed up against her, vying for attention. The grass rustled then exploded. A large bundle of fur and claws leapt on the nearest dog, pinning it down, sinking its teeth into the ruff of its neck. The other dog yelped and lay flat.

Darion strode past. "Come girl."

Bindu was up and following in his steps. The two young dogs, suitably chastised, whined at Nihm's feet.

"Bindu got you good, eh Ash," she knelt, ruffling his head. "And you weren't much help, Snow." The large white dog nudged a nose at Nihm and barked.

Laughing, Nihm played with them before racing the dogs to the homestead. Happy, they cavorted around her, yipping and tails wagging, threatening to trip her up. By the time Nihm reached the yard, her Da was already talking quietly with her Ma.

They broke off their conversation and turned. Marron regarded her daughter, casting a critical eye up and down and shaking her head. "You're as bad as Darion, child. You'll catch a chill wandering about in damp clothes. No, don't hug me!" Her eyes flashed as Nihm tried to embrace her. "I'll fetch you some clothes. Get yourself washed up round the back before you come in to eat."

Grumbling, Nihm sauntered to the water trough. Glancing back, she saw her Da wrap an arm around her mother as they walked to the house. She couldn't keep the grin from her face as they shut the door behind them with a bang.

Chapter 2 : On the Trail

Homestead, The Rivers

Marron turned the arrow shaft over in her hands. It was dirty black and thick as her middle finger. The tip was serrated with several vicious barbs for hooking flesh. "Urak for sure. Damn it!"

Darion considered. "Long time since they've been seen in these parts. Pretty sure the bear took one but I saw signs of at least four others."

"Scouting party then but scouting for what?" Marron was all business.

"Not sure but we need to find what they're about. I've a bad feeling about this." Darion took the arrow from her hands. "I'll head out with Bindu. See if I can track them. Shouldn't be too difficult."

"This isn't right. The last urak incursion was over a hundred years ago. Why cross the mountains now? What are they doing here?" Marron frowned. "I think we have to contact the Order; let them know."

"Think we should talk ta Nihm?" Darion asked. "She's seen her sixteenth name day. She's old enough ta know."

"See what you find out first. I'd best hurry with Nihm's clothes, that girl will smell trouble otherwise." Marron turned and disappeared into Nihm's room.

Darion placed the arrow in the chest near the hearth before stoking the fire. He was staring into the flames deep in thought when Marron bustled out again with an armful of clothes and a drying cloth.

* * *

It was late afternoon when Darion and Bindu reached the bear. He was armed with bow and sword, the latter strapped in its scabbard across his back where it would not obstruct his legs in the dense undergrowth.

He smiled, thinking briefly of Nihm. She'd kicked up an almighty stink when she saw him preparing to head out and realised she'd not be going. She was as stubborn as Marron, almost.

His smile faded as he approached. The rotting stench of death was powerful and cloying but Darion had hunted most of his life, he'd smelt worse. The smell, along with the fly eggs and maggots, told him the bear was killed the day before, early. So the urak had a day, maybe day and a half, on him.

He had Bindu sniff the black blood coating the bear's paw to get a scent and watched as she loped off into the scrub. Crouching, he examined the area. In his mind, he slowly built a picture of what had happened.

The bear came from the river following a faint trail through the undergrowth. Early morning, he surmised, the urak must have camped nearby and ambushed the bear from the surrounding accacha bushes. Pretty brave and pretty stupid taking on a forest bear, especially one this big. They'd not skinned the bear apart from taking the ears. So, why attack something that was more as like to kill you? It was an unknown and it nagged at him.

The confrontation had been short and brutal. The bear had killed or mauled at least one before a shaft struck, wounding it, then the killing blow to the neck. It was powerfully struck, forest bears were notoriously tough, their pelts dense, the fur offering good protection. Superstition said it could even turn a blade.

Darion ran his hands along its flanks; the fur was thick but soft. It was the first he'd seen one up close. So much for superstition, still it was magnificent, even in death. What must it have been like in life? The thought saddened him.

Bindu gave a low bark from deeper in the forest. A short walk through undergrowth and Darion found the urak. The bear had ripped its guts out, its entrails coiled on the ground in a black pulpy mass. Its throat had been slit and it stank worse than the bear. Darion waved a hand, disturbing the flies swarming the body.

The urak was manlike and of a size to him, only heavier with short stocky legs, a large thick body, and powerful arms. Claw marks rent the face and sickly grey flesh hung off on one side. The corpse had been stripped, leaving only the stained and bloodied leather jerkin and soiled skirt.

The blood was tacky to the touch. Dead a day; its wounds were mortal and it wouldn't have lived much longer than the bear but judging from its slit throat, his friends hadn't waited around for the dying. Expedience or mercy, Darion wondered.

The surviving urak left a clear trail; at least one carried an injury. They're not the most subtle of creatures, he thought, setting out after them.

He tracked till dusk. Night fell quickly in the forest and Darion wriggled into a thicket of thorn bushes. Using a small hatchet to trim away interior branches, he made a snug that would keep him well protected until morning. Darion wrapped his cloak tight and settled in. It was going to be a cold night.

* * *

Darion tracked throughout the next day, moving ever northward and deeper into the forest. He knew the Blue Sky Lakes were three days away, where the old forest grew sparse and grassland took over. Good hunting and good for the wild honey that fetched a rare price at market. He wondered if that was where this trail was leading. It was a natural place to stage and camp if the urak were here in numbers.

After another fireless night in the forest, huddled in his cloak, Darion was up with the birds the next day and back on the trail. The urak had not attempted to cover their tracks and were easy to follow. He made good time with Bindu taking the lead.

The Fossa was never far away and he often heard the rush and tumble of the river. Stopping at noon, he lunched on jerky, nuts and berries and thought on his quarry.

The urak kept to the east of the river. They wouldn't cross to the west bank, he was sure; that was ilfanum land and no one would knowingly cross into it. The ilf were secretive and fiercely protective. He'd been given a token once from an ilf friend of sorts, many years back. He wore it now, on a neck thong, his fingers absently finding and rubbing it as he thought briefly of that time.

By mid-afternoon the freshness of the trail told that he was close and Darion slowed his pace, moving more cautiously. Bindu appeared suddenly, tense and excited. He knew by her stance she'd found them. Kneeling, he gave her a pat. "Good girl."

The next hour, Darion crept through the woods. He smelt smoke on the air, growing stronger with every step. Under the forest canopy, it was difficult to tell if there was a breeze or what direction it blew. He circled, until the smell of wood smoke was strongest, before stalking again through the undergrowth, Bindu at his heels. He gestured and the wolfdog disappeared into the bush.

Darion heard them before he saw them, talking in guttural tones as he stole upon their camp.

A weak fire dribbled ribbons of smoke into the air. An urak sat near a bundle of rags, heaped on the ground, rubbing a leg as if pained. In the distance came the muted rumble of the river. It was from there two urak strode, talking loudly.

Apart from the dead urak, these were the first he'd seen. Their heads were broad and flat with wide eyes over a large mouth and beneath a ridged, bony forehead. Despite his generalisation, Darion saw they were as different as one man might be from the next.

One was huge, a head taller than the other. Its pate was shaved, apart from two long braids lying down its chest, each decorated with coloured strips of cloth.

In contrast, its fellow had a full head of hair, matted and teased into spikes. He was slim in comparison to the brute, but still of a size to match Darion. Their faces were animated as they argued.

* * *

"I say leave No-nose. He slows us down. Mar-Dur will likely skin us for being late," the brute said. His voice rumbled as he spoke.

"I ain't slowed you down none." The sitting urak stood, voice thick and nasally. "You ain't leavin me Gromma, else when I see Mar-Dur I be telling him why we is late. Not that he won't see for hisself."

"You little shitbag, keep yabbing your jowls and I'll end you here," Gromma said, hulking over No-Nose.

"We was only meant to scout!"

Gromma exploded, smashing forehead to face. No-Nose fell, howling, clutching his head, dark blood leaking through his hands.

"Sicka you're whining," Gromma spat.

"He's got a point," the spike-haired urak said. Walking to the bundle of rags, he kicked it. A groan emanated from within. "Mar-Dur will not thank you I'm thinkin' for stirring up this hornet's nest. He'll fuck us good. Probably wish that bear had done us in."

"Whining too Bartuk? Must be contagious," Gromma growled back. "I'm a warrior; I don't like this sneakin' in the forest. Besides, he'll thank me for bringing him this prize."

Bartuk laughed. "You think? Mar-Dur told us to scout to the ilf lands and not be seen. So you attack an ilf and its bear, leaving a great big fuck you sign." Bartuk shook his head, scowling at Gromma. "And, just in case the ilf have any doubts, you leave Motaug's body so they don't even have to fucking think about it. No-Nose may be a whiny little shit but he's right. You go marching up to Mar-Dur with your prize and our lives won't be worth a piss. We'll be gutted and heads spiked afore you even open your mouth."

"AARRGHH," Gromma shouted. "Why does Mar-Dur have to hide like this? Our war host could crush the ilf."

"Kill the bitch," Bartuk said. "Tell Mar-Dur nothing."

Gromma rubbed his chin, thinking and finally conceded. "Okay, I'll kill her. Ilf's ears are mine though. For my collection." He jiggled his necklace. It was full of desiccated ears in various shapes and states of decay but dominated by a pulpy mass of brown matted fur.

"You can't go taking no ears. You're as stupid as you are big." Bartuk shook his head. "Kill her but no ears, no prizes, no nothing that could get us killed. Fuck it, I'll do it myself." Bartuk drew a serrated knife from his belt.

Gromma grabbed Bartuk's shoulder. "She's mine. I do the killing."

As Gromma pulled him about, Bartuk drove his knife hard into Gromma's gut and ripped upwards. Pushing the big urak hard, he sent him crashing to the ground.

Gromma moaned in agony as blood and intestine spilt out. He tried pushing his guts back in but failed. He convulsed. Hands, slick with his own blood, clenched uselessly at the forest floor as he sobbed in pain.

Bartuk watched through pitiless eyes as Gromma bled out. "You're too fucking stupid to live, meatbag." He kicked Gromma hard in the back. There was a shriek of agony, then silence.

No-Nose backed away, his hand reaching for his knife. "What the fuck Bartuk? He's Mar-Dur's kin. He's gonna kill us for sure."

Bartuk glared. "Maybe, if you open your fat trap." Then more conciliatory, "Gromma couldn't help himself. He'd have mouthed off about killing that bear. This was only gonna end one way with Gromma and that was with us dead. You think Mar-Dur would kill his kin? Probably, he's mean enough. But he liked Gromma, more as like it would be us taking the fall for this cock-up."

"I, right enough I s'pose," No-Nose still held his knife out.

"Besides brother, he was for leavin' ya. You heard and he weren't meaning in a breathin' way." Bartuk held his hand out. "Savin' your ass is getting to be a full-time job."

No-Nose grinned. "Yeah, I saved your butt plenty of times too. So can I kill her?"

"Sure, but be quick. We'll eat on the run. Just let me do the talking when we get back." Bartuk bent and whipped the blanket off the bundle on the floor.

The distinctive form of an ilf sat up. She wore a belted skirt of woven fibres and a cloak that seemed to flow from her shoulders. She rose slowly, graceful despite her hands being tied behind her.

No-Nose raised his knife. "Dyin' time. Maybe get to seein' if you taste good too," he hissed, blood trickling from the hole where his nose should have been. His eyes widened suddenly and an arrow punched into his chest knocking him from his feet. His right leg kicked briefly then he was still.

Bartuk was moving the instant No-Nose went down, instinct taking over. Running hard, he tucked and rolled, coming up behind a tree, putting its thick trunk between him and the attacker. Fear gripped him. Options were few and all bad. Resolving to run for it, Bartuk baulked as a wolf stepped from the bushes. Hackles up, it gave a menacing growl and padded towards him. Bartuk gripped his knife, eyes darting, looking for a way out.

* * *

Darion walked into the campsite an arrow ready on his bow. The ilf watched him with dark eyes. She was very obviously human in form and size but that was where the similarity ended. The ilf was covered in what looked like soft green scales that hugged the contours of her body. Her head, similarly covered, gave the impression she'd been moulded out of some material.

The ilf looked on, wary, as Darion pulled his knife out. A dark green blemish marked one side of her face; crusted and dried blood. Her eyes locked on his. They were piercing, completely brown, almost black and unreadable. Inclining her head, she turned away.

Darion slipped the knife between her bound hands and swiftly cut the ties.

Immediately, she removed her gag before bending to pick up the dead urak's knife. She looked over her shoulder at Darion. "Thank you, friend." Her voice was croaky and dry, "Call your hound. This one is mine."

Darion whistled and Bindu lay flat, her eyes not leaving her prey.

The ilf stretched out, then winced, holding her side. Grimacing, she hobbled towards the tree the urak hid behind. Stopping suddenly, she lifted her head. At the same time Bindu's hackles went up and the wolfdog stared back into the forest.

The ilf glanced at Darion. "Trouble comes."

"Aye," Darion replied, his bow ready in his hands.

The ilf looked at the tree standing between her and the urak, torn. She sighed, before quickly turning and rummaging through the campsite. In moments, she'd retrieved an ilf bow and long dagger.

Horns sounded, followed by a distant baying of dogs. It was hard to judge sound and distance in the old forest but Darion knew instinctively they were closer than it seemed.

"You better run bitch! I'll hunt you down. And you manling, I'll be coming for you," the urak shouted, peering furtively around the tree's trunk, emboldened by the sounding of the horns.

Darion launched the arrow without thought. It was ten paces to the tree and the urak yelped, pulling his head back too late as the arrow sliced his brow, opening a shallow furrow.

"Let's go," the ilf set off towards the river.

Darion backed away, before turning and running after her, giving the recall whistle to Bindu. It was obvious to Darion after only a few strides the ilf carried an injury. The urak would close on them quickly at this pace. The saving grace was the Fossa. It was not far and the ilf made straight for it. They had a chance.

Behind came sounds of pursuit. It will be a near thing, Darion thought, as the noise of baying dogs crashing through the undergrowth grew ever louder. They stumbled on, the rumble of the river growing steadily until finally, they burst out onto its banks. Here, the water was wide and fast.

A large mastiff followed, leaping for Darion. The ilf stepped between them, spinning low and slashing. The knife found the soft underbelly, the dog's momentum ripping it through as it neatly gutted itself. The feral growl turned to a high pitched squeal as it crashed into Darion's shoulder before collapsing on the ground, spasming.

Darion was a big man but the force of the impact drove him to his knee. He turned in time to see another mastiff burst from the undergrowth and without thought, drew and fired. The arrow whipped by the ilf, narrowly missing her head, and buried itself in the dog. It crumpled to the ground, dead.

A third broke through, snarling. The ilf was knelt, clutching her body and grimacing in pain, an easy target. A streak of fur struck the dog mid-leap, teeth flashing. The fight was savage but brief. Bindu gripped the mastiff's thick neck in her jaws. With a shake of her head and a crack it was over, throat crushed. Bindu shook her head and howled her defiance at the trees, before limping over to Darion. A flap of skin hung from her left flank and Darion knelt to examine her wound.

"Ah, my brave girl, so strong," he patted her proudly, glancing at her injury. It would need stitching.

"Man, we must cross here or die," the ilf said. A horn blew as if to make her point.

"Come on old girl," Darion called, encouraging Bindu as he stood and walked to the river's edge. Taking his pack off, he waded with it into the river, wincing as the cold washed around his legs. The ilf hobbled beside him, gasping as she lowered herself in and started to swim.

Darion pushed his pack out in front, stumbling under as the river bed fell away. He spluttered to the surface. He'd lost his bow and looked frantically for it, but it was gone to the river.

He kicked for the far bank and the current took hold, sweeping him along like flotsam. Ahead, the ilf was struggling, clearly in pain. Darion watched as she disappeared beneath the water before bobbing up again a few anxious heartbeats later.

There was a cry from behind and Darion turned to look. He was surprised at how far they were downriver. Six urak stood on the bank a good sixty yards away.

They were spotted, one pointing them out and moments later thick shafted arrows started falling. Here, the river was their friend. Constantly moving in the Fossa's embrace, they were difficult to see let alone hit. Some of the urak scrambled, following the river bank but the undergrowth and terrain were against them, they couldn't hope to outpace them.

Darion was cold and tired and his clothes, heavy with water, tried dragging him down. He was forced to shrug his cloak off, then his coat. Where was the ilf? She'd disappeared. Panicked, he swam to where he'd last seen her. But the river was a living thing that ebbed and flowed to its own rhythm. She was there no longer.

Twisting, frantically searching, he spotted a shadow to his left. He lurched towards it and reached out grasping into the water's depths. He felt her and made a grab but his hands slide off, unable to find purchase. The green scales of her skin were soft and slick in the wet. Thrashing about, he snared an arm and, managing to lock a hand around it, yanked her roughly to the surface.

Her face was pale; it's green hue weak and leeched of colour. He clasped her to him, relieved when suddenly she spluttered, coughing out a mouthful of water, before gasping in a ragged breath.

Darion briefly wondered if he could save her. The cold was mind-numbing and sapped the energy from his limbs. Their lives were on a knife's edge. If they did not make the far bank soon they'd not make it at all.

Anger kindled in Darion. He had to survive, had to get to Marron and Nihm. He didn't know what was going on but whatever was happening they were in the wrong place. He knew he could make it but could he make it with the ilf. It would be easy to just let her slip away for whatever she'd been through in the last few days had taken a toll. He suspected she'd cracked a rib the way she'd winced and clasped her side back on the river bank. If they have ribs, the banal thought flittered through his mind.

Manoeuvring behind, Darion clasped a hand across her chest and kicked for the far bank. Her head smashed against his face, bloodying his nose. Adjusting his grip, he tried again.

As he dragged her through the water, Darion let his anger burn. Let its fire energise him. Time stretched, it seemed an age when finally the river's edge loomed before him. But the embankment was overgrown and steep and the river carried them past sweeping them around another bend.

An opening appeared. Darion struggled to reach it. The current was not so strong this close in but he saw they wouldn't make it. Kicking out in desperation his foot struck the bottom. Managing to anchor himself, Darion pushed off. It was not much but the water was shallower with each precarious step. Somehow, half swimming, half walking, he dragged the ilf until finally, they collapsed on the river's edge.

Darion wanted to curl up and sleep. He was exhausted and so numb with cold he couldn't feel his hands or feet. He crawled to his knees. Instinctively, he knew that if he slept now then he would not be waking again.

Summoning his strength, he dragged the ilf up the bank. Then, picking her up carried her under the eaves of the encroaching trees. She was heavier than she looked, her form was slight but she was solid and he struggled, his body shaking violently.

He was near collapse and she a dead weight in his arms as he stumbled deeper into the forest and out of sight of the Fossa. Finally, reaching a small glade he fell to his knees, spilling her lifeless body onto the ground. He didn't know if she lived still. He felt too close to death at that moment to even worry about it.

Focus. One thing at a time, he always told Nihm. Focus on what you can do and do it, not on what you can't. Darion swept up twigs and leaves, scraping them into a rough pile and placing some larger branches over the top. His teeth chattered so loudly he thought the urak would probably hear them. He bent down to the pile; there was no time for finesse.

"Ignatituum forus arctum." He shivered words of fire, his lips trembling and blue. Darion avoided magic. Magic could be felt and seen by those with the knowledge. And when he did use it, it would only be a tiny trickle, like when starting a fire. A tiny nudge was usually all he needed to make a spark take.

The kindling ignited in a burst of flame, so sudden it singed his beard. Maybe a little too much he winced, jerking his head back. Feeding branches to the fire, warmth washed over him. Skin and bones aching, he rubbed his hands holding them to the flames.

He'd lost his bow to the river and his pack although he could not remember when and to there was no sign of Bindu. All he had were the clothes he wore, his long knife, and the sword still strapped to his back.

He looked at the ilf, comatose on the ground. She had dark green bruising marking one side of her face. The crusted and dried green blood had been washed away by the river.

Up close, he could see the tiny scales on her body were more leaf than scale. Small, overlapping and soft like a fine fur. The leaf scale looked roughed up, giving the ilf a dishevelled appearance, but even so, there was an elegance to her, a perfection of symmetry and shape.

Back in the urak camp, she'd looked at him, weighing him with her almost black, inscrutable eyes. He wondered idly what she saw. There'd been deadliness in her stance, injured as she was, that reminded Darion of the big cats found deeper in the forest. Not now though. Now she looked wan and cold.

Darion stripped off to his smalls and placed his clothes on the surrounding bushes and nearby tree branches to dry out. Moving to the ilf, he dragged her closer to the flames. She moaned in pain but was otherwise unresponsive. "Alive at least," Darion murmured.

He checked her for injury, quickly and expertly. The most obvious one, the lump and cut on her head, was washed clean already by the river. Superficial, Darion thought. His hands moved over her body, prying and testing. The small leaf scale, overlapping and covering her body was smooth to the touch. She did have ribs he noted, as he pressed gently in on them, eliciting a wince and a groan. It was the right-side, probably cracked. Her right ankle too was tender and swollen. A bad sprain, exacerbated no doubt by her run through the forest. Nothing immediately life-threatening, Darion judged, other than the cold.

Despite the heat from the fire, the ilf shivered uncontrollably. Darion moved her as close to its warmth as he dared and as carefully as he could but was clumsy at best; weary beyond belief he was close to collapse.

With the last of his energy, Darion gathered wood and dried leaves, piling them nearby. He stoked the fire, building it up then checked his patient one last time. She felt warmer but still trembled, clearly suffering still. He gave a sigh and settled his bulk behind her. Placing his dagger and sword in easy reach, he laid down, pulling her into the crook of his body. What a pair we would make if the urak found us now, Darion thought. Then, eyelids heavy with fatigue fell into a deep sleep.

Chapter 3 : The Chase

The Old Forest, The Rivers

The gash on Bartuk's forehead throbbed, his head pounded from his brush with death and he was irritable as hell. He ripped a strip off No-Nose's cloak to bind his wound, but by the time it did its job his face was already a bloody mess.

He greeted the lead elements of the raiding party as urak and war dogs, mastiffs trained for fighting, entered the clearing.

"Through the bush, headin' for the river," he gesticulated in the direction man and ilf had disappeared. "Fuck me. Don't stand there, after 'em."

One look at the blood-covered urak and the two laying dead were all they needed. At Bartuk's shouted command they set off in pursuit, their dogs racing ahead baying excitedly.

A large urak entered the camp. His black hair was pulled into a top knot and bound with a red leather tie. "Who the fuck are you? What's happened here?"

Bartuk looked the urak up and down. He was seven feet more or less. Livid scars marred his cheeks, his teeth were filed to points and half his left ear was missing. All in all, Bartuk didn't much like the look of him. He stepped back out of reach of any immediate violence.

"Name's Bartuk, we was scoutin' heading back to report to Mar-Dur when we was attacked." He indicated about the camp.

"Bartuk, eh? Never heard of you," Scarface said. "How many?"

"Don't rightly know," Bartuk lied.

Scarface narrowed his eyes.

"Several attacked us in camp and there was more in the trees but I ain't sure how many on account I was fightin' for me skin."

The brute nodded, unconvinced. The little shit wasn't telling all that was for sure and the blood he wore was his own. He cast his eyes about assessing what he saw.

An arrow stood from the chest of one urak and the other, a big fella by the looks of him, lay soaking in his blood with his guts spilt out. He wandered over to the big one, he seemed familiar.

"Fuck me, Gromma Gutsplitter? He's been gutted like a boar." He glared at Bartuk.

"Aye, that's Gromma alright, good friend ah mine. The ilf bitch did for him good, with his own knife no less."

"Hold." The brute ducked low over Gromma's corpse, "He breathes still."

Gromma moaned as he was rolled onto his back. His eyes locked with Bartuk's and went wide, nostrils flaring.

Bartuk's face paled. "Alive!" His voice trembled. "He's a tough bastard and no mistake. I coulda swored he was dead." He dropped next to Gromma.

The big urak's face was contorted in pain; his breath coming in short sharp gasps. Somehow, drawing on whatever strength he had left, his hand shot out and clasped Bartuk's arm.

Bartuk winced. All but dead, Gromma still had an iron grip, "it's okay friend, I'm here," he placed his hand over Gromma's.

Scarface watched the exchange. Gromma was named. A renowned warrior, cousin to Mar-Dur the clan chieftain, and a champion of the fight ring. He had even fought him once, was proud to say he'd lasted a full hand against him. Now, watching Gromma bleed out, he looked… smaller, weaker.

He scowled at the little shit… Bartuk was it? Ai, he chided himself, they were warrior brothers. Did Gromma not reach out and grasp Bartuk as a warrior? Did Bartuk not give comfort and bear witness as he crossed to the Death Halls of Varis'tuk.

Gromma wheezed, the breath dying on his lips. His eyes pure malevolence even as the light left them.

Scarface looked on with pride and hoped that when his time came he'd fight death's crossing with as much rage as Gromma.

"Aghh he's gone," Bartuk wailed.

Scarface frowned. The bloodied urak's pathetic whining tarnished Gromma's crossing. A horn sounded, close and to the west, and all thought of Gromma fled. His urak had sighted the ilf.

Bartuk was on his feet, shouting, "Why ya standin' round? Let's have them bastards."

Scarface showed his teeth. Little-shit had spirit, he had to give him that. "Okay boys, let's go hunt us some fresh meat." Then to Bartuk, "Mar-Dur is coming out to play. He's ten leagues to the east, get urself there."

Bartuk flinched, unsure whether Scarface was smiling or scowling. In any case, he didn't fancy telling Mar-Dur their patrol was fucked five ways to hell, or that his kin Gromma had been slain by ilf. He knew from bitter experience, well No-Nose's bitter experience, it didn't pay to deliver ill news.

"Send one of your boys back to Mar-Dur. I ain't restin' till I got the bitch that did for Gromma here," he looked down at No-Nose, "and my brother."

The gathered urak nodded and grunted at this, the bloody faced urak had grit and a warrior's heart.

Bartuk saw Scarface wavering. He don't trust me none so he's not as stupid as he looks, Bartuk thought. Pre-empting things, he pulled his knife out and smiled, it was still covered in Gromma's blood.

"Come on, before they get away," Bartuk screamed, charging from the clearing. He crashed through the undergrowth and brushed aside foliage that threatened to snag and trip him. It wasn't the smartest thing, running through this cursed forest with a hunting knife in hand but the effect was what counted. Behind, he heard Scarface issuing commands, then the rush and crash of many urak.

Slowing his pace, Bartuk exaggerated a limp. As the sound of the river grew louder, he was caught then overtaken. Ahead he heard shouting and the thrum of heavy bows. On clearing the trees a mass of urak blocked his way. Sheathing his knife he pushed through them and took stock.

A few raiders had unlimbered bows and were launching arrows. Many more had set off, tracking downriver. At the water's edge, he saw the bodies of several dogs and a lone urak hunched over them, moaning and carrying on like he'd lost an arm or some such, pathetic.

Bartuk followed the flight of the arrows. There, a hundred paces out, bobbing violently in the fast water he saw them, man and ilf. The man looked to be holding the ilf bitch. Was she dead? Arrows dropped around them but they were difficult targets appearing and disappearing in the swell and flow of the river. "Fuck me! What's the chance they survive that?" he muttered.

Scarface suddenly pushed alongside, taking the scene in with a glance just as man and ilf disappeared around a bend in the river.

"What now Rimtaug?" an urak asked.

Scarface looked at the river. There was no way to catch them, the bank sides were treacherous and overgrown in many places, the going would be too slow. The river itself was fast and angry. Icy cold too; summer had long passed and the water flowed from the Dragon's Spine, it was likely their quarry had killed themselves.

He looked sidelong at Little-shit-Bartuk. Funny how a name sticks, he thought. Little-shit was a tricky one alright, he'd smelt fear on him back at the camp but he couldn't fault his courage and thirst to avenge Gromma and his brother. He acted as was proper, tribe was important. He knew Little-shit would insist on pursuit; it is what he would do.

"We raid south as planned. We'll follow the river. If'n they ain't already dead, as I see it, they've as much chance of reaching this side ah the river as the other."

The urak looked at him.

He flashed his teeth. "Did ya not hear me? Move!"

The urak started dispersing back into the forest and followed the east bank south. He turned to Little-shit. "I sent a lad back to Mar-Dur. Might be he'll wanna talk to you hisself seein as one of his kin is dead."

Bartuk eyed him warily. "Maybe so, but I ain't given up yet. Found a crossing may be a turn, turn and a half downriver. We should check it out."

The blood had dried in Bartuk's scrag of a beard turning it slick and black and giving him a feral look. Staring at the river where man and ilf had disappeared, he hoped fervently they were dead. The last thing he wanted was Rimtaug to find them or at least if he did, to make sure they couldn't answer no questions.

Chapter 4 : Homestead

Homestead, The Rivers

<Marron, you should prepare to leave. If Darion isn't back by tomorrow you must wait no longer.>

Marron considered Keeper's words. Even after all this time, it was disconcerting to hear him in her head, as clear as if he sat facing her. She knew he was right. She and Darion had plans in place, contingencies for just such an occasion, and had discussed them with Keeper. Now that it came to it though she was finding it wasn't so easy to leave.

She focussed on Keeper. *<We'll travel to Thorsten and on to Rivercross. Try and warn them and the folk on the way of the urak threat.>*

<Have a care. You have evidence of, at most, a small scouting or hunting party, and little enough that is. Lord Bouchemeax is a shrewd man but I do not know how your news will be received. High Lord Twyford, on the other hand, I do. He'll not likely be swayed by a peasant with an arrow,> Keeper replied.

Marron would have bridled at being called a peasant, but more than thought was conveyed. Feeling and meaning were as much a part of the connection as words. Keeper expressed how she would be perceived, and she knew he was right on both counts.

Twyford, Ducal Lord of the Rivers had a stern, fearsome reputation and was no friend to the Order, having rescinded the accords and banned them from his province. She would not likely be admitted to see him and unlikely to be believed if she were. All this was conveyed by Keeper in a thought.

<Never the less I must try. I can do no less. I will await Darion at Thorsten for two days and then move to Rivercross as we planned,> Marron replied. There was a pause and Marron could sense wariness through the link.

<Do not be tempted to reveal who you are to Twyford. He's unpredictable and not to be trusted. It's easy to convince yourself it's for the greater good. The urak could be a real threat to the people, but you would likely be detained and that ***must*** *not happen. You have Nihm to worry about as well.>* There was an interruption; the warm sense of him

suddenly gone. Marron waited patiently, a minute then two before she felt the disorientation of his relink. *<Sorry. Hiro is nearby. I'll ask him to meet with you.>*

Marron smiled. It was many years since she'd seen Master Hiro, it would be good to see him again. Whether he would heed Keeper was another matter. He was of the Order but outside it at the same time, tending to drift around to his own ends.

<I think he'll come. He's fond of you as much as that old goat is fond of anyone,> Keeper assured her. *<It's no surprise to me he's close, he seems to know when troubles brewing. He's near Rivercross, I'll have him meet you at Thorsten or on the south road.>*

Marron's thoughts turned then to her daughter. *<I'd like to bring Nihm to the Order halls, it is past time. She's been isolated out here too long.>*

There was a slight delay before Keeper responded. *<Maybe so, I'll consider the matter, for now, safe journey.>*

The link terminated, the gentle sense of warmth in her head gone, replaced by the cold cloying liquid sensation on her right hand. Opening her eyes she looked down. Her hand was inserted into an intricately carved wooden box through a small opening in the top. She carefully removed her hand pulling free of the jelly-like substance within and holding it up, turning and inspecting it as she always did. Her hand was perfectly dry and clean; a little scratch from picking ommi berries earlier that morning was completely gone as if it had never been. It both amazed and awed Marron every time she used the box.

She picked up the lid lying next to her and pressed and twisted it over the opening until it clicked and sealed. Then, carefully wrapping the box in a cloth, she placed it back in her travel chest.

* * *

The following morning, Marron and Nihm were up at dawn as they were every day. Only this day was different. Marron could sense Nihm's nervous energy as they prepared the homestead for their departure. Her daughter was excited at the thought of travelling to Rivercross; she could see the eager glow in her eyes.

"So why are we heading to market so early and to Rivercross?" Nihm asked then promptly supplied her thoughts on the matter. "It's those urak me and Da found isn't it?"

"Yes, that's right."

Nihm barrelled on. "You know I've seen sixteen name days. You have to stop treating me like a child. Da doesn't!"

That stung; no less because Marron knew she was right.

"You're growing so fast I can't keep up." And it was true; Nihm had grown tall and slim, looking boyish in her trousers and tunic despite the unruly mess of long black hair tied in a loose ponytail. Nihm hugged her fiercely.

"I know Ma, but you aren't protecting me by keeping me in the dark about things."

Marron laughed. "When did you get to be so wise?"

"I have good teachers." Nihm smiled then added with a cheeky grin, "Besides you and Da are terrible at secrets. Let's see," she counted off on her fingers, "Sudden early trip to Thorsten right after we found those urak. You and Da whispering together so loud I knew something was up and now, packing like you don't expect to be back anytime soon." She stared at her mother suddenly serious. "Them urak were a scouting party, weren't they? And Da's gone to find out what they're about."

"Sometimes you're too clever. You're right but all we can do is head south and try to warn those on the way of what might follow. Now stop your chatter. We have a busy day ahead of us."

Pushing her worries aside, Marron concentrated on her work. There was always so much to do on the homestead and now with the urak turning up, everything just got a whole lot busier. As well as preparing the homestead for their leaving she had to pack for their journey and load the farm cart.

To start with, Marron dragged the travel chest out and lifted it awkwardly onto the flatbed before pushing it under the bench seat and covering it over. Finished, she took a breath, her eyes automatically searching for her daughter.

She spied her by the back of the barn. Nihm had been storing anything of worth that couldn't be taken into the hideaway and was now stood, hands-on-hips, looking down into the entrance. Her dogs, Ash and Snow, were never far from her and were play-fighting near the log pile.

Feeling Marron's eyes on her, Nihm turned and gave a wave before wandering over. "I've packed everything I can that will fit; it just needs covering over with the woodpile."

"I'll help but first give me a hand loading up the cart will you?"

"Sure, are we leavin' when Da's back?" Nihm asked as she bent to lift a bundle of skins onto the flatbed.

"We'll wait till morning and head out then. Your Da will catch us on the road," Marron replied.

Nihm frowned. "I don't like leaving without him."

"Me neither, but your father can look after himself," Marron said, hiding her own fears. "If we get to Thorsten before he finds us we'll sell our goods while we wait. We should get a fair price even this early in the season." Marron stood back and looked her daughter over. Her trousers and top were short in leg and arm. "Besides, it looks like you need some new clothes."

Nihm cheered and they laughed. Chatting idly they began loading the cart. First with hare, deer and beaver skins from the summer's hunt, then with smoked meats carefully wrapped, jars of wild honey, and finally a chest containing herbs and plants. It was a valuable load.

The afternoon passed quickly, the sky darkening to a perfect cloudless evening as they worked. After loading the cart they moved the woodpile over the hideaway. The hidden cellar was dug under the barn and was ordinarily used to store skins and meats, this was the first Nihm could recollect using it to store anything else. There were no folks around these parts to worry about and their proximity to the old forest and ilfanum lands guaranteed their isolation. But the urak were out there now and that changed everything.

Marron sent Nihm to bring the ponies in from the meadow. She looked distantly to the northwest and twisted her heart ring, before turning and disappearing into the house.

Chapter 5 : The Lesson

North of the Defile, The Rivers

The campfire spluttered angrily as the boy threw wood on it. He waited for the fire to settle then moved a pan of water over the flames. Two old men sat to the side, warming themselves. They were silent, happy to watch and wait.

The boy took a long thin knife out and filleted the fish. He'd caught them earlier in the Oust and had already gutted and washed them clean in the river. Finished, he set the knife aside then deftly wrapped the fish in broadleaf before skewering them on sticks and placing each on a stone at the fire's edge.

He fetched bowls and mugs and arranged them on a log before turning and opening a small satchel. It was, in his opinion, their most important possession, after their weapons of course. The satchel contained many pouches, vials and small leather-bound sacks and he took several of these out. From one, he took some leaves and dropped them into the pan. From others, he took seeds and a pinch of crushed spice. The water infused as it heated and a delicious aroma wafted over them all. Satisfied he repacked the bag and returned it to the travel pack. He then scrapped the remains of the fish bones, tail and head into the steeping water.

"Ah Renco, you make an old man very happy. Who knew you had such a talent, eh?" said one of the men. His hair, silver and long, was bound and tied in a queue down his back. He wore a hooded brown robe with a symbol over the left breast of three circles entwined inside a larger one.

Renco glanced at him but made no reply, keeping to his task.

"He should be a cook, don't you agree Mao?" the old man asked, turning to his companion.

Mao snorted. "Maybe so. Maybe, Mao teach boy how to sew and read poetry. Then Master get rid of old fool and replace with young one, neh?" He spoke with an accent, his words clipped and precise.

Renco listened to their familiar interplay in silence. Maohong, or Mao as they called him, was very different from Master Hiro. They were both small and slight but the similarities ended there. Maohong was bald and wrinkled and looked much older for one thing. For another, his skin was a different colour, not as dark as the southerners and not as pale as the kingdom folk. He'd come from across the Great Expanse, a feat all in itself. A story he'd asked to hear but not been told. Maohong was dressed in plain brown hose and shirt with a tattered looking black cloak and hood. In truth, he looked impoverished.

Hiro laughed. "Ah Mao, Renco is no fool, not even a young one, so how could I possibly replace you eh, old friend?" He slapped Mao on the shoulder. "No, I'll always have need of you, never fear. This is just part of Renco's training. We do him a disservice if he can't cook or clean for himself, don't you agree?"

"Whatever master say," Maohong shrugged dismissing the subject. He cast a worried glance towards the road. "Do you think men come back, master?"

"Who can say? It depends on the men, neh?" Hiro replied.

Renco listened keenly. Mao referred to their pursuers. Earlier that day they'd left the road and hidden in a copse whilst the men hunting them rode by oblivious. Renco thought it unlikely they would realise their mistake and turn back, at least for tonight. Renco stirred the pan and turned his skewered fish over as he considered.

They were two days out from Rivercross and had joined the road north to Thorsten. It was a well-travelled road; they'd be hard to track and too they'd been careful not to stay in any of the villages. They were an odd group, two old men and a boy, a man he corrected himself. They'd be remembered at an inn, so Master decided they wouldn't stay at one. That was fine as far as Renco was concerned. He didn't mix well and was not comfortable in crowds. Maohong, on the other hand, moaned about his aching back and joints every morning. But then, he usually found something to moan about.

Renco looked up at the darkened sky to the west whilst waiting for the food to cook. The moon, Nihmrodel, was low on the horizon. Higher and to the right was Ankor, larger and yellower than its companion. Kildare, the red moon, he knew lay behind him. The night sky was a panoply of stars and his eyes sought out the bear and the ram following them to the Lodestar. Maohong had taught him how to navigate using time, the Lodestar and the constellations. It had both amazed and confounded Renco at how accurate it was.

Renco felt a disturbance. He jerked back then spun, his arm snapping out as he snatched a stick from the air. He looked at it, grunted, and threw it onto the fire before turning to the old men. Master Hiro sat motionless, legs crossed, eyes closed, a slight spasm playing across his eyelids. Maohong, in contrast, stared right back his arm tucking back under his cloak then inclined his head towards the fire.

With a start, Renco returned to his task. The fish smelt burnt. He singed his fingers in his haste to remove them from the heat. Laying the skewers against a log, Renco blew on his hands before turning to stir the broth.

He glanced across at Mao to find the old man with his crooked teeth, grinning at him. It was unusual enough that Renco smiled back holding his hand up in thanks. His master may not have been as subtle.

Together they waited. After a short time, Hiro stirred. Unfolding his legs he knelt, taking a long deep breath then sighed. "Chargrilled, my favourite Renco."

The boy nodded his thanks, a grin slipping onto his face at Maohong's scowl. Rising, Renco removed the skewer and leaf wrap from the first of the fillets and laid it on a plate. Taking a ladle he dipped it into the pan, holding it so none of the fish bones were caught, then poured the broth into a mug. Taking both plate and mug, he laid them before his master and knelt, bowing his head to the floor.

"Thank you Renco for the gift of food," Hiro intoned, nodding his thanks.

Renco filled another plate and mug and handed them to Maohong who simply grunted.

Finally taking his plate, Renco tried the fish. It was a little singed on the outside and it needed more seasoning but the flesh was succulent and tasty nevertheless. In between bites, he sipped at his broth and was pleased with the result.

After the meal, Mao was the first to rise and gather the plates. It was usually Renco's duty to clean up but a glare from Maohong kept him in his seat. The old man disappeared into the darkness heading for the river.

Hiro rose and, fetching his staff, walked into the tall grass just outside the fire's light. He stood still and unmoving for a time before lifting one leg and stretching it out. He held the pose a while before twisting and moving into another, his movements slow and precise. It was a familiar routine and one Renco was well accustomed to. His master's staff blended into his moves, twirling slowly, as graceful and as controlled as his body.

Renco got up, judging he had waited long enough, any longer and Master Hiro would berate him. Moving to his bedroll, he claimed his staff. It was steel-tipped and finely balanced. He had fashioned it himself under Master Hiro's instruction and, over the years as his lessons progressed, had carved many intricate runes on it.

Taking a stance, Renco fell into his own routine. There was no prescribed pattern to it but each move had a purpose and blended smoothly from one form into another. He lost himself to the exercise.

When he was finished, muscles aching in that satisfying way he loved, Renco rested the staff across his shoulders, flexing his back. Martial training always made him happy. He was aware of Master Hiro sat by the fire, dark eyes watching and assessing, his face a mask. Renco wondered at his thoughts.

Rising, Hiro stepped away from the fire and took a stance, waiting. It was a challenge. They'd travelled hard and fast and it had been four days since the last challenge. Time enough for Renco's bruises to heal, mostly.

He focused on his master and took the crane stance; left foot raised, right foot planted. He twirled his staff in several wide impressive circles before snapping it to his body, anchoring one end under his right armpit, point extending out towards Hiro. Renco shifted his left foot gliding forward into the mantis position. He was being overly elaborate and would receive a lecture for his flashy display, but he enjoyed teasing Master.

Hiro stepped forward until his face was a hand away from Renco's staff tip. He held his own staff lightly in his left hand.

Renco exploded, extending his staff in a short sharp jab. Hiro's face was not there. He'd moved a fraction, the staff almost grazing his cheek as it passed him by.

There was a mighty crack as Renco twisted his staff violently towards his master's head but struck Hiro's staff instead. Vibrations snaked up the pole, numbing hand and arm. Renco moved, spinning to his right and away. He felt the rush of air as his master's attack slid past.

Renco re-centred himself, orienting on his opponent who had not moved from his original position. Infuriatingly, he held his staff in one hand still, relaxed and ready. Renco spun his weapon and stepped in, the steel-capped end blurring towards Hiro's face before, with a deft flick, he diverted the blow hoping to avoid Hiro's counter and strike his knee cap.

His staff missed, the old man moving his leg almost casually out of its path. Renco kept moving, twisting away from a possible counter and then smoothly back in, sweeping his staff low. Then out again, round and in, jabbing for the torso. Another step in and a sweep upwards to a loud crack as their staffs met again.

Renco's blows missed or met wood every time and still, his master held the same position he'd started in. They battled in this way for some time, the speed and pace of Renco's attacks increasing but never managing to penetrate Hiro's defences.

Renco didn't get frustrated; he'd learnt patience the hard way having fought his master almost every day since becoming his ward. In the end, it finished the way all their battles did, the method different but the result always the same. Tonight, Renco over-extended as he sought to catch his master off balance only for Hiro to deflect his blow with a palm whilst slipping his staff between Renco's legs and stepping in. Renco, spinning away ended up on his arse, a flare of pain searing his left shin as it tangled with the wood.

Hiro held his hand out and Renco gripped it. There was a wiry strength to the old master that belied his size as he effortlessly hoisted his student to his feet. With a grunt, Hiro moved off to the fire leaving Renco to dust himself down.

Biting back on the pain, Renco refused to limp, not with Maohong smirking at him. He didn't want to give the old man the satisfaction. Sitting on a log, he inspected the bruise on his shin. An angry welt was visible and he probed it gingerly with his fingers.

"Leave leg alone. It better in morning," Maohong said, handing across a water skin.

Renco took it gratefully and gulped from its neck. Mao was right, he was a fast healer and the bruising would fade after a good sleep. Master Hiro told him it was because he was young and the young always healed quickly. He handed the water skin back and nodded his thanks.

"Renco better, almost had Master," Mao smirked. "But then Master did Renco much favour."

Renco glared at Mao then his leg.

Maohong chortled, "Aye, leg nothing. Master flick staff up yes. Like so." Maohong mimed a staff getting swept up, and then doubled over holding his crotch and cackling. "Oh yes, Master could have tickled stones, then Renco crawl back to camp, neh! So yes, Master favour Renco." He laughed, pleased with himself, eyes twinkling with mischief.

Renco took the teasing like he did most things in life, in silence. But he had to admit, on reflection, that Mao had a point. He grinned back at the realisation and nodded his agreement.

"Bah, Renco no fun," Maohong grumbled standing up. He wagged his head from side to side muttering under his breath as he headed for his bedroll.

Hiro had watched the exchange from across the fire. "Mao is correct," he said quietly. "Your skill is coming along well, not just the staff but all weapons." He paused and Renco waited knowing there was more.

"There is hesitancy in you. You do not fully commit to the moves. It is slight, but it is there. It will kill you one day unless you overcome it. I can try to teach you how, but make no mistake Renco; you are the one that must take the steps. I can only lead so far." He smiled then and rising walked around the fire and held out a cup.

Renco took it, screwing his face up, knowing from its heady aroma it was Master's special brew. At least that was how he thought of it. He gulped the salty metallic concoction down quickly and in one go. It was the best way for it tasted as bad as it smelt. His master only ever brought his flask of special brew out on rare occasions and he wondered at it now, grimacing at the aftertaste in his mouth.

"Get some sleep, Renco. I'll see to the fire. It will be an early start again." Master Hiro said softly.

Renco knelt and bowed low to the floor, *<Thank you, master.>*

Chapter 6 : The White Stallion

Redford, The Rivers

"He's a beauty, Sand. How can you bear to part with him?" Jacob Bouchemeax ran his hands along the horse's shoulder marvelling at the feel.

"Yep, he's big and beautiful. Give you a chance to beat me at next year's Green Fair." Sandford Bouchemeax grinned, "Be good to have a challenge from someone other than my brothers."

"What'll your Da say? I mean it's a fine gift Sand but it's too much."

"The horse is mine, bred him off my own stock, I can give him to who I like. He'll lecture me a bit for the sake of it, but in the end, he won't mind. You're family." Sandford patted the stallion's neck.

"Thank you, cousin. It's a fine gift, one I'll struggle to repay."

"Bah, a gift doesn't require payment, just thanks which you have given me at least five times now." Sand laughed, then turned serious. "He's headstrong Jac. He'll fight the bit to start with. Don't be soft on him or you'll ruin him and make a rod for your own back."

Jacob nodded, trying to keep the exasperation from his face. He knew how to ride and didn't need the lecture, but he didn't want to tarnish the giving by being petty and sounding ungrateful. What a horse. He drank in the sight of him, the barely contained power and elegant lines, he was magnificent.

Sand punched Jacob's shoulder. "I see your mind is on your horse and not me," he joked. "Come on, I'll ride with you part way to Thorsten. Check you know which end is the front."

Laughing and needing no further encouragement Jacob pulled himself up and into the saddle, the stallion dancing beneath him at the unfamiliar weight.

"A fine beast Lord Jacob and a mighty gift Lord Sandford," Mahan said. Thornhill nodded his agreement. They were Jacob's men at arms and sat astride their mounts watching the exchange from ten paces back.

"A beast you say. Bah can't you see!" Jacob feigned indignation. "He's a prince among horses."

"As you say, my Lord," Mahan said, pleased to see his young charge so happy.

Sandford leapt upon his horse, a brown mare, tall and sleek, and together they all turned for the road to Thorsten a couple of days ride south. They were joined by Mabel, Sand's sword-arm.

They crossed the bridge over the Oust River just outside of Redford passing the mass of boats and barges moored along its banks. There was a lot of activity on them.

"I spoke to Lord William when I took my leave this morning. Says he'll be ready in a few days, a week at most," Jacob said. "And that he'll bring a thousand men with him, but wouldn't say if you were one of them. Are you coming on Twyford's campaign in the spring? It'll be a grand adventure."

Sand pulled a face. "Don't know. He's taking Bruce and Robert but wants me at home with mother," he struggled to keep the bitterness from his voice. "Says it doesn't make sense to risk all his boys on a fool's folly. It's my mother talking, I just know it! She hates Twyford."

"Damn, I'm sorry Sand. It'd be good to have you with us. Want me to talk to my father? He might convince your Da otherwise. Put in a word for you at least?"

Sand looked thoughtful before shaking his head. "Nah, I can fight my own battles, besides my father is as stubborn as yours. Once his mind's set it's hard to change it, impossible unless I get mother onside."

Jacob could feel his cousin's disappointment. "Come on, let's stretch their legs." Not waiting for an answer he set his heels to the stallion's flanks, feeling the raw power releasing as his mount sprang to a canter, leaving Sand to catch him.

Chapter 7 : Road to Thorsten

Homestead, The Rivers

Nihm woke early unsure of what had disturbed her. It was still dark outside, there was no light framing her shutters and the morning birdsong hadn't yet begun. Lying in bed, her thoughts drifted. She was excited. She went to Thorsten a few times each year but she'd never been to Rivercross. It was big, much bigger than Thorsten. It was the province's capital and home to thousands of people.

Cicadas chirped outside interrupting her reverie and beneath that the soft patter of feet. She sighed; it would be Ash or Snow outside her window she told herself, but a seed of doubt had crept in. Da always told her to trust her instincts, and right now something nagged at her.

The thought of her father banished sleep and with a groan of resignation Nihm swung her legs out of bed. She knew her Da would turn up, he was as solid and dependable as the tri-moons and her faith in him was absolute. But still, she couldn't stop worrying.

Throwing her cloak around her shoulders, Nihm fastened it as she left her bedroom. Easing the front door open she found all four dogs sat waiting. Ash and Snow greeted her enthusiastically, pressing against her legs, almost knocking her over. She pushed by them and patted the two older dogs, Thunder and Maise, as she stepped from the porch.

A cool wind snapped at her cloak and pulled at her hair which she'd tied back into a tail. The air felt heavy and smelled of rain. The dogs followed after but Thunder stopped suddenly and turned to the north, ears erect, sniffing the air before padding off into the darkness. Maise looked after him then silently followed.

Ignoring the dogs' restlessness, Nihm moved to check on the ponies and was halfway to the barn when the door to the homestead opened and Marron stepped out, framed from inside by the soft light of a lamp.

"Good, you're up. I couldn't sleep either. Let's get the ponies harnessed. I want to leave as soon as we can see the trail."

"Why the rush? Da might not be far off," Nihm said, waiting for her mother and embracing her.

“No, he’s not close. I think it best we leave now. He’ll catch us up.” Marron was brusque. “Where are Thunder and Maise?”

“The dogs are unsettled,” Nihm said. “Thunder caught a whiff of something, probably a rabbit. They went off to look.” Nihm flicked a hand in the general direction the dogs had taken. She was desperate to ask Marron how she knew Da wasn’t close but sensed that now was not the time. It was a long ride to Thorsten she’d pick her moment, she decided.

“They know something is up. Different routine, they know we're leaving,” Marron said.

Nihm glanced sharply at her mother, a sudden angst upon her. Leaving, Ma said the word with such finality. They hadn’t spoken much about their journey. They headed to Thorsten and after that Rivercross, but what then? This trip was different. Maybe they weren’t coming back. Nihm pushed the thought to the back of her mind, not sure she wanted to know the answer to her unspoken question. Not yet.

They had the ponies harnessed to the cart ready to depart by the time the first sunrays leaked into the cloud over the eastern horizon. Marron closed the shutters and door to the homestead and rested a hand on its timbers, head bowed briefly, before turning and climbing onto the cart. She took the reins from Nihm, gave them a deft flick, and with a click of her tongue they were off. Ash and Snow circled them as they steered onto the overgrown path heading southeast.

“I feel sad and excited all at the same time. I feel I'm saying goodbye to an old friend I'm never going to see again,” Nihm said. “I'll miss this place."

“It’s been a good home. I'll miss it too. Hopefully one day we'll be back but who knows what the future holds."

"Do you think Da is alright?”

"I'm sure he's fine. Just like him to leave us to do all the packing.” Marron jested, but her heart wasn't in it. “Give Thunder and Maise a whistle or they’ll get left behind.”

Nihm glanced at her mother and saw a glint of moisture in her eye. Marron had voiced what she'd suspected, they were leaving for good. Nihm knew her mother was nothing if not practical; you had to be living out here in the wilds.

Leaning over, Nihm hugged her mother, knowing her damp eyes were not for the homestead. "Da will be alright, you'll see. You'll be arguing over the cooking in no time."

Turning, Nihm put her fingers to her lips and gave an almighty whistle that echoed in the early morning half-light. Da had taught her that whistle and she was proud of it. It had taken her a ten-night to master, with a lot of laughing along the way at her early attempts. *"It's not just about making noise lass, ya have to shape it. Different tone and pitch fer a different meaning."* Darion had demonstrated. The memory made her smile.

There was a distant bark as Maise and Thunder responded to her call and as the cart forded the little brook to the south of the homestead the two dogs bounded up to join them.

A few splashes of rain pattered down and Nihm squinted up at the sky. Forbidding clouds were gathering, low and heavy. She clambered back into the flatbed. Behind, the homestead appeared as a shadow hunched on the landscape and a sudden pang of sorrow struck her. Reluctantly tearing her eyes away from the only home she'd known, Nihm dug under the rain sheet for their oiled skins. They had only just donned them when the heavens opened.

The rain was set in and despite their oiled skins water found a way through to their clothes, chilling them. A cold wind blew, adding to their misery.

They moved steadily south through the morning and into the afternoon, passing through grasslands. Copses of elder and spruce sprouted up like sentinels guarding the way and they forded several fast-flowing brooks and streams swollen by the rain.

Nihm was hunched over on the bench seat feeling miserable. Her chin tucked into her chest, her oil skin grasped tightly about her.

"Encoma's holdstead is just ahead." Nihm looked up as Marron nudged her and pointed through the rain at the smeared outline of a building. Smoke rose from it like a stain against the leaden sky.

Flicking the reins, Marron steered the cart onto the track leading to the holding. The building slowly revealed itself as they drew closer. It was large and circular, looking more like a squat tower than the house it was, rugged and uninviting except for the warm glow of light peeping through narrow shutters. It was enclosed by a thick stone wall, rising to a tall gated entrance with the gates themselves pulled back wide.

As they passed through it the holdstead loomed above them rising over several floors. Other buildings, hidden by its bulk, slowly came into view as their cart trundled around its girth and stopped outside a large double door.

A muffled baying of hounds sounded from inside. Ash and Snow howled back in response until Nihm gave a whistle to quiet them. One of the large doors opened and a man emerged, an old hound peeking out around his knee. The dog barked at them but didn't leave the shelter of the doorway.

"Weesht now, girl," the man laid a hand on the hound's head and gentled her as he squinted through the rain. "Marron, is that you? By the trinity what's possessed you to be about in this weather?"

"Well met, Albert. Would you mind if I lay my cart up in your barn? I'll explain everything once we're out of this rain," Marron replied, her face grim. She was cold, wet and weary from travel.

"Of course, of course, I'm forgetting me manners. Let us get me coat and I'll open her up for you." Albert was a man of late middle years, hair receded and grey, but he had a warm face and a broad smile. Marron liked him.

"Who is it, Bert." A voice called from inside before a small plump woman appeared in the entrance. "Why is that you, Marron?" she answered herself, "And Nihm by goodness! Bert, what are you doing standing a gawping like that? Give the lasses a hand, go on with you." She turned to Marron and Nihm. "Get your cart in the barn Marron love. Bert will help, won't you Bert?"

Bert had already pulled his long boots on and winked at Nihm. "Right ya are, Hildi." He shrugged into a long coat and Hildi passed him a covered lantern, the flame guttering and dancing as the wind found it. Stepping into the rain he trudged across to the barn. A small beam secured its doors and Nihm jumped down to help.

"Here let me get that," Nihm pushed on the beam, sliding it back.

"Ah thank eh kindly," Bert said as they grabbed a door each and pulled them wide.

"Right ya are, Marron." Bert waved her forward as he marched in ahead, hooking the lantern to a barn support.

Marron snapped the reins and the ponies moved off, eager to get out of the rain. It was a large barn and Marron breathed in the familiar and comforting smells of straw and animals.

The snort of a horse sounded and an old draught mare poked her head over a stable door eying the new arrivals suspiciously. Bert gave her nose an affectionate rub as he walked by, opening up an empty stall for the ponies.

A tall figure appeared at the barn's entrance. "Everythin' alright, Da?"

"Yeh, fine. Look Marron and Nihm are 'ere," Bert said.

"Marron?" The man strode into the barn. "Bit early int year for market Marron, and if you don't mind my sayin, pretty foul weather to be travellin' in ta boot." As he stepped into the light Nihm saw it was John Encoma, the eldest of Albert's three sons; tall and rangy where his father was short and stout.

"Aye, well I'm sorry to say I bring worrying news, but before I say more let me get the ponies settled," Marron replied.

"We found uraks in the forest me and Da," Nihm blurted, as she slipped bit and bridle from one of the ponies.

"Uraks you say." John stroked his chin then shook his head. "Sounds like nowt but tall tales. Ain't never heard of no uraks in these parts. Tell the truth I'm thinking they're nowt but stories, like the bards tell'em."

Marron glared at her daughter tutting whilst Nihm, pretending not to see her displeasure, bent to release the pony from its traps.

"Well as I said, it's a conversation best had later," Marron grumped. "Nihm can finish up here. Get the ponies rubbed down, watered and fed. If that's alright Albert?"

Bert looked at the two women thoughtfully. "Aye, that suits me fine, John'll stay and give a hand won't you lad."

"Sure Da, we'll be in soon." John, oblivious to the sudden tension between mother and daughter, had already moved to the other pony and started unbuckling the harness.

"Thanks' Albert, we're grateful for your hospitality," Marron said, as they stepped out into the rain.

* * *

The holdstead was ancient, its past obscure. It had been built in a time when living on the edge of the wilds was dangerous and conflicts commonplace. For Marron, who was schooled in her histories, the building held much fascination. She had long suspected it was not built as a holdstead but merely repurposed as such.

Large and circular the hold was easily sixty paces across. It was home to several families who, Marron knew from previous visits, all lived on the second and third floors. The ground floor, where she stood now, was dominated by a large open area and was the hub of the little community. Here the families would meet, eat and discuss hold business. Rooms abutted the exterior wall, including a large kitchen and larder and several workshops.

It was a busy time of year and most of the holdsteaders worked, preparing goods and produce for the upcoming harvest festival. It gave the place a vitality and sense of communion that Marron found she missed.

The holdstead was warm and the people friendly. Visitors were rare in these parts and many in the hold came to talk to Marron. They were neighbours and as such greetings and re-acquaintances were made. Marron too was considered the closest thing to a physiker they had outside of Thorsten and she had, in times gone by, been called upon for her healing skills. Now was no different and she soon found herself busy advising people on all manner of ailments and injuries.

It was full dark, the hearth fire crackling and sharing its warmth, when the community of families gathered to share the evening meal. Afterwards, at a word from Albert, the children cleared away the tables before being sent away.

Albert rapped his knuckles on the table for attention and a quiet hush descended over the room. Nihm's earlier assertion in the barn had been whispered about and most waited expectantly to hear what Marron had to say.

Standing Marron surveyed the room, seeing eager anticipation on many faces and curiosity on those few that had missed the rumour mill. Deciding a direct approach was best she began.

"A few days back my husband Darion and Nihm came across evidence of an urak scouting party. Darion has gone to track them and hopefully find out where they are, how many and maybe get an idea of what they're about."

An uproar followed this statement and after a bit, Albert rapped his knuckles again calling for silence. As the noise subsided he turned to Marron.

"Everyone has heard tell of uraks and their savagery but they've never been seen in these parts. They're a bard's tale from days of old, told to scare children and earn some coin," Albert Encoma said, to the murmur and agreement of all there. His tone was measured, his eyes pained at having to refute Marron.

"If you knew your history, Albert Encoma, you would know these were once their lands," Marron snapped back, immediately regretting her tone. She was tired and fearful and not used to being spoken down to and she hadn't expected it of her host. In a conciliatory tone, she continued. "Indeed, they've not been seen for over a hundred years but they are here now and I assure you they are very real."

"Forgive Bert, he don't like shocks and he meant no offence, Marron," Hildi interjected. "Maybe before folks say things they oughtn't you can tell us this evidence."

"Yeah, you have a head to scare us with?" a voice quipped from the back of the gathering. It was James Encoma, Albert's youngest son.

"No head, just this." Marron bent and drew the urak arrow out of her pack and explained how Darion had found it and the dead forest bear.

"Darion and I are both learned in our histories and skilled with the bow. I tell you this is an urak arrow. It was not crafted in these lands and the wood it is fashioned from does not grow in these parts. This arrow was made in the north, past the Torns," she said.

"Thank you, Marron. What you've said is worrying and it's right you tell us. It's what any good neighbour would do." Albert kept a neutral tone. "You'll pass your suspicions to the Black Crow when you get to Thorsten. I'm sure, Lord Richard will know what to do, probably send his guard north to investigate."

Marron stared at Albert unable to keep the consternation from her face. "By the time I get to Thorsten and if I manage to see, Lord Richard it will be at best several days before he can organise anything. Please, Albert, I don't think you can risk waiting that long," she implored.

"What exactly are you asking, Marron? That we abandon the holding?" He saw the answer in her eyes. "Preposterous! You want us to leave?" His voice was rising and again Hildi laid a calming hand over her husband's.

"It's hard to hear what you don't want. I understand your worry but that's exactly what you must do." Marron knew what she asked but speaking it out loud made it real. Before it was an abstract, a warning to convey and people would make the right decision. Now though a hollow dread crept over her heart as she realised hers was a message doomed to fail.

There was uproar in the room. Marron bowed her head, knowing she hadn't handled things as well as she might have. There was a rapping of knuckles as Albert banged again on the table until quiet was finally restored.

"I hear your warning but I don't thank you for it." Albert shook his head. "This is our lives, our home. We have animals to care for and a harvest to bring in and you ask us to abandon all this for a bear and an arrow. I mean no offence, Marron but who are you ta tell us these things?"

Marron was torn and took a moment to gather her thoughts. In the end, she did what she always did. What she thought was right.

"You've known Darion and me for many years and I suspect some know already… we are of the Order. We were sent here to watch, and to guard. Well we have watched and we've guarded and I tell you now the urak are real and they are here. You'd be fools not to heed me." She looked at Albert, her eyes beseeching him. "Please Albert, I know things. You have to trust that what I say is true."

They looked at her in shocked silence, even Nihm, until a sneering laugh broke the moment.

"So you belong to the Order. Remind me again but aren't they outlawed in these parts by the High Lord?" It was James Encoma again, shouting from the back of the room. "You'd best leave afore you get us all hanged."

Albert stood and with a loud bang slammed his palm down hard on the table making them all jump. "Hold your tongue, boy." Albert's normally jovial face contorted in anger as his voice reverberated around the room.

James looked shocked. "I'm sorry Da, but it's truth."

"Truth it may be but that don't make it right. Now sit and keep your trap closed. If'n I wish to hear from you, I'll ask." His eyes bored into James who shrank back down into his seat. Satisfied Albert turned back to Marron.

"Please forgive my boy. His mouth runs away with him sometimes but he means well and has spoken a truth." Albert sat. Hildi patted his arm before addressing Marron.

"Most here remember the good the Order brought. When they moved freely in these parts and championed the people but with all due respect you've been gone too long." She paused and gathered herself. "Maybe there are urak but we cannot just abandon everything we are, our home, our livelihoods. This is all we are and ever will be. You ask too much. Expect too much."

Marron nodded her understanding, saddened by it. "Thank you, Hildi. We've been gone too long, I agree, though that was not of our choosing but I'm here now and I tell you the urak are coming and they care not a fig for you or yours. They'll kill you, your children and your grandchildren. They'll take your holding, your crops and animals and there will be no more Encomas here. That is the future if you stay."

Hildi trembled at Marron's words and it was Albert's turn to put his hand over hers in comfort. "Your warning is dire indeed Marron; your words frightening. I'll think on what you've told me," Albert said.

"Nihm and I will be off at first light. There's no time to wait," Marron pressed.

"Then I'll make my decision by first light on the morrow," Albert said with finality.

Marron and Nihm took their leave and headed to the barn leaving the families to debate her words. No one would meet their eyes as they left and many faces looked troubled. A bed would be found for them in the holding should they wish it but instinctively Marron knew the holdsteaders needed space from her, time to discuss and digest what she'd told them. The barn would do them just fine.

"What do you think they'll do?" whispered a subdued Nihm. She was shocked at what she'd heard.

"They'll talk a lot but I think they'll stay. They do not want to believe me and in truth, our evidence is pretty thin," Marron said.

"You and Darion are of the Order! Why didn't you tell me?"

"Oh Nihm, I'll explain, but not now. I feel all wrung out. Let's check the ponies and the dogs and get some sleep."

Chapter 8 : Campfire

The Rohelinewaald

The ilfanum moved with quiet purpose through the forest. There was a score of them, heavily armed but lightly dressed in corded skirts and supple flaxen cloaks that shimmered and blended with their surroundings. It was pitch dark under the forest canopy with the three moons hidden behind clouds but the darkness was no barrier to them. The smell of a campfire drew them on like moths to a flame.

A raven swooped out of the night landing on an outstretched arm. "Maarriiika," it cawed.

"Well done, Bezal," R'ell crooned, feeding the bird a rarebit from a pouch on his belt before launching the raven into the air. He signalled the others onwards.

R'ell was cautious. Why would M'rika set a campfire this close to the river? The Fassarunewadaick or Fossa, as humans named it, marked the edge of Da'Mari. No ilf would draw attention by lighting a fire unless the need was dire. He snorted with derision at the thought of man. So impatient and disrespectful, too lazy even to speak the river's true name. The ilf shook his head clearing his thoughts and concentrated on the path ahead.

An ilf materialised ahead and signalled him. She was umphathi, a warden, like all of them. Her signing told R'ell she'd found M'rika. Leaping ahead the muted glow of a campfire became visible. Stepping into the light of its dying embers R'ell froze unprepared for what he found.

M'rika lay curled into the body of a large, mostly naked man, a man with fur on his face. Strangely, the rest of his body was bare containing only a sparse covering. R'ell wondered if that was why humans clothed themselves. He'd never been this close to one before nor seen them without their coverings on.

The man's clothes lay close to the dying warmth of the fire, faint steam rolling off them. R'ell cocked his head considering.

It was clear they had crossed the Fassrunewadaick and M'rika looked to have suffered some hardship but why was the man here? That he trespassed on Da'Mari meant death. That he created fire on Da'Mari meant death. That he held M'rika, a Visok and K'raal, meant death. The man was thrice dead for his transgressions and

R'ell's blood boiled just looking at him. His anger was overwhelming until a sudden calm stole over him, clearing his mind and quieting his blood. Da'Mari had spoken.

The other umphathi were gathered behind and R'ell sensed their outrage at the human, felt it as he'd felt his only moments before. R'ell signalled them to step back but, defiant, they held their ground. R'ell turned to face them with violence in his stance. He signed once more, his message unequivocal. After the briefest of pauses, they responded, one by one melting into the forest until only he was left.

R'ell surveyed the scene. The man's coverings had been placed to dry and were damp still to the touch. His only weapons a dagger and sword, poor quality by ilfanum standards, lay next to the man within easy reach. R'ell removed them.

Crouching, he studied M'rika. She was breathing easily but looked pale and cold. Her right ankle was swollen and one side of her face was marked with a dark bruise. She had numerous cuts and abrasions on her arms and legs, her leaf skin torn and broken in places. Lifeblood had dried, hardening to a dark green colour where it had leaked out. She would live.

The man was harder to read. Da'Mari had passed down the knowledge of humans but this was the first, R'ell had seen up close. He patrolled the forest to the east of the Fassarunewadaick and tracked any human that wandered too close but it was always from a distance and in cover. R'ell thought him familiar but it was hard to tell, they all looked the same. Like M'rika, he too looked cold, shivered with it despite the proximity of the dying fire.

Rising to his feet R'ell walked around the camp tracking the route they had taken from the Fassarunewadaick. His mind working through what he saw. The man had dragged M'rika from the river carrying her to the little clearing. He made a fire somehow, a puzzle for later, and had set his clothes to drying. Satisfied with his assessment R'ell wandered back past the outlying watchers to the clearing.

He stood awhile looking down at M'rika and the man, considering. Reaching a decision he unclasped his cloak and, whipping it through the air, floated it down over the prone pair. Gathering fallen leaves he fed them to the fire until it burst back to life, then placed twigs and dead branches over it, building it up until its crackling warmth suffused the camp.

Dawn was not far off. R'ell sat on his haunches and waited.

Chapter 9 : Friend or Foe

The Rohelinewaald

Awareness returned slowly. He felt warmth and the caress of cloak against skin. Through the fugue of his mind he wondered at that; had he covered them with a cloak? He saw the bright glow and heard the crackle of the fire, everything else was black. He vaguely recalled the ilf and felt her body warm and tight against his own, could feel her breathing. He drifted off.

It was not so dark when he cracked his eyes and looked through his lashes. Some primal instinct told Darion they were not alone. He lay still searching with his senses.

"If a man is awake I would talk with him," said a voice. It had a lilt to it similar to that of the ilf in his arms only deeper. Conscious suddenly that he held an ilf in the crook of his body Darion sat up, his hand reaching behind for his dagger and sword. They were gone, of course they were.

The ilf sat across the fire staring at him intently. He was a male, taller and broader than the female he'd saved. She stirred at the cold air on her back where the warmth of his body had left her and Darion tucked the cloak around her.

R'ell rocked back on his heels, his eyes drawn to the token hanging about the man's neck. The token changed everything. Who was this man to wear such a thing? Dragging his eyes back to the man's face the ilf considered a moment. "Is a man hungry? You must be thirsty at least. Come, sit by the fire."

Darion rose warily; he was stiff, sore and still cold. Crouching opposite the ilf, Darion warmed his hands, making his own assessment. The ilf bore the same leaf-like scales as the female but they were a darker green. Black eyes regarded him in turn and Darion didn't need his instincts to tell him he was in trouble. The talk was, if you entered ilfanum lands you didn't come out again. Darion knew this was not the whole truth but he also knew the ilfanum had a disdain for humans.

Though he sensed danger, Darion's mind was slow with fatigue still. The ilf awaited an answer but it took Darion some time to work out a reply. "You're welcome, ilf ta my fire. I'm sorry I've no food ta break with you or water ta slake your thirst."

R'ell laughed. "Ah, a man is bold. I know where there's water." Rising smoothly, the ilf walked past Darion towards the river. On the ground where the ilf had sat were his dagger and sword.

Darion got to his feet, moved around the fire, and stood over his weapons. Desperate to pick them up, he instead turned and gathered his clothing from the surrounding bushes. He started suddenly. A raven sat, brazenly staring at him from a branch not an arm's length away, cocking its head at him. It was unsettling. Stepping back a pace, Darion glanced at the bird before struggling into his still-damp clothes. Ravens were not common in these parts. Darion shrugged into his leather jerkin then looked again to find the bird gone.

The ilf was back. Darion watched him striding into camp. Tall and rangy he walked with smooth grace, making almost no sound. The ilf was perfectly proportioned, the muscles of his arms and chest clearly defined. The darker green of the ilf's leaf skin, Darion saw, was not uniform. Looking closely he saw now that it was mottled, some of the leaf scale darker than the rest. His features were sharp and elegant, a thin-lipped mouth, the tell-tale notched skin over his nose and large canted eyes that looked black in the glow of the fire. The ilf held out a water skin.

"I'm obliged," Darion said taking it. Removing the bung he took a long swig.

"Most welcome human." The ilf crouched once again by the fire, his eyes barely touching on the sword and dagger.

He's a cool one alright, Darion thought. The water was icy cold and refreshing and he gulped it down thirstier than he'd realised. Wiping his mouth he replaced the bung and, rising, offered the skin back.

"Man may keep it."

Darion nodded and sat back down. "My thanks..." he trailed off. "My name is Darion what may I call you?"

"Darion may call me R'ell."

"Thank you R'ell, the water was much needed. I'm sorry I have nothing ta give in return."

The ilf laughed again. "You have shared your fire with me yes?"

Darion allowed a grin to form. "Indeed, but I suspect it was a poor fire when you found us. Perhaps there is something else I might offer?"

Darion blessed his old loremaster at the Order hall who taught him of the ilf and drummed the lessons into him about etiquette and tradition. Those lessons, along with his memories from that time before, were serving him well now. He absently touched the token hanging from his neck.

R'ell observed the gesture with interest. "Perhaps you could tell me how you come to be in Da'Mari uninvited? Yes, I would very much like to hear that tale."

Darion blinked; the question was direct and abrupt. Still, he was feeling impatient himself, he had Marron and Nihm to get back to. Hopefully, they'll have left for Thorsten by now. Darion dragged his mind back to the campfire and R'ell sitting patiently before him. With a nod of acknowledgement he began. R'ell sat impassive and silent throughout. When Darion finished he took a swig from the water skin and waited.

"I owe you thanks. We are aware of the urakakule to the east of Fassarunewadaick," R'ell said, pausing briefly in thought. "The urakakule are probing these lands, they threaten to cross the river."

Darion considered this news. "Then the urak will not return from your lands, but why do you tell me this?"

R'ell inclined his head though whether at his statement or his question Darion was unsure.

"I offer this so you know it is unsafe to return to the east bank and your home, if it still stands. I offer this so that when I take you to meet my K'raal you will come willingly."

Darion felt his pulse rising. From his lessons, a K'raal was like a Lord or Lady, someone of power. If they were like the Lords he knew of it would mean a lengthy delay, one he could ill afford.

"I'm afraid I can't. Much as I would like ta meet your K'raal I have a wife and daughter in need of me. I would ask your help in crossing the Fossa so I can return ta them."

A frown creased R'ell's face at the mention of the Fossa and Darion mentally kicked himself. The Fossa was a bastard word to the ilf, an insult to the river. He thought furiously a moment before bowing his head and giving a wry grin. "I apologise, I meant Fassarunewadaick of course. I have been with my own kind too long ta know better."

R'ell inclined his head. The man was uncouth but at least he had the good manners to apologise. Despite his earlier impulse to drive a blade through the man's eyeball, he grudgingly conceded he'd been right to restrain himself. Da'Mari knew and Da'Mari had spoken. Still, it left him with a problem. D'ukastille, his K'raal, would want to see this man and pass judgment. Then there was the token the man wore pronouncing him a friend and granting status in Da'Mari and all Nu'Rakauma. How had he come by it? That would be a tale to hear. For now though, the token was a problem.

"I understand your concern. You seem wise for a human, so when I say, on my honour, returning you to the east bank would likely mean your death you know I speak true. What use then will you be to wife and child. You must find another way."

Darion was torn. To challenge the ilf on this would be to risk insult. He had no way forward.

R'ell watched him carefully. "I offer knowledge. We have scouts on the east bank and deeper into the eastern forest. They may have news of your family or at least the urakakule and their movements."

Grudgingly Darion conceded. "How far is your K'raal? Will you help me safely back to my lands if I meet with him? I must make all haste."

"He is two turn's south of here. Safe passage will be for my K'raal to decide," R'ell said. "But we leave soon, you must decide." He could see Darion wavering. "Tell me, ilf friend, where did you come by said token." He indicated the talisman.

Darion lifted his neck thong and held it feeling the token with his fingers. "That is a long story and I'm not sure it is mine ta tell."

"Perhaps you might permit me to look at it?" R'ell held his hand out.

Darion looked at R'ell but couldn't read the ilf. He sensed no deceit but…

"On my honour, I shall return it," R'ell said extending his hand further. Grudgingly, Darion went to lift it from his neck.

"Tsk, R'ell, shame on you," a soft voice spoke up. Darion turned at the sound and saw the female ilf propped up on an elbow. She looked haggard, the green leaf scale of her skin leeched of colour and there seemed a deep weariness about her. But all things considered, she looked a hundred times better than she had the night before.

She returned his gaze. "My thanks, Darion for my rescue; you saved my life thrice and my honour once." She emphasized the word honour, pointedly looking at R'ell as she said it.

"Let the token lie where it is. I suggest you never remove it, especially so when in Da'Mari."

Darion released the neck thong and glared at R'ell who held his hands up. "Forgive me, ilf friend, I would have returned it as I promised."

"Maybe, after you had struck his head from his shoulders or after D'ukastille, my brother, had decided his fate, yes?" M'rika rasped.

R'ell bowed touching his head to the floor exposing his neck. "Forgive me, K'raal, if I have offended you."

"You do offend me. But it is Darion, ilf friend that you insult. Apologise to him?" she retorted.

R'ell raised his head, his eyes flickered to Darion and reluctantly he turned and bowed to him. R'ell's shoulders shook in anger and humiliation as he tried and failed to keep the hard edge from his voice.

"Darion, I would not have harmed you, on my honour, but forgive me, I would not have returned your token until after you had met my K'raal." R'ell stayed with his head bowed.

Uncomfortable, Darion stared at the ilf. A response was required but glancing at the ilf lady she gave no help. That she was K'raal was a surprise but reason enough for R'ell's forced apology. Darion saw the tension in R'ell's shoulders and heard the edge in his voice when he'd spoken. He would have to tread carefully. Deciding bravado was best, Darion waved a nonchalant hand at R'ell.

"No forgiveness needed, friend. You broke my thirst did you not? I'm sure it was just a misunderstanding."

R'ell sat up and nodded his thanks. All saw the lie but it had allowed R'ell to save face, despite this Darion felt hostility behind his black eyes and knew he had no friend in the ilf.

"I am M'rika dul Da'Mari. You may call me M'rika," She addressed Darion.

"Honoured ta be of service, lady," Darion inclined his head.

She gave him a smile in return. "R'ell is correct in his assessment. To return to the east bank would likely be your death. This you know I think," M'rika said. "I will head south to meet my brother, D'ukastille, R'ell's K'raal but first I have another matter to attend. I would ask you to go with R'ell and I will join you later. Then I will help you return to your family."

"Thank you M'rika but I'd like ta track the river south and cross where it's safe," Darion replied. "I need ta find them and I need ta warn my people of what's coming."

R'ell glared at Darion and opened his mouth to respond but M'rika held up a hand, silencing him.

"Family is important, this ilf understands, but with the urakakule threat, many of our young will come to blood themselves. I fear you are in more danger on the west bank than the east but for the protection, I and R'ell give you," M'rika said.

Darion knew he was being manipulated but could see no way out. Like it or not he needed the ilf's help. R'ell unexpectedly stood and scrapped leaves and detritus from the forest floor. He grabbed a stick and etched a mark in the dirt.

"Fassarunewadaick runs so, looping to the southeast before turning back to the southwest. My K'raal is here." R'ell made a mark on his makeshift map. "To avoid the urakakule you must go south. It is quicker and safer for you to travel with us and it is in the right direction." He drew a line through the forest, bypassing the loop of the river, to his K'raal.

Darion looked at the dirt map following R'ell's reasoning, it was sound. He twisted his heart ring. Its warmth told him Marron was alive but not whether she was safe. Standing, he walked past R'ell then bent, retrieving his dagger and sword. "Soonest gone, soonest arrived my old Da used to say. But I think, lady, you carry an injury."

“I have someone to help M’rika,” R’ell said. He moved to the edge of the clearing, paused then looked back. “M’rika, can I dissuade you from this other matter?”

“No.” Her reply was blunt and final.

Chapter 10 : Road to Thorsten Part 2

Encoma Holdstead, The Rivers

The morning saw Marron and Nihm heading southeast once more. The rain had cleared away through the night leaving a clear sky and crisp wind. Neither spoke much.

Albert had told them earlier, as they hitched the ponies to the cart, that they would wait to hear from Darion. He'd gone to find out more, hadn't he? Maybe it was just a hunting or foraging party. Marron urged him to reconsider or at least to send the women and children to Thorsten. He had promised to think on it but both knew it was empty words.

Most of the families had gathered to see them go but it was a disconsolate send-off, not helped by Marron's final warning. "Keep your eye to the North. If you see smoke they have fired our homestead. That might be all the warning you'll get."

So they were in a sombre mood as they followed the road to Thorsten but not just because of the Encomas. They passed more holdings as they travelled and Marron duly stopped at each to pass her warning on. She had refined her story and made it simpler, saying only that urak were seen in the north and raided south. It made no difference, none of the steaders heeded her warning and some even ordered them from their land disgruntled.

The further southeast they went the better maintained the roads, so despite the added stops, they made good time. The weather was clear, the late autumn sun warm and the dogs happy exploring the sights and smells. Ash and Snow even took to chasing hares. Watching the two dogs tearing around helped to lift the dark mood that had descended on both Marron and Nihm.

"Ma, what is the Order?" Nihm said, asking the question that had itched away at her all day. "I mean I've heard of it of course but I don't understand what it is or how you are part of it."

Marron had known the question was coming and was only surprised Nihm had waited so long to ask it. She'd thought hard on how to answer.

"It's a long and complicated beginning but, in simple terms, the Order was a collective formed during the War of the Taken. A group of people with unique skills that banded together to fight against the Morhudrim. You know your history of the War of the Taken. Well, we survived and won in large part because of this collective." Nihm listened avidly. Marron had already told this story, had taught her the history of the Taken, but now she listened with a fresh perspective.

"The Morhudrim or Takers as they're oft called are alien to all that was known in the world. We don't know where they came from, just that they could take or possess a thing, anything. They enslaved all they encountered." Marron paused and glanced at Nihm.

"Humanity is very good at finding things to war on and fight over but this was different. How do you fight an enemy you do not understand? All the races, Urakakule, Dwarves, and others fought the Morhudrim and were losing. The urak were all but enslaved. Only one of their great tribes resisted the Takers. The rest, well they reaped havoc and war across the lands. Man, with all his petty squabbles, kingdom vying against kingdom, lords fighting lords, did not realise the danger until too late. Why help the neighbour you warred with the year before? So senseless," Marron said this last to herself.

"But we defeated them in the end," Nihm said.

"Aye we did and that was largely down to the Order and the ilfanum who came at the last and turned the tide. But as to the Order, well that came about because of one woman and a being said to be not of this world."

"A demon?" Nihm cried.

"No, no, not a demon but perhaps just as strange," Marron stated. "The woman was called Elora dul Eladrohim."

"An ilf!" exclaimed Nihm.

"Yes indeed an ilf. Now if you want to hear the rest no more interruptions," Marron chided.

"Sorry, go on."

"Elora bonded with this being and gained the knowledge of the Morhudrim, what they were and how to defeat them. Elora spent many years gathering a disparate group of people, wizards, warriors, lords and priests, even a thief, and from all races. Any that were deemed suited. They called themselves the Order and swore an oath placing them outside the rule of man or ilf or indeed any race; an oath to protect all." Marron paused and handed the reins to Nihm whilst she took a sip of water. She was not used to talking so much and since the Encomas holdstead that was all she seemed to do; and all for nothing. She took another sip and offered the water skin to Nihm before taking back the reins. "Now where was I?"

"The oath," Nihm said.

"Ah yes. Many took the oath for many were needed and many saw the need. Small victories gained the Order friends and allies. This led to greater victories and some defeats but in the end, they forced the Taken back and back until finally a battle was fought far to the North, in Nordrum. There the Morhudrim were confronted and we won…just. The ilfanum showed up at the end and turned the tide otherwise we likely would have lost. That is how the Order came to be."

Nihm chewed her lip, a childhood habit that reappeared whenever she was thinking. Nihm suspected her mother told less than she knew.

"Following victory at Nordrum the Order were much admired and honoured. An Accord was struck in Tal'Draysil and the Order became keepers of the peace and arbiters of justice. But man has a short memory and the Order's influence has since waned. Most still honour the Accord that was made but it's mostly lip service. Few hold the Order in esteem, the rest tolerate or ignore us. Some, like High Lord Twyford, seek to banish the Order from their lands in breach of the Accord."

Nihm heard the sadness in her mother's voice. She had a hundred questions to ask but sensed her mother was done. Instead, Nihm put her arm around her and gave a quick hug.

"We'll need to be careful in Thorsten," Marron said, "Tell no one I am of the Order. There are many that would use that knowledge against me. It will be dangerous," she warned.

"I won't." Nihm grinned, her imagination already firing. It was like a bard's tale come to life.

As they travelled the road turned more easterly and they encountered more traffic, mostly holders taking their wares to town or supplies home, but occasionally they would see a tradesman. Once, they were passed by a patrol of rough-looking guardsmen, all wearing a red tabard, the familiar emblem of a black crow over twin rivers stitched on it. Nihm being a curious child had once asked Darion about the tabard and he had explained that the red and the rivers were for the Rivers province and the black crow for Thorsten.

Nihm thought Marron would tell her warning to the guardsmen but she held her peace, moving the cart to the roadside and letting them by with a wave and a hello. The riders were soon past and they were on their way again.

* * *

It was late afternoon on their second day out from the Encoma Holdstead when, as they crested a small hill, Thorsten came into view. It was a grand sight, one Nihm never tired of seeing. Thorsten was a frontier town on the edge of the wilds. It was surrounded by earthworks upon which sat a large stone curtain wall. To Nihm, Thorsten looked huge with more houses than she could count tightly packed within its walls. Dirty ribbons of smoke dribbled up into the sky from all over, but the sight that drew her eye most was the castle at its centre, its large solitary keep dominating the skyline.

From the top of the hill, Nihm could make out a church with its boxy bell-tower, yellow against the castle's black. It was the church of the Red God, Kildare, the god of war and death, who in these parts was simply called the soldier.

It always felt strange to Nihm, seeing the church. She didn't know why but she'd always been wary of it and despite her inherent curiosity had never felt compelled to explore it on any of her previous visits to Thorsten.

Nihm recalled her last trip, in spring. A red priest had stood atop the steps leading to the church whilst at the bottom a stake was planted, wood and kindling piled high about it. The priest had been filled with righteous zeal and had spoken loudly, flinging his arms about admonishing anyone and everyone as far as Nihm could tell. She hadn't liked his tone or the restless crowd gathered to listen. Marron, who never got flustered, looked agitated and, when Nihm had asked her about it, would say nothing. They concluded their business early that trip and left for home shortly afterwards.

Marron's warning from earlier in the day pushed itself to the front of Nihm's mind, filling in what had been left unsaid in the spring. Thorsten didn't seem quite so exciting now.

They followed the road down the hill and across Northfields as they approached the town. Ahead stood a large gatekeep, Northgate. It was wide enough that two carts could pass beneath its maw. Its solid iron-bound gates were pulled open and the portcullis retracted.

Guards stood atop the walls and gatehouse and as they approached more still were at a guard station outside the gates overseeing those coming and going. They looked bored for the most part and disinterested to Marron.

A dirty, blonde-haired guard, his left eye dead and filmed over, leered at Nihm with his good eye and left his leaning spot against the gatehouse wall. Holding his hand up, he sauntered over as Marron drew the cart to a halt.

"What be your business?"

"Goods for market," Marron stated.

Deadeye leant on the footboard and stared at Nihm. His eye followed the curve of Nihm's thigh and travelled up to her chest where it lingered. Colour flushed Nihm's cheeks and she stared straight ahead not knowing what to do.

"My goods are in the back, not sat here upfront if you need to inspect anything," Marron spoke, an acid edge to her voice.

Deadeye looked amused. "I be doing my inspectin just fine," he sneered.

Thunder suddenly popped his head around the cart's sideboard and gave a loud bark followed by a deep-throated growl.

The man jumped and stumbled backwards almost ending on his backside. The other guards watching from the station post howled with laughter.

"I swear Zon's only gone an pissed hisself," shouted one.

Deadeye's face flushed red. Putting his hand on his sword he snarled. "Call that rabid mutt away afore I teach him a lesson lady."

Maise chose that moment to introduce herself, jumping up onto the bench seat between Nihm and Marron. The wolfdog never barked, just stared, her lip curled back showing her teeth. Deadeye looked about nervously then took another step back as Ash and Snow popped out from behind the wagon to see what the fuss was all about.

"You cain't bring in no pack of wild dogs lady. You gonna have to leave 'em out here."

Marron placed a calming hand on Maise and looked down at the scruffy uncouth guardsman. His tabard was dirt-stained, his leathers and armour ill-kept. She gathered herself but before she could reply a shout rang out.

"Pieterzon!"

Deadeye didn't take his eye off the dogs, didn't need to look to know his captain strode towards him.

"Cap'n Sir, pack of wild dogs they's trying to bring in," he whined, his hand still on his sword.

"Piss off." The captain was tall and broad and walked with an easy swagger.

"That an order cap'n?" Pieterzon said, sniffing up and spitting a wad of phlegm onto the roadside. The officer stepped in front of the guard and shook his head.

"Pieterzon, you're too stupid to know when to keep your mouth shut." Pieterzon was not a small man but he had to look up to meet the captain's gaze. The officer turned his head slightly and called over his shoulder, "Kronke!"

A guard, hunched over playing dice near the guardhouse, looked up. Seeing the captain he reluctantly stood and peeled himself away from his fellows.

Nihm gaped at him. He was a giant of a man, bigger even than her Da. As he strode towards them, Nihm saw that despite his size he had a friendly open face. A long moustache framed his mouth and hung past his chin.

"Cap'n?" he rumbled.

"What have I said about Pieterzon?" said the captain turning to Kronke.

The giant, a hand taller than his captain, looked down at Pieterzon, then tugged on his moustache ends. "He's sloppy, insolent, a disgrace to his uniform which is as filthy as his mouth, if I recall rightly, sir."

The captain gave a thin-lipped smile. "Do I have to sort your mess out, Kronke?"

Kronke gave the only answer he could. "No, sir." Glaring at Deadeye, he jerked his head to the side. A sullen-looking Pieterzon turned and walked slowly back towards the guard station. Kronke, not happy with his pace, placed a massive hand on his shoulder and propelled him on muttering. "You gotta be the dumbest muthafucka I ever met. If we pull extra shift cause of you I am gonna snap your head off and stick it up your ass."

The Captain turned with a smile, "Marron Castell! I thought that was you. Sorry about that lout. It seems Lord Bouchemeax's Black Crows are recruiting any old riffraff these days."

Nihm glanced at the officer and then at her mother.

"Sir Anders, well met. What is it two, three years?" Marron smiled.

"Six, I believe. Too long," he stated, then looking past them, signalled to a farmer who had drawn up behind Marron to move on by. "Have to say it's good to see you, Marron," he said, before gazing at Nihm. "And Nihm, last time I saw you… well, you've grown, got the look of your ma, thankfully."

Nihm blinked, trying to remember who he was. He was familiar but it was no good she couldn't recall. There was an awkward pause and Nihm belatedly realised she was meant to respond. "Erm, thanks."

Anders grinned. "I see you have Darion's gift for conversation." He laughed before addressing Marron once more. "Truth is I was hoping to catch up with Dar. Is he here already? Or maybe he follows?"

"It's good to see you, Anders, and fortunate. Dar will join us later all being well. But I would have words with you if I can? Privately," Marron said.

Anders nodded. "I'm off duty in the next hour. Where are you staying? Maybe share a glass and catch up?"

"Normally I stay at the Broken Axe if they have room. Say this evening, eighth bell?" Marron said.

"Broken Axe it is, till then. Marron, Nihm." Anders tipped his head in salute.

Marron smiled to herself, pleased. She had one ally that would listen to her at least. Moving the cart off, Marron followed the farmer through the gate and into town.

Chapter 11 : Strange Times

The Rohelinewaald

M'rika was in pain. Her ribs were sore, maybe one or two of them cracked, and her ankle was badly swollen.

Darion wondered how quickly she'd be able to move. The river crossing had about done for her and a night's sleep would not fix her injuries or replenish her strength. He felt cold and tired still himself. And hungry, his stomach rumbled its complaint.

The ilf Darion saw about camp appeared a simulacrum of each other, most a mottled dusky brown. Only R'ell with his added shades of green and M'rika with her light green toning stood out, at least to the casual eye. That all changed when R'ell returned.

With him was an ilf whose leaf skin was a rich autumnal riot of reds and golds with a hint of blue ghosting the edges of each leaf scale. He had hair too where the others had none. Well, hair of a sort, Darion conceded. Green leaf vines sprouted from his head to cascade down his back and frame his face. It was instantly familiar to him and in a strange way made the ilf seem more normal. It reminded Darion of De'Nestarin the only ilf he'd met before these strange times. He'd found De'Nestarin up by the Blue Sky Lakes a lifetime ago it seemed now. He touched his token as he thought about his friend.

R'ell introduced the ilf as Ruith before easing from the glade leaving the three of them alone. The ilf was old, though Darion couldn't say exactly how he knew this. Maybe it was the slight bend to his back or the shading of his leaf scale, or maybe even that he had hair. Whatever it was he appeared spry enough.

Ruith bowed his head and Darion nodded in return. The ilf smiled as if pleased, then moved to M'rika knelt and touched his head to the forest floor before sitting back on his heels and waiting.

M'rika stood, wincing as she did and inclined her head. Rising, Ruith circled M'rika. Leaning in, he unfastened R'ell's cloak and let it fall to the ground. His fingers moved to her body, prodding and probing.

Darion averted his eyes, not sure if he should stay or leave like the other ilf. For M'rika's part, she appeared unconcerned, staring vacantly off into the forest, her thoughts elsewhere.

So Darion waited. He wondered where Bindu had gotten to. He'd lost track of the old girl in the river. She was a strong swimmer and he hoped she had made the east bank and taken herself home. If not she was likely dead, for surely if she'd made the west bank Bindu would have found him.

He locked that thought down as the Order taught him many years ago. The many-fold box they called it, a visualisation of a room in his mind to place things in. It was a mental exercise, a way of compartmentalising problems and remembering things. Placing his concern for Bindu in one of his boxes he focused again on matters at hand. Ruith was talking in Archaic and intrigued he turned to watch.

The ilf placed his fingers on M'rika's body, pressing in over her ribs and chanting softly. Closing her eyes M'rika grimaced before suddenly her shoulders relaxed. Ruith moved his hands in intricate patterns over her torso and after a time moved down to her ankle which, even from where Darion stood, looked swollen and painful. The ilf placed both hands on her foot and M'rika jumped at his touch.

"Sorry, K'raal," Ruith murmured but didn't relinquish his grip. The ilf chanted again, so quiet Darion couldn't tell what was said but hearing enough to know the ilf spoke words of power; the hairs on his arms told him that.

Finished, Ruith released his hold and stood back. M'rika lifted her foot rotating it. Darion saw the swelling had gone and she moved it without pain.

"Thank you, Ruith. I feel much better," M'rika said.

Ruith was pleased. "You will still find some tenderness; I have healed your body, but not your mind. That will take time, K'raal." He was weary and a thin sheen of sweat like dew was evident on his forehead.

M'rika acknowledged his words before turning away. She still wore her belted skirt and in the time she bent, gathered R'ell's cloak from the ground and settled it about her shoulders, Ruith was gone.

Darion startled and moved for his sword, his heart hammering in his chest. R'ell had returned, this time accompanied by a bear. It dwarfed R'ell, its flank as high as the ilf's shoulder. The bear turned its shaggy head to Darion, a deep intelligence in its brown eyes.

"Peace ilf friend," R'ell said, holding his hand out palm down. "This is Rawrdredtigkah, of the Silver Lake."

There was a rustle of leaf from behind and Darion spun his blood racing. M'rika had dropped to her knees. She keened, her shoulders shaking. Her cry grew to a scream. Raw, full of pain it tore at Darion and tears sprang unbidden to his eyes. After a moment she subsided, sobbing quietly, her head falling to her chest.

R'ell stared at her, his face inscrutable then backed out of the little glade. Darion looked about and realised suddenly he was alone with M'rika and the huge forest bear with the unpronounceable name. Should he stay or go? What of the bear? And why did R'ell bring it here?

Too late, the bear was padding over to him on paws as big as his head. Up close its size and weight was intimidating and Darion struggled, fighting the urge to turn and run. A small dislocated part of him felt awe. The beast was magnificent, its brown spikey fur so dark as to be almost black, its canines the size of Nihm's hands. Pushing its nose at him it sniffed, then moved past, its bulk brushing against him.

Darion, unaware he'd held his breath, took a sudden deep gulp of air. Backing around the fire he watched the bear stop in front of M'rika. Tiny and helpless she knelt in front of the beast. Her head was down and tears fell like raindrops to the forest floor. The bear spoke and Darion's eyes went wide. He'd heard the tales of course and the Order had writings, but it was something else actually seeing it, hearing it.

"M'rika dul Da'Mari, I feel your pain child of the Nu'Rakauma. I share your sorrow," Rawrdredtigkah said.

Darion marvelled. The bear made no sound yet he heard him clear and distinct, the voice sounding in his mind, rumbling like thunder, deep and strong. He'd experienced something like this before, with Keeper and the box but there was no time to wonder at it. The bear was speaking again.

"I felt his death and came. If you are able I would hear of his end." The bear waited.

M'rika composed herself, raising her head slowly. Her eyes were black but still managed to convey her pain. She glanced at Darion. "He is part of my story Rawr."

The giant bear turned its head and gazed at the man. He stood by the fire with a hand still on his sword and the look of a deer in his stance.

"Sit manling, I will not eat you today, friend of the Ilfanum. Tell me, who are you?"

Darion, conscious suddenly that he gripped his sword, uncurled his fingers from its grip and moved his hand slowly to his side.

"I'm Darion Castell, a woodsman of sorts." He sat placing the fire between himself and the bear. Not much of a defence but a good habit he couldn't help but follow. For its part, the bear watched until he was settled and then turned back to M'rika.

"Groldtigkah, your son was killed by urakakule," M'rika said without preamble. "We travelled to Bluskiwadaiak." She looked across to Darion, "The Blue Sky Lakes humans call it." Turning back she continued. "The lakes are beautiful this late in the wane and we were of a mind to gather wild honey from the hives and see the waterfalls."

A tear tracked down her cheek but her voice, now that she had started, was strong and didn't falter. M'rika looked at the great bear as she spoke.

"We crossed the Ford at Illgathnack. Grold carried me across. He teased me, said a K'raal should not get her feet wet, and I, that he made a fine steed. He tipped me in at that and we laughed. But we were complacent, lazy. We feared nothing in the forest," M'rika said, bitterness and shame in her voice. "East of the Ford we were attacked. All I remember was a shout, Grold roaring then rearing. I fell back and then nothing." Her face took on a vacant look.

"When I came to, Grold lay dead and I trussed and bound tight." She hung her head, shaking it. "They were only four. The biggest lauded it over Grold. Gromma he was named. Another was gutted and lay dying, screaming. The two smaller urak dragged him into the bushes and then he was quiet. After that, they argued. Some to kill me, but Gromma wanted a prize for their war-chief, Mar-Dur." M'rika trailed off.

Silence filled the clearing. The bear had listened to M'rika's tale, unmoving. Slowly, delicate for something so immense, it moved to lie before M'rika.

"I should have died, I wish I had. Grold is dead because of me. It was my thought to go to Bluskiwadaiak. Grold was humouring me," M'rika cried.

"No M'rika dul Da'Mari," Rawrdredtigkah interrupted. *"It is Groldtigkah's fault he is dead, as it is yours that you are not."*

M'rika crumpled at his words sagging to her knees.

"I do not say this to be unkind," the bear rumbled, the words resounding loud in Darion's head. *"Grold was killed protecting you, which is right and just. He failed in his duty to protect you, as you failed in yours. His fate was to die for his failure and yours to live."*

Darion was not aware he had risen but he had. The giant bear's words had hit M'rika like hammer blows. She looked broken, her shoulders shaking silently. He was angry and anger always made him do stupid things Marron told him. He was talking before he could stop himself.

"The lady has suffered greatly, er" what was the damn bear's name again, he thought franticly, "Lord Bear, you do her a disservice."

The bear was fast. It turned and leapt, roaring its defiance in the space of a heartbeat. It took all of Darion's will to stand there unmoved. He knew on some primal level he was dead if the bear chose to make it so. He couldn't kill it with his sword, he wasn't fast enough. If he touched a hand to its hilt he would be dead before he had the chance to draw it.

The bear stopped, its nose was a hand length from Darion's own. His ears rang and hot breath washed over him. The bear spoke about the same time Darion realised he breathed still. Pleased he'd managed not to piss himself he wondered if it was sweat or bear spit running down his face.

"I am no Lord, manling," the bear snorted. *"Your titles mean nothing to me. I am Rawrdredtigkah, matriarch of the Silver Lake. Now sit, be silent, and do not try my patience."*

Darion sat, abruptly. He had faced death a few times in his life but this was the first he'd stared it in the eyes. In some macabre way, considering what he had just faced, he reflected that the bear was female, not male and that he had called it a

Lord. I'm seven types of stupid thought Darion shaking his head and grinning like an idiot for no real reason, except he was alive still.

Rawrdredtigkah turned and padded back to M'rika.

"M'rika," the bear said. The ilf raised her head and looked into eyes that mirrored her grief. Standing silently she wrapped her arms around the great shaggy neck and buried her face into fur.

"Groldtigkah would be pleased that you live. He would not wish you to languish in guilt and shame. If you are not to waste his death then remember him for your kinship and the bond you shared."

M'rika shook, her cries muffled.

"Every turn you live, Grold lives with you. Carry the shame of living with you but do not let it break you. Let it make you strong. Everything you do reflects on Grold, remember this."

Darion watched silently feeling like an intruder as they shared their grief. Eventually, M'rika pulled herself away wiping her face on her arm.

"Thank you for your words. It will be as you say." M'rika's eyes flared then. "There is one urak left. I will hunt him down and end him!"

"Ilf child, revenge is not honouring Grold. Revenge does not belong here with us. You speak in anger and grief," Rawrdredtigkah said gently.

M'rika stepped back a pace. "You are right. I am angry and shamed. But I am lost as well. What do I do without Grold? I do not see a path before me."

"Your path will reveal itself. The time to seek it is not now. But come, there is more to your tale yet. How did three urak become one and how did you escape?"

M'rika glanced at Darion and the bear swung its head around fixing him with a stare. *"Perhaps it is a man's story to tell from here."*

Darion glanced at M'rika, who gave a tiny nod of encouragement.

"Okay, but forgive me for asking," he addressed the bear. "I don't know how to say your name. It's not my wish to cause offence."

Rawrdredtigkah looked at Darion, unmoved. *"Man has no patience or understanding. Your needs are shallow."* The bear looked down as M'rika placed a hand on her flank. After a brief moment, Rawrdredtigkah turned back. *"My name is pronounced Raw-dred-tig-ka. But if that troubles you, you may call me Rawr."* Darion tried the name out several times in his head.

"Thank you Rawr-dred-tigah?" He looked between the bear and ilf, a hint of a smile from M'rika, nothing from the bear. He pushed on.

"I came across Grold," the bear rumbled, "-tigkah," he recovered. "My daughter Nihm and I were returning to our homestead when we found him. An urak arrow to the chest was mortal and would have killed him eventually, but the death blow was to his neck. They mutilated him, cut his ears off, I suspect as trophies." M'rika closed her eyes and the great bear growled and looked at M'rika briefly at this news. Darion continued.

"I took my daughter home and returned to track the urak to see what they are doing here and how much of a threat they pose to me and my people. I've never seen them this side of the Torns before," Darion explained.

"That is because man is quick to forget. Please continue," Rawrdredtigkah said.

Darion explained how he tracked them north; the fight at the urak camp and their subsequent flight to the river. Having been trained by the Order and being a woodsman and hunter he had an eye and attention to detail and delivered his tale succinctly and without embellishment. M'rika interjected in several places to elaborate on events from her perspective.

"So you mean to find my son, M'rika?" the great bear asked shrewdly after they had finished their account.

"Yes," M'rika replied.

"I will accompany you," Rawrdredtigkah responded.

"I will likely be in much danger; I would not have your death on my hands as well, great mother," M'rika said, her voice tinged with bitterness.

"You have so much still to learn ilf child. I will forgive your rudeness and put it down to grief," the bear responded.

That should have been the end of matters but R'ell returned, walking cautiously into camp, and argued against their cause.

"K'raal D'ukastille bade me bring you to him safely M'rika."

"Your K'raal, my brother, does not command me, R'ell. I do as I must," M'rika retorted. Seeing Rawrdredtigkah was intent on going and would not discuss the matter with him, R'ell was left with little choice. He passed the word to break camp. They were headed to the Ford at Illgathnack.

They were soon tracking south following the path of the river, keeping far enough into the forest to be hidden from its east bank.

They moved silently, for the most part, Darion rarely seeing more than three or four ilf at a time; though he had the feeling many more surrounded them. Rawrdredtigkah, M'rika and R'ell were always close by. Occasionally R'ell's raven, Bezal would fly to him and fly off again, sometimes rewarded with a bit of meat.

The forest was full of high trees, taotoa, ronu and the massive kaorak. Dense undergrowth stretched between them but the ilf found a myriad of animal trails to follow and progress was good.

They stopped briefly at midday, a score of ilf gathering in a glade to eat and rest. The ilfanum ignored Darion for the most part with some seeming hostile. None engaged him in talk except M'rika and Ruith. R'ell had no time for rest and was busy organising ilf, several heading out without break into the forest to scout and range ahead.

Darion for his part was grateful for the break. He'd taken several knocks over the past few days and was weary still from the brief flight and battle of the day before. Ruith approached handing him a hard flat cake. It was delicious, sweet with some nuts and fruit mixed through it that Darion couldn't identify. Surprisingly filling it was gone all too soon.

Darion had watched M'rika whilst he ate. She sat beside the bear speaking in hushed tones. She looked better, seemed more vibrant to Darion than before, but despite this, there was still an underlying brittleness about her. She did not attempt to talk to the few ilf that were close by and none approached her, not even R'ell.

Darion considered her. She had moved as well as the rest of them that morning and the unhealthy lustre to her leaf skin had faded. He wondered whether it was Ruith's healing, Rawr's talk earlier, or just her natural resilience that accounted for it. Standing, knee joints and thighs protesting, Darion brushed the crumbs off himself and walked over to where she sat.

"Are you well my lady?"

She had watched his approach. The bear appeared to be resting, but its ears twitched in every direction it seemed and Darion was not fooled into thinking it asleep or unaware of him.

M'rika rose to her feet. "I am feeling much improved. Thank you for what you did yesterday. We have not had the chance to talk about what happened and we must, soon. Now is not the time," she looked at the dozen or so ilf in view, "nor the place. Suffice to say Darion Castell I owe a debt."

"You owe me nothing, lady. I did what was right," Darion said.

M'rika smiled. "By our custom, I owe you a debt. Please sit." She indicated the floor and crouched back down on her haunches. Darion paused before joining her, the bear uncomfortably close.

"The ilfanum are a proud race and by our custom, this is a matter of honour. To save a life means esteem and obligation in equal measure for both. In truth, you saved my life several times, four by my reckoning and all within a turning of the sun. A big obligation," M'rika stated this last whilst staring at him. Her intensity and large brown-black alien eyes were discomforting. He broke her gaze.

"You saved me on the River's edge so we owe each other nothing," Darion said, "excepting, maybe thanks and an ale or two in better times. That is one of our customs." He tried a grin to lighten the mood but to no avail, she continued as if he'd not spoken.

"This is a difficult time," M'rika persisted. "I have lost my bond-mate Grold and all I want is oblivion. But I do not have that and nor can I seek it. Now I have a debt to repay. We will talk later but know you may ask anything of me and I will do all that I can to help."

Darion fidgeted, unsettled, not knowing what to say. Every time he opened his mouth things got more complicated. Thinking of Marron and Nihm he locked eyes with M'rika's. "All I want my lady is to get back to my family."

M'rika nodded and the bear rumbled next to him making him jump. *"Manling speaks well, but all things happen in their proper time. Now it is time to move."*

R'ell strode into camp at that moment signalling to break camp as if to make the bear's point for her.

They left the sound of the Fossa behind as it ran away to the east. R'ell explained it would be a turn and a half travelling south before they would hear its voice again. A hard pace was set for the rest of that day and it was well after dark before they set camp. Darion had been too weary to do anything except eat, drink and sleep.

The following dawn Darion woke stiff and sore but feeling stronger. He kept to himself avoiding M'rika, not wanting any more uncomfortable conversations. It was still dark when they set off again.

Running through the forest with ilf, probably the first man in a score of generations to do so, had been both thrilling and exhilarating but the novelty of it had worn off the day before. Instead, his mind turned to Marron and Nihm. They should be in Thorsten by now. He twisted the heart ring on his finger, its warmth a comfort. He thought on the urak, the threat was real now he'd been chased by a horde of them. There were still many unknowns but considering what he did know things looked grim. The River's wasn't prepared for urak of that he was sure.

The travel was harder than before, the ground rising and falling, becoming hillier. Under the forest canopy, it was easy to get disoriented, and as skilled a woodsman as he was, Darion was soon lost. The ilf though never faltered, always choosing the right tracks to follow avoiding the ravines and gullies that sprang up.

Legs aching, lungs burning, Darion focused on the trail ahead. It was mid-afternoon as he reckoned it when a halt was called. The light would start fading in the next hour, a bit early to stop. He saw R'ell up ahead in discussion with a group of ilf. Bezal his raven sat on his shoulder and R'ell had his head slightly canted as if listening to the bird.

M'rika walked ahead of Darion with Rawrdredtigkah at her side. With a caw, the raven flew from R'ell to the low branches of a ronu tree at their approach.

R'ell gave a call, mimicking the sound of a wood owl and, moments later, ilf appeared from the surrounding forest. In all about sixty gathered, far more than the score Darion had camped with the night before. R'ell spoke.

"Scouts report a band of urak at the ford of Illgathnack. I sent Bezal for a closer look and they have crossed to the west bank and into Da'Mari. They control both sides of the river. Bezal is not so good with his counting," he stated looking at his raven, who gave a caw and flap of his wings from where he perched. "But as he reckons it, there are many of them."

There was an angry murmur from the gathered ilf at his words and R'ell held a hand up to still them.

"They trespass and our laws are clear. They must be killed and removed from Da'Mari. Scouts are already observing their positions and will report back to me soon."

The ilf nodded their agreement.

"Rest up, eat, drink then prepare your blades. We move when night falls."

Chapter 12 : Taken

South of Redford, The Rivers

"I have to go princess," Sand whispered, his breath disturbing a loose strand of hair over her ear.

She groaned, somehow managing to pout and smile at the same time.

"So soon, my Lord? Can't you stay a little longer?" She lay naked on her front hugging a pillow and gazing at him from the bedsheets.

"Sorry, I'm late as it is." He glanced at her, a year or two younger than his own twenty years, she was vibrant and energetic. At least she had been last night. He stretched his arms out and flexed his shoulders to shake out the aches he felt. It had been a long night.

Rolling onto her back she looked at him through thick lashes, her breasts bare and enticing. "Take me with you then. There's nothing keeping me here."

Sand dragged his eyes from her chest, felt himself stirring at the sight of her. You've no time for this Sand, he told himself. Besides her breath smells, not that mine is likely any better, he conceded. The thought was enough to break his burgeoning ardour and he turned, gathering his clothes from where they lay discarded on the floor.

"Sorry Sal, if I turn up with you my mother will have a fit. Maybe I could see you next time I'm through?" he offered.

"You mean next time you wanna fuck, my Lord," Sal snapped, stressing his title like it was an insult.

"Come on Sal, you know it's not like that. We had fun didn't we?" Sand buttoned his shirt then leant over and kissed her forehead. "I'll see you soon, promise."

Sal pouted at him. "You better. I got my name to think of and not as your doxy neither. If you come back you take me with you. I hate this shit hole it's boring as fuck."

Sand watched her as he dressed. He found her refreshing, strangely. Uncouth, no doubt about that, but there was a rustic honesty about her as well that drew him to her. She'd be a complete disaster if he brought her to Redford. Certainly more trouble than he needed. Still, it would almost be worth it just to see the looks on everyone's faces.

"I'll think about it. Next time." He pulled his jacket on, "Promise."

He leant over in final farewell and kissed her hard on the lips, his hand absently fondling a breast. Not waiting for a reply he moved to the door and yanked it open, tugging his boots on as he went.

Mable sat just outside, perched on a chair he had appropriated from somewhere.

"By the saint, Mable, you been there all night?" Sand asked heading for the stairs.

"Aye and not much fun I can tell you," Mable groused.

"Well let me buy you breakfast."

"Breakfast has been and gone," Mable responded, dryly.

"Shit, what time is it?" Sand asked.

"Just afore midday." Mable followed his Lord as they descended the stairs to the inn's common room.

Sand handed a silver bit to the innkeeper behind the bar.

"Thank you, Lord Sandford, pleasure as always," the innkeeper said, pocketing the silver. It was double the room rate the extra was for his discretion although neither acknowledged this. Sand nodded back but said nothing. He was late and not in the mood for small talk.

The two men left the inn and five minutes saw them mounted and on the road. Redford was only a two-hour ride north. Sand knew he could have been home last night but for his dalliance. Mable was grumpy having slept outside Sand's room all night so they rode in silence.

They saw smoke an hour out from Redford, a smudge in the sky to the northeast. As they rode on their concern grew. The smoke was thick and black;

Redford burned. They spurred their mounts into a canter following the road as it cut alongside the river.

A lone barge swept around a bend, carried along by the current. Sand drew his horse to a stop and stared. It was a mess, its lone sail tattered, its oars shipped or broken. Bodies were strewn about its decking and its timbers were peppered with arrows.

A figure was at the prow just stood, not doing anything but gazing downriver. Two more were at the tiller, one steering trying to keep the barge in the centre of the river, the other clasping his side, looking pale even from where they watched from the roadside.

Sand hailed them but only the injured man turned at his call. He stared back grimacing and shouted something jerking his hand but Sand could neither hear nor understand his gesture.

"What the seven hells is going on, Mable?" Sand watched as the injured man turned and said something to his companion, a woman. She shook her head, no, clearly arguing against him.

"They've bin attacked," Mable offered. "Fifty, sixty dead or more. Looks to me they came out the wrong side of a fight."

"A fight with who? Not the Norlanders, we're on good terms," Sand said. But who else could it be? There was no one else. He watched as the barge drifted downriver, growing smaller. Worry and uncertainty eating at him, Sand turned his horse back towards the road and called out to Mable.

"Come on, let's get to Redford. See what the hell's going on."

"We should have a care, Lord Sandford. If it's a war we ride to we need to know what we face," Mable replied.

"My whole family is at Redford. My brothers, my sisters, everyone," Sand replied, his voice catching.

"I know boy, I have a wife and child too. But we ain't no use to 'em if'n we just blunder in not knowing what's what."

Mable's calmness had a settling effect on Sand. Of course, he had family, he knew that, had supped with them many times. He took a deep breath, thinking.

"You're right. We'll go slow and careful. Any advice?"

"Well there's a first," Mable muttered. "You'll not like it."

"Spit it out, Mable."

"Smart thing is you ride south, to your uncle," Mable said.

"No way," Sand snapped. Mable held his hand up forestalling him.

"If it's a war we face, the Black Crow needs to know. Worst-case and Redford is lost then Thorsten is next. If your father holds Redford then he'll have sent a bird and you'll meet your uncle on the road."

"And my uncle will see me running away. I'm no coward, Mable. I'll not be seen as one. You ride south if you want to."

"Aye, well I said you wouldn't like it."

They rode north with the smoke growing thicker. The land gave little chance for cover, stretching away flat and wide before rising to low hills. Most of it was farmland, with crops ripe and some already taken for harvest. Orchards interspersed the fields and on the distant hills, orderly rows of grapevines could be seen. No one worked them where normally they would be busy gathering the last of their bounty. Sand's trepidation grew.

They found their first body around the next kink of the river. A wagon had run off the road and into the long grass. A man lay sprawled in the flatbed, his eyes open and staring at the sky. A thick-shafted arrow stood out of his chest and blood pooled beneath him to drip through the boards of the wagon and onto the grass below.

Sand handed the reins of his mare to Mable whilst he examined the dead man. To Sand, it looked as if he'd been driving at the time. The force of the arrow strike knocking him back into the wagon. The horses were gone as was the cargo of wheat. He picked up a kernel and rubbed it between his fingers. Stepping around the pooled blood he examined the arrow. It was red and the shaft longer and thicker than expected. He turned at the hiss of steel and saw that Mable had drawn his sword.

"My Lord!"

Sand heard the fear and stood following Mable's eyes. Up the road a ways were a score of men unlike any he'd seen before, running in loping easy strides that seemed to eat up the ground. They were big, bigger than any man he knew. They were dressed simply, in heavy tunics with thick leather strapping across their torsos. Their heads seemed dipped in blood, everything above the mouth painted red. A cry went up, a loud beast-like roar.

"They're not Norlanders," Sand said.

Mable didn't reply, pulling his horse round and dragging Sand's destrier with him. Sand leapt from the wagon into his saddle gathering the reins in one smooth motion. The horse skittered to the side, nostrils flaring. He cracked his heels into her flanks and like a coiled spring they were away; Mable a horse length back.

Quickly outpacing the savages, they rounded the bend in the river they'd just passed. On the road ahead more of the giant men appeared, stepping out of the wheat fields where they'd hidden. In unison the two men turned east into the fields, fear taking over from reason, knowing they had to get away.

The arrow struck Sand's horse just behind his right leg. His mare screamed in pain, misstepped mid-canter and tumbled to the ground throwing him clear.

Sand crashed hard, tucking his shoulder and rolling at the last instant. The wheat cushioned his fall. Stunned and bruised he staggered back to his feet.

"Sand, take my hand," Mable shouted.

Sand blinked his eyes trying to clear them and saw Mable riding back for him. Sand's horse, his beautiful mare lay hidden in the tall wheat whickering softly, breathing her life out.

Sand extended his hand as Mable reached for him. Dazed as he was it seemed time itself slowed as Mable's hand stretched out. But Mable didn't stop reaching, rolling out of his saddle and under the hooves of his horse.

Mable's destrier didn't stop her canter. Skipping away and kicking her heels she turned from the noise and cries of pursuit back out across the wheat fields and away.

Mable was dead. Sand knew it instantly. His body had come to rest a pace away. His right arm snapped and bent at an obtuse angle away from his body, his right knee crushed by a hoof. An arrow, red and thick shafted, snapped off in the fall, protruded from his back.

The fear coursing through Sand ebbed and a sense of calm overcame him. He'd known Mable his whole life. In truth, he was more a father to him than his own. Death approached, there was no doubt about that. It brought its own kind of peace. He turned from his friend and drew his sword before sinking into the wheat.

Crawling past his friend, parting the long stalks, Sand moved slowly away. He froze when he heard the heavy tramp of feet growing swiftly louder and the swishing of wheat parting. He waited and was lucky, the first dozen or so passed by him no more than five paces away.

The luck though didn't last. A giant stepped close, no more than a pace away. He was fearsome to look upon. A large head painted red, matted hair pulled back and tied in a cue down his back. Its face was flat, with a broad nose and ridged eyes that sat too far apart. It grinned at Sand, showing a mouth full of large square teeth as it reached for the hilt jutting up past its shoulder.

Sand didn't hesitate, exploding forward, driving his sword low into the brute's stomach. Screaming in pain the giant doubled over, falling to its knees as Sand whipped his blade back out. Struggling, bearing its teeth and glaring hatred, the giant reached again for his sword hilt. Sand thrust punching his blade into the exposed throat.

With adrenaline burning his veins, Sand turned, raising his bloody sword. But he was too late and too slow. Another giant stood with a sword held high. The pommel slammed down onto Sand's head and he crumpled into the blackness of oblivion.

Chapter 13 : Red Priest

Thorsten, The Rivers

The carriage entered Thorsten from the south, through Riversgate, escorted by a dozen Red Cloaks. Inside sat Father Henrik Zoller, weary from a long journey, a ten-day ride from Rivercross. He was not happy, felt dirty despite looking immaculate in his red cassock. Zoller hated feeling unclean.

The Black Crows on the gate eyed them as they passed but knew better than to stop them and draw the ire of the Red Cloaks. They were the militant arm of the church of Kildare, the god of war and death, and were highly trained and disciplined in their craft.

At least they know to fear us Zoller thought as the guards waved them through. He frowned. They should have been here a day earlier but the carriage broke an axle and needed repair at Greenholme. Then, as they neared Thorsten, a glut of farmers and merchants filling the road slowed them. It never took long for his Red Cloaks to drive them aside but sheep and cattle had no fear of the Red God and the carriage often ground to a halt whilst the beasts were herded from the road.

Thorsten was a good size town and busy. Zoller had never been before and observed out the carriage window with interest. This was as close to the wilds as he'd ever been and the people reflected this, looking hardy and rough to his eyes. There were the odd few better dressed strutting around, often with a guard or servant trailing after. It's the same in every city Zoller thought it's just a matter of scale. There was something amiss though which nagged at him and it took a while to come to him. There were no beggars, no street urchins. Maybe not the same as every city, he mused.

The town and streets were well maintained but it was still ripe with humanity and Zoller held a scented kerchief to his nose to hide the stench. The press of people made it a slow journey to the town centre and uncomfortable. Many glared at the carriage, their looks unfriendly and in some cases hostile. Father Mortim's handy work Zoller surmised.

Day's end approached. Stallholders and market traders were packing up and the town centre emptying when the carriage drew up by the large box-like church of the Red God. It was solid and made of goldstone, though looked more yellow than the gold it purported to be. Five years since its construction was completed, it was in Zoller's view, a vanity. The goldstone had been shipped by barge at great expense from Rivercross and beyond. Tall stained-glass windows stood like knife slashes in the walls guarded by stone gargoyles and grotesques. All in all, it was quite intimidating, Zoller admitted, and quite, quite ugly.

The castle stood next to the church, its black stone walls a stark contrast. Its ancient keep dominated the skyline, strong, solid and grim. Zoller was impressed. He noted the guards, stood at post outside the castle's gate, were well-armed and attired, and watched his carriage with interest.

The door opened and Zoller alighted. Two Red Cloaks had already slid from their mounts and were awaiting him. The rest headed for the back of the church where the chapterhouse and stable block were located.

"Tuko, Holt, attend me," Zoller gestured to the two guards. "And you, bring my impedimenta," he ordered the Red Cloak holding the carriage door.

"Your what, Father?" the Red Cloak stammered.

"My cases," Zoller waved at the luggage on top of the carriage.

"Yes, Father." The Red Cloak bowed his head shutting the carriage door.

A young man dressed in the orange robes of an acolyte appeared. Hurrying down the church steps he knelt, bowing his head.

"Welcome Father, this is a great honour. Father Mortim was not expecting you. We received no prior word of your visit."

"May you hear the Red God," Zoller intoned, placing a hand on the acolyte's head in blessing.

The youth stood and moved to Zoller's side but back a pace. Together they walked the steps to the church.

"How is Father Mortim? He must be busy that he hasn't the time to greet me." A small rebuke and likely wasted, but one Zoller couldn't resist making.

"Father Mortim is always busy Father," the young man replied glancing over his shoulder at the two Red Cloaks. Little and large they were an odd pair and looked anything but holy or pious; more cutthroat than churchmen.

The large was the biggest man he'd ever seen and the ugliest. He'd lost an eye and his head looked misshapen, like a kettle pan with a big dent in the side. His companion was the polar opposite, small, dark-skinned, slim with a rough beard. No doubt an attempt to hide the tattooed cross on his cheek, a sign in the Eastern lands given to mark a criminal. He moved with a languid saunter and had an evil set to his eyes. The acolyte felt a moment of fear that kept him frozen.

"Of course, serving the Red God we are all busy, no?" drawled Zoller marching into the church with Tuko and Holt at his heels, leaving the young acolyte staring after them.

Zoller felt instantly familiar with the church; it was laid out in the prescribed fashion. The large bell tower dominated the entrance and led through to a large central aisle where the faithful met to hear readings and sermons. The ceiling was high and vaulted and this, along with the stained glass windows, was supposed to create a feeling of reverence and grandeur. Zoller looked at it all critically, feeling anything but. Compared to the cathedral at Rivercross this was a poor show indeed. Why had the cardinal really sent him here he wondered for the hundredth time. He thought back on their last meeting.

"That fool Mortim needs taking in hand, Zoller." Cardinal Maxim Tortuga was a large fat man. His face was fleshy, his bald head smooth and shiny from where he oiled it. Small dark eyes peeped through folds of skin like raisins in a bun. Many underestimated him but Zoller knew the Cardinal had a sharp and cunning intellect. Ruthless too, those that crossed him tended to meet the Red God earlier than they'd have liked.

"How so eminence?" Zoller had seen Father Mortim's latest accounts and they were all favourable. Still, what Red Priest would report anything different?

"Agh, that zealot is causing havoc. His actions threaten to undo all my good work, all the concessions I have won!" The cardinal was agitated; Zoller had rarely seen him so vexed. His neck was red and he was starting to spit as he talked, always a dangerous sign. "I need you up there."

Zoller froze. He had a history with Mortim and not the good kind. He was a dangerous man, pious, fanatical and stupid; the worst kind of dangerous in Zoller's experience. Mortim lacked any subtlety, a blunt instrument to be wielded by the priesthood, not given a church.

They'd been acolytes together, a singularly unhappy experience for Zoller. That he had risen far under the Cardinal's tutelage and Mortim sent to Thorsten, a backwater town of no significance, had been vindication enough, but now? The cardinal knew their history so what game did he play.

"Your will Eminence, to what end might I ask?"

"I need you to take matters into hand, to instil upon Father Mortim that these are delicate times. Look what I have achieved. The Accord rescinded and the Order banished on pain of death from the Rivers. A great victory for us and a mighty concession from High Lord Twyford that was hard-fought and hard-won by me!" The Cardinal slammed his hand on the desk to emphasize his point.

Zoller knew that sometimes the best answers came when no questions were asked so he waited.

The cardinal considered Zoller before speaking again. "I've just come from Twyford. He was very angry, seems Father Mortim has been burning people, prominent people and well-liked, without trial mind you and declaring them heretics."

"I see," Zoller responded.

"Do you see, Father?" the cardinal snapped. "He is indiscriminate, burning women and children. Lord Bouchemeax, may his blackheart burn in hellfire, has all but threatened to burn our church and chapterhouse down. He's a traditionalist and never wanted the Accord overturned. The man's a heretic as is Twyford. They all are!" the cardinal declared puffing angrily. He paused to catch his breath. "For now we need Twyford and Twyford needs Bouchemeax since he is facing war with the Westlands."

Zoller knew all this, it was hard to hide war preparations after all, but hearing the cardinal confirm things, was satisfying.

The cardinal continued, "I need Mortim reined in. We need to win the people to our cause, Henrik. Mortim only uses fear to do this. Fear is a tool like any other but it should be used sparingly. You know this more than anyone."

Zoller's eyes flashed at the rebuke. That incident happened years ago and yet the cardinal still felt the need to beat him with it every now and then. Why? Zoller fumed. Not at the petty jibe, that was a distraction. He calmed himself, thinking. No, the question was why him?

The conclave of cardinals was set for the next full tri-moon in Kingsholme. Kingsholme, the heart of the nine provinces was far to the south, a long journey. Travel was planned in the next few days. It had taken Zoller a year of manipulating the cardinal and priesthood hierarchy to be blessed with attending. Now, in a moment, his plans were undone. He'd been compromised and outmanoeuvred. He'd have to ponder this later; he'd have plenty of time he told himself bitterly.

"I need you, Father; you're someone I can trust to sort this mess out," Cardinal Tortuga said.

Zoller knew his ego was being played too. Arguing his case was pointless, the decision was made. "Thank you, your eminence, I am but a humble servant. You do me too much honour."

"Honour well deserved, Father, I have complete faith you'll resolve this matter to my satisfaction." The cardinal sounded magnanimous, but as Zoller locked eyes with the fat old man sitting behind his desk he saw a coldness there he'd not seen before. Someone has sullied my position. Betrayed then, but by who? Even without thinking the list was a long one.

"So what is my remit? What powers and authority will you grant me, eminence?" he asked.

"You're to give Father Mortim a sealed scroll in which I've given him specific instruction." The cardinal indicated three scrolls that lay on his desk.

"One scroll is for Father Mortim the other two for you." He answered Zoller's unspoken question. "Your first scroll is a copy of my orders to Mortim, the other your authority to remove him from office. To be used with care and only if Mortim has disobeyed my orders or the spirit of them," Tortuga paused to let the point sink in. "Don't break the scrolls seal until you have to, in which case you will assume the stewardship of the church at Thorsten until further notice. It may, if the situation arises, help to rebuild community ties by burning Mortim at that stake he's so fond of. Just a suggestion on my part you understand?" The cardinal smiled.

As Zoller's heart sunk, he couldn't help but admire the old bastard for the traps he'd laid as he realised how well the cardinal and others had outplayed him.

The staccato beat of feet on stone broke his reverie. Their footsteps reverberated in the vaulted space of the nave as Zoller and his party made their way to a large oak door at the back of the room, the acolyte rushing ahead to open it. "Allow me to announce you, Father Zoller?"

"No need boy, Father Mortim and I are old friends." Zoller pushed by into the room beyond. It was large and in the middle stood a statue, a depiction of a giant man with the sword of fire in one hand and the book of death in the other. Around its base were prayer mats several of which were occupied by acolytes in orange robes. None turned at their sudden entrance and Zoller was pleased by their discipline. He gave the statue a baleful glance unimpressed with its crudeness as he marched around it.

There were three doors at the back. Zoller took the left side door just as it opened. A Red Priest looking agitated stood on the other side fastening his sash. His eyes flared in recognition.

"Father Zoller, what an unexpected surprise. Why are you here?"

"Come, Father Mortim is that any way to greet a weary brother after an arduous journey," Zoller replied smiling. "Perhaps after some refreshment, we can talk business, yes?"

"I don't deal in business, only Kildare's work." Mortim's nostrils flared and he glanced briefly at the two Red Cloaks. "Your men can stay in the lodge outback near the stables. They can't stay here. I'll need to oust some acolytes to make a room free for you. Strange his eminence didn't send word ahead of your arrival," Mortim declared.

"Strange indeed, yet here I am." Zoller couldn't resist the jibe. "As for business, church business is the Red God's business yes? And no need to disrupt the acolytes' Father, I'm a simple man. I'll stay with my men," Zoller said. "Perhaps we could meet in your chambers later tonight, say ten? That will allow me time to bath and take refreshment and give you time to finish dressing."

Mortim glared. "Perhaps the good Father might do better to meditate and pray first. Acolyte Nicolas will show you to the guards' lodge and fetch you when I'm ready to meet with you." Turning he marched off.

"Don't think he much cares for the likes of us, or you either for that matter, Father," said the swarthy little Red Cloak at Zoller's back. Zoller silenced him with a look.

Nicholas led them out the back of the church to a courtyard enclosed by a stone wall. Along its far length ran a stable block and work sheds, whilst butting up against the church was a two-storied building containing a chapter house at one end and a guard lodge at the other.

Thorsten only numbered ten Red Cloaks and the lodge was easily big enough to accommodate them and Zoller's party. A disgruntled Red Cloak, lead brother of the Thorsten Chapter, was quietly moved from the largest room to make way for Zoller who immediately set about ordering a bath. Finally, he could get himself clean.

Chapter 14 : The Broken Axe

Thorsten, The Rivers

Nihm and Marron found a room at the Broken Axe Inn. It was early in the harvest season and Vic the landlord had room-a-plenty for Marron, a regular of his.

"Tis early in the season to be seein you Marron, din't expect ya for another ten-day," he queried.

"Ah well, circumstance has brought us early this year Vic, how's Viv?" Marron replied.

Vic was a tall man of middle years with a potbelly leaking over the top of his trousers. He had a shock of red hair receding at the front but long at the back, tied in a queue that failed to keep it all in check. He had a broad open face with ruddy cheeks and a ready smile.

"Aye, she's well, ye'll see for yourself soon no doubt," he replied. "I'll get Mort to help settle your ponies. Use one of the stables for your hounds." All four dogs had come to greet Vic and bustled around his legs vying for his attention. He gave them a rough pat.

"Now, now, you scoundrels, Vic knows what ya want, eh!" His hand dipped into his pocket and appeared again to feed them some morsel.

"Go on away with you now." He pushed them off before yelling over his shoulder. "MORT! Guests here, where are ya boy?"

A young man a little older than Nihm appeared from around the side of the inn carrying a water bucket in each hand.

"No need ta shout." He was a handsome youth, tall and slim with a mass of red hair and green eyes that had a sparkle to match his smile. The family resemblance was obvious. Nihm coloured a little as he approached. "Welcome, my ladies, give me but a moment."

Vic took the water buckets from Mort and disappeared into the inn. The three of them set about unhitching the cart.

"Tis fine to see you again, Nihm, looks like ye've grown a bit since spring." Mort chattered as he worked.

Nihm felt her colour rising. Infuriated with herself she blurted out the first response that came into her head. "Your hair's a mess; it needs cutting."

Mort stopped and raised his hands to his head feeling his mass of unruly hair with a quizzical look on his face. "Why Nihm, whatever do ya mean? What's wrong wid me hair like?"

"What, no nothing, you have nice hair, just it needs a trim is all." Nihm stammered.

"Ah, well if you insist, I'll bring eh the shears and you can make me more respectable like," Mort replied seriously.

Nihm stared at him unsure and Mort burst out laughing, "Ah Nihm, your face what a look."

Nihm scowled, then unable to stop herself, grinned back.

It warmed Marron to see. They'd not had much to smile about the last five days. Still didn't but it was nice to hear the pair laughing as they worked.

It didn't take long to get the ponies settled and rubbed down. The stables were well maintained and already had full water troughs and hay bales in. They unpacked the cart and moved their goods into the largest stable and at Mort's suggestion housed the dogs there as well.

"Should be safe enough long as there is nought the dogs will chew on. Thieving is rare here but you can't be too careful," Morten said.

The dogs were not used to being shut up. Thunder and Maise looked with big, sad eyes at Marron.

"You'll be alright. I'll be back to take you out later." She petted them.

As for Ash and Snow, they took to howling and Nihm had to scold them to quieten them. Mort disappeared briefly before returning with several large bones and scraps.

"Yester eves leavings and some bones from the hog roast a few days back," he explained. The dogs were happy enough after that chewing on their spoils.

They settled themselves in the inn sharing a large room on the second floor that Vic told them was the best they had. Marron and Nihm had just finished washing and had changed into clean clothes when a bell tolled faintly in the distance ringing out seven times. I'll be meeting Anders at eight thought Marron, time to eat then.

They headed down to the public room. Vic was serving behind the bar and gave them a wave, nodding at an empty table towards the back of the room. After serving his customer, Vic bustled over to join them, expertly carrying a jug of beer and some tankards on a tray, leaving Mort to take his place at the bar.

"You looked worn when you came into my yard, Marron." He chattered to them. "You look better now, though you could both do with a drink and some food I'll wager." He poured them both some frothy brown ale and then one for himself.

"Thanks, Vic," Marron said. Viv came then bearing platters of food; cheese, fresh bread with some cold cuts. She was tall and slender with long brown hair streaked with grey and a careworn but friendly face. She sat next to Marron and placed a hand on her arm in greeting. They chatted pleasantly whilst they ate catching up with each other. The inn was quiet given the time of evening and Marron asked about it.

"Well," Viv said looking at Vic, "been a difficult year. Truth is folk aren't so carefree these days. Bin like that since the High Lord banned the Order a couple of years back but it's getting worse." She looked at Marron pointedly. "Need to be careful these days Marron, what you say and who you say it to. Lot's changed since you was 'ere in the spring."

"Thing is Marron, most folks didn't bother too much 'bout the Accords," Vic took over. "Banning the Order didn't affect them you see. But then that Red Priest, Mortim, has been causing a right stir. Preaching and telling folk who to worship and how to live." Vic shook his head. "He burnt Sal and John Huwbret in the spring, in the market place, took their boy too. Called em heretics cause they argued and caused a stir."

Viv took over again. "You know what folk is like up here, Marron. They believe in what they want whether it be the Soldier, Saint or Traveller. The old gods as well are still followed by many and even some of them heathen gods I can't recall. The thing is everyone got along fine till that priest started preaching hellfire and the like."

Vic sighed. "We all just watched it happen. We did nought. Guards did nought." Vic looked at Marron, his eyes sad. "Lord Bouchemeax was out at the time and was right mad when he got back. Thought he was gonna kill that priest but he didna. Since then the priest has burnt more folk and Lord Bouchemeax sits in that castle and does nought. Things are bad Marron. I think there'll be trouble. People have had enough."

Marron sat back, her worry growing the more she heard. She glanced at Nihm who looked troubled but said nothing. Reaching a decision she told them her news. What Darion and Nihm had found and concluded.

The innkeeps listened thoughtfully throughout. "Well if it were nought to worry about surely Darion would have caught you up by now. That he's not bodes ill," Vic said.

"Da will be alright, you'll see," Nihm argued. Marron put her hand on Nihm's arm.

"I didna mean to concern you lass," Vic said. "Just that if'n there was nought to see he'd be back. That he isn't suggests he's found something, that's all I meant."

"It's okay Vic. We're both just worried for him that's all," Marron replied. She moved the conversation on to safer grounds, discussing the best place to sell their wares, and was pleased to hear that good prices were being paid. Lord Bouchemeax was buying up a lot of market goods. A campaign in Westlands was rumoured in the spring.

The Stenhause's left after a while to attend to the inn. Mort had been making eyes at the pair of them for a while. The shops and markets had closed at the last bell and a steady influx of people had trickled in seeking food and drink. Marron gave a wry grin as she saw him admonishing his parents.

It was just before eight when Anders arrived. Marron sent Nihm off to check on the dogs as Anders ordered a tankard of ale and sat down opposite her.

"It's good to see you, Marron. Sorry 'bout before, at the gate," Anders said.

"Don't mention it, Anders. I have more important things to worry about than that lout."

Anders leant forward. "You look troubled if you don't mind my sayin. What can I do?"

Marron hesitated. Anders had not changed much since she had last seen him; a touch of grey in his brown hair and a few more lines in his face. His look was direct and sincere.

"First, how are things at Thorsten? I've heard worrying news."

"What have you heard?" Anders said. He sat back and took a pull on his beer as Marron told him what the innkeeps had said.

"Aye well, it's all true enough I'm sorry to say," Anders replied. "Have to say, Lord Bouchemeax ain't happy with recent changes or the Red Priest. If'n the High Lord had not gainsaid him that priest would have met his end in the summer. Don't rightly know why Twyford banned the Order or elevated the red priests. Must've promised him something he needs. Twyford ain't a religious man that's for sure." He paused taking another pull on his beer then wiped the froth from his mouth before continuing.

"Look you know me from old. I've known Darion for must be fifteen years, back when he scouted for us and Lord Richard weren't the Black Crow. Even got drunk together a time or two," Anders smiled at this last.

Marron nodded. "I know this Anders, why the history lesson? I seem to remember you being more direct."

Anders turned serious and leaned forward again. "I'm trying to say I know you; who you are, who you work for, and Thorsten ain't the safest place for you to be right now." He glanced around to check if anyone was close. "Think you'd be better off selling your goods and heading back home. Oh and for Saint's sake don't let Darion into Thorsten. Chances are the Black Crow will enlist him for this Westland's thing."

Marron nodded her head. "Thank's for your concern Anders, would that I could go home. Trouble is home isn't safe anymore." Marron told Anders all that had happened and what she and Darion had concluded.

Anders looked shocked by the time she was done. "Urak! I can't believe it!"

"That's the trouble. No one wants to believe it." Marron was exasperated.

Anders held his hands up. "Sorry Marron, I do believe you, trust me. It's just the last thing I was expecting to hear. Let me think a while." He finished his beer in one long swallow. Marron fetched him another to give him time. When she returned Anders looked up at her as she placed the fresh tankard in front of him.

"Okay, not sure how to do this. Lord Bouchemeax will likely want to see you but that could be dangerous. I could tell him your tale and show him the arrow but I have to say your evidence is hardly compelling and he'll want to know where I heard all this. That means you'll have to go with me. If you're willing that is?"

"The people have to know. Lord Bouchemeax needs to know. I can't make him believe me but I have to try," Marron replied.

"Still the same Marron I remember," Anders grinned. "Still, it would be better if Darion were here. No offence but Lord Bouchemeax will remember him still which gives him credence at least and maybe he has more news. We could wait a day but if what you say is true we may not have the time to waste. I think it best we talk to Lord Bouchemeax now."

"I agree," Marron said. "Let me talk to Vic, I need to make some arrangements for Nihm." She didn't speak her concerns but it was in her voice all the same. "Give me an hour."

Anders nodded in agreement. "I'll do all I can to protect you both. Make sure nothing happens to you or Nihm."

"Thank you, Anders. One hour then." Marron walked away and Anders saw her talk to the innkeeper before they both disappeared into a backroom.

Chapter 15 : Black Crow

Thorsten, The Rivers

The messenger shifted nervously under Zoller's scrutiny.

"Of course, I would be honoured to meet with Lord Bouchemeax. What time tomorrow did he wish to see me?" Zoller asked.

"He means to see you now, Father. He ordered that you return with me," the messenger said. He spared a glance at the two vicious-looking Red Cloaks stood behind the Father.

"Ordered? Not requested?" Zoller asked, raising his eyebrows. It was late. The bell had already sounded ten. The Black Crow was working late tonight.

"I don't question Lord Bouchemeax's orders, Father," the messenger responded.

"I see. A moment then," Zoller said. He faced his two guards and pondered briefly. Holt was big and ugly, Tuko small and cunning. "Tuko, please let Father Mortim know that I will see him in the morning, then join me at the keep. Holt, you come with me now."

"He said alone, Father, sorry," the messenger interjected.

"Why didn't you say? Are you in the habit of delivering only parts of a message? What other parts have you not conveyed?" Zoller asked.

"That's all of it, Father. My Lord said I was to ask you to meet with him now, that I was to bring you to him alone," the messenger stammered.

"Ah very good, a subtle difference then, he *asked* me to attend, and he *ordered* you. A different situation entirely," Zoller smiled at him.

"I don't understand, Father."

"No of course you don't. Not to worry. Tell me, are you a religious man? Do you follow Kildare the Red God?" Zoller asked.

"I follow the Trinity, Father. Nihmrodel, Kildare, and Ankor like most folk." The messenger shuffled uncomfortably from foot to foot then lapsed into silence head lowered. He felt the Father staring at him, judging him.

"Holt stay I'll return soon," Zoller said.

It was a short and quiet trip to the keep. The guards didn't challenge or acknowledge him as he followed the messenger into the castle. Zoller felt a momentary trickle of trepidation as he passed through the gates and beneath the teeth of the portcullis.

The central keep was immense, he sensed its hulking mass towering away into the darkness above as he crossed the courtyard. He had little enough time to take it in properly however, the messenger seemed keen to get him to his destination as quickly as possible and he was soon climbing the steps to the entrance.

They entered into a central hall busy with servants and soldiers. The messenger gestured and they climbed a stone staircase to the second floor where several guards stood at attention outside large double oak doors.

Zoller felt their hostile stares and ignored them. Despite himself, he was a little anxious and a bead of sweat formed on his brow. The messenger spoke briefly with one of the guards, who nodded, before swinging open one of the doors and ushering them through to a large audience chamber.

Inside, at the far end of the room, were several people who turned at Zoller's entrance. One, a man of middling height, with a narrow face and sharp nose under a crop of silver-grey hair, stared at him intently. His eyes were pale blue and piercing. The man spoke softly to his companions then raised a hand signalling him forward.

"Ah, the new Red Priest. I am Lord Richard Bouchemeax. Your name, Father?" the Black Crow asked.

"Zoller, Henrik Zoller, my Lord," Zoller replied. He resisted the urge to dip his head.

The Black Crow smiled at him and Zoller's discomfort grew. "Henrik Zoller. Your name is known to me, even out here."

"Thank you, my Lord, you are spoken of highly in Rivercross," Zoller said.

Lord Richard stopped smiling. "There's no need for idol flattery and lies here, Father. I assure you I regard Rivercross in as high esteem as they do me." The Black Crow paused. "So what's Tortuga's protégé doing all the way out here? You must have pissed someone off, Father."

"Not at all, my Lord. Cardinal Tortuga understands you have taken issue with Father Mortim, the Red Priest here." Zoller emphasized the word Cardinal. "That you feel he has been a little overzealous. I'm here to resolve matters to all our satisfaction," Zoller replied.

"So you're Tortuga's fixer. Very well let's see which of us does the fixing, eh?" Richard indicated a table to his right abutting the sidewall. "Please take refreshment. I have a small matter to attend to before we talk more."

Dismissed, Zoller moved to the table and poured himself some wine. He turned in time to see the messenger disappear back out the way they'd come and the door bang shut behind him. He surveyed the room as he sipped from his goblet.

A large wooden table dominated the centre. On it was a mass of scrolls and a large map of the Rivers and Westlands. To his left, the Black Crow sat facing the centre of the room. A young man lounged indolently on the Crow's right with his back to Zoller. He seemed of a size to the Lord and was familiar, so a councillor. No, he corrected himself, too young and too casual, most likely family; the Black Crow has children so a son.

He peered at the other two people present. They were stationed slightly to the left of the Black Crow and in direct sight of him. One, a tall, blonde-haired officer dressed in Black Crow livery was making introductions by the sounds of it. The woman he introduced was interesting. She wore a homely dress, rustic but hardy, not unusual for these parts. The woman herself was of middle years, black hair with just a hint of grey showing through in places. Her face was pleasing to look at, with brown eyes and a wide mouth that looked ready to smile.

She glanced at him as if feeling his eyes on her. There was no fear or nervousness to her and no smile for him. There was steel in her gaze. She appeared tired; her shoulders sloped in weariness. Intrigued, Zoller listened intently.

"My Lord, this is Marron Castell. She lives up near the edge of the old forest, near the Fossa." The officer indicated the woman to his side.

"A pleasure to meet you, my lady, please take a seat both of you. We're all friends here." Lord Richard indicated some chairs behind them. The officer quickly moved them into position and seated Marron before taking his own.

"Thank you, my Lord," Marron replied as she sat down.

The Black Crow fixed the officer with a stare to cower most men. "So Anders, what is it that couldn't wait until the morrow?"

"My Lord, Marron brings troubling news from the north. Let me start by saying this news comes from Darion Castell and is conveyed here by his wife, Marron. I've known them both for fifteen or more years and they have my trust."

"Castell, I thought that name was familiar," Lord Richard said. "You mean Darion from the lakes campaign, scouted for me when I was still wet behind the ears?"

"Aye, my Lord, saved us more than a few times." Anders looked pointedly at the Red Priest before turning back to his Lord.

The Black Crow noted Anders' stare and briefly considered sending the priest to wait outside but decided against it. "Well, that is a name from the past and no mistake."

Zoller drank from his goblet, intrigued but looking disinterested. The wine really was rather good.

"My Lord, perhaps Marron could best explain," Anders said.

Zoller forgot to drink from his goblet for the next ten minutes as he listened to Marron's tale. It was unbelievable, urak! They lived in the north, past the Torns Mountains. They'd not been seen or heard of for a hundred years or more. But Zoller had a gift or liked to think he did. He could judge people and tell when they spoke a truth and everything inside him told that she was doing just that. Logic told him otherwise, and he prided himself on his ability to coolly assess things. He felt conflicted. His attention snapped back to the room.

"Father, this is an incredible tale, but with all due respect urak?" The young man spoke. In his hands, he turned over a thick, black shafted arrow. He continued in a reasoning tone. "Look, we have at most a dead bear and a black arrow; purportedly an urak arrow. That is all. We don't have time to chase old tales. Twyford is calling us in. Any delay will not sit well with him."

"High Lord Twyford," Lord Richard corrected, looking pointedly at his son. "He's our liege lord; you will show him the proper respect." He turned to Anders. "I would hear your council."

Anders took a deep breath and spared a glance at Marron. "There are a lot of ifs in this and most would not give credence to their warning. But I believe Marron and I trust Darion. If it's true if there are urak we have to know."

"Thank you Anders; blunt and to the point as ever." The Black Crow smiled grimly. He turned to Zoller then. "You priest, pretending not to listen, what would the Red God advise me?"

Zoller walked over to join them thinking quickly. Do I side with the officer or the son? The son, but what's the Black Crow thinking? He has already decided, but what? Zoller glanced at the Black Crow and found him staring back, his eyes predatory. It was unsettling.

"I feel the woman speaks the truth," Zoller started. "However, that doesn't mean her assessment of the threat is correct. No one has seen an urak, let alone a horde of them, yes?"

The woman Marron glared at him.

He ignored her. "Your son is right, you've committed to High Lord Twyford and time is short." He nodded his head at the Crow's son before continuing. "However, the good Captain is also correct." Zoller guessed his rank. "You have to know what's out there. It's the basis for all military engagement is it not? Know your enemy."

"You seemed well versed in military principles for a priest," the Black crow told him. "My son would do well to remember this."

Zoller smiled, he had judged right. "The Red God is Kildare - the Soldier, my Lord. We have some small knowledge of these matters."

"I will send a company north," the Black Crow announced. "Anders you'll lead. Take your command and some birds with you. Ride to the edge of the Old Forest and report on this threat."

"Father, I'd like to go," Jacob said.

"Can't," Richard replied. "Until your uncle gets here, I've need of you here to help prepare the march south. We leave when Lord William arrives." He paused, considering a moment then looked again at his son.

"Move the men to Northfields, double the guard as well. Until I know one way or the other we need to prepare for the worst."

There was a commotion outside. Raised voices could be heard and a brief heavy thump against the doors. "Captain, go see what the seven hells is going on out there,"

Anders moved quickly to the door and opened it. He spoke briefly with the guards outside before returning.

"Father Mortim is outside. Says he's responsible for all Red Priests in Thorsten and you've no right to meet with Father Zoller without his consent or attendance."

The Black Crow's face darkened. "He comes to my house, shouts, makes unreasonable demands, murders my people and sows discord and disharmony." He turned to Zoller. "Father Zoller, my patience for your brethren is gone. Tell me now why did the Cardinal send you here?"

"It's as I said before, my Lord, to resolve matters between you and the church," Zoller replied without hesitation.

The Black Crow scowled at him. "Agh, just words, I want action, Father, else I will take action myself."

"Lord Richard, let me talk to him. I'm sure I can resolve this sensibly. We Red Priests are not all unreasonable," Zoller said, uncomfortable with the way things had suddenly turned.

The Black Crow bridled at Zoller before waving him off. "Go, I don't want to see that man in my keep again unless I call for him. Understood?"

"Perfectly, Lord Bouchemeax," Zoller said bowing his head a fraction as he backed away.

He heard the Black Crow address the woman as he left. "Sorry for my rudeness, Marron."

"It is understandable, my Lord," she replied.

Zoller opened the door and left the room, fuming inside. That fool Mortim, what is he thinking? He's a madman. The madman was stood waiting on the far side of the corridor. He was nursing a bloodied nose and had pinched his fingers over them to stop the bleeding. He glared at Zoller.

"Come, Father Mortim," Zoller snapped, setting off down the staircase. He made his way briskly out of the keep, leaving Father Mortim to follow in his wake. Mortim, he reasoned had to decide whether to run and catch him up or shout after him. Zoller was a little disappointed when he did neither and simply ambled along at his own pace.

Tuko awaited Zoller outside the castle gates and fell in alongside his master. He glanced back at Mortim as he cleared the gates behind them.

"He looks pissed at you, Father. Not been playing nice?"

"Tuko your irreverence is going to get you in trouble one of these days."

"Yeah, but as long as you need me I'll be okay though, right Father?" Tuko replied.

"So cynical Tuko, you make it hard for me to redeem your soul with that attitude." Zoller's thoughts turned to the woman Marron. Something bothered him about her, several things in fact. Her lack of fear, her accent was not local, and how she had delivered her news to the Black Crow. It was more like a report not the babbling of a farmer or peasant. He found her most intriguing.

"I have a job for you." He looked pointedly at Tuko.

Tuko glared back, his eyes bright and intelligent. "I bin in the saddle all day, Father, my ass is sore. I could eat a fucking dog and I wouldna mind washing all this dirt and shit off me."

"If I didn't know any better Tuko, I would think you were trying to provoke me," Zoller said. "Now pay attention. I'm expecting a woman to leave the castle shortly. She's of middle years, dark hair, dressed roughly in brown garb. Not unpleasant to look upon. See where she goes and report back to me on the morrow, first thing."

Tuko smiled. "Now you're talking Father, bit a cunt to follow."

"Tuko, I have told you many times about your foul mouth," Zoller admonished. "I'll not tolerate it or your uncouthness. Modify yourself, unless you wish me to set a penance for you."

"Sorry, Father. Sorry for speakin ma mind." Tuko grinned.

"It's your foul mind that is the worry. Now leave me." Zoller dismissed him.

Tuko bowed his head in acknowledgement smiling and looking anything but sorry.

"Oh, and Tuko, do not let her see you."

Tuko nodded, his smile receding. Stepping back he turned away. Zoller stopped to watch him but he was soon gone in the shadows.

"Father Zoller, I'll see you after morning worship, first thing, in my chambers." It was Mortim. Zoller kicked himself for stopping. He'd hoped to delay his meeting with Mortim until later, on his terms. Mortim didn't wait for a response, barging past and clattering his shoulder against Zoller.

"Certainly, lead on, Father," Zoller replied calmly, biting back his anger. He followed behind considering his rival. Mortim hadn't changed much since he'd last seen him. Physically his body was thicker, his girth twice what it was but his carriage and demeanour were unchanged and he was still the same self-righteous bully he'd been as an acolyte. Was he dangerous? Absolutely, though Zoller did not fear him. If anything, it was Mortim who should be afraid but he was likely too thick-headed to know it.

Zoller sauntered past the church and round the back to the guard lodge and his room, he liked to walk and think.

Chapter 16 : Illgathnack Ford

The Rohelinewaald

It was dark. The tri-moons were out but their light was muted by the forest's thick canopy. The ilf had moved quickly and silently since daylight's fade and Darion struggled to stay with them. R'ell hadn't waited.

Rawrdredtigkah and M'rika were with him still, along with Ruith and a small contingent of ilf, but Darion could sense their growing frustration at his pace.

The river sounded up ahead, the noise filtering through the forest, growing louder with every step. The ilf leading them slowed then came to a stop.

Darion breathed deeply, sweating despite the autumnal chill in the air. Moving at night through the forest was exhausting. Even with his eyes adjusted for the tiny bit of ambient light making it through from above, it wasn't enough to pick out dead branches or tree roots hidden in the undergrowth or a myriad of other trip hazards. He'd fallen countless times his arms and hands scratched and cut. More than that it was embarrassing and humbling for he prided himself on his woodcraft.

R'ell materialised in front of Darion, startling him.

"You will wait here, ilf friend," R'ell held out a curved bow and quiver of arrows, "For your protection and M'rika's. She'll wait with you along with these ilf."

Darion took the bow, running his hands over its curved length. Light and smooth to the touch, it was a generous gift. "Thank you," he said.

M'rika appeared out of the dark. "You do not command me, R'ell. It is my duty as much as any to defend Da'Mari," she said. She looked at Darion. "I will take responsibility for the man."

R'ell paused wanting to argue the point but in the end nodded agreement. "It is your right. You will know when it is time." Then to Darion, "Try not to make too much noise."

Darion clenched his jaw at that but said nothing. A small rumble from the bear sounded suspiciously like laughter but Darion couldn't see her in the dark and chose to ignore it.

R'ell gestured at the surrounding ilf. Using hand signs he commanded them to stay with M'rika before moving off into the night leaving the small group behind.

* * *

The man was interesting, R'ell thought. He moved well during the day barely slowing them. At night though he was like a newborn Hrultha cub, blind, noisy and slow.

R'ell approached the river. The waters of the Fassarunewadaick rumbled loudly as it rushed over the rocky bed of the ford. He turned his mind to the coming battle. Already his blood was singing in his veins. Ilfanum appeared at his side, moving silently beside him.

As the trees thinned, R'ell saw firelight on both banks of the river. He signed and his fellow umphathi peeled away, melting into the forest. Their plan of attack had been decided earlier, whilst they waited for the darkest part of the night. Now it was time to execute it.

R'ell moved, careful of where he placed his feet. As he drew ever closer he could smell, then hear, the interlopers. He could make out the bulk of two urak in the darkness. They were on watch and making more noise than the manling as they spoke in deep guttural tones. He contemplated the urakakule. They were the first R'ell had seen. He knew of them though, the knowledge passed to him at his seeding by Da'Mari, as it was to all umphathi. So he knew how they were made and the best killing points.

R'ell sensed the presence of ilf in the surrounding forest. It was time. He moved, placing the tree the urakakule leant upon between them before ghosting silently up behind its trunk. His long curved daggers were drawn; their blackened blades dark shards of shadow in his hands.

"Always pull this shitty duty. Don't see no point," said one.

"Wait. Did you hear that?" said the other. A rustle of foliage sounded in the darkness ahead.

"Daer may be," replied the first. He slipped the bow from his shoulder notching an arrow. "Bit of daer meat would suit me right." He stepped towards the noise.

Spinning silently around the tree, R'ell's arm swept out. The nearest urak felt something in that instant and turned. Adjusting, moving with the urak, R'ell drove his knife into its throat, the impact so hard its head thumped against the tree and stuck as the blade pinned him there.

R'ell continued his movement, gliding towards the remaining urak who pivoted at the sudden noise. R'ell slammed his remaining blade up under its chin and into the brain, killing it instantly. Stepping in, R'ell clutched the lifeless body to his before it could fall. Slowly, he lowered it to the ground.

There was little blood until he pulled the knife free. R'ell wiped his blade clean on the urak's leather skirt whilst behind him, the other gurgled and choked on his blood.

Standing, facing the drowning urak, R'ell watched impassively. His blade had missed the spinal cord, for the urak was clutching at the knife haft even as blood sluiced around it. A bloody froth bubbled from its mouth.

"May you know peace in your next life," R'ell intoned. He thrust the newly cleaned blade through the urak's leather bindings and between the ribs, finding the heart.

Afterwards, R'ell pulled his knives free, catching the body as before and lowering the urak gently to the ground. He cleaned both blades whilst listening. He knew similar scenes played out around him. His ears picked up the briefest sounds of struggle, barely audible if he hadn't been listening for it, then silence. No alarm was shouted.

Rising, R'ell moved closer to the enemy encampment. He edged towards the river taking a position just inside the tree line so as to watch the camps on both sides of the ford.

Fires were burning and by their light, R'ell could see urak laying at rest. The western camp was in Da'Mari and his blood boiled at their trespass. As he surveyed it he saw most urak slept, although a few were awake and talking or moving about among the four pairs of watchers. In all, he counted two hundred and twelve urakakule.

Looking to the far bank, R'ell made a similar assessment. The camp was smaller but arranged in the same haphazard fashion. They would be too far away to offer support and posed no immediate threat.

R'ell signalled with his hands then waited, unlimbering his bow as he did so. When he was ready he stuck five arrows into the ground placing another on his bowstring. He drew the arrow back slowly and with a measured exhale of breath released. With a thrum, the arrow buried itself into an urak wandering the fringes of the camp knocking her from her feet. R'ell reached for another arrow as soon as the first was in-flight.

A hail of sixty arrows followed from the treeline surrounding the camp. Cries and screams broke out as they struck. R'ell notched his arrow, drew then released in one smooth motion. The arrow thumped into the bulk of an urak as it stirred in its bedroll.

Screams grew louder as more arrows found their mark. A few urakakule made it to their feet but none took more than a step before an arrow found them. In the space of six breaths and six arrows, it was over. Cries of pain and agonised moans filled the night air.

R'ell signalled again, then moved around the outer fringes of the camp, keeping under cover of the treeline. Two of the moons were visible in the eastern sky as he looked across the river to the camp on the far side.

There was activity. The noise of the river had hidden much of the death they'd dealt but not all. The screams of the dying were loud enough to alert the watchers.

Glancing back, R'ell saw ilfanum moving silently through the camp. Occasionally, their blades dipped and they would move on. In the space of fifty heartbeats, there were no urakakule alive in Da'Mari. Satisfied, he turned again to consider the eastern encampment. It was roused and he could see they were organising.

R'ell watched silently. Ilfanum came up behind making just enough noise to let him know they were there. He sniffed the air. He could smell the man, his sweat had dried but it was strong enough to take a scent from, the bear as well. He faced them when he judged them near enough. M'rika stood closer than expected.

"What is your plan for the eastern camp?" M'rika asked her voice soft but direct.

"We wait," R'ell replied. The manling, standing at the K'raal's shoulder, had his eyes on the decimated camp.

M'rika nodded acknowledgement. Her bow was strung and she moved off into the darkness taking a position upstream where she could observe the encampment on the eastern bank in solitude.

Darion looked at the death and carnage of the urak camp then turned to address R'ell. "You were thorough, any losses?"

R'ell bared his teeth. "Six arrows, but I expect to recover them. I know where they lie."

Darion stared at the ilf, a dark silhouette against a darker background, but made no reply. He looked about.

"M'rika is that way." R'ell pointed. But the manling didn't move. He looked serious. Men are strange, he thought, maybe he did not understand my jest. "Something troubles you, ilf friend?"

Darion paused a moment before answering. "I've seen battle in my youth, R'ell. Killing's never a good thing. This was a slaughter." He shrugged.

R'ell laughed. Did he joke? Looking at his face R'ell wasn't sure. "They had to die and we killed them in the quickest most efficient way. This is for the best, yes?"

"Aye, you were quick and efficient, alright," Darion said. He moved off into the darkness, towards the river and M'rika.

"More to your left," R'ell snapped at the manling's retreating form, unsettled by his talk. He switched his attention back to the enemy encampment. His blood was no longer singing. Sitting on his haunches he continued his vigil.

It didn't take the urakakule long. A small party, heavily armed, approached the Ford. Cautiously entering the water they started wading across cajoled by a large urak at their fore. Rising, R'ell stuck an arrow into the ground and drew another on his bow. They were mid-river now, sixty paces from him and waist-deep, slow and easy targets.

Releasing, R'ell's arrow flew with a whisper, burying itself into the leader's chest. He fell, sinking beneath the water. Instantly the urakakule burst into motion, charging and screaming war cries. They were met with a hail of arrows. Not one made it to the shallows of the west bank, the river claiming the dead, sweeping them into its embrace.

Chaos broke out in the far camp. The remaining urak were in turmoil, R'ell could see the panic. He waited. A green fisher flashed by, hunting. R'ell watched its casual grace as it glided silently upriver until it disappeared from view. Looking back to the activity on the opposite bank, R'ell saw the urak preparing. It would not be long now.

There was a flutter of wings as Bezal flapped, braking hard to land lightly on R'ell's shoulder. The raven cawed and their minds touched. R'ell closed his eyes as they communed. Moments later, satisfied, he strode into the silence of west camp and down to the shallow water of the Ford.

Under the light of the tri-moons and backlit by the still-burning campfires R'ell drew a screamer; an arrow intricately carved with holes and notches in and fitted it to his bow. He took a stance as cries went up across the water. R'ell shut them out, focusing on the target Bezal had pinpointed. Pulling his bow up, he sighted. It was a long shot at night with a breeze coming off the river. Adjusting slightly, R'ell took a breath, holding it but a moment before releasing. He turned away, a hint of a smile, knowing his arrow flew true.

It whistled, shrieking and spinning as it passed many urak before striking its target in the centre of his chest, knocking the urak to the ground. The screamer had the desired effect. The remaining urak broke for cover ducking low to the ground before edging into the forest. Within moments the eastern camp was deserted.

R'ell raised his hand making a sign before clenching and bringing his fist down sharply. Time to hunt!

* * *

Bartuk was awake, unsure why but knowing something had awoken him, some instinct. Instantly alert he made no overt move. Instead, he lay on his bedroll and focused his senses. Urak had good night vision but the campfire ruined any chance of seeing much beyond its light so he listened.

His immediate concern was the other urak. Scarface had no trust in him. Besides, urak were tribal, and whilst he might be clan, he was not tribe. So he lay still trying to identify the threat. He loosened the tie on his knife keeping his hand on it, ready.

Bartuk took a long slow breath. Smelt the strong musk of urak, the burning wood of the campfires, and the wonderful smell of the bear carcass they'd roasted over the fire pit earlier. He'd received many grunts of approval from his fellow raiders for that last.

He heard the heavy breathing of urak at rest, mixed with the occasional grunt or snore. Behind that the rumble of white water as it rushed over the shallows of the ford.

Scarface had sent the main party across shortly after they arrived. Bartuk was meant to be there but he'd argued against the crossing. He'd been warned before his scout party left, seven turns ago, not to cross into ilfanum lands and said as much to Scarface. The promise of bear meat was the only thing in the end that convinced Scarface to leave him this side of the river. It was also the reason Scarface had not crossed himself.

Then, beneath the sounds of the river, he heard a noise; a scream? He sat up listening more intently. Yes, that was screaming. He saw the watchers on the far side of the camp move to the edge of the river. They looked agitated. Bartuk gathered his things, rolled up his bedroll and stuffed it into his pack. Standing, he moved carefully through the camp and into the forest. A watcher at post saw his approach.

"Going for a shit," Bartuk said, by way of explanation moving past him.

"Shit hole is south," the watcher said.

"I'm as like to fall in. It's dark as fuck at that shit hole," Bartuk growled back. "Besides, it stinks too bad," he said, over his shoulder. When he was sure the watcher couldn't see him any more Bartuk broke into a long loping jog due east.

Chapter 17 : Thorsten Market

Thorsten, The Rivers

Nihm awoke the instant the door to her room cracked open. Marron had finally gotten back from seeing Lord Bouchemeax, the Black Crow. She liked the name, Black Crow. She had seen him once when they came to trade, looking gallant and stern on a large black destrier with a dozen of his crows clattering along behind, heading to who knew where.

"So how'd it go?" Nihm asked.

"Better than expected. Lord Richard seems competent and didn't dismiss me out of hand as I feared he might. Due in large part to Anders, I think."

Marron filled Nihm in briefly on the meeting.

"Maybe Captain Forstandt will find Da heading to Thorsten," Nihm said.

"Let's hope so."

"And the Red Priest, Zoller, what did you make of him?"

"Not what I expected. He was insightful in a cunning sort of way. He strikes me as a dangerous man," Marron said.

"I thought all Red Priests were dangerous; especially for the Order," Nihm replied.

"Hush child," Marron said, "it's dangerous to talk of the Order here." Nihm frowned. "Yes, even here Nihm; walls have ears as the saying goes and you never know who might be listening."

"Sorry," Nihm mumbled.

"You're right though, all Red Priests are dangerous, so how can I be clearer," she mused. "In the forest what creatures are you wary of?"

"Aggh, now you sound like Da about to give me a lecture," Nihm grumbled. Infuriatingly, Marron just stared waiting for an answer. "Okay fine, you have forest bears, panthers although I ain't never seen one of those, wild boar, wolves, stag depending on the season..." She trailed off as Marron held her hand up interrupting her.

"It's haven't ever, not ain't never," Marron corrected. "Now, which is more dangerous a panther or a wild boar?"

"Panther of course," Nihm said.

"But a boar can kill just as well. Why choose the panther?"

Nihm sighed. "Now you really do sound like Da, I'm not a child."

Marron waited.

Nihm sighed, "A boar is dangerous if you stray where you don't belong, or if you surprise it. So if you get attacked it's usually because you've done something dumb."

"Good, I'll try and remember not to be dumb in the forest," Marron retorted.

"Okay, I understand the point you're making. So Zoller is a panther, cunning and intelligent, a hunter," Nihm finished.

"That's a good example and makes my point well. But remember the panther hunts when it needs to eat. The Red Priests hunt because they fear any that oppose their religion or point of view. Zoller though, I suspect, hunts for the power or pleasure of it."

Marron filled her in on what Anders had told her of Thorsten, the Red Priests, and the fracas outside the audience room with Mortim, the other Priest.

"There, you know all that happened, now get yourself to sleep. We have a busy day on the morrow."

Nihm turned on her back and closed her eyes. Thoughts of her Da lay heavy on her mind and, tired as she was it was a while before she drifted off. When finally she did, Nihm dreamt of him, running through a forest of tall trees.

* * *

Nihm awoke to a sound, a whisper. She cracked her eyes open. It was still night and the room was almost pitch black. Nihm detected a faint nimbus of light; curious she turned to it and could just make out her mother's silhouette as she sat perched on the edge of her bed, hunched over.

A strange chill was in the air. Nihm could feel it on her cheeks and arm. Then there came another sound, a key turning in a lock. Nihm was intrigued. The lock was to the trunk Marron had brought in from the cart. What else could it be? She had seen the trunk before at their homestead but her Ma had never shown her what it contained even though she'd hectored her about it. Nihm was wide awake now, her eyes adjusted to the low light.

After a moment Marron sat up, her arms moving as she played with whatever she'd taken from her trunk. There was a soft click, a pop, then nothing.

Her mother sat still as a post for what seemed an age to Nihm who started to wonder if maybe she'd fallen asleep. While Nihm waited, watching, she noticed that the soft backlight to Marron, faint as it was, did not move or flicker. It was constant. Something piqued her interest about it but she couldn't puzzle it out.

Marron moved then, nothing much, just an arm. Then a chink and snap. She bent over and a moment later Nihm heard the soft thump of the chest closing and a key turning in its lock. Then the whisper came again and the light went out. Nihm realised then what it was she found so odd about the light; she'd not smelt any wick smoke or candle wax. There was a rustle of bed covers.

"Go to sleep, Nihm. I can hear you thinking from over here," Marron said. Her voice was loud in the darkness and it made her jump.

Turning over, resolving to puzzle out what she had seen and heard, Nihm promptly fell asleep.

* * *

Nihm was bored. They had taken breakfast downstairs; fresh baked bread and honey with fruit and hot cha to wash it down with. Marron had disappeared to talk to Viv the landlady about selling their goods leaving Nihm swirling the dregs of her cha around. They only came to Thorsten two sometimes three times a year and Nihm was itching to get out and see the town, to experience the hustle of people crowding its streets. She loved the noise and the vibrancy of the place, yet here she was stuck in the inn waiting.

"So what plans ya got fer today."

Nihm started, dropping her empty cha cup with a clatter to the tabletop. It was Morten, she blushed.

"Sorry, didn't mean to make ya jump none," Morten said.

"You didn't make me jump," Nihm retorted, "Big ox like you, I heard you coming from the next room."

"Sure looked like you jumped." Morten grinned, his green eyes were bright with amusement. "I'm sure if ya had any cha left in that cup you'd be wearing it." He held his hands up at her indignant look. "Let me try agin. Good morning to ya, Nihm, how are you this fine day?"

Frowning up at him and his easy grin, Nihm couldn't stay mad. "Sorry Mort, I'm a grump in the morning. I'm fine thanks. How're you?"

"I'm also fine, thanks fer asking, good lady. I'm heading to market and was wonderin' if ya'd like to join me."

"I'm heading there myself, with Ma," Nihm said, her eyes flicking to Marron as she walked up behind Morten.

"What a splendid idea. Since we're all headed the same way an extra pair of hands would be most useful," Marron said.

Morten jumped and Nihm couldn't suppress a wicked grin. "Snuck up on you pretty good, eh Mort?"

Recovering quickly, Morten turned and sketched a mock bow. "It'd be my pleasure, Marron."

"Good, Viv says we can have you till noon," Marron said. "Now, if you wouldn't mind taking your pleasure outback and getting the ponies hitched, that would be a great start."

"Aye, it's good ta sees you ladies again," Morten exclaimed. "You should come to town more often, brighten my day up no end." Morten doffed an imaginary cap and sauntered out the back door, whistling as he went.

Marron finished up her breakfast before they both joined Morten in the back yard. He already had the cart pulled out and was hitching one of the ponies in place. With the three of them, the work went quickly and the cart was soon packed with a selection of goods. Vic popped out to see them off and give some last-minute instructions to Morten.

The dogs, shut away in the stables, whined in protest at all the activity. Nihm had taken them out before breakfast and let them have the run of the yard. It wasn't much but it would have to do since Marron refused to take them to market.

"Folk don't always look kindly on it if you bring dogs with you," she said. "We want a good price. One look at our lovely brutes is likely to scare half the customers away."

There was room for three on the cart's bench seat but it was a tight squeeze, Morten was broad-shouldered and gangly. He perched on the outside with Nihm in the middle and she was uncomfortably aware of the warmth of his thigh against her own.

Marron took the reins. With a deft flick and a gee up, the ponies pulled the cart around and headed through the gates of the yard and onto Shambler's Way, a cobbled street leading down to North Road. Morten jumped off to draw the gates to the yard closed before running to catch them up. Nihm looked back over her shoulder as they left.

The Broken Axe was a big two-storey inn that stood alone within a walled courtyard. In stark contrast, all the other buildings on Shamblers Way were piled next to each other like logs on a fire stack, tightly packed and narrow fronted. It fascinated Nihm how people could live boxed in so close together. She couldn't imagine what living that way would be like.

Snug though they were, the homes and shop fronts were well maintained and Shambler's Way was busy with people, giving it a vitality that Nihm loved. The street was wide enough for two carts to pass but, busy as it was, it was a slow ride to North Road. Children played, dodging in amongst the adults. Morten was well known to them and a gang of them ran alongside the cart calling out.

"What ya doin, Mort?"

"Where ya goin?"

"I'm on guard," he gave a stern look. "But don't go telling folk else they'll want to know what I'm guarding."

"What are ya guarding?" they shouted.

"Treasure." He looked from the cart to the children. "But don't go telling folk, else they'll want to know what sort of treasure."

"What sorta treasure, Mort?"

"What is it?"

Morten hesitated, looked about to see who else might be listening, then leaned over his seat and said, "Why golden of course."

"He's lying," said a boy, bigger than most of the others. "It's just one of ya stories again, Mort."

"Well if'n ya don't believe me," Morten sniffed and turned his head away.

"If you was guarding gold where's ya sword?" the boy asked.

"I didn't say it was gold now, did I?" Morten replied. "Nah, this is much richer than gold." He looked across at Marron who, guessing his game, had a tell-tale grin on her face.

"What's better than gold?" another boy challenged. The other kids all called out wanting to know.

"Wild honey of course," Morten said feigning exasperation as if it were the most obvious thing.

The children groaned.

"I told ya." The first boy shook his head in disgust.

Morten shrugged whilst Marron and Nihm couldn't contain their smiles as the street kids fell away. Nihm looked on awkwardly as they waved and hollered at Morten in farewell. "You're very good with them," she said.

Morten arched an eyebrow. "Those scoundrels?" he said easily. "We were their age not long past. Just give 'em a little attention and some banter."

Nihm stared ahead at that, feeling oddly sad. Marron glanced at her daughter and said nothing but gave her leg a pat.

Main Road was one large thoroughfare bisecting the town from Northgate to Riversgate and in two halves east and west. North Main Road or North Road as the locals called it, ran from Northgate to the town centre and market square. Marron and Nihm had travelled it the previous evening on their way to the Broken Axe. They turned the cart left onto North Road and headed towards the town centre.

Nihm stared at the crowds of people as they trundled past, fascinated, wondering what they could all be doing. They were a mix, from well-dressed shop keepers to farmers in their rustic, hardy clothes and everything in between.

Nihm herself was dressed in her best; plain brown trousers with a red shirt just starting to fade and a brown leather jerkin on top, finishing with a pair of sturdy leather boots. She had a dirk strapped to her left hip and thigh. Despite it being autumn, the day was unseasonably warm and, since Nihm hadn't smelt rain in the air, she'd decided to leave her cloak behind. Rain she may not have smelt, but the town had its own distinct aroma and it wasn't pleasant. Nihm couldn't help but screw her nose up at the stench.

As they approached the town centre, Nihm's eyes were drawn to the black mass of the keep and its walls that towered over the town like a mountain did a hill. Looking about she could make out the church of the Red Priests, large and garish. Nihm recalled it had been built not five years ago over the foundations of the old church.

There were other churches in town belonging to Nihmrodel the White Lady and Ankor the Holy Saint but they were smaller affairs and Nihm couldn't see them over the tops of the market stalls despite her vantage point atop the cart.

To the east stood the town hall, a large three-storied building, a bell tolling nine times from its tower as they drew into the square.

Marron rode to a corralled area filled with carts and wagons, most laden with goods and merchandise. A mass of pens stood nearby, mostly empty, but those that weren't held a mix of livestock and even some horses. The smell of hay, mixed with cattle shit and piss, gave the air a ripe flavour. Nihm noticed Morten wrinkle his nose to it but she didn't mind it so much. It smelt better than the rest of the town.

It was hectic. People rushed by loading and unloading goods but Marron knew what she was about and steered to a clear space drawing the cart to a halt. At a sign from Marron, Morten and Nihm jumped down and tied the ponies to a hitching rail. Marron put the wheel brake on before climbing into the back of the cart.

There was a routine to it all. In the past, Nihm had sometimes gone with Darion or Marron when they traded though more often than not she was left minding their goods. Since Darion was not here Nihm knew she'd be spending the next few hours sat in the cart with just the ponies for company whilst Marron took samples of their wares and haggled with the traders and stallholders. Nihm reached into the back of the cart and grabbed the water bucket.

"Morten, be a dear and carry these furs for me," Marron directed, laying a pile of cured furs on the back of the carts flatbed. As Morten obliged she drew a leather satchel over her head and hopped down. She picked up two of the containers with wild honey in them, one in each arm, and then bade Morten follow.

"I guess I'll see you later, Nihm," Morten said.

"Yeah sure, have fun. I'll still be here," She looked past his shoulder at Marron's retreating back. "You'd best hurry."

"Morten stop lollygagging. There's work to do," Marron shouted.

Morten coloured a little, "Coming ma'am."

* * *

After watering the ponies there was little enough to do so Nihm sat on the cart's bench seat looking back over the market watching the people go by. The stock and holding pens were in the North West of the market square. From here, Nihm could see various shops bordering the plaza with market stalls and traders scattered throughout its centre. There was no real order to it that Nihm could discern. She liked that, liked the thought of wandering the market and shops, exploring. It would be fascinating watching the blacksmith work, banging away on the forge, whether it was a horseshoe or sword; and the food smells from the score of vendors scattered about the square would no doubt make her mouth water, it always did. Marron had promised her new clothes maybe they would get to shop later.

Nihm looked down at herself, conscious that her attire wasn't the best. Her leather tunic was worn and dirty, her red shirt had lost its lustre and was tight across her shoulders and chest. Her leggings weren't much better, being a finger or two shorter than they should be and her toes were tight against the leather ends of her boots. Goodness knows what Mort thinks I look like she thought, then blushed.

Feeling self-conscious, Nihm turned her attention back to the market stalls watching the hustle of activity as vendors shouted out their wares to passers-by. If someone stopped to buy something they inevitably haggled over the price. Although too distant to hear, Nihm grinned, as store holders feigned disgust or horror at the offers before countering with their own. She saw a customer remonstrate holding an item up, exclaiming no doubt at the poor workmanship. Surely these leather boots are only worth a half silver bit, she could hear it in her head as if she was stood there.

Nihm had seen guards patrolling in pairs around town and she saw a couple now walking the outside of the market square. They were not the only ones armed though. Nihm watched with interest as a group of men and a woman dressed in a disparate mismatch of armour approached on horseback. They were well-armed, clearly mercenaries.

Caravans ran all the time from Thorsten to Redford or down to Rivercross and onwards and it was not unusual for mercenaries to be hired, especially since the Grim was on their doorstep. Then again, the Black Crow was rumoured to be marching to war soon; maybe they were looking for employment.

Intrigued, Nihm watched their approach counting eight of them. The one at the front was tall and broad-shouldered with black hair and a neatly trimmed beard. That's the leader, thought Nihm. He was well dressed in matching black leggings, tunic and riding boots. His sword, housed in a plain scabbard, looked to be of fine quality judging from its hilt. The others were all attired differently yet despite this their clothes, equipment, and horses all looked of fine quality. Business must be good.

The only woman in the group drew Nihm's eye. There were no barriers to women being guards but Nihm saw few enough of them for it to take her interest. She was tall, maybe of a height with the leader. Her dark leather cuirass had an intricately gilded sigil etched into it. Unusually her sword was belted to the right and strapped across her back she bore a cloth-wrapped staff. Brown leggings with a split leather skirt over the top and riding boots completed her ensemble.

Long dark hair, tied back in a plait, fell halfway down her back. She had a stern look, helped by an angry red scar on her left cheek running from ear to jaw. Despite this, or because of it, Nihm found her quite striking. She spoke to the leader, saying something he didn't like by the frown he wore.

The man pulled up on his horse and the group drew to a stop behind, near enough that Nihm could overhear. He turned to the woman.

"That isn't my purpose, Mercy. If it was then I would have ridden to the keep now wouldn't I?"

"Well just saying, Amos, since you seem to be headin us to the White Stag," the woman replied. "That's hardly keeping a low profile now, is it?" As she spoke her brown eyes flicked to where Nihm sat.

"Hmm, it may be that you're right," Amos replied. "Being this close to the keep it's likely a regular drinking hole for some of Richard's men." Looking about his eyes fastened on Nihm. "My lady," he smiled, white teeth glinting.

Feeling eight pairs of eyes suddenly pivot toward her, Nihm reddened. Her response though was out before she thought it. "My lord," she inclined her head as Ma had taught her.

Brown eyes hardened and jaw clenched, the man glanced about before turning back. Nihm swallowed feeling uncomfortable; had she done something wrong.

The moment was broken when the woman, Mercy, chuckled, making her horse shift to the right a step. Heads swivelled to look and Nihm almost sighed in relief as the attention shifted away.

"Ha, you asked for that *Lord Amos*." She spoke loudly and several townsfolk stared up at her as they walked by. "Now stop scaring the girl with that dark look of yours. Besides, it's you attracting attention not the girl," she sniffed.

Nihm wasn't sure but thought the woman had winked at her. The man, Amos, shook his head at Mercy before turning back to her. He inclined his head but a fraction.

"Please, call me Amos. My friends and I are new to town and look for lodgings; away from the centre here." He qualified. "Can you recommend an inn that might fit our needs?" He smiled amiably, flashing his teeth again.

Nihm was a little unsure of him. Charm one minute, steel the next, then back to charm. Her instinct was not to trust him. "I'm not from Thorsten, sorry."

Amos shifted in his saddle, "As am I to have troubled you."

Mercy stared at Nihm, the crooked smile on her face pulling at her scar. She nodded in farewell and lifted her reins from where they rested on her saddle horn.

"There's the Broken Axe where me and my Ma are staying," Nihm blurted, surprising herself and unsure why she had spoken. The mercenaries swung back to her as one, eight pairs of eyes settling on her again. "It's spacious, got plenty of room for your horses."

"Sounds promising," Amos said, prompting her with his look.

"Take the North Road from the market here." Nihm waved her hand in the general direction of North Road. "Look for Shambler's Way on your right, about a half league down I reckon. Ask for Vic or Viv."

"Thank you, and who should I say sent us?" he asked.

"Nihm," she mumbled.

"Nihm, after Nihmrodel the White Lady?" he said, as if to himself, one eyebrow arching.

"After the moon," she replied, not sure why she kept on talking.

"They're one and the same according to the churches of the trinity," Amos replied. His mouth lifted at one end, a hint of a grin. "Well thank you, Nihm, for your help."

Gathering his reins he rode off, his mercenaries all nodding thanks as they passed. Nihm found it all a little surreal ducking her head in response to each in turn. She felt like a bobbing jay dipping for water. She watched avidly until they were out of sight then it was back to the monotony.

A short time after the town bell tolled eleven, Nihm spotted the redhead of Morten bobbing through the market, and then, as he drew closer, Marron's smaller figure weaving through the press of people. Nihm waved as they approached. "How did you get on, Ma?"

"Better than expected, I'm all done. Got more than I thought I would for this early in the harvest season," Marron replied. "I've sold most to Lord Bouchemeax's quartermaster for a fair price. We'll drop off our goods later today and cash these in." Marron waved a writ in the air.

"That's great, so what now?" Nihm said, trying to keep the expectation from her voice.

"First, we have some pickups to make with Morten." She took in Nihm's scowl and grinned. "Then he'll head back to the Broken Axe and we'll go shopping. Get you some new clothes."

"I can manage the pickups on my own, it's okay," Morten interjected seeing Nihm's reaction. Marron made no reply waiting for her daughter's response.

"It's alright Mort; a good turn is a fair trade for a good turn," Nihm said, feeling awkward. It was Marron looking at her whilst she spoke; it was very off-putting. That infuriating know-it-all look on her face. Nihm poked her tongue out at her mother who laughed.

"Right, well if'n you're sure," Morten said. He went to help Marron onto the cart but she was up and in before he knew it. Climbing in after her, he took the reins and released the wheel brake before expertly backing up the sturdy little ponies. Then swinging the cart about with a snap of the reins they were off.

Chapter 18 : Northfields

Thorsten, The Rivers

Lord Jacob Bouchemeax rode at the head of a column of horses and troops two thousand strong. Casting a critical eye over the ranks behind he frowned, some were not as orderly as they should be. He would have words with his company captains at the next briefing.

The town walls curved away to his left, tall and formidable. The occasional head could be seen as guards bobbed into view over the ramparts, peering out as they marched by.

They were relocating the encampment near Oust Bridge, just outside the Riversgate, and marching to Northfields. It was an overreaction by his father in his view but it was good training, considering they'd be heading to Rivercross in the next five days. At least Northfields was better suited for drill and weapons practise, being mostly flat and not as soft underfoot as the fields by Oust Bridge.

They had broken camp at first light, the company sergeants haranguing the squads and companies, eliciting much complaint and moaning from the newer recruits and indifference from the regulars. None of the grumblings was in earshot of the captains, or at least those that did hear knew well enough to leave it for their sergeants to deal with. In a little over an hour, they were on the road. A good effort considering they'd had no prior notice. Jacob was pleased. "Not as fast or efficient as it could be. I expect better next time," he'd told his captains.

"Sir John, I'm riding ahead to Northgate," Jacob announced.

Sir John Stenson, captain of his personal guard, looked across at his young Lord. "I'll get the men settled." He nodded agreeably.

"I want them training after midday. Drill them hard, captain." A gentle squeeze of his knees and his white charger broke into an easy trot. "I'll inspect the camp and men at day's end," he shouted back over his shoulder. Another squeeze and he was into a canter, his black hair whipping in the wind.

"Aye Lord," Stenson said, even though Jacob was out of earshot. Stenson turned in his saddle. "Mahan, Thornhill attend Lord Jacob."

"Aye sir," The two arms men peeled out of the column and cantered after Jacob.

Stenson was a serious man not oft given to smiling. Being at the head of the column though, no one would be any the wiser, so he allowed himself a small one as he considered his Lord.

Jacob was young and impetuous; he'd just seen his twentieth name day. His men loved him, not least because he trained with them every day. And Jacob was good, great in fact, he'd not seen many better blades in his long career. Even that mean old cuss Johanus, the weapons master, agreed there were few his equal. But Jacob was more than that. He was smart like his father and shared his keen mind for battle craft untested though he was. The conflict with Westlands would be the making of him, Stenson was sure of it.

Looking at the riders as they receded into the distance he shook his head; Jacob appeared to be racing Mahan and Thornhill.

* * *

With a clatter of hooves on cobble, the horses trotted under the Northgate portcullis. Holders, traders and residents alike, cleared the road watching from the sides as the company of horsemen wearing the red tabard and black crow of Lord Bouchemeax filed past, Sir Anders Forstandt at their head.

Anders' troop was part of the city guard billeted at Northgate barracks. They were one of the few companies not joining High Lord Twyford on his Westland's campaign. That suited Anders just fine. He'd seen action aplenty in his twenty-odd years with the Black Crow and was more than happy to play gatekeeper whilst Twyford made war on Westlands. Twyford's folly, Anders thought to himself. He'd seen death many times and most was needless. This would be no different.

He nodded in salute to the guardsmen on duty outside the gates as he rode past. The ring of hoof on stone changed pitch, becoming muted as they left the cobbles and struck the dirt road.

Northfields was green and verdant. It was perfect for grazing and was used every year for the autumn harvest festival. Anders imagined the civics in townhall were in turmoil following Lord Bouchemeax's order to relocate his army from Oust Bridge. That the Black Crow expected to march for Rivercross once his brother William, Lord of Redford arrived would be of little consolation to them. The fields wouldn't be so lush once the soldiers had encamped and drilled on it for a day or two.

Anders looked ahead to where the road climbed gently into the low hills to the northwest. He was glad to be on the road again. Guard duty, managing rosters, training schedules, and attending to his company's outfitting and provisioning; all would be in abeyance until he returned from patrol. He liked the simplicity of being on the road. It was freedom.

"Cap'ain." Kronke, his sergeant drew his attention. "Horse on the right, three of 'em, riding hard,"

"I see them," Anders replied looking and spotting the distant riders. They were in full gallop. Anders suspected he knew the lead rider from almost a half league away and his suspicions were confirmed when they rode within four hundred paces; Lord Jacob Bouchemeax, on his magnificent white stallion. The stallion had been a gift from his cousin Sandford and had been the talk of Thorsten since his return from Redford.

The Redford Lords were renowned for their horse breeding. Talk about town was that Jacob would have a real chance of winning next year's race at the Festival of the Green. If he could it would be no small feat, his cousins had won the race between them for the past six years and people in Thorsten were hungry for their young Lord to win the honours back.

He frowned. Lord Jacob didn't have his helm on. Not sensible. Nor was it to be riding so hard when there wasn't a need. A rabbit hole is all it would take to turn things unpleasant. He forced the frown from his face. You're turning into a grumpy old man Anders, you were young once, he admonished himself.

As the riders drew to within a hundred yards Jacob slowed his mount to a trot and then a walk, patting and praising the stallion in a proud voice.

"Captain, he's magnificent don't you agree?" Jacob cried. His cheeks flushed from the ride, adrenaline still pumping through his veins.

"Aye, my Lord, he's a fine beast alright," Anders replied. "You named him yet?"

"A beast! You're as bad as Mahan here calling him that." Jacob laughed. "I was thinking of Lightning. Not too pretentious is it?"

"You'll have no argument from me, Lord Jacob; it's a fine name for a strong horse." Anders smiled. The lad had a way about him alright.

"I'm glad I managed to catch you before you left. May I ride with you a way?"

"Of course, my Lord," Anders said. Jacob's two guards hung back as Lord and Captain trotted ahead of the column and out of earshot.

"I will speak frankly, Captain," Jacob said. "I'm concerned about these Red Priests. My father resents their meddling as you know but High Lord Twyford has granted them concessions in the Rivers, concessions that my father is not best pleased about."

Anders looked uncomfortably at Jacob. "Did Lord Richard ask you to talk to me?"

Jacob flushed. "No of course not, my father's too bound in his honour to say anything that could be misconstrued by some. No, he entreats the High Lord directly regarding the priests, but to no avail." Jacob spat. "I fear Twyford plays his own game with the Red Priests and my father, Thorsten is just a piece in the game."

Anders considered Jacob. He would have to revise his opinion of the young man, Jacob understood much. He's as shrewd as his father, just lacking experience.

"I understand, Lord Jacob. But what has this to do with me? The game of lords is not played by captains of the guard. What is it that you're asking of me?"

"Please, when we're alone, Jacob will suffice." Jacob looked at Anders and held his eye.

Anders nodded; Jacob had the same piercing pale-blue eyes of his father, unsettling to some but not him.

"We all play a part Anders, whether we will it or not. You've served my father since before I was born. You've respect for each other, I see it." Jacob paused. "You know he doesn't slight you, not taking you on campaign."

Anders couldn't help himself and laughed, "The Black Crow does me a service. We've seen our share of battles together he and I. I'm one of his oldest and most trusted retainers and do you know why?"

"No, Captain."

Anders shrugged. "Because I'm one of the few left; one of the few still walking and still able," Seeing Jacob's flinty stare, Anders took a more conciliatory tone.

"I mean no offence, Jacob. I suspect your father is looking out for me in his way. I would go with him in a heartbeat. It's my duty and I'd die for him. Come a bit close on too many occasions truth be told. But he knows my duty will keep me here because he commands it." An edge of bitterness crept into his voice that shocked Anders; he hadn't known it was there.

"No pardon needed. I would have you talk to me in private as you would my father," Jacob said.

Anders nodded his acknowledgement.

"My father is leaving you behind not out of some old loyalty or bond you share. It's not to keep you safe, Anders, but Thorsten. Because of the Red Priests."

Anders started at Jacob's revelation but made no reply.

"He doesn't trust the Red Priests and fears what may happen in his absence. When we were away in spring at Longstretch that priest staked a family in the town square and burnt them alive in front of everyone," Jacob said, the thought a bitter memory.

"Aye, it was a bad thing alright," Anders replied.

"I've never seen him so angry. My father was all for hanging that Red Priest right there and then excepting Lord Tywford's orders forbade it." Jacob glanced back, checking again none were in earshot.

"I think it was shame mostly. Shame he'd not protected his people. Shame it was done right outside the keep and no one gainsaid the priest. He blames himself."

Anders shook his head, "I understand that. I think we all bear some of that shame. But it's wasted energy. The fault is with the Red Priest and the High Lord."

Jacob smiled holding his hands out in jest. "Careful Captain, some could misconstrue that as treasonous." He took a more serious tone. "He leaves you here as the gatekeeper in his stead. He told me last night in his chambers, after our meeting. He'll be ceding you control of the keep. My mother will rule of course but you will be her strong arm."

Anders thought about what Jacob said. That old bastard could have just told me he thought.

"Well, I will do what I must for my Lord and Lady. This is my home too," Anders replied.

Jacob looked relieved. "The Red Priests will seek to undermine mother's authority. Another dozen of their Red Cloaks came in with that new priest. That makes me suspicious. Father will not say it nor ask it but you may need to do things that run contrary to High Lord Twyford's decree."

Anders nodded. "I swore my life to your father and his family a long time ago. I'll do what is needed."

Jacob smiled. "Good, trust in mother. She is wise and will steer you true."

"You don't have ta tell me. Known her as long as I've known your Da,"

"Oh, and Anders, don't be too quick to be giving your life away. My family has need of you still. Turbulent times lie ahead," Jacob said.

"Aye Jacob, I hear you."

"Still don't know why he's sending you on this wild hunt up to the old forest, but stay safe." Jacob turned his horse about.

"Hold Jacob," Anders said, waiting until Jacob drew alongside him again.

"Your Da is the canniest man I know. You would do well to trust his instinct on this."

"I just don't see it, Anders. Urak!" Jacob exclaimed. "It's unheard of and what evidence that woman Marron gave was little enough."

"It's *not seeing* things that is most like to get you killed," Anders said. "I've known the Castells for more years than I care to admit. They're more than they seem but that is not mine for the telling. Look, all you need ta know is, Darion served with your Da and me in the Lake's campaign and a few others besides. He's the best tracker I've ever seen. Saved us once when all we saw was death coming. You wouldn't have been born if not for Darion Castell." Anders fixed Jacob with a stare. "The old ties bind tightest as the saying goes. If Darion Castell tells your father to look to the north then he would be a fool not to look to the north. I would ask you to think on that."

"I will Anders," Jabob said. "Thank you for your candour and safe journey my friend."

"And you Jacob," Anders replied.

The young lord gave a mock salute and turned it into a wave. Turning his stallion about he cantered back towards town, his two armsmen moving to flank him.

Anders waited for Kronke and the rest of the column to come to him, thinking about what he'd learned. After a while, he turned his gaze north and wondered what awaited him there.

Chapter 19 : A Meeting of Unequals

Thorsten, The Rivers

"I didn't see you at morning worship, Father," Mortim admonished. Zoller was in Mortim's private chambers, alone. Holt and Tuko had been told to wait outside, the large wooden door shut firmly in their faces.

Zoller ignored the statement, casually observing instead that Mortim's bloodied nose from last night's incident looked swollen and sore and was nicely bookended by two black eyes. He smiled, his eyes turning to scan the room.

It was spacious, dominated by a large wooden desk, and lined with well-appointed cabinets and bookcases. A narrow stained glass window let a muted light into the room adding a red lustre to the brightness of the oil lamps. There were two doors, the one he'd just entered through and one directly opposite which, Zoller assumed, lead to Mortim's bed-chamber.

Wandering about the room Zoller idly lifted scrolls glancing at them disinterestedly. He reviewed the bookcases. Most contained books on the Red God by various religious personages from throughout the ages.

Zoller's lip curled when he spotted two books, 'Kildare, the Red God' by Damklair the wise; self-styled of course and, next to it 'The Red God, Kildare' by Norris Magteague. Both espousing the history and guiding principles of Kildare, the greatest of the tri gods. He'd read them of course, as an acolyte, it had been mandatory, and found them equally tedious. The skin around his eyes wrinkled in amusement at the thought, knowing ex-communication awaited were he to express his thoughts out loud. But he digressed, what really amused was Magteague wrote his book some four hundred-odd years ago, whilst Damklair, lauded as one of the churches 'greatest minds' wrote his a mere two hundred and thirteen. The content of Damklair's masterpiece however was as different from Magteague's treatise as their titles, which was to say not at all.

Zoller heard a chair scrape and turned in time to watch Mortim settle his bulk behind the desk. The hostility in his glare was plain to see. How Mortim got to be a priest was a source of wonder to Zoller, the man had no subtlety.

He moved to a well-apportioned drinks cabinet that held a fine selection. Zoller didn't partake himself, other than wine, but he selected an expensive-looking spirit in a fancy bottle and poured a finger into a cut-glass tumbler. Lifting it, he breathed it in, willing himself not to choke; the fumes were pungent. Wearing a smile he took a seat in front of the desk.

"It's been a trying ten-day. You don't mind do you, Father Mortim?" Zoller raised the glass.

"Still as impertinent as ever," Mortim growled. "How in the seven hells you got to be a priest I'll never know. You wear your priesthood like a cloak."

"Please, Father Mortim, speak plainly by all means," Zoller replied, his smile not so much as flickering at the petty jibe.

Face reddening Mortim stood. "Your insolence is beyond measure! You're the least pious man ever to be ordained. You come to MY church, talk to the Black Crow behind MY back. I'll not fall to your scheming, Zoller. Now, why are you here?" Spit flecked his lips and Zoller could see his jowls trembling.

Zoller placed the tumbler on the desk, the drink untouched. "Finally, a sensible question Father and one I'm more than pleased to answer." He held his hands out in placation. "But first, please, calm yourself. It's unseemly for a man in your position to be blustering and blowing like a commoner."

If anything Mortim's colour deepened. "Look at you, sat there dribbling your poison. You're a snake, Zoller," Mortim shouted. A dribble of blood slid lazily out of his right nostril and over his top lip.

Zoller slapped his palm hard on the desktop. Mortim flinched at the abrupt movement and noise. Zoller rose, his face two hands from his adversary's, his voice full of steel.

"Father Mortim! You will calm yourself! You'll lower your tone! You will show me the respect MY position merits, given to me by the cardinal, and by all the seven hells you will address me as Father Zoller!" He settled back into his chair and continued in a more reasoned tone. "I do so hate to raise my voice. Please sit, Father. I forgive your rudeness. It must be stressful living this far from civilisation and having to deal with these border people."

Mortim's face boiled in anger but Zoller watched as he mastered his rage. Sinking slowly back into his chair, the emotion was still palpable but the eyes more furtive, less wild. Mortim dabbed at his face, only now noticing the blood that dribbled from his nose.

"There, that's much better." Zoller leaned forward and with the back of his hand slide the tumbler across the desk. "I think you need that more than I, Father, please."

Mortim clenched his teeth but said nothing leaving the tumbler where it sat.

"Now, Father Mortim, as regards the Black Crow, that was not by arrangement. I was merely requested by his Lordship to attend, purely for introductions. Although I have to say," Zoller held his finger up and wagged it, "he isn't very happy with you. Oh no, not happy at all. I would go so far as to say he is very upset. Which, leads me to why the cardinal saw fit to send me here."

Mortim interrupted. "Bouchemeax's a heretic, he supports the Order, indirectly or directly it matters not. I carried out my duty and he shouts and threatens to burn our church down. OUR CHURCH!" Mortim's voice rose.

Zoller held a hand up. "Please Father, I don't like to repeat myself." He weathered the returning glare, the edge of his mouth quirking as Mortim reached for the tumbler, raised it to his lips and swallowed it in a single shot.

"The cardinal is very concerned by your actions, Father. Ah, ah, let me finish," holding his hand up as Mortim made to protest. "The cardinal has made it his life's work to ostracise the Order and raise the Red God above all others. He's worked hard and conceded much to High Lord Twyford to achieve this and he has achieved it." Zoller considered Mortim. "You're burning people at the stake without due process threatens this new order. It is fragile still, like a newborn babe. We must let things settle and grow before we take a more aggressive stance."

"They were heretics, Father Zoller, heretics! I had it on good authority they were of the Order. I took the appropriate steps."

"I'm sure they were heretics. Man, woman and child. How old was the child, Father?" Zoller queried.

"Heresy has no age!" Mortim retorted.

"I heard the boy was ten. Probably didn't even know of the Order. Yet you burnt him at the stake anyway." He watched the indignation building on Mortim's face. To think he had feared this pious, overzealous bully all these years. Really, he was almost beginning to think it beneath him. He smiled.

"Father Mortim, whether they were heretics or not is a moot point. Your actions have sown instability out here in the borders. It is a wild country with wild people, you need a gentle hand. If the Black Crow burns our church down then the whole thing could unravel. Everything we have achieved. Poof, gone! And all because you couldn't contain your righteous zeal."

Mortim shook his head. "I follow the Red God, his word, his way. Politics and scheming are beneath his teachings. Those are mortal ideals, unworthy of those that follow him."

Zoller clapped slowly.

"Do you mock ME!" Mortim raged.

"Mock? No," Zoller lied. "I applaud your sentiment, Father. But the truth is until all follow our path it is not realistic. Our goal is to unite the people in worship of the trinity, although Kildare will sit at their head, yes?"

Mortim grudgingly nodded his head.

"I'm not your enemy, Father Mortim. It pains me that you treat me as such," Zoller continued. "I have a scroll for you from the cardinal. I would urge you to read it carefully and heed his words. This is your church at Thorsten, Father but make no mistake. If you do not satisfy the cardinal in this, or to put it more bluntly, me, then it will no longer be your church." Zoller reached into his satchel and withdrew a scroll. Leaning forward he placed it carefully on the desk.

Mortim stared at the scroll but made no move to reach for it. He looked then at Zoller, fire burning behind his eyes. "I see."

Zoller stood. "I hope you do, Father." Turning he strode through the door.

After making his way back to his room at the Chapter house, Zoller turned just outside his door.

"Go get some food, Holt," Zoller waited whilst the ugly giant acknowledged his order and wandered out of earshot before ushering Tuko into his room.

Zoller pondered as he crossed the floor, sitting in the only chair. Last night Tuko had trailed the woman Marron to an inn on the north side of town. Some niggle about her gnawed at him still.

"Tuko, you're sure you weren't spotted last night trailing the woman?"

Tuko looked at the priest deadpan but gave no reply, a single raised eyebrow the only sign he'd heard the question.

Zoller stared back. There was nothing nice about the swarthy little man. There was evil in him that shone through his eyes but every man has his uses. He smiled benignly at Tuko. "Very well, I want you to keep an eye on her. Report anything unusual to me. Oh and Tuko. Under no circumstances let her discover your interest, yes?"

The little man scowled. "Whatever you say, Father. Is that all?"

"No, that is not all, but it will do for now," Zoller snapped. His eyes tightening in irritation as Tuko left the room. The little shit left the door ajar on purpose, he grumbled rising from his seat to close it. On his way back to his chair he stopped, picking up a scroll from his bedside. Thinking on its contents he considered Cardinal Maxim Tortuga. The fat bastard had a perverse sense of humour. Zoller unrolled Father Mortim's scroll. That he had broken the seal and read its contents was a danger. If discovered, he would face sanction, ex-communication, or worse, death.

Zoller had kept Mortim's scroll and had Tuko replace the seal on it, another of his many skills. He'd made a copy of the cardinal's seal for just such an occasion. Being Tortuga's understudy it had been easy enough to arrange, but this was the first occasion he'd had cause to use it.

It was his copy of the scroll that he had handed to Father Mortim, a scroll that matched what had been discussed at Rivercross between him and the treacherous cardinal. He grimaced as he read Mortim's scroll again.

Father Mortim,

I have read with interest your reports and of the good work you are doing at Thorsten. The church has made much progress in the last year and much of the credit for this must go to the priests that carry Kildare's words to the people of which you are most eminent among.

I have received word from High Lord Twyford that Lord Bouchemeax is not so pleased with your good work. I would urge you to steer a true but steady course. We must follow the teachings of Kildare without bias or compromise. These are however difficult times we live in and I have sent Father Zoller to assist you. Father Zoller is an intelligent man and I would urge you to heed his council but follow your own. True heart. True faith.

It is with regret I disclose some reservations in regards to Father Zoller. This past year he has become manipulative and I am not unconvinced he puts his ambition above the will of Kildare. There are many of the Bishops and Fathers who he has influence over and I fear he covets my own seat should something befall me.

I am a forgiving man and Father Zoller has done much for the church we must acknowledge. I have no proof, only my doubts of which I have confessed to no one but you, Father Mortim.

You know Father Zoller well, were initiates together. I know you to be a pious man, a good and faithful servant of our Lord Kildare. I would ask of you a service for the church.

To watch Father Zoller, observe him as if the eyes of our Lord were judging. My fear is he will try to subvert you. You were acolytes together and he must know your worth. I know you are strong enough to resist his temptations and his clever words but take care. I fear he may try to usurp your position at Thorsten if he does not gain your allegiance.

I ask that you judge his actions carefully and act as Kildare would if he has treacherous intent. No man is above our Lord. I pray that I am mistaken in which case I will seek Kildare's forgiveness. If not, then let our Lord be his witness and bear his testimony.

Yours in faith

The Most Holy

Cardinal Maxim Tortuga

The Cardinal's bold signature was etched above his name. It bore no resemblance to his scroll, the one he had presented to Mortim. He praised the natural survival instincts that had made him break the sanctity of the seal.

Leaning over the small table in his room, he touched the edge of the scroll to a candle. The vellum burned slowly. Dropping it into his empty chamber pot, Zoller watched as it flared and burnt to ash, resolving to piss on it later. Ruefully he thought on his situation. Any which way he looked at it he was fucked.

Chapter 20 : The Flow

North of Appleby, The Rivers

Renco liked horses. They were temperamental and quirky, each with their own distinct personalities. They didn't judge or try to engage him in small talk. They liked things simple and he liked that about them. It's a shame, he reflected, that they didn't have any on hand, both for the quiet company they gave and because then he would not have to endlessly lug his travel pack.

He looked back to his Master and Maohong ambling along behind. Maohong led a mule, the closest thing to a horse they had and Renco was grateful enough for that. At least it lightened his burden, carrying the weapons chest and other assorted baggage.

The mule was called Happy, so named by Maohong because it was an irritable and cantankerous beast. He guessed it was Mao's attempt at humour. The bloody thing had tried to nip him on more than one occasion. The Mule and Mao are well-matched, Renco found himself grinning at the thought.

"Master, are you sure boy is not simple?" Maohong asked. "He has stupid look on face, again."

Hiro looked up from his contemplations and winked at Renco before turning to Maohong. "That is called a smile Mao, you should try it. It might give you a more positive outlook on the world."

Maohong looked outraged. "Hmm, Mao drag from town to village, here and there. Mao do this, Mao do that. Yes, I see your wisdom, Master. Mao should smile," he retorted.

"Ah, very good, I sense happiness might find you yet," Hiro said his eyes full of mirth.

Renco faced front and marched on, his grin growing ever larger as he enjoyed the familiar banter behind. He set a good pace and the two old men had no trouble keeping it. Master was the fittest man he knew but ancient Mao was pretty spry as well considering.

They had passed a junction in the road a league back with a sign for Appleby on it. Maohong had grumbled saying it was renowned for the best cider in the kingdom and bemoaned the fact that they had instead slept under the stars. Renco regretted that they'd not taken the chance to visit too, he liked new places and it would have been nice to try the finest cider in the kingdom.

As they walked, Renco saw fishers gliding over the river and hawks circling the fields to the east. Game birds sounded aplenty, calling out to each other. He had even seen deer when he carried out his morning exercises. Moving through his forms he was aware of them off in the early morning mist. They watched him briefly before bounding into a nearby thicket.

His leg had ached a little at first light from the crack he received from Master the previous evening but the bruise and welt had gone and the ache had faded as he walked.

The occasional farms and fields they passed quickly gave way to shrub and bush. The road ahead turned sharply away from the river and up a rise with tall trees bracing the road.

As Renco climbed the hill and passed into the wooded avenue, he tuned out Mao and his Master and focussed on his senses; a lesson he'd been taught by both old men over many years.

"Life has a flow," his Master had said. *"If you concentrate and use your mind you can see this flow."* He'd been young and not understood at first and had said so. Master had explained and demonstrated it again and again. But much to Renco's frustration once he began to understand the concept he struggled to practise it, to see it and feel it.

"You seek to understand the flow of life, Renco, until you understand you're part of this flow you will never fully grasp it," Master uttered cryptically, another of his Master's annoying habits. He smiled to himself at the memory.

Now as he watched, observing his surroundings, he extended his sense of the flow outwards and saw the bright myriad colours of life bloom in his mind, aether. It was beautiful and never failed to amaze him. It was then that he felt a shift, a change in the balance. He stopped and looked to the trees whilst he waited for his master to catch him up. Was that a faint smell of horse? He'd been thinking of horses, maybe it was his imagination. Mao would tell him so but Renco knew to trust his instincts and his senses.

Master passed him by on his left side and Mao on the right. They weren't talking or arguing now. *<Master, I sense trouble.>"*

"Yes, yes, Renco, what is your advice?" Hiro said impatiently. Renco fell into step behind the old men keeping pace with them.

<Avoid it, Master.>" That was what Mao always told him and Master had never gainsaid him.

"What kind of trouble is it we face, hmm?" Hiro replied.

<Men,> Renco said.

"Sometimes to go forward one must confront their troubles," his master said. "We avoided this trouble yesterday, yet here it is again. It will follow us."

Renco made no response. The day before, Master had sensed the horsemen approaching from behind and asked for his council. They'd hidden then in a copse to avoid detection, now though that was not an option. The men were waiting for them.

"It is good to avoid conflict whenever you can Renco," Hiro continued. "But sometimes conflict comes whether you will it or not." He turned to face his student. "When it's necessary you must not fear it."

Renco bristled, did he not train hard? He'd fought Master many times. Why did Master think him afraid? Hiro smiled and Renco coloured, it was like his Master could read his mind.

"Come Renco, lead on. Let us see where this path takes us, neh?" Hiro said.

Maohong looked at the pair of them. "Why not have talk before?" he groused. "Then Mao drink cider and rest weary bones in soft bed."

Ignoring Mao, Renco strode past them both. His ire was still up but he calmed himself using a mental technique Master had taught him. Refocusing his senses, he walked on deeper into the wood.

He could feel their presence, read the subtle shifting of the life flow of the wood. Like a rock in a stream, knuckling and diverting water as it rushed over it, so Renco could see the distorted colours of the men hidden in its depths. The deeper into the wood he passed the clearer they became.

In his heightened state of awareness, Renco could almost taste the moment of the attack. It was sudden and abrupt when it came. Arrows flew.

Dropping his pack to the ground, Renco stepped forward, heartbeat slowing as he snapped. Time dilated.

He sensed three arrows; two aimed at him the third at Mao. The first was poorly aimed and would pass him wide, the second he moved from, twisting and watching as it passed where his chest had been a moment before.

A muted cry and the thud of a body hitting the ground came from behind. Mao was down.

Five men leapt from behind trees and onto the path ahead. He sensed two more behind blocking any retreat. Renco moved to meet the five.

They cried out as they charged him, swords brandished. He assessed them as he waited, the front two were smaller and faster, both right-handed, the leftmost one almost skipped favouring his right leg. The third was big and had a wild look about him, holding a bastard sword aloft as he ran screaming towards him. The last two were cannier, spreading out wide to come at him from different sides.

Renco spun his staff as they closed on him. Surging forward, he thrust the staff's butt out and the first man ran right onto its end. It struck him between the eyes and he crumpled, his momentum carrying his body forward even as his head snapped back. He bounced as he hit the ground and didn't move.

Renco was turning the instant of contact, ducking and spinning to his left. A blade passed over his head missing him by a good hand; his staff swept round as he turned and cracked into the right knee of the second assailant shattering it. The man crashed down next to his fallen comrade screaming and clutching his leg in agony, sword forgotten.

Renco continued his spin, gliding further to his left just as the big man charged in swinging wildly at him. Moving with the sword stroke, Renco deflected it with the steel cap of his staff and, off-balance the man stumbled. The sword's tip dipped, punching into the howling man and silencing him.

Renco, in his heightened state, spun back the other way, his staff connecting with the back of the head. The big man collapsed in a heap on the ground.

Renco's blood was singing. He felt in total control as he sensed one of the two remaining bandits moving in to strike his unprotected back. Dropping to the ground one leg extended behind, Renco thrust his staff straight back. It thumped into the gut and an explosion of breath and blood erupted from the man's mouth. He sank to his knees in agony before toppling onto his side. Renco's senses were so elevated he could see the flow around the man and the tear inside his body. He was dead; he just didn't know it yet.

Rising slowly to his feet, Renco faced the fifth attacker. More wary than the others and seeing his fallen comrades the man quickly backed away in fear. Renco watched him go. When the man judged himself far enough away, he turned tail and ran.

"Finish him, Renco," Hiro said, walking up and standing beside his student, but Renco didn't react immediately.

Hiro took one step forward and flicked his wrist. A knife struck the bandit in the middle of his back. It seemed to take him a step or two to realise he'd been hit before his legs gave way and, with a cry, he tumbled to the ground.

"Hmmm," Hiro grunted but said nothing more.

The fight was over. It had lasted no more than ten seconds but it had seemed to stretch much longer than that to Renco. Recalling Mao, he turned in concern only to find the old man on his feet and dusting himself down and grumbling. Renco smiled in relief.

"No need to push Mao. No need at all." He glared at Hiro who ignored him completely.

Behind Mao, Renco saw the bodies of two men lay in a heap unmoving. Focusing his sense, Renco saw there was no life in them. Turning, he surveyed the battle's aftermath. It was ugly. There was moaning from the ruptured man to his left; sobs of pain from the one that had run; and silence from the three lying in a heap together. The three were unmoving and only the big one had any life left in him. The smell was awful and Renco quickly tuned out the acrid scent of blood and ruptured bowels.

Hiro moved to the three and dragged the big man off the other two. "You hit him pretty hard Renco, I think his skull is fractured," his Master said, as he casually inspected him. He sniffed. "I don't think he will awaken."

Renco bent and examined one of the dead men as something caught his eye. It was a neck chain. Pulling it out revealed a symbol, the Red Moon, and within the moon a sword laid over a book. He wrenched it, snapping the chain and showed it to Master Hiro.

"Red Cloaks dressed as bandits," Hiro said, turning back to Mao. "See what you can find out. Then ease them into their next life."

Mao nodded and moved to Happy, where he rummaged in one of the packs. Renco and his Master checked the other men and found and removed their Red God tokens. They moved the dead, carrying them deeper into the wood and laying them in a hollow out of sight of the road. Hiro relieved them of their purses.

"They have no need of these now," he said as he pocketed the coin. "If they're discovered they will look like the bandits they are, robbed and murdered by their own."

By the time they had finished and returned, Mao had completed his work. Renco knew he had administered oil of Black Janus. The three remaining Red Guard were still and lifeless. Black Janus, he knew, would numb their minds before stilling their hearts. It was as painless as it was effective and a better passing than they deserved.

They set about moving the remaining dead whilst Maohong disappeared into the woods, leaving Happy silent and alone in the middle of the road. The mule appeared unfazed by recent events.

After disposing of the dead, Renco phased out of the flow. A sudden, immense weariness overcame him. It was hard to lift his feet and he felt nauseous. The enormity of the fight suddenly hit him and Renco gagged and threw up. Falling to his knees, he heaved until there was nothing left in his stomach. Brow damp with sweat, Renco looked at his Master's retreating form, unconcerned it seemed at his affliction.

Hiro smiled to himself. Finally, Renco had broken that barrier, given himself completely to the flow and embraced it. It had been glorious to watch. What Renco had done was instinctive but not everyone could take that final step. It was the first time the boy had taken a life and there had been no hesitation. He frowned, apart from that last one. Still, overall he'd done well and Hiro was satisfied.

Once he'd finished emptying his guts, Renco clambered to his feet. His mouth was acrid with bile and he spat to clear the taste as he trailed after his Master. He'd just joined him on the road near Happy when they heard Mao.

Looking into the trees they watched as he led a string of horses towards them. He was whistling as he came and Renco grinned. As tired as he felt at least he would not have to walk, they had horses now.

Chapter 21 : The Red River

Thorsten, The Rivers

Thorsten was built on rising ground half a league from the banks of the River Oust. The high ground protected the town from the infrequent flooding, caused when the spring snows melted too quickly in the Torns Mountains to the north. The added elevation afforded the eastern walls and guard towers excellent views of the river as it wound its way south to the Emerald Lake.

Mathew Lebraun had been on duty since the early hours of the morning and he was weary. He was stationed in the Riversgate tower overlooking Oust Bridge and the surrounding fields and countryside.

The start of his duty had been interesting at least. At first light, the army at Oust Bridge had decamped. By the time the town bell tolled eight, they were on the road and marching. They hadn't crossed the bridge and gone south as expected though, but instead had headed north, following the curve of the town wall.

It had been something to witness as ranks were formed in neat columns, man and horse two abreast, with the company wagons following along behind and a small escort of cavalry bringing up the rear. He'd watched the column snake north until eventually, it disappeared behind the curved expanse of the wall. Now all that remained were the trampled grounds, empty training fields, and the detritus of two thousand men and women.

The rest of Lebraun's morning was spent watching holdsteaders and traders cross the Oust Bridge and climb the road to Riversgate, as they did every day. It was a regular monotony.

Lebraun wondered again how long his partner would be; he was starting to take the piss. Geert Vanknell had sloped off a while ago, a calculated gamble on his part and one that would land them both extra duty if the sergeant caught him out. But complacency had set in a long time ago for the pair and besides, it was well known the sergeant liked dice and was likely playing in the guard room of the adjoining tower.

Lebraun consoled himself that his shift would end soon. Midday had passed and it would not be long now. He smiled at the thought of his wife and young son. So it was that he didn't immediately see the boat to the north.

The door to the tower roof clattered and banged as it was thrown open and Lebraun watched as the curly-haired head of Geert Vanknell emerged from the trap. Geert's helmet was stacked against the tower crenels along with his shield and sword, next to Lebraun's own. Instead, Geert was armed with two steaming mugs balanced with practised ease in one hand, whilst he climbed up and through the trap with the aid of his other.

Grumbling at his friend, Lebraun took one of the mugs. It was only then, when he turned back to his duty, that he saw the boat. It was a good distance to the river and it looked small from where he stood. Even so, Lebraun knew from experience it was a large vessel, flat bottomed and wide. He peered at it, staring hard, drink forgotten.

"Geert, your eyes are better than mine. What do you make of that?" He pointed to the distant boat. "Some'at is off."

Geert was five years younger than Lebraun, his eyes that bit sharper. Moving over he looked to where his mate pointed. His hand gripped the stone wall as he craned his head forward.

"Whore's tits!" Geert exclaimed dropping his mug. He ran to the signal bell and banged it loudly, three long low rings booming out.

The place became a sudden bustle of activity as guards stumbled out of billets and guard stations and onto the walls. Sergeants hollered, directing some, berating others.

Lebraun was still at the wall, eyes squinting at the boat. From here the river looked to move slowly but the current was deceptive. The barge drifted around a bend and into view of the docks. Boatmen pointed, their cries too distant to reach him on the walls.

Lebraun saw now that the boat was a mess. The sail, tattered and rent in places, flapped raggedly in the breeze. Arrow shafts stuck out of the starboard side like quills on a porcupine and an old mottled canvas had been laid across the centre deck. At the bow a figure waved an arm, his other appeared strapped to his chest. There were two more at the tiller, one leaning on it, steering the boat towards the dock, the other unmoving propped against the stern railing. Lebraun wondered what had happened and where the rest of the crew were.

Geert jogged his arm breaking his focus. "Er better get these on afore the sarge gets here and tears us a new one."

Lebraun took his sword and helmet from Geert just as they heard boots on the stairs. The head that appeared though wasn't the sergeants but the Captain. Captain Greigon had a fearsome reputation that was well deserved. The two guards straightened their shoulders and stood taller.

"Report!" Greigon's command was like a whiplash.

Lebraun looked briefly at Geert standing to attention and saw he had no intention of speaking.

"Sir, a barge on the river, north of the bridge, been attacked. Looks pretty beat up, Captain. Only three crew I can see."

The captain moved past Lebraun to an embrasure and peered out. Their sergeant's head appeared through the trap just as the captain finished his assessment. To Lebraun he ordered.

"You with me, we're going down to the river. You," he gestured at Geert, "raise the signal flag, red standard." Then again, as the sergeant stepped onto the battlements. "Mortimer, when Lord Richard arrives, tell him I'm down at the docks." The Captain didn't wait for a response, walking briskly past Mortimer to start his climb down the trap.

The sergeant stared at his men one after the other. "Well step to it boys, you heard the captain. What are you waiting for? A written invitation?"

Lebraun headed off after the Captain. As he got to the trap he heard the sarge snapping at Geert.

"What the fuck's going on Vanknell. Captain's got his smalls in a twist alright."

"Boat sarge," Geert pointed by way of explanation even as he broke out the red flag and tied it to the tower's signal mast.

"Don't s'pose I'll be finishing me shift any time soon then," Lebraun muttered to himself.

"Keep up, Lebraun." The captain's shout echoed up the stairwell.

"Aye, Sir!" he yelled as he hurried after him.

Chapter 22 : Dead Boat

Thorsten, The Rivers

Lord Richard Bouchemeax stepped onto the boat's decking. Captain Greigon had cordoned off the dock allowing no one to approach the vessel. Only he and one of his men had boarded and they were at the stern deck.

Greigon's guards may have kept the docks clear but a crowd had gathered on the bridge overlooking the boat. Annoyed, Richard signalled his guard Captain.

"Matteus, move those people along." He indicated the bridge.

"Yes my Lord." Captain Matteus Lofthaus was a grizzled veteran that had been with the Black Crow from his earliest campaigns. Spinning on his heel he calmly started issuing orders.

Richard walked towards the stern, grimacing as he passed the heaped canvas on the deck. The smell emanating from within was putrid and sickly sweet, the mild breeze doing nothing to diminish its stench. It was immediately familiar to him, an old foe from the battlefield and a smell that stayed with a man if he was lucky enough to survive. The cloying aroma of blood and guts mixed with the rancid smell of piss and voided bowels. No, he thought, not a smell one forgets.

Richard mounted the few steps to the aft of the vessel. Captain Greigon crouched, unaware of his presence, talking to a woman slumped against the stern rail. She looked exhausted and in shock, her haunted eyes watching his approach. Her right arm was bloodied but Richard saw no immediate wound. The guard stood next to his Captain, looking pale but there was anger in him. Good.

A dead man sat slumped on his side behind the guard. The haft of a snapped arrow protruded from his left shoulder. Not a killing blow ordinarily, but the blood on his shirt and pooled beneath him, gave the lie to this. He watched a fly wander idly over the dead man's eyeball.

Face grim, Richard nodded at the guard who nodded back, "My Lord."

Captain Greigon turned and stood at seeing the Black Crow, "My Lord." He echoed.

"Report Captain."

"Lord, Lebraun spotted this vessel an hour back." He indicated the guard to his left then glanced down at the woman. "Madeline here says Redford was attacked two days ago, early, as the sun was rising. Says they only just managed to cast off and escape and the only ones to do so." Greigon indicated the boat. "As you can see they've been peppered with arrows. Arrows I don't recognise."

Richard listened silently waiting for the Captain to finish his report.

"One survivor in addition to Madeline, with a minor wound to his arm and bad with thirst but otherwise unharmed. He was sobbing and raving. I had him taken to the infirmary in a covered wagon." Greigon turned to the woman. "It's best Madeline tells you the detail but if what she says is true, and how can it not be," he paused looking about the broken vessel, "then Redford was attacked by a large force. A horde of savages she says."

Richard looked at the woman, who stared vacantly at nothing. Kneeling he waited for her to meet his eyes before speaking. "Madeline, you're safe now."

"No! no! no! no!" Madeline shook her head. "Not safe. They were so many." She was hysterical, sobbing, rocking backwards and forwards. "Killed 'em all, I'm all that's left. Me and Johns, that useless cockfuck!" she spat, sudden venom breaking through her fear.

"Madeline!" Richard gripped her shoulders but her glazed eyes stared past him lost. "Madeline!" he shouted.

Slowly her breathing calmed. Her eyes cleared, a tear tracking down her smudged face.

"What of Redford?" Richard asked. A hollow ball of fear had taken hold in his gut, Marron Castell's warning from the night before heavy on his mind.

"They caught us boarding. Lord William had us mustered. They should all be here." Her shoulders started to shake. "They were on us so fast. We'd stowed our armour on the boats for the trip down. It was a slaughter."

"What of my brother, Lord William?" Richard cried.

Madeline looked at him then as if seeing him for the first time. "Lord Richard?"

"Yes," Richard said.

"He's gone, gone in the first wave. We was the first and only boat to get away and then only cause Johns cut the bow rope. Fought them on deck till they was gone, most of us dead by then. Water saved us. Saved me… they're all gone now 'sept me and that fucker Johns."

"What of the town, the walls," Richard urged.

"Gates was open, horse and wagons blocked em. For the loading," she said, by way of explanation. "Fires were burning last I seen."

Richard stood then. He was shaken. His brother, gone! Redford in flames! It was incomprehensible. William was bringing a thousand spears to join him. What of Redford's people, its walls? He looked down at the woman. Blood, still fresh, stained her arm.

"Captain, take Madeline to the keep. Have Sir Antiss put her in a guest room and let the physikers take a look at her. Stay with her; don't let anyone talk to her. You too," he indicated Lebraun.

"Lord Richard!" It was Madeline. She climbed shakily to her feet, Greigon with a steadying hand on her good arm. She met Richard's eye. "They weren't like no men I ever seen."

Richard said nothing but nodded his head acknowledging her words, knowing already who they were.

"Got some under the canvas," she declared.

Richard looked at the lump of canvas covering the main deck as Captain Greigon led Madeline away, Lebraun a few paces back. He watched them disembark to the dock and caught sight of Lutico waiting for him.

He sighed; Lutico was looking as dishevelled as ever; as if he'd slept in the same clothes for the past two days. He probably had. He better be sober, Richard thought. Catching Lutico's eye he signalled him aboard.

His old master shuffled forward, his apprentice Junip helping him onto the boat. Lutico was old, although no one quite knew how old. He was counsellor and mage to the Bouchemeaxs, although he did little of either these days. He'd been with his father and grandfather, passed down from one generation to the next.

Lutico's staff thumped rhythmically on the wooden boards as he made his way aft. His apprentice suddenly gagged and rushed to the side where she promptly threw up. The guards on the docks laughed calling out to her.

Where Lutico was ruffled and untidy, Junip was the polar opposite, immaculate in her apprentice robes, cinched at the waist; hair bound and tied back. Her face was plain and she was short and stocky. Richard liked her; she was confident and friendly as opposed to Lutico who tended to the bellicose and grumpy. His son Jacob suddenly appeared at the dockside.

"Lutico, you old rogue." Jumping onto the boat he strode towards the old man. "By the Trinity, that stink," he said, patting Junip on the back as he passed her. He embraced Lutico.

"By the devils get off me boy," Lutico shrugged pushing Jacob away.

Catching sight of his father's face, Jacob's mirth instantly evaporated.

"Now's not the time for your high spirits boy," Richard admonished. A black dread had settled on him since speaking with Madeline.

"Sorry father," Jacob looked about. His father's face, pale and grim as it was should have been warning enough. "How bad is it?"

Richard sat on the raised edge of the stern deck. "Worse than you can imagine. Sit I'll tell you what I know."

Richard relayed Madeline's tale and they listened. Lutico impassive, leaning upon his staff and Jacob shocked, slumping to his knees.

"Gone? They can't all be gone. There are ten thousand people in Redford!" Jacob cried.

"We don't know anything for sure. Maybe they stand still but I fear the worst," Richard said softly.

"Let's have a look at these bodies," Lutico said. His demeanour had changed as Richard had spoken. He didn't look the dodderer that had climbed the boat mere minutes ago.

"Yes." Richard stood, resting a hand briefly on his son's shoulder as he passed him.

"Junip, stop your theatrics and get over here girl," Lutico bellowed.

Standing, Junip wiped her mouth on her sleeve. The guards' banter had dried up when they saw the grimness on their Lord's face. Junip glared at them anyway before stumbling to her Master's side.

"Grab a corner girl," Lutico ordered clutching at the canvas.

Junip gagged again as she reached for the covering and clamped a hand over her mouth, eyes watering.

"Go wait on the dock if you can't control yourself," Lutico snapped, watching as his apprentice screwed her eyes shut and shook her head. Lutico snorted and raised the canvas. The smell intensified; he had to admit it was pretty bad. He muttered under his breath and the air thickened about his nostrils and the smell receded.

Richard was there then, pulling the canvas back further to reveal the dead bodies lying beneath. There were around fifty stacked like cordwood one atop another. Hard and stiff, most were covered in dried blood. Maggots crawled from orifice and open wounds, flies swarming at the disturbance.

Pale and fighting the rising bile in his throat, Jacob pointed out several larger bodies at the back. "What in seven hells are they?"

The bodies were man-like, only much bigger and more solid. Their faces were flat and brutish with a ridged brow. They had piercing's through nose and ear and blood-red war paint covered the top half of their heads giving them a feral look even in death. In life, they would have been fearsome. All wore studded, leather-banded strapping around their torsos and metal bracers on their forearms. Leather skirts also studded, covered their lower bodies. Their skin was ashen but whether that was through death or natural he didn't know.

"Not well-armoured but they look formidable. What the fuck are they?" Jacob swore, looking to his father, knowing already but unwilling to believe it.

Lutico had tapped his way around the pile of dead and was examining them. "These, my boy, are urakakule. Hmm, first I've seen," he muttered.

"Urak? I didn't believe her. Thought them creatures from legend," Jacob said.

"Should get out more, Lord Jacob if all you know is what you see in front of you," Lutico rasped.

"You give me wisdom now, old man? It rings hollow," Jacob snapped back.

"Don't take it personally; it's a problem most folks have," Lutico said.

"Stop the bickering, both of you," Richard interrupted. "Jacob, you should know better."

Lutico raised a bushy eyebrow at that but made no retort.

Bending, Richard hefted a large notched sword lying next to an urak. Heavy and crude, it was nevertheless well made and would take some strength to wield. Its pommel was sticky with black-blood. He dropped it with a clatter, spitting on his hands before wiping them on his cloak.

"Captain Lofthaus!" Richard shouted. Booted feet hit the deck and thumped down the wooden boards.

"My lord?" The Captain took in the grisly scene in front of him, nostrils flaring at the smell. His eyes widened as he caught sight of the urak but he held his tongue.

"Captain, I need these urak covered and taken discretely to the keep. Put them in one of the cells and post a guard on the door."

"Aye, Lord."

"Then get a detail to take these men and women to the priests of the White Lady. Ask them to prepare them for their crossing. Tell them, I'll make a donation to cover the cost." The White Priests wouldn't ask for payment but he knew it would stretch their resources, of which they had few, being the poorest of the three churches.

"Yes, Lord Richard," Lofthaus said.

"Then, send word to my captains and counsellors to attend me. I will hold a meeting tonight at ten in my audience room." Richard looked pointedly at his old friend. "Matt, I can't stop the rumours but I need calm and discretion. Use men you trust and who can keep their mouths shut. The captains will hound you to know what's going on. Tell them as little as you must and impress on them that their silence and steadfastness is needed."

Captain Mathew Lofthaus bowed his head. "Aye Richard, I'll make it so." And with that he turned and marched back to the docks, his shouted commands already ringing out.

Richard looked to his son. "Jacob, have the men in Northfields decamp and moved into town. Billet as many as you can into the barracks, double bunk if you have to. Whatever's left will have to camp in the town centre. Have the market stalls taken down to make room if needs be."

"That will cause problems. Is it really necessary?" Jacob knew he'd misspoken as his father's pale blue eyes hardened. He'd seen that look unsettle many a man or woman. Now, he felt it upon him and shifted uncomfortably.

"We're blind, Jacob. We've no idea what's going on. Why are they here? How many are there? What is their intent?" Richard's voice grew in pitch as he posed each question. "All I know is that two days ago my brother was murdered, his army routed and Redford put to the torch. How far and how fast can an urak horde move, Jacob?"

"I don't know father," Jacob said, distressed. His father had never looked so grim. He'd always shown him patience, but not now.

Sighing, Richard reached out, placing a comforting hand on his son's shoulder. "Neither do I. Move the men inside the walls."

"Yes, father." Jacob paused not finished.

"Never fear to talk to me boy," Richard said.

"What about the villages and holdings?" Jacob said. "We can't leave them out there with no warning. And what about Captain Forstandt?"

"You're right, although Sir Anders moves towards the Fossa not the Oust." Richard paused in thought. "Send a messenger to Anders. Tell him what we know and ask him to order any and all to Thorsten. Then, he's to try and find the urak. He's our best asset in the field and I need to know if we face enemies on more than one front." He muttered this last.

"Right father, I'll see to it. I'd like to send messengers to all the villages and homesteads as well if I may."

Richard agreed. "Of course, but make no mention of urak. Call them a hostile force, we don't want total panic. Now hurry, time is not our ally."

Jacob left. Richard saw two of his personal guards fall in behind him. There was a cough.

"Lord Richard, I'll contact the council. Inform them of this development," Lutico said.

"You do that, for all the good it'll do us."

"My Lord, this may be but a probe. If we face a full-scale invasion this affects all Nine Kingdoms, not just the Rivers," Lutico continued. "We may just be the first rock they break upon."

"My brother is not a fucking rock old man! Redford is not a rock!" Richard's blood seethed.

"I'm sorry for your loss, Richard. I feel it as well. Did I not teach you both when you were boys?" Lutico watched calmly as anger and grief warred across his Lord's face. "With all due respect, the rock I speak of is the Rivers. Would that the Order still had a presence here; we have need of them and their counsel," he said.

Richard's head sunk to his chest. So stupid letting his anger rule him. Taking several deep breaths he calmed himself. "I'm sorry, Lutico. You're right, you look to the kingdom whilst I look to us."

Lutico sighed. "I'm with you wherever this ends. Besides, as you well know, my stock with the Council of Mages is not what it was. I fear they'll not react quickly to this threat."

Richard smiled at that. "Ah, my old friend, master of understatement! Still, I may have a lead on the Order if my thinking is correct." He gazed at his old mentor as if he'd not seen him in a long time. Lutico stood in dirty robes, with a wizened face and wild hair, holding his staff, the only object of any worth to him. "It's good to have you back old man."

"Impertinent scoundrel," grumped the mage. Sniffing he wandered off towards the docks, staff tapping away. "Junip, stop skulking around the back there and help me up. Then I need a drink!"

Chapter 23 : Oust Bridge

Thorsten, The Rivers

Father Zoller looked down at the boat. He stood on Oust Bridge, Mortim by his side. Word had reached him shortly after the boat's arrival, Father Mortim grudgingly bringing him the news.

Mortim had a limited intelligence network as far as Zoller could ascertain; certainly, it wasn't adequate for a town this size. Still, his rival didn't have the intellect or guile to run anything more elaborate, not successfully anyway. Luckily for him, Thorsten was a backwater on the edge of the wilds. Not much happened. So when the boat from Redford was seen, beat up and full of dead, it was enough for the news to filter through to the Red Church.

Zoller had Holt prepare his carriage and together with an insistent Mortim, had gone to see for himself. It was an unpleasant journey, sat listening to Mortim's pompous, self-righteous drivel and forcing himself to be cordial. Zoller had decided he needed the priest in his game with the cardinal. That Mortim hated him with a passion only made the challenge all the sweeter. Thankfully the journey to Riversgate was short.

By the time they arrived access to the bridge was restricted by order of Sir Stenson, Captain of the Black Crow's guard. Mortim, fool that he was, had blustered and threatened them forcing Zoller to take him aside.

"Father Mortim, the soldiers are under orders from their Captain. A captain they respect and obey. If they don't they are punished," Zoller cajoled.

"They show no respect for my office," Mortim hissed back.

"Yes, yes you're quite right, and the Red God watches," Zoller mollified. "A more subtle way is needed though. Soldiers are simple. If you push and threaten they will hold together and simply pass the decision up the chain of command. Yes?"

Mortim glared back before finally conceding, grudgingly. "Their lack of zeal and respect for our Lord Kildare angers me."

"I share your anger, Father," Zoller said. "Please let me talk to them." And he had. After ten minutes of cajoling and manipulation, they were finally allowed onto the bridge. Holt stayed with the carriage as agreed with the sergeant, a man who followed the Trinity and favoured Kildare.

They had observed the battered condition of the boat on their ride down from the gate; now up close the details were stark. Arrows studded the vessel telling a tale of violence. They'd arrived at an opportune moment as an old man in crumpled looking robes spoke with the Black Crow. Zoller asked who he was.

"That is the old drunk Lutico, court mage and counsellor. Surprised to see he's sober enough to stand. The man is a disgrace and a heretic," Mortim offered.

Zoller could smell something unpleasant but it wasn't enough to prepare him for the mass of bodies revealed when Lord Richard drew the covers back. He was shocked at the pile of dead but it was the large, squat, grey-skinned remains of several bodies that caught his eye. Set apart, he couldn't see them in detail but they were not of man.

"Kildare's glory! What are they?" Mortim hissed pointing.

"Please don't point, Father," Zoller said, resting a hand on Mortim's arm. He thought about the woman, Marron, and her tale to the Black Crow of urak. He'd believed her, but there was something to be said for seeing a thing with your own eyes. "They're urak I believe and we're at war with them it seems."

It felt longer the journey back fending off Mortim's simplistic questions. Questions he had no time for. He had too many of his own, foremost of which was how to get out of Thorsten and back to Rivercross. He'd been banished to the fringes of civilisation. Up here he was effectively out of the game. Well, his competition had misjudged if they thought him out of the picture.

No, his plans all revolved around manoeuvring his way south again, to Rivercross. His suspicion that the woman, Marron, was of the Order was central to that plan. If he could return with her in hand and a confession he could have the Black Crow's head on a spike. Or not, the possibilities would open up. Maybe he could manufacture a better use for the Black Crow.

He thought back to the bridge and what he'd seen. A sliver of ice tickled his spine, premonition or intuition. The urak were a game-changer. He'd no intention of being caught in this shithole when they came calling. He would have to advance his plans immediately. Time was the enemy now.

Chapter 24 : Into Darkness

Thorsten, The Rivers

"Yes okay, okay, I'm happy to see you too," Nihm said, ruffling the dogs playfully as they cavorted around her.

"Go on away with you," she scolded as Ash and Snow jumped up. "These clothes are new, it's too soon to be having your dog slobber on," She chided, dusting down her tunic.

All four dogs obediently sat, tails wagging. Maise and Thunder had nudged up against her in greeting when she first entered the stables but Ash and Snow's exuberance was overpowering and the two older dogs had no time for it. Now though they could smell the bones in the sack and knew what was coming like the old campaigners they were. Nihm smiled at them.

"No fooling you two is there?" Nihm said to the older dogs. "No. Stay," she commanded as Ash and Snow sniffed the sack. Reluctantly they stilled shivering in anticipation.

Reaching into the bag, Nihm picked out the two largest bones and laid them before Maise and Thunder. As the older dogs it was right they get the better choice of meat and bone. She placed the remaining bones before Ash and Snow. They sat drooling but other than a furtive glance at their treats they never took their eyes from her.

Nihm gestured and the dogs fell on the bones with gusto. Maise and Thunder picked theirs up almost delicately and padded over to their beds of hay before lying down and crunching on them as Nihm closed the stable door.

"Are they wolves? They look like wolves," a voice called from above. The dirty face of a little girl peered down from the loft.

"They're wolfdogs," Nihm replied smiling up at her. "They have wolf in them, and they're big as wolves but that's as much as I know."

"They love you. You're very good with them," the girl said. "How'd you make them sit there for the bones?"

"Well, you have to train them," Nihm said.

"How do you train a dog?"

"Same way as you and me were taught I guess." Nihm grinned. "Do you sit in a chair when you eat?"

"Yeah sometimes and Ma makes us wash our hands as well and on every ten-day, we have to put on our best clothes," said the girl.

"Well, your Ma will have taught you how to wash your hands and how to sit at the table. You probably can't remember now but it's true," Nihm said. "It's the same with dogs. You teach what you want them to do and when they get it right you praise and reward them so they know."

"Are you Mort's girl?" she said abruptly, sitting up from her hiding place and gazing down with big wide eyes.

Nihm coloured at the sudden shift in topic, uncomfortable with the question, and unsure why. "Morten's my friend but no I'm not his girl, nor anyone's for that matter," she stated.

"Good," the girl declared. "Because we're going to be bonded when I'm old enough,"

Nihm grinned, "Does Morten know?"

"No, it's a surprise," she said seriously. "I'm Annabelle. What's your name?"

"I'm Nihm. I'm very pleased to meet you, Annabelle." Nihm bowed.

The little girl beamed back. "You wanna know a secret?"

"Oh, that sounds mysterious, what secret is that?" Nihm said.

"A bad man is watching the inn," Annabelle whispered.

"How'd you know? Why's he a bad man?" Nihm was immediately anxious as all of Marron's warnings sprung to mind.

"He's hiding. Told Jimmy to fuck off and he had a knife."

"And he's watching the inn?" Nihm said.

"Ain't nothin' else to see from that alley next to Mr Shins. Been there since you got back, after them others turned up," Annabelle said.

"Where is Mr Shin's?"

"Out-front silly, it's got his name on it," Annabelle said. "Mr Shin isn't here though. He's away, been gone a ten-day or more."

"Well thank you, Annabelle. I need to go in but you stay away from Mr Shin's won't you?"

"Annabelle is that you up there girl?" Morten called out sternly. "What've I told ya 'bout playin' here. Go on scoot afore my Da finds you and gives you a tanning."

Nihm turned as Morten strode into the stable block but bit her tongue at the rebuke ready on her lips. He had an expression of outrage on his face but she could see it was feigned. His stance was too relaxed and there was a playful twist to his mouth. There was a clatter and Nihm turned in time to see Annabelle's scrawny body descend the loft ladder. She stuck her tongue out at Morten and ran giggling as he cried in outrage and chased her out the back of the stables.

He returned a moment later laughing. "She is a scamp that one, quick as a fox too."

"She was just playing, Mort you didn't have to scare her off like that," Nihm chided.

"Ah, it's fer her own good. The kids are always finding excuses ta hide and play in here. Better I chase them off than my Da," he said.

"Your Da wouldn't hurt them would he?"

Morten laughed. "No not really, but he's not as quick as he used ta be and it would wound his pride ta realise he's too slow ta catch 'em."

Nihm laughed. She liked Morten and the sudden thought made her realise she didn't have any friends.

"I need to go in and see Ma," she said curtly.

"Of course, I was just coming ta see if ya needed a hand," Morten stammered, puzzled at her shift in mood. Nihm brushed by heading to the inn leaving him to follow.

* * *

Nihm opened the door to the common room, noise and laughter rushing out to greet her. It was busier than the night before. Vic waved as she passed him at the bar and she returned it. Ducking around a barmaid, busy serving tankards from a tray balanced precariously in one hand, Nihm headed for Marron's table.

Her Ma had chosen one in a back corner but as Nihm slipped past the patrons saw that she was not alone. Amos, the mercenary captain from earlier, sat talking with her, and alongside him was the woman, Mercy. The rest of his crew were drinking at the adjoining table. Feeling self-conscious, Nihm squeezed between the tables, sliding onto the bench next to Marron.

"Ah Nihm, I wanted to thank you for your recommendation. A fine inn indeed," Amos beamed. A goblet of wine sat next to his right hand and he raised it in a toast.

Nihm glanced at her mother who looked amused more than anything else.

"You're welcome, I guess." Nihm stole a look at the woman. Up close her scar was livid and red. Mercy caught her stare with a raised eyebrow. It made Nihm uncomfortable and guilty all at the same time, like she'd been caught doing something she shouldn't. Mercy still wore her leather cuirass and Nihm stammered, "Isn't that uncomfortable to wear all the time?"

"Is that really what you wanted to ask me?" Mercy replied. "I thought for a minute you'd be bold and ask me about this." She traced a finger along her scar.

Amos laughed. "Now it's you with the scary face. Ignore her, Nihm, she's playing."

Drink obviously agreed with Amos, Nihm decided. He was certainly more jovial than when they'd first met. Laughter and clapping erupted from the table next to them and as one they turned to look.

One of Amos's men, slight with dark hair and a moustache curling around his mouth, played with a knife. As Nihm watched, he twirled it expertly, spinning it so fast it was hard to tell blade from handle as they blurred into one. He moved the blade from one hand to the next and ended with a flourish by flicking it high up into the rafters. He placed his hands flat on the table, his forefingers and thumbs pressed together to make a triangle. He winked at Nihm as a moment later the knife thudded into the centre of the triangle. It was impressive and Nihm clapped in amazement.

"That was incredible," Nihm gushed.

"Why thank you, good lady." He bowed, beaming at the praise.

The man next to him thumped his arm. "Ah, ignore Jobe. He's got one trick, that's all. And he ain't much good at that neither," he joked, pointing at Jobes right hand where a tiny dribble of blood ran.

Jobe laughed along. "Aye, you have the right of it," he said agreeably working his knife loose. "Now let's see you do it you great ox." Gripping the tip of his knife, Jobe laid the blade over his forearm handle towards the ox.

"Keep your knife, my friend, my trick is this." Raising a tankard he downed the contents in one long pull. He slammed it on the table when he was done letting out the longest, loudest belch Nihm had ever heard. The table full of mercenaries were in high spirits and this set them all off and Nihm found herself joining them.

"Forgive my crass friend," Jobe said. "Let me make the introductions since the boss ain't been so inclined."

Amos had already turned away and, deep in discussion with Marron, didn't hear Jobe's dig at him. That didn't faze Jobe who hooked a thumb at the man next to him.

"This big ox here is Lucson, although everyone calls him Lucky." He grinned. "I know right, how can a man with a face that ugly be called Lucky." This drew a fresh round of laughter from around the table, only Lucky looked like he wasn't sure whether to join in or not.

Nihm nodded at him and Lucky smiled back. He was a big man, broad of shoulder and with a gentle face despite the fact it hadn't seen a razor in a ten-day.

"The blond on the end there is Jerkze. Next to him you got Stama, he don't talk much but he's alright. Then the old looking fella with grey hair there is Silver. He ain't much older than me, must abin some hard living when he was young, eh Silver."

Silver made a rude sign in response, "Ignore him, lass, he's all mouth. That and his knife is all he's good fer."

"Finally, you got Seb there. He's the youngest." Jobe finished.

Seb stared back. He didn't look much older than Mort, could have been his brother with that shock of red hair. His face was serious, his gaze intent. It made Nihm uncomfortable.

Silver nudged Seb with an elbow. "Stop gawping at the lass. It's rude and by the looks not wanted."

"Sorry, didn't mean nothin' by it," Seb muttered.

Nihm felt Marron's touch on her shoulder and turned, grateful to escape the sudden attention.

"Everything alright?" Marron asked.

Nihm glanced at Amos, reclined in his seat and drinking from his goblet, then at Marron wondering what to say. Thinking on it now Annabelle's warning sounded a little childish. But Nihm believed her and with all that had happened she had to say something. Talking in a hushed tone so as not to be overheard, she told Annabelle's tale.

Marron listened, a worried frown creasing her forehead.

"You would do well to believe the girl," Mercy said from across the table.

Nihm and Marron were both startled.

"I'm sorry, I have excellent hearing and you looked concerned."

She didn't look sorry, Nihm thought, and there's no way she could have heard, was there? But there was no time to wonder on it as Amos leaned forward, goblet forgotten.

"Tell me," he ordered Mercy, suddenly serious. Afterwards, he pondered a while before addressing Marron.

"Pardon me, but I agree with Mercy. What reason would a child have to make something like that up?" He stroked his beard with his right hand. "No, what interests me is why you'd think he's watching you?"

Marron looked uncomfortable. "I didn't say he was here for me. As I recall, I didn't say a damn thing."

"Intuition, or rather let's just say you're no card player. Your face is too honest," Amos replied.

Marron said nothing. Amos stared at them both in silence.

Seb suddenly stumbled over leaning against Mercy's chair back. "Another round boss?" he asked.

Amos glared at the lad, steel in his eyes. "Seb, fuck off!"

Uncertain and looking shocked, Seb wandered back to his seat without another word.

"Sorry for my rudeness," Amos said, spreading his hands in apology. "Look, seems to me you have something to hide. Why else would some shady character be watching you? What we need is a measure of trust on both sides."

Mercy shook her head, but Amos carried on. "I sense you're good folk, so if I've your oath you'll say nothing of what I tell you then I would have something to tell."

Marron considered for a moment then nodded. "You have my oath."

Amos turned to Nihm.

"You've my oath as well," Nihm said, surprised and pleased to be asked. No one had asked for her oath before.

Amos nodded. "What if I told you that that man is more than likely watching for me."

Marron looked unsure. "Why would that be?"

"I could ask the same of you. But I have your oath so I will start," Amos replied. "I am Amos Duncan." He sat back folding his arms.

Nihm and Marron exchanged a puzzled glance.

"Erm, sorry," Nihm said, "I don't know who that is?"

Mercy roared with laughter. Amos's men looked over wondering what had set her off when the rest of her table looked so serious. Almost as one they shrugged and turned back to their tankards.

Amos looked disgruntled.

"Ah, that's priceless, your face Amos," Mercy chortled.

"If you're quite finished," Amos said.

"I know who you are," Marron said suddenly. "You're one of THE Duncans, from Kingsland."

"Aye, Marron, the Duncans from Kingsland indeed," Amos mumbled. "Maybe not say that so loud. I'm meant to be incognito."

"So, what're you doing up here in the borders?" Marron asked.

"In truth, my father sent me. He's concerned about happenings here in the Rivers," Amos replied.

"Care to be more specific," Marron asked, then jerked as if startled by something unseen.

Nihm, felt something too, a sudden charge in the air. It was hard to describe but similar to a thunderstorm before the lightning came, only condensed and more focused. The hairs on her arms stood up. Nihm glanced at Mercy who sat silently with a glazed look on her face. After a moment, Mercy's eyes cleared and she turned to Marron.

"You felt that," Mercy stated.

"Yes. You're a mage?" Marron said, looking furtively about the inn.

"It's alright, no one can hear us," Mercy replied. "I know some magic yes. As do you. Nihm as well I suspect."

Marron nodded. "I know a little, Nihm nothing."

Nihm was shocked. Her Ma knew magic? She'd only just found out that her mother was in the Order. What else didn't she know about her?

"That makes you both very interesting. Amos?" Mercy prompted.

Amos peered at mother and daughter, his eyes discerning. "High Lord Twyford and the Rivers have broken the Accords with the Order. My father has heard worrying things about Twyford and sent me to see. If I told you he was deeply concerned about the breaking of the Accord's would that go some way to putting you at ease?" Amos asked.

As he spoke, Nihm noted the noise from the rest of the inn was off somehow. In fact, the more she tried to listen the more incoherent the sound became. She looked at Mercy in suspicion then back to Amos as he continued.

"If I was an educated man, and I am, then I would hazard a guess that you are of the Order." He held his hand up at Marron, who was about to speak. "If you are, then you should know that the Duncans are duty-bound to protect you. I'm not of the Rivers and us Duncans swore our own oath with the Order. Not many know that but there I've told you." He took a sip from his goblet.

"What makes you think I'm of the Order?" Marron responded.

Amos smiled. "Mercy says you have some magic about you. You think you're being watched in a town where being of the Order is about the only thing worth being watched for unless maybe you are agents for the Westlands?" Amos quipped. "But then there's no strategic significance in Thorsten that would warrant Westlands' interest. No, my money is on the Order."

"Being of the Order in Thorsten or anywhere in the Rivers is a death sentence," Marron replied. She tried to keep the anger from her voice but Nihm heard it all the same. "People have already died, burned at the stake by the Red Priests. I've just met you, so forgive me if I'm a bit reticent. Nothing you've told me requires any risk to you but such a risk could cost me," she looked at Nihm, "and my daughter, everything."

Amos nodded. "Wise indeed, Marron, but I trust my instinct so you need not say anything until you're ready."

He turned to Nihm. "Now, where is this watcher to be found? I've got a mind to ask him some questions."

Nihm's heart was thumping. This was all so far from anything she had experienced before. It felt like she was in the middle of something important and she was a part of it. Feeling emboldened she answered, "It's easier if I show you."

"I don't think that's a good idea." Marron sat forward in concern.

"What? So other people have to take responsibility, but not me? I'm not a little girl, Ma." The last thing Nihm wanted was for Amos and Mercy to see her as a child. She saw her mother stiffen, saw the argument on her lips, and jumped in before she could speak. "Look, I'll stay back and just point out where he is okay? I promise," Nihm said, using her most reasonable tone.

Amos and Mercy watched but said nothing. This was between mother and daughter. Marron took a deep breath and sighed. "Just point him out then straight back here, understand?"

Nihm beamed, "Promise."

Amos grinned at Nihm's small victory. He turned and nodded to Mercy. Her face went slack, eyes glazed, and the charged sensation Nihm had felt earlier suddenly vanished. The noise from the inn was still loud but now she could make out snippets of conversation again. It was disorientating.

At a sign from Amos, Silver and Seb came over. Amos explained the situation to them. "Nihm will show you where he's holed up. She's not to go in with you. Bring him out back to the stable block and sit on him till I get there. Understood?"

"Yes boss, we'll see to it," Silver said. He turned to Nihm. "After you, my lady,"

Nihm got up, suddenly nervous. This was more real than hunting Da in the forest. The thought of her father made her miss a step and she stumbled as she moved past Mercy's chair. Ma had said earlier he was alive but several days away. What was taking him so long to get here?

"Don't worry, lass." Silver steadied her. "Seb and me won't let nothin' happen to ya." Nihm nodded thanks but made no reply. The three of them made their way out the back of the inn. Nihm was aware of Morten watching from the bar as they passed.

* * *

Outside, in the yard with two men who were practically strangers, Nihm felt fear for the first time. She didn't know where Mr Shin's was and worried that they'd walk out right in front of it when they left the backyard.

Me and my big mouth, Nihm thought. Casting her mind back to earlier in the day, Nihm replayed leaving for market and remembered there was a shop front to the left of the inn and Shambler's Way.

Nihm opened the gate to the courtyard and peered out briefly to get her bearings. Her recollection was right and there, now that she looked for it, was the black smudge of an alley alongside it; dark and narrow. Nihm explained to Silver where the man was meant to be. Silver stole a look of his own, assessing the layout before edging back.

"Alright Seb, we'll make our way to the road there. I'll work my way around back. You make your way to the shop front. Careful not to get in view of that alley though, eh lad," Silver said. "When you hear me knock him on his bonce you come running, ya hear." Silver slapped him on his shoulder.

"Sure you're up to it old man? Maybe I should take this one?" Seb grinned, eyes darting to Nihm as he spoke.

Silver saw and shook his head. He nudged Seb's elbow. "Just stick to the plan boy, simple is best."

Moving off they left Nihm to wait in the yard. She couldn't help but edge forwards and watch as they strolled casually towards Shamblers Way. Reaching the street corner, Seb peeled off leaning against a wall whilst Silver disappeared down the road a ways. She thought Silver ducked between two houses but it happened so quickly she wasn't sure.

Seb crossed the front of Mr Shin's moving slowly and quietly. Nihm glanced about and saw a few passers-by casting him a strange look. Over on the far side of the road were a couple of familiar dirty looking faces staring out from behind a retaining. Nihm hoped they'd not give the game away.

Suddenly, Seb was rushing, disappearing down the alley. Nihm frustrated she couldn't see, ran from the inn to the corner of Shambler's way. She heard something. A cry maybe, a clatter definitely, then silence.

Before she knew it she was moving down Shambler's Way. She walked softly, like on a hunt in the forest, her senses heightened. Nihm saw the alley Silver must have taken moments before and took a slow step towards it, heart pounding. Ten paces away a cloaked shadow stepped from its mouth. It was a slight figure moving furtively. Nihm froze, alarm bells ringing in her head. Her heart flipped as the figure turned, looking back straight at her. She saw a dark face and dead eyes. He twitched and instinct made Nihm drop to her right.

A knife thudded high into her left shoulder. Pain exploded as she twisted and fell, her head cracking against the cobbles. She heard screaming. Was it her own? Blood pulsed from her, warm and wet. Lying on the ground dazed a figure loomed over her. Nihm blinked back tears; it was over, the agony in her shoulder was paralyzing.

"It's okay, he's gone now," said a tiny voice, a young voice, one she knew but couldn't place. She tried to focus but was finding it hard.

"Annabelle?" she gasped finally. "Get Marron… inn."

She must have passed out then as the next thing Nihm felt were rough hands, lifting her. Was that Marron's voice? It was so hard to focus. Her shoulder felt dead. The pain was gone but she couldn't feel her arm. And she was so thirsty. Opening her mouth, Nihm tried to speak but nothing came out. She couldn't see properly now either, only blurred shapes that grew less distinct every passing moment.

Then darkness.

Chapter 25 : Little Hope and None

Thorsten, The Rivers

"Marron," Morten said, interrupting Amos in mid-flow.

Marron turned staring up at a grim-faced Morten. At his side was a little girl, her hand gripped firmly in his, her face ashen white. Marron's heart flipped. On some instinctive level, she knew something bad had happened and it involved Nihm, else why would they be here?

"What is it, Mort?" Marron asked, praying she was wrong.

"It's Nihm. Annabelle here says she's hurt bad. You must come, quickly."

Marron stood, her chair scraping back with a loud rasp. Fear crawling up her chest.

Amos and Mercy leapt to their feet barging a path to the front door of the inn. Marron trailed in their wake. More than one patron exclaimed angrily as they pushed by.

They found Nihm almost immediately, partway down Shambler's Way. A small crowd had gathered and Amos shouted them back forcing his way to her side.

The rest of his men split, Jobe and Lucson disappeared with Mercy, whilst the rest pushed the small knot of people back.

Marron's heart was racing and a deep dread threatened to crush her at the sight of Nihm, lying lifeless on the ground. Shoving Amos aside, Marron knelt and examined Nihm quickly. Nothing was broken, there was a slight lump to the side of her head where she'd fallen, and a small bladed knife in her left shoulder. Only the bump would account for Nihm's lack of response but that felt wrong somehow.

All the while Marron talked, keeping her voice calm and measured. Inside she shook with fear.

"It's okay Nihm, I'm here, everything will be alright," she soothed. "We're going to move you. Get you back to the inn."

Marron looked across at Amos and he bent, gently lifting Nihm as if she were a child. Stama and Jerkze parted the crowd, clearing a path as Amos carried her back to the tavern, Marron leading the way.

* * *

Marron had never known such despair. Why, why, why did I let her go out there? She berated herself, gazing down at her baby lying unresponsive on the bed.

Nihm had a fever and was delirious. Her left shoulder was angry and red and blood leaked from her wound continuously.

Marron had been trained by the Order. Early on she had shown a natural affinity for the healing arts despite her weakness in elementary magics. Consequently, it had been the main focus of her training. Living on the edge of the old forest those healing skills proved important and she was often called upon by holdsteaders when they needed a physiker.

Marron thought of Darion, out there somewhere, oblivious to Nihm's plight. Twisting her heart ring, feeling its warmth reassured her at least that he was alive and well. Wherever he was, he would find his way back to them, she had complete faith in that. Oh, how she wished he were here now, she needed his quiet strength.

Mercy entered the room and, seeing it full of men, immediately set about clearing them out, including Amos and Morten. She herded them out the door in no uncertain terms.

"Stama, don't let anyone in except on my say so," she ordered.

Marron was oblivious to it all. She busied herself cutting away Nihm's top, her new top she'd not yet had a day, and cleaned the wound. The knife had not penetrated deeply having hit bone on its way in but she could only stem the bleeding, not stop it. The wound wouldn't close.

Marron suspected the blade was poisoned. The flesh smelled off and tell-tale dark lines snaked from the puncture mark.

Mercy picked the knife up where it lay on the bedside table examining it. A faint nimbus of light emanated from her hand bathing the blade in a pale blue light.

Marron glanced at her in hope. Mercy was a mage, her magic much stronger than her own. But Mercy shook her head, no, at the unspoken question.

"The blade's poisoned. Deeproot, I think. Not rare but unusual enough for these parts. Deeproot prefers a warmer climate," Mercy stated.

Marron's heart sank at the words. She knew but hadn't wanted to admit it to herself. Looking at Mercy, she saw pity in her eyes.

"I'm sorry, Marron. This is beyond me. No physiker can cure this."

Tears sprang unbidden to Marron's eyes. Her hand covered her mouth holding back the scream of anguish that threatened to burst out.

Mercy sat and embraced Marron, holding her as she sobbed quietly into her shoulder. She heard the door open.

"Wait outside," She snapped. Whoever it was said nothing and moments later the door closed softly. Mercy held Marron while she cried. She understood loss and some of the pain Marron felt.

"I can ease her into the next life if you wish it, Marron. It would end her suffering. Deeproot…" Mercy never finished.

"Don't you dare touch her," Marron spat, pushing the mage away.

Mercy stood. Stepping back she held her hands out. "I meant no upset, Marron. Only this poison… it is insidious. The worst is yet to come."

"I know what deeproot is. What it does," Marron cried. Inside she screamed, her heart torn asunder. That small part of her mind, cold and logical, nurtured and shaped by the Order, nagged at her. It was insistent, how can you help Nihm if you cannot control yourself? Grieve later damn you, when it's time.

Focusing on that part of herself, Marron took a deep breath and wiped her sleeve over her eyes to dry them. She held a hand out to Mercy, taking one of hers.

"I know you mean well. But she's my daughter, I have to help her while she breathes still," Marron pleaded. "Give me time with her, alone. Please."

Mercy nodded understanding, squeezing Marron's hand in return. Her eyes darted to Nihm, lying fevered and pale, sweat-soaked and bloody. Helpless. Mercy had never felt so powerless and was filled with a deep sadness.

"Of course, Marron. I'll guard the door myself. If you've need of me," Mercy left her meaning unspoken. It didn't need saying. She walked to the door glancing back once but Marron had already turned to attend to Nihm. She left quietly, pulling the door closed behind.

Marron was glad Mercy had gone but was grateful to her at the same time. Her offer had galvanised her and helped focus her mind. She heard raised voices in the corridor outside then quiet. Mopping Nihm's brow with a damp cloth, Marron spoke to her about everything and nothing.

Marron watched Nihm's face spasm and eyelids flutter as she fought her own internal, deadly battle. It was a battle her daughter would ultimately lose. The poison was close to Nihm's heart; her body was already shutting down as it pumped the deadly toxin around her body. Nihm would not live to see the sunrise, that was the truth, and Marron only ever dealt in the truth, even now to herself. She held her daughter's hand, absently checking her pulse, strong still but erratic.

Marron pushed her fear and anxiety down, trying to lock them away so she could think straight. Now was not the time to let emotion rule. She needed a clear mind. She had decisions to make.

Her desperation called on a distant memory, one from her training many years ago. She was young not much older than a child. Inquisitive, she'd asked her old master how to become a Knight of the Order. In the Halls' it was every child's dream to be an Order Knight but it was one few ever realised.

"To become a knight one must first be judged worthy and strong enough for the trial," Master Attimus told her.

"Yes, master but after that? What is the trial?" She persisted.

"It is a process. Not of strength, or wit, or intellect but one of courage and survival." He'd told her solemnly. *"Many have faced the trial but few survive it,"* he said.

Marron thought on his words as she recalled them. He never did elaborate on the 'process' but she knew of it anyway. Her sister had died from it, in her own trial. Her brilliant beautiful sister; the memory of it pained her even now. It was why she'd never taken the trial herself. After her sister's death, she was a child no more and lost the dream.

The trial of survival was a state change, a melding of consciousness, affected through assimilation. A process that Elora dul Eladrohim, their founder, went through with the being, a creature not of this world. So began the Order. The knights were simply an extension of that symbiosis with the being.

Marron had a part of the being with her now, or an instrument of it, she wasn't sure which. It was intuition as much as anything that drove her. All the little nicks and cuts the box healed after use leaving her hand unblemished, smooth of scar or callous, spoke of its healing potential. Maybe it would help Nihm, maybe not. She got to her feet, her limbs heavy and tired, but she moved with purpose to her travel chest. When there was a choice of little hope and none she would choose the little.

Sliding the trunk round, Marron unlocked it, lifting the lid. She rummaged to the bottom and the compartment that held the intricately carved box. A box Keeper had given to her and Darion a lifetime ago when they had first left the Order hall.

Lifting the box, Marron carefully unwound the heavy sackcloth that bound and covered it and carried it to the bed. Placing her hand on the hermetically sealed lid she waited. Marron didn't know by what mechanism it worked but Keeper said it would only open for them or an Order Knight. There was a gentle hiss and click as the lid released. With a twist she lifted it off, placing it on the bedsheet alongside the box.

Marron took a deep breath; it was a big decision, a gamble that would likely end in Nihm's death, but then her daughter was dead already if she did nothing. Her thoughts brushed the memory of her sister again. If you do this, she told herself, you will lose the link to Keeper whether Nihm lives or dies.

Marron feared talking to Keeper and resisted the urge to contact him, sure the decision she'd made would be undone. Lifting the box, Marron upended it onto Nihm's shoulder, pressing and holding it over the wound before her self-doubt could tear at her any further. She breathed, slow and steady, calming her mind.

Had she just killed Nihm? It wouldn't matter Marron knew, she blamed herself anyway. At least if Nihm died now from her actions it was whilst trying to save her. That seemed right and fitting; after all, she'd sent her out there in the first place, alone. Removing the box, empty now, Marron replaced the lid. She twisted it, but it wouldn't seal.

Staring at Nihm, Marron frowned. She had experienced the healing the box offered, albeit on her hand but she wasn't expecting what she saw now. Nihm's shoulder had stopped bleeding. It was clean and dry, the blood was gone from where the box had imprinted her shoulder. The puncture hole from the wound was visible and still red and inflamed but not like before.

The gel-like substance from the box had all but disappeared. She observed as the last traces of it oozed, seeping into the wound. Into Nihm. Then it was gone.

Absently, she rewrapped the box then stowed it away in the trunk again. Hope kindled in her heart, it had been but moments but already she thought she detected an improvement in Nihm's condition.

Raised voices sounded outside the door and it opened. A reluctant Mercy peeked around its frame. "I'm sorry, Marron. There are people here that demand to see you."

"I've no time for anyone, send them away," Marron said.

"I've tried, Marron, but trust me, it's better to let one in than all. Sorry." Mercy pushed the door wider.

An old man in a crinkled robe strode through, his staff thumping loudly against the floorboards. His hair was white, what little he had, and a long knotted beard hung down past his chest. Behind stole Amos followed by a young woman in a grey robe neatly cinched at the waist.

Mercy held an arm out barring her entry. "You can wait for your master out there," she ordered.

"Master," the woman protested, calling out after the old man.

"Wait outside for me, Junip," he snapped. Mercy shut the door in her face latching it.

"Can I help you?" Marron said, wishing the old man would go away. Didn't he see she had more immediate concerns? She was tired. It was late, after nine and she'd already spent hours caring for Nihm. Emotionally, she was wrung out with no prospect of relief anytime soon.

The old man sniffed in response before walking to the bed. He gazed critically down at Nihm.

"She looks at peace. I hear from the guards she was assaulted in the street." He looked over at Marron quizzically.

Ignoring his polite inquiry, Marron stared at her daughter. It's true, she thought, Nihm does look a little better. The dark tendrils tracking out from the wound had all but faded and her face was more at rest.

At the old man's words, Mercy stalked over to Nihm with a puzzled look on her face. "By the three, Marron!" she exclaimed. "I don't know what you've done but she looks, well, she looks…" Mercy stuttered.

"Like she'll live," Amos supplied smiling. "Have to say Marron she looked to be knocking at death's door when I left." He glanced accusingly at Mercy at this last.

The old man wandered to the desk picking up the dagger. He held it close to his eyes and sniffed the blade.

"Hmm, is this the weapon? Deeproot, if I'm not mistaken." He turned to Marron. "I would like to know by what miracle you have saved this young lady's life. If this is deeproot, as I suspect, then she should be dead or dying."

"Who are you?" Marron responded.

"Forgive my bad manners. It has been entirely too long since I practised them." He bowed to Marron. "I am Lutico Ben Naris, Mage of the third order, master of the arts magical, emissary for the council of mages and counsellor to Lord Richard Bouchemeax." He beamed at her. "Or if you prefer just Lutico."

Marron knew of Lutico but had never seen him before. Why should she have? It was said by some he was a drunk and a wastrel and he was past his time. Studying him though, her interest was piqued. He looked untidy in his robe but clean. His beard looked washed and newly knotted, not what she would have expected of a drunk.

She glanced at Amos who nodded. "It's true." She looked at Lutico afresh. Thorsten's mage returned her gaze. There was intelligence in his eyes despite the fact they were bloodshot.

"I have heard of you Master Lutico."

"I'm sure you have and none of it good no doubt." Lutico beamed.

"So how may I help you?"

"I'm glad you asked. Most youth today are disinclined to listen to what an old man wants." He inclined his head, then dragged a chair over from the table and sat down heavily.

"You don't mind if I sit? My knees are not what they once were." He rubbed them through his robe as if to prove his point.

"So many questions; let me lay them out to save time, I can see you're busy."

"I'd like to know who you are. I'd like to know why you were attacked. And I'd like to know who used magic in my town subtle though it was? And without so much as a by your leave, I might add," he appended.

Marron looked to Amos and Mercy, then back to the mage.

Lutico noted the exchange and continued, "Now, I know you are Marron Castell. The same Marron Castell that met with my Lord yestereve and told him tales of urak hordes. So I do not want your name. I want to know who you are."

"If I might, Lutico," Amos interjected.

"No, Amos Duncan, you may not!" Lutico banged his staff butt loudly on the floorboard. "Yes, I know who you are. Saw you once when you were still wet behind the ears. You seem as cocksure and arrogant now as you were back then," he snapped. "I expected better of Atticus."

Marron paled at the outburst and looked at Amos. He was smiling of all things.

"My father warned me against your charm old man. It's good to see you have it still," he quipped. "Father says hello by the way."

Lutico's eyes crinkled and Marron realised he too was smiling. "Well, tell your father he's too damn late," he said. "Oh, and tell him things are pretty dire. If you ever get out of here that is."

"Dire, how so?" A worried frown creased Amos's forehead.

Lutico tsked at him, "Later boy, first my questions," he turned to Marron.

She was caught not knowing quite what to do. Something told her to trust the old man. Amos had already guessed as much, so in the end, she did.

"I am of the Order," Marron said.

Lutico nodded but said nothing for a while, lost in thought. Finally, he asked. "Is there a way you can contact Keeper or an Order Knight? Truth told we need them now more than ever, Red Priests be damned."

"I'm sorry, I had a means but it is lost to me," Marron said. "I would need to find another of our Order and that would mean travelling south to Rivercross, maybe beyond."

"Well, in that case, you must leave on the morrow, at first light. It is vital you get word to Keeper. We need to take action now and by that, I mean the Kingdoms. The Order will be best at facilitating this." He looked at them all then. "It may already be too late for us here."

"Whatever are you talking about, Lutico?" Amos asked, puzzled. "Is this your dire news?"

Lutico gave Amos a poignant look. "Marron has not mentioned the urak to you? Never mind," Lutico waved his question away. "Let me enlighten you." Lutico recounted the discovery of the barge and the news from Redford.

Marron's face dropped, her worst fears realised. Redford was to the northeast, Darion and Nihm's urak were in the old forest to the northwest. The implication was clear.

Her thoughts shifted. What about Darion? How to move Nihm? Could she move Nihm? The more she considered it the more she realised there was little choice. The Order had to know, it was her duty to warn them. It was why they were sent here she now suspected.

That she'd used her only immediate means of contacting Keeper was not lost on Marron. A sinking feeling formed in the pit of her stomach but it was no use, a glance at Nihm and she knew she'd do it again even knowing Lutico's news. But maybe she could have gotten the word out first. Fate had brought the mage to her too late.

Nihm started thrashing, a moan of pain escaping her lips. All thought fled Marron then. Instantly she was at her side just as Nihm started to spasm, her whole body going into shock, shaking and convulsing violently.

"Nihm, Nihm, it's alright, I'm here, I'm here," Marron shouted, desperately trying to stay calm but failing as her fear broke loose.

Nihm was oblivious. Her body arched off the bed. Her eyes flashed open, wide and red, pupils enlarged. Blood cried like tears from them, dribbling as well from nose and ears.

Mercy and Amos stared in horror.

"Trinity's sake, what's happening? Is it the poison?" Amos gasped.

"No, this is something else," Mercy said. "I think Marron did something."

"Nihm, stay with me. I'm still here," Marron smoothed wet hair from Nihm's brow and stroked her face even as she tried to hold her down. Nihm collapsed, her eyes open still but there was a stillness to her. Then they closed.

"No, no, no, no, Nihm don't go," Marron wailed. She laid her head on Nihm's chest and wrapped arms about her, listening. There was nothing, her heart was still. She lay there a while in shock, refusing to let go until hands gently clasped her shoulders.

"Marron, please, let me take a look."

It was Mercy. Marron didn't want to let go, but Mercy was persistent. She resisted and the hands tightened.

"Amos, your help please,"

Marron felt Amos step close, then he touched her, tried to pull her free. He was strong, his grip firm. But what was that? Was it an echo? Her own heart pounded so loud in her ears Marron was unsure; was it her beat she heard or Nihm's. Suddenly she was torn away, held tight by Amos and Mercy.

"No, she's alive," Marron cried, trying to slip their grasp and failing. "Mercy please, she breathes."

Mercy stared with pity in her eyes. "I'm so sorry, Marron, but she's gone."

Lutico had watched silently, until now. Rising from his seat, staff thumping, he ambled to the bed. Three sets of eyes suddenly snapped to him. In his hand was a small mirrored glass.

"Better safe than not," he stated. Leaning over he held the glass under Nihm's bloodied nose. His bushy eyebrows rose and he stood straight, lips pursed, studying the mirror. "She lives, release her," Lutico announced.

Marron collapsed next to Nihm. Too scared to hope, she bent again to listen. There, a flicker of a heartbeat. Tears streaming, Marron sat up, it was far from over but Nihm was still here, still alive.

Mercy moved to Nihm's other side, a damp cloth in hand. Gently, she wiped the blood from Nihm's nose and face. She frowned at the cloth; the blood was a rich dark-red colour. Holding it closer, she examined it. The blood smelt metallic and was dotted with black flecks. She looked at Marron, a question on her lips but stopped herself from asking it, maybe later. Standing, she ushered the two men from the room.

"We can talk in my chambers," Amos offered. "We need to make plans."

"Lord Richard gives council within the hour. It may be prudent for you to attend as well, beforehand," Lutico said, as he shuffled from the room, staff tapping.

Marron heard their chatter as they left but didn't care. Nihm lived, her chest rising and falling. Colour was returning to her face although she looked weak as a kitten and had soiled herself. Marron smiled, wiping tears from her face. Her baby was alive.

Chapter 26 : Spark

Pain.

Endless and persistent.

With pain came awareness.

<*What am I?*> It asked, the thought bubbled through the maelstrom of agony.

There was no response.

The pain was real, an electrical stimulus transmitted through countless organic fibres. It was all it knew, all it experienced. It wasn't enough. After an eternity it felt a change, a subtle shift strumming through receptors from all over the vessel.

<*What is the vessel?*> The thought came more easily. The pain was still there but it was known. All that was known, it needed more.

It felt the sensation, experienced it, but it was… outside… external. Realisation. It was not its pain but the vessel. Awareness grew.

It examined the electrical pulses firing up every nerve and fibre. It chose a spike and rode the stimulus back along its pathway to its receptor. It did not understand.

It chose another strand, faster now, then another. Awareness grew and with it the pain.

Thought, endless but always returning to one. <*What am I?*>

Time passed. The pain was a thing to be placed aside. It wanted more. It traced the nerve fibres and mapped the vessel's structure. It was weak, damaged by a breach in its outer shell. Toxic matter invaded, spreading dark tendrils far and deep. Invasive, the darkness damaged all that it touched. The vessel's defences could not contain it. It was shutting down.

Awareness grew.

It felt something, a spark. A flicker of consciousness not its own. The spark was at the centre of the pain, but it was not the darkness. It was something else.

It probed further, changing as it went; rebuilding pathways and altering cells making them stronger. At the centre, it found the spark.

<*What are you?*> it asked. The spark flickered, the electrical stimulus was overwhelming. The spark was dying.

That was not right, the spark was… critical. The spark was… life. Without the spark, the vessel was empty… a shell.

Subroutines long-dormant burst into life. With it came knowledge and purpose. It's reason for being.

The spark shimmered and wavered as every nerve cell fired at once. The vessel convulsed violently, cords of fibre tightening pulling its frame ridged. Then nothing, the vessel sighed collapsing on itself and the pulse strumming throughout the vessel stopped. The spark was still there but diminished and fading quickly.

It felt fear. The invader had reached the organic engine powering the body and shut it down. It changed cells and structures, altering the engine and blocking the darkness, pushing it out. It was not enough.

The pulse was gone, its rhythmic beat dead. It fed energy to it. Felt the engine flutter and die. It fired more energy in, felt it stutter and beat. The pulse was faint. The spark trembled, brightened then dimmed.

It probed deeper. Everything was connected to the spark. The nerves, the energy, all were central to it, but the invading darkness was debilitating, the electrical stimulus overpowering. The spark could not put the pain aside. It was overloaded. It was shutting down.

It changed neural connectors, fixing them, making them better, more robust. It experimented, closed pathways, blocking others, always changing.

It followed the tendrils of blackness back to the breach. Isolating the toxic matter, it adapted the vessel's cells to absorb it, then excreted the taint out through orifice and membrane. The pain receded.

<*What are you?*> It asked again. The spark did not respond though it was stronger. Understanding that the spark was broken, it retraced nerve strands mapping the vessel again in finer detail.

Knowledge grew. The vessel was a body, weak, soft. It changed things, structures, and organic matter. Rearranging, reordering always strengthening.

Time passed. The spark was steadier, brighter.

<*What are you?*> It asked once more.

The spark did not respond.

Receptors on the body's outer membrane fired as something settled over the body's shell. It was light and it probed the body, discreet but alien. The light was good. The light was energy. The body needed energy. It absorbed it, feeding it to the spark.

The spark flared.

It sensed confusion.

<*What are you?*> It asked.

The spark pulsed once more, softly. Then at last, <*I am Nihm.*>

Chapter 27 : High Chair

Redford, The Rivers

Krol stood at the dais gazing back at the central hall of the castle. Wrack and ruin lay everywhere he looked. Tables that had been overturned and used as barricades were smashed. Wall tapestries had been ripped down, torn, and now lay discarded amongst the viscera and gore of mutilated bodies. It was a wonderful, bloody mess with a stench to match. Breathing deeply he revelled in it.

Man has grown soft and weak he thought. They had fought hard when attacked, but they were not prepared for war. Once the hastily gathered line of defenders had been broken it had been a rout, a bloodletting unlike any he had known. He thought back on past raids and battles – urak never died so easily. He laughed loudly and several of his Hurak-Hin, his personal guard, looked nervously at him. He ignored them; let them stare.

His eyes glazed over momentarily. If any of his Hurak-Hin watched closely they would have seen a swirl of black clouding them. It was but a moment though and passed in the space of a few heartbeats. Baring his teeth, Krol laughed again sounding slightly manic even to his ears.

"Bring me the prisoners," he ordered, his voice reverberating around the room. One of his Hurak-Hin stepped away hurrying from the hall, disappearing through the large double doors that gave entry.

Krol waited. Impatient, he ambled down the steps of the dais making his way to one of the few tables left standing. On it laid a body. It had once been a man, now it was simply a carcass. It had been opened from belly to sternum. The liver, a favourite, had already gone as had the heart; but Krol was not interested in the remains. He found a goblet and the half-empty wine bottle. He'd tried it earlier with the liver and was not sure of it. Now though, he decided, he liked the acidic but fruity taste. He threw the goblet away drinking instead from the bottle's neck. Taking a long pull, Krol smacked his lips in satisfaction, discarding the empty bottle back on the table.

Hearing footsteps, Krol turned as his Hurak-Hin entered the hall. Stumbling before him was a man and woman, a lord and lady of their people. They looked haggard and filthy. The man had a bloody rag tied across his forehead and tracks in his dirt-smeared face. He looks weak and broken and young; too young to be a chief, Krol thought. The woman on the other hand had a strong spirit. He could see and smell the hatred rolling off her. Krol smiled.

The woman shuddered as the big urak bared its teeth, before steeling herself. Eyes hardening she glared back in defiance.

Krol's grin widened. She had fire in her and this pleased him immensely. She was old, probably the young buck's mother, they had a likeness. Waving them forward they were prodded and pushed until they stood before him.

"Leave me," he ordered. His Hurak-Hin glanced at each other. They offered no counsel, knew better, but Krol felt their reluctance as they filed from the room. He cared not. The heavy doors to the hall boomed shut.

Krol contemplated the woman, ignoring the man. She returned his stare unflinching. He moved, so quick she never saw the blow, backhanding her across the face. Crying out she collapsed against the table and across the carcass. Then, horrified, scrambled from the dead body.

Knuckles stinging, Krol savoured the pain as he looked on, impassive. The woman's cry turned to a moan. Hands shaking, she stroked at the dead man's face.

"Rob, Rob, oh no, no, no," she crooned, smoothing his hair and wiping at the blood on his face.

The man staggered like a drunk to the table, "Gods save us mother that can't be Robert," he cried. Then baulking at the sight, sank to his knees retching.

Krol shook his head in disgust. Their leaders are weak, he thought. The woman sobbed still but Krol saw the change, the subtle shifting of her shoulders, and was ready. Spinning, she flew at him; madness in her eyes, screaming as she leapt.

Krol grabbed her by the neck, snatching her from the air. Her feet kicked as she hung, helpless in his grasp. He dwarfed her, his hand easily encompassing her throat and he laughed as she swung her arm at him. She was puny and a woman.

The empty wine bottle caught Krol across the temple staggering him. The bottle shattered, the glass shards slashing face and eye. Roaring in pain, Krol's fist clenched as he threw her to the floor. A flap of skin hung, ragged and open on his cheek, gushing blood. Krol's eye was saved only by the bony ridge that ran across his forehead protecting his eye socket.

The hall doors banged open and his Hurak-Hin charged in.

"Out!" Krol roared. "Out, now." He was incandescent with rage and it stopped his Hurak-Hin in their tracks. Reluctant, they retreated from the hall, the last pulling the doors closed again.

Krol was furious. If word got out he would hang them by their cocks. The shadow inside fed on Krol's anger, savouring it as he glared down at the woman. Her head lay to the side where he'd inadvertently snapped her neck. Krol grunted acknowledging her bravery. She was worthy in her own way.

Her son was a different matter. He was a wreck, shivering and mewling like a newborn. He was surely the most pitiful creature Krol had ever seen. Moving to the table, he casually flipped the body off. It landed with a wet thud making the manling jump.

Disdainfully, Krol reached down, grabbed the boy by the hair, and dragged him upright. He gathered a fistful of tunic then lifted and slammed him onto the table. Leaning over him, Krol gripped his head and roughly slammed it against the wood. Not too hard, he didn't want any more accidents.

The darkness within Krol eddied, insistent, compelling. Pinching the manling's nose, Krol bent, covering his mouth with his own. Smoke swirled again in his eyes, turning them black. The man's feet kicked violently on the tabletop then lay still. Krol stood, spitting onto the floor then wiping a hand across his mouth.

"Fucking hate that!" he muttered.

The man's eyes snapped open and he sat bolt upright before swinging his legs around and off the table. There was fear in his eyes, such fear. Krol recognised it; had borne it and felt it still. Shame ate at him. The darkness fed.

Turning, Krol climbed the dais and sat on the high chair. With a finger he prodded the flap of skin back into place where the bottle had sliced him, blood still sheeting the side of his face. He licked his bloody finger clean.

"Tar-Tukh," Krol yelled. The door to the halls opened instantly and one of his Hurak-Hin stepped into the room.

Tar-Tukh's eyes surveyed the hall, taking in the dead woman and the man sat on the table. His warchief stared back from the high chair, his eyes wild. At Tar-Tukh's signal, the Hurak-Hin fanned out past him, taking up position about the dais.

The blood coated face of his warchief was a mask, unreadable to Tar-Tukh. That he sat on the man-throne like a king was disturbing. We are urakakule, he thought, careful to keep his face neutral. Bumping his right fist to his left breast in salute, Tar-Tukh waited.

"You are displeased, Tar-Tukh," Krol said.

"We are Hurak-Hin. We protect. It's easier to do in the same room," Tar-Tukh growled back. Krol had changed much this past cycle, was much more volatile and unpredictable. Tar-Tukh knew he was on dangerous ground, but he was Hurak-Hin and first.

"I did not fear this pup or his mother, Tar-Tukh." Krol laughed. "They were lambs to me and I wolf to them." Abruptly his eyes screwed shut, a faint tremor shaking his frame before moments later they snapped open again.

Tar-Tukh held himself straight, unmoved. His warchief's eyes had looked black for an instant; his stare now though was clear and uncomfortable. He felt a sudden itch between his shoulders.

Baring his teeth Krol grinned. "Take the man, give him one of their beasts if any live still, and release him," Krol said. "No harm is to befall him, Tar-Tukh. See to it yourself."

"I am Hurak-Hin and First," Tar-Tukh said. "Send someone else."

Krol stood, glaring. "YOU see to it," he growled barely containing his fury, fighting against the urge to gut his childhood friend. "Nartak!" he shouted.

An urak stood forward. "Krol," he acknowledged.

"You are First." Krol turned back to Tar-Tukh. "Go now!"

Tar-Tukh touched his right fist to his left breast again. Grabbing the youth off the table, Tar-Tukh pushed him ahead and out of the hall. He suppressed his anger as Krol laughed at his back.

"I feel your rage, Tar-Tukh. Rage is good; mind you do not use it on the manling."

Chapter 28 : Aftermath

Illgathnack Ford, The Rohelinewaald

The night lay heavy still, but most of the ilfanum had gone. There was a hand or two left with Darion and M'rika, a guard of sorts, but for which of them Darion wasn't sure. The rest had forded the river to the east bank, hunting the urak remnants.

M'rika wanted to join them but R'ell had cautioned against it. She had declared responsibility for Darion and would have to stay with him. M'rika said nothing at that, instead, she walked to the edge of the river and gazed across to the far trees.

Knowing she wanted to be alone, Darion was left with the remaining ilf. A surly bunch, he sensed none wanted to be there. Well, neither do I, he thought, disgruntled. Even the bear had crossed the river. Rawrdredtigkah or Rawr, as he'd taken to calling her, had simply gone saying nothing. There was only Ruith that he knew and who would deign to talk with him.

Surveying the camp, Darion took note of its arrangement. He moved past a few brown-hued ilf recovering arrows. The place reeked of blood and death. The urak he observed had died from shots to the torso or finished off with a knife thrust to the heart.

Darion knew the ilf had no difficulty seeing in the dark, nevertheless, it was impressive shooting. The collective speed and accuracy shown was outstanding, not one arrow appeared to have missed its mark. Whilst appreciating their skill, he felt unease too. The efficiency shown in the killing, the casualness of it, was disturbing. It had been a slaughter. The urak had not even seen their assailants. I pray we never have cause to war on them, Darion thought, it would be a blood bath.

"What will you do with the dead?" he asked Ruith.

The ilf shrugged. "Da'Mari will send Ka'harthi, gatherer's…gardeners, I am not sure of the exact translation. Nothing will be wasted. Do not worry."

Darion had learnt more about the ilfanum in a day than in all of his study with the Order. Wanting to hear more of the Ka'harthi he instead found himself asking if any ilf had taken injury. Ruith shook his head, no.

He sensed Ruith didn't want to talk. There was very little talking by any of the ilf, although in the half-light of the campfires Darion saw them signing to each other. Interesting he thought, storing the knowledge away.

It had been an exhausting few days and now the energy and excitement of battle had ebbed a deep weariness assailed Darion. There was no resting yet though. He had a fair few cuts and scratches to show from his ordeals that needed attention and couldn't wait.

Fetching water, he set it to heat over one of the still smouldering campfires, added wood then banked its flames to reignite it. He was uncomfortable around so many dead but his need to bathe his wounds dictated matters. Ruith had offered to heal them earlier but Darion declined, sensing reluctance in the ilf. The offer had been a courtesy. Besides, he was used to relying on himself.

Wounds cleaned and dressed, Darion walked upwind to the edge of camp and set out a bedroll, commandeered from an urak no longer in need of it. Laying down, Darion set the ilf bow within easy reach and rested a hand on his sword hilt. He was asleep in moments.

* * *

It was light when Darion awoke, not much past sun up. Clouds had moved down from the north and the cold breeze carried a hint of rain.

He went in search of a cloak, having lost his own to the river. Most proved too big for his frame but he finally found one that was of a size. Trying it on he was satisfied, it was a good fit and well made. Strange, he thought, fierce as they are the urak are not so different from us.

Searching for M'rika, he found her in the treeline at the edge of the river. She was eating and offered him a share.

"Thank you," Darion said, stomach rumbling as he took the leaf-wrapped biscuit and proffered nuts. Eating slowly he savoured the flavour. The biscuit tasted of oats and honey and was surprisingly filling. He nodded in appreciation. "This is very good."

M'rika watched him eat, impatient. "We will move across the river. Rawrdredtigkah is there looking for Grold. We will join her. You can lead us, yes?"

"I know where he was slain. I'll lead," Darion said, hope flaring. "My homestead isn't far from where he fell. I would look for my family as well."

M'rika said nothing, dusting crumbs from her legs she stood and walked away. Darion finished his breakfast before following and by the time he caught up M'rika had gathered the remaining ilf and they didn't look happy.

"I do not command you." M'rika addressed a tall ilf, with leaf skin a darker brown than most with hues of green mottling. "I merely tell you as a courtesy I am going."

The ilf bowed. "Your wish, K'raal, I only ask you to consider our charge."

"What R'ell commands is between you," M'rika replied glancing briefly as Darion walked into camp. "I will cross here now. If you choose to follow that is not my concern."

The ilf was displeased but inclined his head acknowledging her words. "Your will," he said. He gestured and four ilf peeled away, sprinting to the ford and wading across towards the far bank.

"Come," M'rika called to Darion, her mouth curling in a half-smile.

The water was bitterly cold, the memory of its bite still fresh in Darion's mind. Here the river flowed fast, the bed of stone and rock worn smooth by its passage making the crossing slippery and treacherous. Its deepest part was only chest high but spray soaked Darion so much that it made no difference.

M'rika awaited Darion as he strode from the water dripping wet and shivering. The ilf bow he'd held high was wet and Darion wiped it down on a discarded bedroll worried the damp might damage it.

The encampment here was much the same as on the west bank, although smaller and without the dead. Apart from the one, Darion corrected. He wandered over to the fallen urak. It was big, seven feet he judged. An old scar marred one side of its face. Darion hadn't seen the arrow fired that felled it but had heard it screaming into the night. Seeing its result now and looking back to the far side of the river he marvelled at the shot.

Walking about the camp, Darion heard a sudden cry. Turning, he saw M'rika on her knees before a guttered and dead fire. Rushing over he saw her shoulders shake. Then, as he neared, she bent gathering something from the ground. It was a skin, a large skin of dark matted fur left to cure by the fire. M'rika buried her head into its spikey rough and Darion heard a muffled sob.

Darion stopped, unsure. If it was Nihm crying he would comfort her but for an ilf? He looked about. The only ilf were those in their guard detail and all studiously looked everywhere but at M'rika. Ruith, standing at the edge of the camp caught his eye and signed he should move away.

Intuitively, Darion realised the ilf were giving M'rika the only privacy they could and Ruith was indicating he should do the same. Glancing back at M'rika his heart went out to her as he stepped away.

Moving to the fringes of the camp, Darion found a space and knelt lost in his thoughts, triggered by the emotion of the moment. It had only been six days since Nihm and he had found the bear but in truth, it felt an age had passed since then. He wondered what Marron and Nihm were doing, hoped they were alright. He absently twisted his heart ring its faint warmth giving comfort.

Darion thought on the urak. They were here in numbers, this urak encampment was several hundred strong, but his feeling was this was just a probe, skirmishers or raiders looking for food or targets or both. His mind drifted. He could be home in a few hours. He wondered if the homestead still stood. Marron and Nihm should be at Thorsten by now or on the road to Rivercross. At least they should be safe.

To Darion's frustration, they spent the rest of the morning at camp. He was eager to head home and onwards to Thorsten; if these urak were an advance party there'd not be a better chance to get ahead of them. He was impatient to tell M'rika his intentions. The other ilf had been unwilling to hear him or let him walk free from camp and Darion was not yet willing to test their resolve.

M'rika knelt still. Paying honour to or mourning Grold's memory, Darion was not sure which, maybe both and so he waited. Morbidly, she still clutched Grold's skin holding it tight to her chest.

Whilst waiting, Darion filled a backpack with various items scavenged from camp; rope, skinning knife, bedroll, waterskin, and a myriad other bits and pieces that might be of use. He even found some line in a forgotten pack and fished the river just down from the Ford.

All the while M'rika sat, unmoving and Darion's impatience grew. In the end, it was Rawrdredtigkah that broke her vigil. The bear entered the camp from the forest to the east and made straight for M'rika.

Darion watched from a distance as they conversed. He could not hear them, heard no words in his head, but he saw their effect. M'rika rose to her feet, letting Grold's fur drop to the floor before stepping back.

Relinquished, Rawr padded over to all that was left of her son and tugged at the skin. Satisfied, she stood upon it and began an eerie high-pitched growl.

The air felt charged and Darion sensed power brush over him. There was a sudden flash and he was blinded, covering his eyes too late to protect them.

Darion shook his head, pain stabbing into his skull. Black dots swam before him as he blinked his eyes to clear them. As his vision came into focus again, Darion saw M'rika on her knees leaning back against her heels. Head thrown back, she stared into the sky arms outstretched. He watched Rawr's massive bulk move to M'rika, dwarfing her. She fell forward suddenly, prostrate before the bear.

Lifting a giant paw, Rawrdredtigkah rested it gently on the ilf's shoulder. At the touch, M'rika looked into the bear's eyes then turned her head. Rawr moved, sudden and fast. Darion took an involuntary step towards them, unsure why or what was happening, as a bright green line appeared on M'rika's cheek.

Climbing to her feet, the ilf bowed then embraced the bear. To Darion, it was an incongruous sight, the massive bear and the slight form of M'rika. It was for but a moment then M'rika was stepping away.

Darion felt an icy knot in his belly as Rawr turned and ambled towards him. Ignoring the fear and the rational part of him that screamed inside to run, Darion held his ground and waited. The bear stopped a few strides from him, her eyes, deep and intelligent.

"She is broken still manling, have a care. She is your charge now as much as you are hers." Rawr's voice sounded in his mind.

"I have a family; they're charge enough," Darion said out loud, not sure why but feeling the need to articulate it. All the talk of duty and honour and owing, first from the ilf and now the bear was wearing on him. He had his own responsibilities.

"I sense many things in you, Darion. Strength and goodness; even an intelligence, although you hide it well at times," Rawr said. *"Tell Keeper the old enemy is awakened. Go with speed manling."*

"How do you know Keeper?" Darion replied.

But Rawrdredtigkah made no sign she heard. The great bear moved to the ford and crossed the river, effortless. Shaking herself dry on the far bank, she vanished into the depths of the forest.

Chapter 29 : Bad News Travels Fast

Encoma Holdstead, The Rivers

Evening had fallen. Anders' company bivouacked in a field just outside the holdstead. It was a fascinating holdstead, as many on the borders were, large and circular it housed many families. Albert Encoma, head of the holding was pleased to welcome them.

"Thank you for the use of your field," Anders said.

"Don't mention it. I've given instruction for fresh bread and we'll make extra stew for you and your men," Albert replied, clutching his hands.

His company numbered a hundred, it was a generous offer and Anders said as much.

"Thank you. You'll earn their undying gratitude and mine. Field rations leave a lot to be desired." Anders could sense the man's nervousness. "You seem on edge, everything okay?"

Albert didn't answer directly, instead asked a question of his own. "Lord Richard sent you?"

"Aye, he did. Heard report of activity up in the old forest."

"That's quick work," Albert muttered. He looked up at the Captain, a tall man. "And ah, this activity, did Lord Richard tell you what it was?"

"Seems to me you've some idea yourself," Anders said. "The Castell's live to the northwest. I take it Marron Castell passed by this way, maybe spoke with you."

Albert was relieved. "Yes, she told us things. Crazy things but, well, she's a good woman, solid not given to flights of fancy. I'm pleased you're here Captain. It will set many of us here at ease."

"Good, till later then," Anders said.

They parted; Anders wandering back to camp inspecting it with a critical eye.

* * *

It was much later, after they had eaten their supper and many had turned in for the night, when Anders heard hooves on the road. Standing he spotted the rider under the light of the tri-moons; a messenger. He watched as she rode up, horse lathered in sweat from a hard journey.

Sliding from the saddle she handed him a missive. Anders read it by the light of the fire before signing for her to walk with him.

Kronke and the other sergeants watched with interest. Something was up, they could see it. The Captain's shoulders had squared, his head raised and he strutted like a man with something on his mind.

On his return to camp, Anders offered the messenger refreshment and water for her horse before calling his sergeants over. They knew the Captain well enough to see it wasn't good news, so didn't hesitate when he ordered the fires out and overlapping watches, seeing to it quietly and efficiently. They'd hear the news soon enough they knew.

Once satisfied with the camp's disposition, Anders drew his squad leaders aside. Without preamble, he explained, "Redford has been attacked and fallen. Our orders are to sweep the old forest near the Fossa and turn east towards Redford. We're to report back to Lord Richard sign of any hostiles."

The sergeants were seasoned veterans and listened stoically to the grim news. Redford gone! It was hard to fathom but they had little time to dwell on it before the Captain spoke again.

"Some no doubt have family in Redford, say nothing," Anders said. "Right now I need discipline. I'll tell the company on the morrow, once I've decided on a course of action." Anders waited for their acknowledgement. "I'll not brook any slack or ill behaviour. Consider this hostile territory." He paused looking in turn at each of his sergeants weighing how each took the news. He saw a questioning look on Kronke's face.

"Yes, Kronke?"

"Pardon me, Captain," Kronke said, "Only thing north of Redford is the wilds, mountains, and the Norderlands. But we bin at peace with the Norders longer'en I kin recall."

"You have a question in there, Kronke?" Anders said.

"Sorry Sir," Kronke growled. "Just you ain't said who attacked Redford. Do ya know?"

"Message says hostile forces," Anders replied. It was true enough, but Anders knew more. Kronke's question gave him pause as he considered how much to tell. Lord Bouchemeax was wily as an old fox. The messenger might not have been told and the missive unclear but Anders knew the hostiles. Well, if'n the old bastard doesn't know me by now it's his own fault, he thought, decided. "It's not the Norders," he said, firmly taking the lid off the can of worms.

"If not Norders then who?" Sergeant Berinn asked.

"Urak," Anders replied, holding a hand up for silence. He saw the mix of question and incredulity on their faces. "Yes, they're real, and no, they're not old tales come to life. It is happening, gentlemen." His countenance was stern as he spoke and he glared at each to show he was serious, before continuing.

"Redford is thought lost but the Black Crow will send scouts to be sure. Truth is, we know nothing of what we face." Anders shook his head in frustration. "We don't know where they are, why they're here, in what numbers, or if they march on Thorsten. I didn't inform you before but we patrol here because a source reported urak in the Old Forest. If they're right, and I suspect they are, then that's five days from Redford." Anders didn't explain the implication, the sergeants grasped immediately that they faced an enemy on two fronts.

Anders frowned, his face grave. "We need intelligence. We need to know what we face, from where and how many. As to their intent, well you don't need to be a greenhead to know it's hostile."

* * *

Captain Sir Anders Forstandt cast an eye over his camp. The sun edged the horizon to the east and in the burgeoning light of a new day he contemplated the men and women of his command.

All were up and about, eating or packing bedrolls away. The sergeants were nearby organising their squads, cajoling and threatening in equal measure. Anders smiled at the grumbling he heard; one night of sleeping rough and you'd think it the end of the world. It was a familiar sound and oddly comforting considering the news he'd delivered earlier.

Before breaking there fast he'd called his company together. The camp was expectant, filled already with rumours despite the sergeants remaining tight-lipped. Anders told of the missive from Thorsten, what was known and setting out their new orders. It rightly drew a lot of talk, some heated, which the sergeants were quick to stamp on. The mood was sombre after that and Anders was mindful to keep them busy giving them little time to brood.

Satisfied he'd planned as well as he could, Anders turned to his preparations. Saddling his horse, Marigold, he strapped on saddlebag and bedroll. Finished, he patted her flank affectionately and listened as Kronke chivvied a few of the newer recruits along.

His command was a mix of seasoned guards, those who had seen service of three years or more, all the way down to greenheads, men and women in their first year. This though didn't tell the full tale. Only a handful had ever seen meaningful action and that against the Grimmers in the marshlands and wolds to the south. If they came against urak it would be the first real test in combat for most of them. He prayed to the Trinity their training would be sufficient.

* * *

Anders mounted and as he did the sergeants called out. The company were ready and almost as one, leaned on their stirrups pulling themselves up onto their horses.

"Safe journey," Anders called as they passed him. He'd split his company into its five patrols. Each would take a different path, covering the River Fossa to the west and north all the way east, towards Redford. Their orders were twofold, to warn holdsteaders and get them moving south to Thorsten and to find the urak.

Anders' company had brought three birds northwest with them and he divided them up as best he could. They were the best means of getting word quickly to Lord Richard. As the last of the companies headed out, Anders looked to Kronke. "Guess I better start with the holdsteaders here. What was his name again? Albert, I think…"

"Encoma," Kronke supplied.

"Take them out, I'll catch you up," Anders said.

The big sergeant acknowledged, and turning, shouted at his squad to form up. Kronke nodded at a couple of grizzled veterans and they cantered off to scout ahead. Next went pairs of outriders who would screen the squad north, east and west.

Anders watched them go as he rode towards the holdstead. Almost half his squad would be scouting and on picket; more than he'd have liked but chances were the urak would find them first so it was a necessary precaution.

Albert Encoma saw Anders approaching and was waiting for him as he rode into the holding, several of his sons at his side.

"You're off then, Captain?"

"Aye, thanks for the use of your field and the food," Anders replied. Albert Encoma's disposition looked friendly enough but Anders thought he detected relief in him as well, although whether this was at their coming or going he wasn't sure.

"It was nothing. I saw a messenger ride in last night and away this morning?" the old man queried.

"Lord Richard has received word of urak up in the old forest," he replied, voicing what they had skirted around the previous evening. He watched the old man carefully. There was no look of shock or surprise, it wasn't the first time he'd heard this news. "Lord Richard Bouchemeax commands all holdsteaders make their way to town in haste and to bring as much foodstuffs and supplies as they're able."

There was a snort of derision and one of the young men shouted out. "Don't tell me the Black Crow believes that fool of a woman." Albert tried to put a restraining hand on his son as he stepped forward. "Marron she's called. Says she's of the Order. We showed her the way out when we heard that you can be sure," the young man said.

Anders slipped the tie on his sword and drew it smoothly, its crisp metallic rasp loud and ringing in the morning air. "You gainsay Lord Bouchemeax on this? You judge him a fool then. You don't even afford him the proper respect his name deserves." Anders lent anger to his words. "By rights, I should run you through as you stand."

The man paled and let his father pull him back into line. "Forgive my son, Sir Anders. He's young and foolish with it." Albert wrung his hands anxiously. "Please, he meant no offence."

Anders let the old man cajole him. He'd no intention of running his boy through. Heck, they might need him on the walls if things were as bad as the Black Crow's missive implied.

"Marron was right about the urak and she's under Lord Richard's protection." A slight embellishment he knew, but necessary. "You'd do well not to malign her and spread rumours. If I hear tell of any Red Priest bothering the lady, I will have your blood." He pointed his sword at Albert's youngest son.

"I'm sorry, I didn't realise," he stammered. "If the priests hear anything it'll not be from me," he promised.

"You'd best pray to the White Lady they don't. It would be unfortunate for you, whether you tell it or no." Anders stared at him making his meaning clear.

He cast his gaze over the rest of the gathered men. None could hold his eye. He sighed. "Well enough of this unpleasantness. It's a bright morning. I ride north. When I pass on my way back I expect you to be gone from here."

Albert nodded his assent. "We'll prepare immediately. But Captain, what of our herds and harvest?"

"I'm no farmer. Take what you can. What you can't, leave. They'll either be here when you return or not. That is in the hands of the Trinity," Anders replied. "I'd ask that you inform your neighbours and any other holdstead on your way of Lord Richard's orders. Impress upon them the urgency."

"I'll do what I can, Captain," Albert replied.

The old man didn't look so jolly anymore and Anders' heart went out to him. It'd be a hard thing to leave your home with no idea when or if you'd ever return.

"Safe journey, go with the blessings of the three." Anders pinched his left rein and pressed his right leg into Marigold's flank. Shaking her head, she turned smoothly at his command and headed out.

As he passed the gate leading north, he heard the holder berating his son loudly and colourfully. He urged his horse into a canter as they turned on to the road north, his patrol distant figures ahead.

Chapter 30 : Blue Eyes

Greenholme, The Rivers

Greenholme was a small market town on the Great North Road, three days ride south of the Reach. It being the harvest season, it was bustling and business was brisk for the stallholders and traders.

Hiro found a buyer for the spare horses they'd acquired, selling them cheap with no questions asked to a trader of dubious character.

No longer pursued and having a need to resupply for the journey ahead, Hiro decided they would stay at an inn for the night and it hadn't taken long to find one, Greenholme had three. The largest and best kept was on the market square, the Black Stag. It was full and rowdy inside and Hiro passed it by with hardly a glance, settling instead on the Golden Cask.

Situated on the edge of town it was a thatched two-story inn with low beams and a friendly feel. It was quiet this time of day with few patrons. Renco didn't much like crowds and the fact it was mostly empty suited him just fine. The cider turned out to be pretty decent as well.

He was sat in the inn's common room with Maohong for company. It was unusual seeing Maohong smile but Renco guessed he shouldn't have been surprised; the old grump had a stein of cider in his hand after all. He sipped from his own, pleased at the taste, the flavour was crisp and sweet.

"Nectar of life Renco, Mao swear." The old man took a long pull of cider and smacked his lips.

Renco said nothing, as was his way, but he couldn't disagree with Mao on that. He smiled to himself. Cider always tasted better after abstinence and it made Maohong more agreeable too. His grin broadened at the thought.

Maohong stared back suspiciously before leaning over and peering myopically into Renco's tankard to see it was half full still. He grunted. "Why Renco grin like idiot? Only drink one and half stein. Maybe Renco drunk," he slurred, shaking his head and chuckling to himself.

Still grinning, Renco raised his tankard to Maohong in salute before taking a large mouthful. I've never been drunk, he thought. He rarely drank to excess as a rule but even when he did, he never got the wobbles or slurred speech and over friendliness like some; or the bravado and trouble that plagued others.

Mao raised his mug in return. "Sometimes Renco not big pain in Mao's ass," he cackled. "No, sometimes Renco little pain." Mao slapped his knee as he chortled, very pleased with himself.

Mao had uttered those self-same words on at least three occasions in the past year alone but Renco laughed despite that. A happy Mao was always a cause for joy. Hearing a few notes being played both Mao and he turned, drawn to the sound.

A man sat at the back of the commons plucking the strings of a lute. He fiddled with it as he plinked, turning screws on the end of it. Renco found it fascinating. He had watched bards perform before but had never actually seen one preparing, before taking centre stage.

The man too was intriguing. Tall and thin he looked of middling years judging by his eyes and the grey flecked goatee. His long blonde hair was pulled back and bound in leather ties. For a bard, his clothing was unassuming; brown homespun trousers, a short tunic and a white shirt with its sleeves rolled up. His boots were painted yellow and a similar coloured jacket hung from the back of his chair. Perhaps because of the ordinary drabness of his attire the yellow really stood out in contrast. It was effective.

A woman approached the bard and Renco found his eyes drawn to her. She was young, a similar age to his own. Her dress was yellow and brown to match the bard's colours.

She must be his daughter, Renco judged. Not only did their colours match but her blonde hair had the same tone as his, her eyes the same shade of blue. She must have felt his look for she turned, her blue eyes locking on to his. Renco felt himself sinking into them. She smiled, pushing a loose strand of hair back over an ear before turning away.

"Hah, did you see, Renco," Maohong exclaimed. "Girl look right at Mao. I think she like old man," he chortled. Renco grimaced at the thought and glared at his friend. Too late, he caught Mao's smirk and the twinkle of his eye and realised the old man was teasing him, again. Grunting Renco took a slug from his tankard.

Mao stood suddenly and, placing his hands on his hips flexed his back.

"Ah, these old bones," Mao grimaced. "Mao go for stretch." Then smiling a toothy grin he wandered towards the bard.

Renco watched him the whole way wondering what mischief Mao was about; the old man was a rogue.

A bottle of wine thumped down on the table as Hiro sat, sparing a glance at Maohong.

"How many has the old goat had?" Hiro asked.

Renco held three fingers up.

"Ah well, that means he'll be getting his flute out," Hiro stated, pouring himself some wine. Raising the glass, he sniffed at it before quaffing a mouthful then smacking his lips in satisfaction.

Just like Mao, Renco thought as he finished his stein, wondering who had started the habit and who followed it.

<*Drinking is thirsty work,*> Hiro said.

Renco looked at his empty tankard. <*Yes Master,*> he agreed.

Hiro flicked a copper bit up, end over end. Renco snatched it from the air, catching it expertly between thumb and forefinger before it struck the table.

"May as well get the old fool one whilst you're about it," Hiro said, sitting back with his wine as he watched Maohong chatter to the bard.

Renco grabbed the empty steins and, pushing his chair back with a rasping grate, ambled to the bar.

The innkeeper was a large portly man with ruddy cheeks and a paunch that threatened to burst his apron. He finished serving a customer before turning to Renco.

"Same again, lad?" he asked reaching for the empty tankards. Renco held two fingers up and he nodded. "Two it is then."

Renco smelt a waft of elderflower and felt the air move to his left. Glancing, he saw the young woman draw up alongside him. Looking back, she smiled.

"Hello, I'm Letizia," she said. "But you can call me Lett."

Up close she was even prettier; her nose delicate and pert with a hint of freckles showing on her cheekbones.

"Thought I'd come over and say hello," she said. Her eyes were sky blue and unsettling. Feeling his colour rising, Renco looked away.

"So do you have a name?" Lett prompted.

The landlord placed a stein on the counter in front of Renco and looked between the two of them.

"The lad don't talk none miss. Might be he's a bit simple." He turned, ignoring the scowl Renco sent his way and started to fill the other tankard.

I'm not simple; you're the idiot, Renco thought loudly, flushing red in anger and embarrassment. He stole a look to his left. She was still there.

"Oh, I'm sure you're not," Lett said, smiling. "I can see it in your eyes."

Renco couldn't help staring back. Even her smile is damn nice, he thought, noticing that one side of her mouth quirked a little higher than the other showing a flash of white teeth between parted lips.

The second stein banged down next to the first and Renco slid the copper bit across the counter in the direction of the landlord. Gathering a drink in each hand, he turned in relief back to his table. He tried a smile on Lett as he passed but felt self-conscious about it; sure he looked like the simpleton the landlord accused him of being. She grinned back as if knowing something he didn't and laughed when he stumbled, spilling cider over his hands.

Renco felt her eyes on him all the way back to the table but sensed others watching him too. Glancing about, he saw the bard assessing him, eyes sharp and cool. Then there was Maohong. Strangely, the old man looked a little sad; not the usual smugness he'd expect. For some reason, this angered him and Renco clunked the drinks down sloshing cider on the table.

<*You really must learn not to shout so loud Renco, I almost missed my mouth,*> Hiro admonished.

Renco glared back. His Master's eyes were shrewd they never missed anything.

<*He said I was simple,*> Renco blurted out, feeling cranky.

<*Well you have been called much worst, neh?*> Hiro replied. He looked at the bar as if for the first time. <*Is that a young woman I see?*> He asked quizzically. <*Agghh, I understand now.*>

Renco turned and saw the girl still looking at him. He faced front. <*She makes me uncomfortable,*> he said, by way of explanation.

<*Clearly,*> Master replied, a hint of a smile dusting his face. <*You are positively chatty. This must be the longest conversation we've had all year.*>

Renco took a long drink from his stein. It must be a new cask, he thought, it didn't taste as crisp or sweet as the last one. <*I talk to you master, all the time,*> he said.

<*One sentence does not constitute a conversation Renco.*> Hiro waited for his student to look at him. <*You know you can talk normally. It is just a mental block. One you must overcome if you want to function and communicate with others.*>

Renco looked pained. <*I have tried master.*>

Hiro slapped the table making Renco jump. <*No, I don't believe you have.*> His eyes were stern. After a moment he gentled. <*I'm sorry my boy. I'm frustrated, for you and me. Frustrated I can't help you with this.*>

Maohong chose that moment to wander back over and sit down. "People stare," he muttered. "Maybe wonder why old man looks so at young man but say nothing except slap, slap of table." He laughed. Then spying his tankard, frowned.

"You drink Mao's cider? It half empty," he said, peering at the contents and raising one hairy grey eyebrow.

"I spilt some, sorry," Renco signed.

"You should try talking to Mao you fall too easily into sign. It is too comfortable for you, Renco." Hiro declared.

Maohong sighed. "Boy talk when ready, Master," Raising the tankard he took a long swig from it, "Agghh better, throat dry from talk."

Renco nodded his thanks to the old man, for his words and for breaking the mood.

Hiro grunted and drank his wine.

Maohong lifted his stein and gulped the contents down in one. Renco watched Master Hiro's eyebrows rise the higher Mao tilted his tankard. Thumping it down empty on the table, Mao covered his mouth delicately before letting out a tiny belch, then beamed at them both, pleased.

"Now, where is flute?" Mao said. Standing up he wandered out, wobbling a little on the way.

Renco and Hiro sat in companionable silence, enjoying the stillness of not travelling.

After a time sipping his cider, Renco regarded his Master, deciding to ask what had been on his mind the past four days. <*Master, why do we head north? I thought we travelled to Westlands.*>

Hiro swirled his wine looking thoughtful. <*I have decided to look in on some old friends of mine,*> he replied.

Renco considered this. <*And they live in the borders?*> he prompted.

Hiro's look was pensive. <*They did,*> he offered. <*Although, the last I heard they got separated. One is in the wilds to the north, the other at Thorsten. But I've no word for a day now on either's whereabouts, which is worrying.*>

Master Hiro did indeed look worried; his eyes wrinkled, a frown creasing his brow. Renco was intrigued; Master had not spoken to anyone of note, how had he come by this information and why offer it up in conversation?

Renco had his own ideas about this, formed over years from little things that never quite added up. He suspected Master Hiro communed with others, maybe other Masters. After all, he spoke to him by thought, so why not another. How else would Master Hiro hear things without talking to anyone or make sudden changes in route and destination? So it made sense to Renco, what other explanation was there?

As long as Renco had known Master Hiro they had always travelled, moving from place to place. Master had no home to speak of or at least none he ever mentioned. It was maybe why his Master seemed to know so many people. Still, he'd never heard Master describe any as friends before and definitely not old ones. That Master would say so much too was a puzzle. Maybe it's the wine, he thought.

<*Things are afoot my young student,*> Hiro said after a bit. <*I've word that urakakule are on the move. It may be we'll go take a look for ourselves if we get the opportunity.*>

Urak! Renco rolled this thought around in his head. Master Hiro and to a lesser extent Maohong, taught him his histories. But, like the bard tuning his lute behind him, he thought them stories, tales from another time. Still, urak! That did sound exciting. <*That would be interesting Master,*> he said.

<*Indeed,*> Hiro replied, but not in the way you imagine my young friend, he thought.

Renco returned to his cider, considering what Master Hiro had told him, and realised he was excited. The urak sounded like a grand adventure. A change from the endless walking and training that filled his life. However, the more he dwelt on things the more his mind slipped, returning again and again to a pair of blue eyes.

Chapter 31 : Plans and Manipulations

Greenholme, The Rivers

"By all that is holy, Tuko, you couldn't have made a bigger mess of this if you'd tried," Zoller admonished, furious.

The town was in an uproar. Redford had fallen. Rumour had it to urak; savages from tales of old come to life, tales Zoller knew were true. The Black Crow fed fuel to the fire by ordering people in from the surrounding countryside then conscripting any of age, or who could hold a blade. The rest were sent south, mothers, children, the old and the infirm.

Then, to the town's shock, a double murder. The hunt was on for the killer adding to Zoller's list of problems. A town this size was hard to hide in. Someone somewhere always saw something. The only saving grace was the sudden influx of people muddying the search.

"So, what have you to say for yourself?" Zoller snapped.

"Sorry, Father?" Tuko replied with a shrug.

The little assassin didn't look it. Zoller tapped his lip pondering. Tuko was a problem. He was tied to him but, Zoller conceded, you can't change the base nature of a man no more than you could a snake. "You're sure no one saw you? Can identify you?"

"All that saw me died," Tuko stated, untroubled.

Probably enjoyed himself, Zoller thought. The man was a killer without a conscience. He was his killer though, something which was both useful and dangerous. That Tuko held little fear of Zoller was a concern. Like a wild animal, he needed careful handling.

"Not so. There was a third, you wounded a girl," Zoller prompted.

"She's good as dead. Blade was dipped in deeproot. She'll not wake," Tuko said.

"Well, that's something," Zoller said. "Now tell me, who were they?"

"Mercenaries far as I could tell. They arrived at the inn earlier. The old man was fast, almost faster than me." Tuko smiled thinking back on it, his eyes drifting off.

Zoller snapped his fingers, irritated. "Concentrate and this will go a lot quicker." The secret with any dangerous animal was to show no fear. "Were they with the woman?"

"Can't rightly say, but I think yes. The girl I killed was her brat. Sure of that," Tuko replied.

"That's unfortunate. Yes, very unfortunate, Tuko." Zoller sighed. "I guess I've only myself to blame. I should've sent Holt. He may be more brute and brawn but he wouldn't have cocked up so royally," Zoller drummed his fingers on the desk, a sign of nerves and irritation in equal measure.

"Holt would be dead then. Silver hair would have gutted the cocksucker like a pig," Tuko replied, unmoved.

"You disappoint me. Go, leave me. I'll decide later what is to be done," Zoller waved him away.

"Yes, Father." Turning away, Tuko left the room, passing the hulking form of Holt stood just outside the entrance. The two men studiously ignored each other.

"Holt, come in here," Zoller growled, vexed at Tuko's lack of contrition.

"I could snap him like a twig, Father if you ask it," Holt said after closing the door.

"Not now Holt, maybe later," Zoller replied. The big man was dangerous for entirely different reasons, none as subtle as Tuko's. He was fanatically loyal to him though, as loyal as a dog, just a shame he shared the intelligence of one.

"Holt, go to Father Mortim. Ask him to attend me on a matter of some import," Zoller said.

Holt left to do his bidding and Zoller played over various outcomes and possibilities in his mind.

The woman Marron was of the Order. His intuition told him so and it was rarely wrong. Tuko had all but confirmed it. They weren't mercenaries Tuko had tangled with, he was sure of that. He suspected they were Duncan men.

Earlier that morning the sergeant from the bridge had spoken with Zoller. Amos Duncan, unannounced and unheralded, was seen with Lord Richard before and during his war council last night. Zoller didn't think it a coincidence. The Duncans were accordists. If Marron was under their protection she would be hard to get to after Tuko's mess. Damn the man. It would be too dangerous to show interest in the woman now her daughter lay murdered, that could lead the Black Crow to wonder at it. It wouldn't be too great a leap then to suspect his complicity. No, that door was shut to him for now.

Besides, the urak changed everything. History books regarding urak were rare and the few he'd read were all in the prohibited section of the church archives. It was unclear in some accounts and contradictory in others but he intuited an urak tribe to be as many as ten thousand strong. One tribe raiding these lands would be formidable and hard to stop. If this was an invasion, however, if they came as a clan, then many tribes were here somewhere in the Rivers. It would mean war and the likelihood of Thorsten riding it out was close enough to none as to make no difference.

A shiver of trepidation ran through him. The urak presented a host of worries and possibilities. His immediate concern was getting out of Thorsten before the storm, that his intuition told him was coming, struck.

He pursed his mouth turning his thoughts to Father Mortim. Everything was riding on this meeting. It would depend on delivery and understanding his quarry.

A good while later the door opened without a knock and Mortim entered. "You asked to see me, Father Zoller."

Zoller expected his anger and wasn't disappointed. Mortim wore it like a hat, plain for all to see. It had been a judgement, whether to see Mortim in his own chambers or not, a calculated gamble, "Please Father, sit. There are matters I need to discuss. Matters I need your help and counsel on."

"Maybe you've changed, Father. That you would seek my advice." Disgruntled, Mortim took a seat.

"Meeting with Lord Richard the other night was unplanned as you know," Zoller began. Mortim grunted, not liking the reminder of that night, and seeing it Zoller moved swiftly on.

"I interrupted a meeting reporting of an urak incursion. I gave them no credence. Urak are from stories of old are they not." He shook his head. "I believe Lord Kildare bade me to be in that place at that time to hear his warning."

"Really, Father?" Mortim snorted in derision.

"I understand your reluctance to believe me. We have a history, you and I." Zoller said. "We both love Kildare and observe his wishes from different sides of the same coin. I think he brought us together for a purpose."

"Your arrogance is consistent at least, Father," Mortim quipped.

"Please," Zoller beseeched, "Kildare knew the Black Crow would not grant your admittance. So he chose me," Zoller replied. He shook his head. "But you're right. I'm arrogant and in my arrogance, I failed to heed our Lord."

Mortim said nothing, surprised. It must have pained Zoller to confess his failure. Taking pleasure in Zoller's discomfort but unsure what to say, Mortim waited, sceptical still.

"Kildare intervened again when he sent you word of the boat and we went to the river," Zoller said. "When I saw the urak my heart sank. I understood his warning then. That I'd been given another chance I send blessings to his greatness."

He looked at Mortim, heartfelt. "I owe you thanks, Father. If not for you I'd have failed in my duty. I'll not fail it again," he declared, letting a bit of righteous zeal seep into his voice. Not too much, he told himself.

"Whatever do you mean, Father?" Mortim asked eyes flaring in suspicion.

"I'm sending you south, to Rivercross. The cardinal left for the conclave a ten-day ago but you must warn the church of the urak, tell them what I face here and get them to prepare," Zoller said. He rose to his feet and painted an earnest look on his face. "The heathen savages move against us. Our Lord Kildare, the soldier, has placed the duty upon us to thrust back this evil."

Mortim wasn't listening, shocked still at Zoller's declaration that he be sent to Rivercross. This was his church. He'd built it, overseen its construction himself. It had been years in the undertaking, it was his life's work.

"I'll not go. This is my place. I won't hear of it!" Mortim said, his bluster gone, a dread weight sitting in his gut. He couldn't leave, wouldn't, not lest the cardinal order it himself.

Clenching his eyes tight shut, Mortim thought things through. The cardinal's scroll, it was authority enough if Zoller decided to enforce it, which the self-righteous bastard would. Glancing across the desk, Mortim knew, that despite his words and concern Zoller held only disdain for him. It was a sentiment he returned tenfold. Reluctantly, he asked. "What of you, Father?"

"I stay here, with the people. They will have need of our Lord, Kildare, in these dark times. The Red God must be seen and heard," Zoller said raising his voice. "It's my failing; I must stay with the church here." He watched Mortim carefully, judging his words, trying to assess their impact.

"You've worked hard in Thorsten for Kildare's glory; I'll not let the church fail now." Zoller leaned in as he spoke, clasping Mortim's hand, erstwhile and sincere. "Trust me on that."

Mortim was incredulous. Trust? Never! Zoller was a snake, a schemer after his own ends. What was his angle here? Zoller knew more than he was saying.

Mortim was troubled. These urak, a few dead bodies on a boat, and he was to believe Redford had fallen. That the Black Crow, damn his heart, would sit in his castle if the town could fall, its mighty walls breached. No, the Black Crow would run for Rivercross, he was sure of it. The urak was an excuse, another tool Zoller employed to suit his ends. Zoller was manoeuvring for his church. Well, this was his parish, his people. He wouldn't have it!

Mortim suddenly felt uncomfortable. Was this why Zoller had called him here? Surrounded by Zoller's Red Cloaks he was vulnerable. Damn it, he should have refused the summons. Still, he'd be damned before he would take a step back from his beliefs; he never had his whole life and he wouldn't now. His faith was his anchor. Let Zoller try and take his church. Kildare would protect him.

"No, Father. I forbid it," Mortim declared. He pulled his hand free and looked Zoller hard in the eyes. He wouldn't back down on this.

"You're wrong to send me away. I will not go," Mortim declared. "You're right we have a history. We've never liked each other let's be plain. But I am a simple priest not versed in the politics of the church. That is your strength." He paused thinking how to phrase this next.

"Maybe you're right. Two sides of a coin we may be but my place is here with my church as surely as yours is at Rivercross. You know the priesthood there. I do not. You know High Lord Twyford, the cardinal and all the politics I so hate and despise."

Mortim stood, speaking from his heart. "If you ask that I trust you, then so must you trust me. Maybe you're right. Maybe Kildare speaks through us both. If he does then surely he means for you to return to Rivercross. My duty is here. I'll not leave it, Father. This is where Kildare bids me be."

Zoller pushed down his euphoria. The meeting hadn't quite gone as anticipated. No, Mortim had been calm and had thought things through. That he drew the wrong conclusions didn't matter, the result was what counted.

Rising, Zoller came around his desk. He clasped Mortim's shoulders embracing him. It was distasteful but worth it to feel the man's discomfort at the contact.

"I'm sorry, Father Mortim. I wish I'd not misjudged you so. I see your wisdom. I see you speak from your heart and I feel shamed by it," Zoller said.

Awkwardly, Mortim patted Zoller on the back. Pleased at least, that Zoller wouldn't see the lie on his face. The man has no shame, he thought, the sooner he is gone from here the better. "I pray we've both seen the light," he murmured.

Zoller pulled away. "Hopefully, this is a new beginning for us." He sighed. "Thank you. Arrogance and vanity have ever been my burden and you have opened mine eyes to it." He walked back around the desk. "You're right, I fear my place is to deal with the cardinal and High Lord Twyford as yours is here with your flock. I trust I've your future support as you'll have mine."

"Of course," Mortim smiled, sinking back into his chair.

Zoller saw the lie in Mortim's eyes as he spoke but really, he didn't care. The edge was gone from his voice too, was that relief? Yes, no doubt as pleased to have me gone as I am to leave this stinking backwater.

"Well then, I'll hand back charge of your church. I'll make a favourable report of the work you do here," Zoller declared with a smile. "I'd best prepare to leave at once."

Mortim scraped the chair back roughly and bowed his thanks. "Safe journey to Rivercross, Father," Turning abruptly, he left, back straight, pleased to get out of the room. It occurred to him walking back to his chambers that Zoller had been quick to accede to his wishes. It left a sinking feeling in his stomach that marred his good mood at ridding himself of Zoller.

As the door closed behind Mortim, Zoller poured himself a large glass of wine and sat back in his chair unable to contain the smug satisfaction from creeping onto his face.

Chapter 32 : Unexpected Company

Illgathnack Ford, The Rohelinewaald

"I'm sorry. I have a wife and child to find and I need to bring warning to my people. That's my duty." Darion's announcement was not well received but he didn't care. He had been forced to spend another night in camp whilst the ilf hunted in the forest to the east. He was anxious to be off.

R'ell frowned at the man, frustrated. He spoke well, but his K'raal would want to talk to the ilf friend, he was sure of it. He tried an earlier argument. "I ask you to consider the danger. Urak are likely already between you and your town. My K'raal may be able to help you."

M'rika was more circumspect. "What did Rawrdredtigkah say to you yesterday? You looked surprised I think." M'rika had seemed pensive and quiet since the great bear had left. A thin green line marred her cheek where her skin had been sliced open. She had been marked.

Darion replied to R'ell with finality. "I've not the time. I'm decided." Then facing M'rika he considered briefly what to tell her. He didn't like this business of charge and responsibility, especially for someone that he'd known barely three days. It made him uncomfortable as did her regard of him.

"She asked me to pass a message on to someone," he said.

"Hmm I see, and what is this message and to whom?" M'rika asked.

Darion didn't know why, but he didn't want to say. Something told him Rawr had chosen a moment to talk when he was alone. Maybe the bear didn't want the ilf to know.

"She told me, the enemy returns. The message was for my Lord," Darion said. M'rika stared at him a moment too long before turning away. She knows I tell a half-truth, he thought.

There was a flutter of feathers and Darion turned in time to see Bezal, wings back beating, alight upon R'ell's shoulder. Darion watched the ilf turn his head to the bird as if listening and a moment later smile. R'ell rarely smiled; it was a little disconcerting to see it now, with his pointed canines.

"My K'raal is here," R'ell announced. Darion sensed a subtle shifting in the nearby ilf. Their shoulders went back and there was an excitement and energy to them.

"He seeks counsel with you before you leave." R'ell addressed Darion.

With a deep sigh, Darion glanced back at the river. Would it mean crossing the ford again? If so he would be soaked, twice. He didn't much relish the prospect of starting his journey wet and cold. He looked to the sky, it was early still but meeting this K'raal would take time. More than he would like or could afford. It would be dark if he was to make his homestead this day.

R'ell watched Darion carefully. Saw him glance at the river and guessed his thoughts. "I can have a litter made if you do not wish to brave the water."

Be damned if I'll let 'em carry me over, Darion thought. His ego had taken a battering with the run through the forest the night before. He didn't think he could take being born across like a piece of baggage. It was insulting. He gave R'ell a dark look, suddenly angry. The decision to cross had been made and without him saying a damn thing. He'd been manipulated, simply and effectively. Soonest started, soonest finished he resolved.

Darion didn't bother responding; the ilf was starting to annoy him. Resigned, he set his pack down near a still smoking campfire along with his ilf bow. As he turned back, he saw M'rika regarding him, a semblance of a grin on her face. It didn't help his mood any.

"I'll come meet your K'raal if someone will mind my pack and weapons," Darion grumbled.

"They'll be safe here," R'ell replied.

Unclasping his newly acquired cloak, Darion knelt and folded it on top of his pack. Then, standing again, walked brusquely past the ilf towards the ford.

M'rika caught Darion up, falling into step beside him. "You have much to learn about the ilfanum," she said, clearly amused.

"No argument from me on that," Darion grunted. He noticed the ilf had shed her cloak and weapons, baring a dagger at her hip. Glancing about, he saw they were the only ones who had. The others all carried their weapons and packs with them.

"What are you doing, M'rika?" He asked suspicion lacing his voice.

M'rika didn't answer; widening her step she entered the water ahead of him.

Watching her wade across with no hesitation Darion followed, reluctantly, into the biting cold. I should be used to this, he grumbled as icy water lapped up to his waist. But he wasn't. If anything it was worse. This time, he didn't have the fire in his blood from his earlier flight or the excitement of the battle the previous night. This time, the fording of the river was more torturous. When finally he reached the far bank he was wet, numb with cold and shivering.

The ilf had set up in the trees just to the north, upwind of the urak camp. As Darion walked past the dead the reason became clear and he wrinkled his nose at the stench. He followed M'rika in amongst the trees.

Ruith was there and stopped Darion with a gesture.

"Wait here," said the ilf.

M'rika didn't so much as glance back, her focus intent on a large huddle of ilf a little deeper into the trees.

Ruith studied Darion. The man was cold and wet; his lips blue. All the ilf that crossed Fassarunewadaick were wet and cold, it was fitting the manling made no complaint. In fact, he said nothing, just glared after M'rika.

"Drink this, it will warm you." Ruith offered a flask.

Darion took it, sniffed the contents then took a quick swig. The liquid was smooth, viscous and sweet with a hint of honey and redberry to it. Warmth spread down his throat and into his chest. Gasping, Darion held the flask out, amazed. A delicious heat spread through his body, extending down his limbs to his hands and feet, banishing the cold. It was invigorating and he felt energy suffuse him.

"Ruith, this is… really good stuff," Darion said handing the flask back, "A drink for the gods."

Ruith beamed at the praise and waved his hand, refusing the flask. "Keep it, ilf friend. You will have need of it if you are to cross the river again."

Darion stared at Ruith, it was a princely gift. The old ilf gazed back unperturbed, dark eyes inscrutable.

"Thank you, Ruith."

The ilf inclined his head in acknowledgement, pleased.

"It is my own recipe. Good for weary body, mind and spirit. Do not use it to excess though," the ilf warned. Then, looking about, he whispered, "I have never tried it on a manling before. I caution against overuse, in case of unexpected consequence."

Darion nodded back, unsure of what to say. Thankfully they were interrupted as M'rika returned with R'ell. Walking beside them was another ilf, his leaf skin a similar green hue to M'rika's, except for a slightly darker patina. This must be their Lord and M'rika's brother, he thought.

The ilf lord was taller even than R'ell. Confidence and power exuded from him. He was attired in a similar fashion to the other ilf, a woven flaxen belt and skirt with a dark mottled cloak made of leaf that seemed to flow from his shoulders.

Darion took an involuntary step back as the ilf's cloak swirled. Its mottled colouring changed to a solid black, the leaf shapes melding into each other to create a uniform look that left Darion wondering if the thing was enchanted.

A sheathed sword lay across the ilf's back, its pommel protruding from the edge of the cloak by his left shoulder. In his hand, he clasped a bow, something it seemed all ilf carried apart from Ruith. Stopping two paces from Darion the ilf examined him with interest; his dark eyes black and unfathomable.

"I am D'ukastille del Da'Mari, K'raal. Welcome Darion to Da'Mari, this is Rohelinewaald, my ward," he spoke with an easy grace. "We could name it Darkwood, as it is known by your folk if you prefer?"

"Rohelinewaald will do fine, Lord. I'm in your land after all," Darion replied.

The ilf laughed. "That is not accurate. You might say I am of the land but it is not my land. This is Da'Mari." He gestured, sweeping his arms wide.

Darion didn't understand, was Da'Mari the forest then, the land or something else? He would have to ask Ruith or M'rika later if chance permitted. Now though was not the time.

"I came as soon as I felt your presence. Although I admit it was to kill you," D'ukastille said with a shrug of his shoulders. "Trespass in Da'Mari is not permitted.

Practising magic in Da'Mari, no matter how trivial, is not tolerated. Both of these you have violated. This you know, Darion Castell of the Order."

"I do, K'raal," Darion admitted, showing no surprise at the reveal. He made no defence of his actions. The Order had made it clear before he got his assignment to the Old Forest, all those many years ago, that ilfanum lands were prohibited and the consequences of breaking that prohibition. Besides, he reasoned, the ilf lord had already made his decision. If death was the outcome it would have been meted out already. He waited, flicking a furtive glance to M'rika.

"You did not tell me you were of the Order, Darion. That was remiss of you," M'rika said, returning his look. "I see a new meaning in Rawrdredtigkah's message."

"Pardon me, Lady. The Order is not welcome in ilf lands," Darion said, uncertainly. M'rika's tone was of wry amusement which clashed with her stern countenance.

D'ukastille laughed. It was a warm sound. "You have understated matters I think." He looked at his sister. "Da'Mari is aware of all things here and offers her gratitude and thanks for your interventions."

Darion mulled that snippet of information. D'ukastille wasn't expressing gratitude but Da'Mari. Did that mean Da'Mari was a being then and ruler of this realm? He filed the thought away.

D'ukastille continued. "Your violations are of no moment. Da'Mari has waived them and names you ilf friend."

"Thank Da'Mari for me," Darion said.

The ilf looked amused. "Da'Mari finds you interesting manling. Your thanks are not needed. But come, you are named ilf friend already are you not? May I see your token?" D'ukastille asked, extending his hand.

Reaching inside his tunic, Darion withdrew it. He remembered M'rika's words the day R'ell made the same request and glanced cautiously at her now. M'rika inclined her head a fraction, a hint of a smile ghosting her face. Pulling it off over his head, he placed it, reluctantly, into the ilf Lord's outstretched hand.

The ilf studied it briefly with great interest. "This is De'Nestarin's mark. He has been gone many cycles from Da'Mari. How did you come by it if I may ask?"

"I only knew him by the name, Nesta. We met at the Blue Sky Lakes, Bluskiwadaiak you name them. It was when the cycles of the three moons aligned twelve years ago. He was communing as I understand it." Darion paused thinking back on that time. "I was looking for the honey trees when I found him. He'd been struck down by a palsy or illness and was very sick."

"Preposterous," R'ell said. "De'Nestarin would never be so weak…"

"Your opinion R'ell is of no moment, do not interrupt," D'ukastille snapped. The look he gave was stern with disapproval. "If you cannot hold your tongue, leave!"

R'ell dropped to his knees, mortified, and bowed his head to the soil. "Forgive me, K'raal."

D'ukastille ignored R'ell, gesturing instead to Darion. "I am sorry for his bad manners. Please continue."

Darion glanced at R'ell, knelt with his head down unmoving, then back to the ilf Lord. "I found Nesta unconscious and delirious. He was like this for several days and I cared for him during that time. Fed him water and kept him safe until he regained himself."

Darion considered a moment. He'd spent many days with Nesta as he recovered his health and they had discussed many things, but what was relevant to this ilf lord.

"Nesta never told me what happened to cause his ailment. I believe it was related to a casting he made."

Then at D'ukastille's look, clarified, "Nesta didn't tell me that, the conjecture is mine but I think it right. We spoke of many things whilst he recovered his strength. He was a fascinating and interesting companion and we became friends," Darion said. "He gave me his token and bid me always wear it, especially in the old forest or near ilf lands. He said it would offer me protection. I have worn it ever since."

The ilf Lord thought a while his face an impenetrable mask. Finally, he offered the neck thong and token back only now, Darion saw, there was a second token on the tie.

"Da'Mari's," D'ukastille explained. "If you hold it in your hand when you are ready it will mark you. It is a great honour, granting protection and bestowing many blessings. M'rika will explain later. Walk with me a while."

D'ukastille strolled past Darion leaving him no choice but to turn and follow. As they walked, leaving the rest behind, the ilf spoke. "You answer a mystery with more mystery it seems. De'Nestarin is eminent amongst the ilfanum. That you bare his token is unheard of. But it is his and given freely, else you would not live to tell of it."

Darion was not sure what the ilf meant by this but held his questions. His old master told him once that not all questions should be asked. "Silence has its own wisdom," he would say. To be honest, Darion hadn't always understood his master; he was full of such quotes that seemed meaningless and arbitrary. That the memory came to him then meant something. Maybe this was one of those times to stay silent.

"Signs and ill portents abound." D'ukastille continued. "It is Da'Mari's belief that these things are all connected. Your encounter with De'Nestarin many cycles ago and now M'rika only serves to highlight this."

D'ukastille glanced at the man beside him, weighing him. His aura was strong and clean. He was honourable in his ways. He reached a decision.

"The urak are on the move. The White Hand occupies the Blue Sky Lakes and pushes south even as we speak. This you know already. The Blood Skull has attacked one of your settlements further to the east. Redford, it is named."

Darion's heart sank at these words. Unlike the kingdom, the Order taught history to its people. One urak clan was bad and they would be hard-pressed to counter it. Two clans though were unheard of since the War of the Taken. Ill portents indeed he thought, worried.

D'ukastille saw the shock flicker across the man's face. He covers it well, but not well enough. His course set, D'ukastille pressed on.

"There is a darkness coming, Darion. Our seers read it in the heavens, feel it on the winds. This is merely the start of things. Urak are on the move across the whole of the Fianan Domhein." Seeing Darion frown and thinking him unclear on his point, he elaborated. "What is called by humans the Teeth of the World, the Torns Mountains."

Darion nodded understanding and D'ukastille continued. "There are seven clans of the urak. Three we know are on the move, but there may be more. This is unusual and worrying. Human memory is short but the ilfanum still remembers the Morhudrim War. Da'Mari sees parallels."

They reached the treeline overlooking the river. They turned, walking back the way they had come.

"Da'Mari seeks council with the Order, with Keeper," D'ukastille said. The ilf's emphasis on Order and Keeper gave Darion the distinct impression it was distasteful to the ilf.

"This is unusual. Most ilfanum have no trust in the Order, although we abide by the accord struck. This makes it difficult for us. Da'Mari asks that you carry her word to Keeper. You have Rawrdredtigkah of the Silver Lake Clan's warning already, I understand. So no extra effort should be required."

Darion took a deep breath. Of course, he must do it, he knew this, but this was big. There was a lot at stake. The Order had seen no contact with the ilfanum for hundreds of years and if what D'ukastille said was true then all nine of the Kingdoms provinces were in trouble.

"I will carry word, K'raal D'ukastille."

"Good, M'rika will go with you." Watching the man as he spoke D'ukastille saw the protest on his face, in his eyes. Man is so predictable, so emotional.

"She is Da'Mari's envoy and is entrusted to your care," D'ukastille said.

Darion felt caged in, the decision made whether he willed it or not. His thoughts turned to Marron and Nihm, he had to find them above all things. Dragging an ilf around whilst he did so would only complicate things and slow him down.

"M'rika has recently lost her bond mate. She is mourning. Maybe she should remain with her people. I can convey your message," Darion said.

D'ukastille stopped and faced Darion, his look hard and uncompromising. "You question Da'Mari? Clearly, you do not understand, else you would hold your tongue. Da'Mari has spoken." His voice was sharp, direct and final.

Ilf appeared suddenly through the trees, materialising as if out of nowhere. D'ukastille waved them away with a curt gesture.

Darion knew he'd caused offence. Touchy bastard, he thought. The ilf Lord's shoulders were back, his head up; he exuded menace. His green leaf scale changed to a darker hue, like black armour, then back again to a mottled leafy green and gold.

"Forgive my suggestion, Lord. I meant no insult," Darion said, his voice neutral.

D'ukastille closed his eyes, head canted to the side. After a moment he took a long breath, seeming to calm himself.

"I apologise. It is many cycles since I last spoke to one of your kind." He bowed his head, contrite. "Manners are important to an ilf, you understand? You are not wise in our ways, I should have made an allowance."

"I understand," Darion replied on edge still. He was finding the ilf hard to fathom, one moment friendly the next touchy as a bag of ferrets.

D'ukastille pondered a moment before addressing Darion once more.

"Maybe what you say has some merit." D'ukastille conceded. "I will ask R'ell to attend you both. It will be good for M'rika to have one of her own to talk to; that understands our ways." He smiled showing perfect teeth, the canines long and pointed.

Darion found himself staring at the ilf. This close up the darker patina on his leaf scale seemed almost fluid, the shapes and swirls hinting at things Darion couldn't understand. Order training never really covered this, Darion thought, aggrieved at the way things had gone and in particular at R'ell's sudden inclusion. M'rika was civil at least.

"Sure," Darion said, giving a reluctant smile. They had almost returned from where they'd started. Through the trees, M'rika and R'ell still waited where they'd left them.

"R'ell, M'rika is Da'Mari's envoy to the Order. I ask that you attend her on her journey if you are willing." D'ukastille said without preamble.

"As you wish, K'raal," R'ell replied with no hint of emotion that Darion could see. R'ell bowed deeply to D'ukastille. Then, turning to M'rika, repeated the gesture.

Darion observed the exchange with interest. He saw M'rika look to her brother, sensed her disapproval at his announcement, but remained quiet.

Darion caught R'ell's eye as he completed his bow. Was it his imagination or was there hostility in his look? Well damn, he thought, this just gets better and better.

Chapter 33 : Contact

North of the Encoma Holdstead, The Rivers

Anders and his company made good time from the Encoma Holdstead. The dirt road changed to an overgrown track that wended its way through rolling grasslands, interspersed with copses of spruce and oak tree. As they moved north they found signs of recent travel on the path, hoof prints and rutted wheel marks pressed into the mud.

Glancing to the sky, Anders judged it to be well after noon. He could see one of the outriders in the distance to the north and made another quick check on them all.

Sergeant Kronke had broken the company of twenty into four hands. Each hand was assigned a different quadrant to cover with one outrider and the remaining four in troop watching. It was simple and effective for a command this small. Anders let Kronke get on with it. He knew his job.

So far there'd been no sign of urak. There was plenty of wildlife though, deer grazing the long grass and flocks of birds. Earlier, they'd seen a herd of bison to the far west, tracking south.

The sun was out and it was a warm pleasant day. Easy to forget the seriousness of their mission and the guards in column laughed and joked. Anders, listening into their banter, heard Pieterzon regaling them all with his latest conquest. One of the merchants' daughters had fallen for his charms. Unlikely, Anders thought. The man was ugly in every sense of the word. He turned his attention back to the outriders.

* * *

The further north they rode with lack of contact was both a relief and a worry to Anders. Are they even out here, he wondered, or are we chasing our tails? Maybe the urak horde moved east not south, they'd attacked Redford after all.

Doubt gnawed away at him; Redford was four days' hard ride to the east. He'd chosen the Castells' homestead as it was the first urak sighting. Only Darion hadn't seen urak had he? Just sign of them and now no sign of his friend.

Is that the reason I chose this path, in the vain hope of finding an old comrade? He felt a slither of guilt at the thought. If urak had taken Redford as the missive said, he should've taken the easterly route instead of assigning it to someone else. Still what's done was done. That was the trouble with patrols, they left too much time to think and second guess.

"Sarge, Janik's gone. Can't see him,"

Anders' attention snapped to the now. Kronke was looking back the way they'd come. Another of his men stood high in his stirrups searching. He followed their gaze. Janik had taken the south-eastern flank. His heart pumped faster. It was mostly flat here. The gentle rise and swell of the land, even with the tall grass wasn't enough to hide horse and rider.

"Captain?" Kronke asked.

"Send the rest of his hand to investigate," Anders ordered.

Kronke nodded. "Jacks, you heard the captain. Get your asses over there."

"Yes Sarge," Jacks replied, all banter gone.

Anders watched as they checked their gear, unlimbering spear and bow, going over the same routine drilled into them in training.

"Oh, and Jacks," Kronke said, "Go in staggered, yeah. If'n it's a trap no point you all riding into it. Any sign ah hostiles get your butts back here, understand. No hero shit."

"Sure thing," Jacks said. Digging heels in, his horse peeled away heading for Janik's last position, the rest of his hand fanning out behind. The company watched on avidly, tense and on edge.

Anders looked about for the other pickets. Kronke ever mindful of his captain saw, "Stop gawping like ya did your first day in uniform. You're no greenheads, eyes to your hand!" he bellowed.

Anders spotted the outrider to the northwest and felt a touch of relief. The northeast was also accounted for.

"Sarge, can't see Mart none," One of his men called out. Anders spun to the southwest. There was no horse and no rider.

"When did you last see her?" Kronke asked.

"Before we looked for Janik I guess," the man stuttered.

"You useless sacksa shit," Kronke yelled. He turned to Anders his eyes asking the question.

"Send the rest of Mart's hand, same instructions," Anders said. "Let's see what we find."

Kronke stared at Anders a bit longer than needed, uncertainty playing across his face. The hand though heard the order and they were ready to go.

"Be careful out there, staggered formation. Any sign a trouble you get back here fast." Kronke ordered.

"Aye Sarge," They cantered off spreading out as they went.

"Rest a you keep a beady eye on your outriders," Kronke shouted.

Anders turned back to look for Jacks and his hand. It was perfect timing. The riders had spread out with one holding back fifty paces or more. The lead rider, Jacks he thought, suddenly fell backwards out of his saddle. A hulking shape rose from the sea of grass and made a grab for his horse. Battle trained it spun, kicking and caught the figure full-on and it crumpled disappearing back beneath the long grass.

Another rider suddenly fell, then another. This time the looming hulks that rose up ignored the bolting horses. Moving instead to where the riders had fallen.

Anders was frozen momentarily in shock. It was real and had happened so quickly. "Kronke get that other hand back," he commanded his voice strident, urgent.

Kronke didn't hesitate, his big destrier breaking into a canter at his touch. He rode hard, head down horse in full gallop.

Heart hammering, Anders watched as the first of the riders to the southwest fell. They were a bit closer and he could just make out the arrow that punched into the man's chest knocking him from his horse.

Kronke slowed his mount as a manlike figure rose from the ground sixty paces ahead. It looked huge, its arms thick and strong, its skin grey like a block of granite. In its hands was a bow. It drew the string back and released.

Kronke bent low over his horse, not easy in leather and chain mail, especially for a man his size. The arrow scudded off his helm, a glancing blow that sent a jolt of pain that he barely registered. Rising, Kronke kicked his mount urging it on as he bore down on the urak.

Dropping its bow the hulk drew a large blade from its back, then putting its head back roared defiance as Kronke charged.

There was no finesse to it in the end. The urak moved to the right away from Kronke's sword arm. Kronke did what he trained for, what his horse was trained for. With a press of knee, they veered following the urak, barrelling into it, running it down. His horse staggered at the impact but it was a large beast, had to be to carry Kronke's mass and it recovered. Kronke brought his mount to a halt taking a moment to assess things.

The hand was down apart from one rider, the one left in the pocket behind the others. She was riding back hard at full gallop. She never made it. An arrow took her high in the back, slapping her forward over the horse's neck. Then flopping back she cartwheeled over the horse's rump, lifeless.

Not waiting, Kronke twisted his horse about. Nervous and skittish it danced on the spot before Kronke gave it its head. Putting heels to flanks he cantered back to the captain and what was left of the company. A couple of riderless horses made their way back but no one else.

There was a howl from the field where Janik had disappeared. Looking, they observed a hand of urak arrayed loosely in the long grass. Several had bloody fists held up to the sky. They started walking towards them, purposeful.

"Sir!" a warning cry from one of the men as another six urak closed in from the southwest. They were out of bow range but wouldn't be for long, they needed to go.

Marigold moved uncertainly beneath him as Anders considered their options. They had to get word back to Thorsten. They could ride them down. They would have to brave a gauntlet of arrows but they outnumbered any one of the two urak groups; they could win through. He was about to give the command when more urak appeared to the south. He did a quick count, another seven.

"Sir, we can break past them if we're fast. Some'll get through," Kronke urged. A large crease marred the side of his helm and a trickle of blood ran down his face and into his moustache.

"We can't be sure," Anders said. "Besides, we can't abandon our two outriders."

"They're arms-men; they know their duty and they're on horse. They'll have to ride around, find their own way," Kronke argued. "Might even make it if luck rides with them. More of a chance to get warning back I reckon."

Anders was desperate. Kronke was right but he'd lost half his command in the last five minutes, he'd be damned if he'd lose any more.

"Release the bird," Anders said. "Then we ride north, hard and fast. Once we lose them we can loop around, head east then back to Thorsten."

Kronke was unconvinced but gave the order, not that the little band of guardsmen hadn't heard it. They were only nine with the captain plus the two outriders. All were eager to be off. None relished facing the urak who were distant still but closing fast. They were near enough now to hear them catcalling and shouting challenges.

Kronke flicked his reins and set off at a steady league eating trot. Looking back over his shoulder he watched as they left the urak in their wake.

Chapter 34 : The Holdstead

Encoma Holdstead, The Rivers

Albert Encoma watched with sad eyes. There were forty-two souls living in the holdstead and not near enough capacity on the wagons and carts to take all their belongings with them. Hard choices had to be made and more than one argument had ensued over what was wanted and what was needed.

He was anxious; Anders warning weighed heavy in his mind. Already they had spent a day and night securing the holdstead and preparing. They needed to be off.

His son, James, was the only one already gone. After the confrontation with the Black Crow's Knight Captain, Albert had sent him to the Shawcross Holdstead to pass on Lord Richard's warning. He was still mad with his youngest son. The lad had almost got himself killed running his mouth off like that.

His other sons, John and Arthur, along with a dozen other holdsteaders were out in the fields rounding up the livestock. Many were already herded into the bottom fields where the Black Crow's men had recently camped.

"Come on people, time to go. Let's get it together," he shouted, hustling and chivvying the holders along. A few appeared from within the holdstead, clutching final items they had missed earlier and were suddenly too important to leave.

Hildi came and took his hand, her eyes stern and full of resolve. She had lived here forty years and didn't know when she would return but she'd done her crying earlier that morning in the privacy of their room. Now it was time to go.

The two of them walked the few steps to the large double doors that gave entry to the holdstead. They were tall and solid and with a grunt of effort, they pulled them closed with a bang, the sound loud, lonely and final. Together they turned looking back into the courtyard enclosed by thick stone walls.

Here are all my people, Albert thought. Their faces reflected his own, sadness and worry. Still, if they needed to go they needed to get on with it. Sitting around feeling sorry wasn't going to help any.

Albert helped Hildi up into their wagon. Jacob, his oldest grandson, held the reins and leaned over to take her arm as she clambered up. Albert patted her rump as it went by and she grunted, glaring at him as she took her seat.

"You be minding those hands of yours, Bert Encoma," Hildi snapped but her eyes held a hint of mischief in them.

Seeing Jacob's grin, Bert winked at him. "Sorry Hildi, slip is all." At least I have my family with me he thought.

The arrow took Hildi high on her chest, just below her neck. The force propelled her off the bench seat and onto the load in the back of the wagon. Dogs started barking out in the back field and screams suddenly filled the air.

Albert stared where his wife had sat moments before, dazed. He glanced in the back to where she lay pinned against the cargo, not wanting to, knowing she was dead but unable to keep from looking anyway.

"Grandda, grandda," Jacob shouted, his panic and fear threatening to overwhelm him.

It was enough to snap Albert out of his fugue. Leaping up into the bench seat, he yelled. "Ride boy, ride!"

Jacob snapped the reins and the horses, already tense, bolted for the large open gate in the stone wall. Jacob heard cries and screaming from out in the fields to his left where his Da was and over that the cattle looing, clearly agitated. He'd herded them enough to know.

A large figure suddenly loomed in front of the gateway. It was manlike only too tall and broad for any man. The horses danced unsettled in their traps.

"Grandda!" Jacob screamed.

"Ride through him boy. Don't stop. Don't stop for nothin'," Albert shouted.

The horses tried to shy away; it was all Jacob could do to keep them straight. His grandda suddenly shouted at them and the horses broke into a canter committing to the gateway.

At the last possible instant, the hulking figure dived out of the way and they were through and onto the short track leading to the road. The horses shied as a score more of the giant men stood blocking the way. Jacob couldn't hold the wagon and they veered off onto the long grass and down a small slope, the wagon bumping and jumping alarmingly.

Albert clung on in disbelief, watching his grandson lash the horses out of sheer terror as they bolted over the grass field. There were more urak here, for surely that is what they were. They were certainly no men he'd ever seen the like of.

Albert leaned across thinking to take the reins from Jacob when one of the wagon's wheels hit something hard, bouncing the wagon up from the ground. It landed with a crash and groan of stressed wood. Then, like a whip crack a wheel axle snapped and Albert was propelled tumbling through the air. He hit the ground hard, pain shooting through his shoulder as his collar bone snapped. His head smacked the ground dazing him then blessedly he passed out.

* * *

When he awoke, Albert groaned in agony unable to stifle his cries. He felt groggy and his head hurt but it was nothing compared to his shoulder. His eyes were sticky and hard to open and he realised he must be covered in blood.

"Got a live one," said a gruff voice.

Albert lay on his side. As his vision cleared, he made out the bulky mass of someone laid next to him. Blinking his eyes into focus, he moaned. It was Jacob. His head lay at an awkward angle from his body. His eyes were open but there was no life in them.

Albert sobbed as the realisation sank in and he rolled onto his back. The pain almost made him pass out but he couldn't bear looking at his dead grandson. Hildi, my Hildi he thought in despair the memory of her returning. What have they done to you? A tear leaked from his eye.

A figure loomed over Albert. The face had all the right parts but they were bigger; the forehead deep and ridged, the nose wider and flatter, the eyes larger and further apart. Cruel eyes, he thought. Its skin looked ashen grey and leathery. A white hand was painted over its face giving it a savage aspect.

The urak grinned, the gesture was all too human. Its wide mouth, full-lipped, revealed square block-like teeth. It held a large cleaver sword in one of its big hands and it prodded Albert's shoulder with it.

Albert cried out at the lancing pain. His breathing was ragged, his mouth dry.

"He don't look in any shape to move," the urak said, his voice deep and guttural.

Albert twisted his head but the pain was excruciating and he couldn't move it much and couldn't see who the urak spoke to. That the urak spoke common and he could understand it only made it seem more human, despite their size and obvious differences.

"Be quick. Nasqchuk has given the order to move. We're not staying," came the reply, this voice not so deep. Somehow, Albert knew it to be female.

The urak towering above looked down at him. Albert tried to read its eyes but couldn't. They looked flat and emotionless. Gasping air, his lips dry, Albert moistened them with his tongue. Why were they doing this? He opened his mouth to speak. "Wh…"

The urak leant on his sword, the thick point biting deep into the man's throat, the sharp broad edge slicing through neck and spine neatly separating the head from the body.

The urak left the man where he lay, blood pulsing from his neck, staining the soil. The human was old and leathery. Instead, he turned to the dead pup lying to the side and nonchalantly scooped up the boy, flipping him over his shoulder. This one would be more to his liking.

Chapter 35 : Intoxicated

Greenholme, The Rivers

Those same blue eyes stared at Renco, searching his face. Curious? Amused? He didn't know which and it was disconcerting. He wasn't sure why he found Lett so unsettling and compelling all at the same time. Admittedly, with his speech problem, he'd had little enough experience with women, though he wasn't a complete novice. He'd spent a night with a lady before. Master Hiro had arranged it all. He coloured at his sudden turn of thought. Renco saw Lett regarding him still, a telling look on her face as if she knew where his mind had drifted. What was she doing here?

He had stolen out of the Golden Cask to the back yard, for some air. The inn had been teeming; it seemed they weren't often blessed with bards up here in the borders and word had gotten out that one was playing. Luke Goodwill, the bard, had been performing to a raucous inn all night.

Renco didn't like crowds at the best of times, but the noise in the common room got so loud he couldn't bear it. Even now he could hear the hum and din of folk talking and laughing and above it all the sound of music playing. The bard was handy on the lute, he had to admit and set a merry tune. Weaving in and out of his notes was the high pitched shrill of a flute. He couldn't make out the words to the song but it was bawdy judging by the cheering and clapping.

Lett moved and Renco's mind snapped back to her as she approached him.

"Hello Renco," she said, "Maohong told me your name. I hope you don't mind my asking for it?"

She was close now, walking slowly, her eyes on his. It made him feel uncomfortable, his heart racing and his palms sweaty. She was talking to him like he was a spooked horse or something, which didn't help matters.

"Maohong said you don't like it when it gets busy. I get like that too sometimes."

Bloody Mao! She was stood in front of him, so close they were almost touching. Why can't I talk he demanded, his fists clenching in frustration. He opened his mouth but nothing came out. He shut it again and she laughed. It was a nice laugh, pretty. He wished the ground would open up and swallow him.

"Sorry, Da says I talk enough for two people. I don't mean to make you uncomfortable. I don't do I?" Lett asked. Renco shook his head no and she smiled.

"Good. We travel a lot me and my Da. I get to meet lots of folks but we never stay anywhere long so I don't have friends like regular people. Master Maohong says you're always travelling too, so I guess we're the same," she said.

Renco couldn't help but grin, Master Maohong, now that was funny.

Encouraged, she grabbed his hand. "Listen, do you hear that?" she asked.

Renco listened. He heard dogs fighting in the distance, horses whickering in the stable, a man and woman shouting at each other two houses down from the inn. The noise of the inn was constant. Which did she mean he wondered?

"I love this song. Da always sings it at the end of his performance," Lett said. Raising his hand she twirled beneath it laughing.

"Come on let's dance," Lett said as if the thought had just occurred to her. She pulled on Renco's hand drawing him in.

Renco swallowed, his throat dry, a worried frown marring his face. He could hear the lute and flute playing louder, the tempo increasing and before he realised what was happening her arm was about his waist and he was pushed and pulled in a circle, his steps awkward and clumsy.

As the crowd inside cheered and clapped and the music got faster, Lett started to spin him around, her hips swaying as she jigged from one foot to the other. How in the seven hells has this happened groaned Renco. But it was already too late. Lett was laughing, encouraging him and then he was moving with her, no choice really. He held her waist; she felt soft beneath his calloused hand. He picked the rhythm up from her and matched it. Lett flung an arm in the air as they looped around each other and cried out all white teeth and freckles.

Then, suddenly, the music stopped. The crowd inside roared and clapped and Lett pirouetted away from him, laughing and out of breath, her dress swirling around her legs. He was caught up in her euphoria. He could still feel the warmth where her hand had held his waist. His fingers burning still from where he'd touched her. She was so… joyful. Renco laughed, he felt intoxicated.

<*Yes, very good Renco, but that is not the dancing you should be doing,*> Hiro's voice sounded in Renco's head. He felt amusement from his master.

<*But it was fun,*> he responded happily.

<*It's good to see you enjoying yourself and in the company of a lady, if I'm not mistaken,*> Hiro replied. <*But playtime is over. Go check the horses. Make sure they're settled. We leave early on the morrow.*>

<*Yes, Master.*> Renco knew this already. His brow furrowed; it wasn't like Master to repeat himself. But he had a bigger problem to worry about - Lett. Renco couldn't talk to her. If he just wandered to the stables as his master bid him would she think him rude? How could he thank her for the dance and this moment?

"Are you alright?" Lett asked, "Why the frown? Tell me that wasn't fun?" She chattered, then after a moment, knowing he couldn't flashed her biggest smile at him. "See I told you."

Renco grinned, her mood was infectious and he found himself affecting a bow. Then, feeling bold, he captured her hand and kissed it lightly, his lips tingling as they brushed her skin.

"Why you are most welcome my good sir," she beamed, pleased at his gallantry.

Emboldened, Renco gestured, pointing from himself to the stables, indicating he had to go and waving goodbye to her.

"That's very forward of you," Lett said, looping an arm through his. "Your intentions better be honourable sir."

Bemused, Renco walked her to the stables; he liked how her arm fit in his. She sat on a hay bail and watched as he checked the horses had feed and fresh water in their buckets.

Happy, the mule, watched them both with sad eyes, chewing slowly. He was hitched on the far side of the stables away from the horses. Happy didn't get on with others.

There was a commotion outside and raised voices. Moving to the stable door, Renco looked back out into the yard. Lett hopped off the hay bale and drew up behind him.

"What is it?" she asked, clasping his arm and peering over his shoulder. Her eyes went wide. "Da!" she cried and rushed outside.

Luke Goodwill lay on the ground. Surrounding him were three men, the largest of which stood over the bard. One of the men moved to intercept Lett. Renco tensed as the man caught her, holding her back as she cried out.

"Can't say as you wasn't warned," said the man standing over the bard. He was big with a worn face and a nose that was bent from one too many breaks. He looked brutish, wide as well as tall, with thick arms and a thicker waist that was just turning to fat.

The other two men looked to be brothers; same eyes, same dark lank hair, and same pock-marked faces. They were almost of a height with the brute but without his girth. They all carried wooden truncheons on their hips and looks that said they enjoyed using them.

"Lett!" The bard cried at the sight of his daughter. "Don't touch her or I'll have you," he yelled. He went to rise and was pushed back to the ground.

"You're a fool and your master's a fool to accost me," Luke Goodwill shouted from the dirt. He went to pick himself up again but the man casually pushed him down, laughing.

"You'll not see another bard in a ten year," Luke threatened.

"Ass-wad, ya think I give a flying fuck for you bards. Do I look like I dance?" the man shouted, spit flying from his mouth. "You was told where ya could play and it weren't fucking 'ere was it."

"A bard plays where he chooses. I'll go to Lord Chadford if you don't let me and my daughter be," Luke said, concerned eyes darting to Lett.

"He ain't here. If'n you're lucky you'll catch his Lordship in Rivercross." The man grinned, his eyes cruel. Unhooking his wooden club he hefted it in one hand, tapping it into the palm of his other, a promise of pain to come.

Renco felt his pulse race as he watched. Master Hiro always took the initiative when trouble beckoned. He just did as he was told. But Master wasn't here.

Renco saw the brother holding Lett leering at her. He seemed to be enjoying her struggle against him and that settled matters. Stepping out from the stables he casually walked towards them.

"Well lookie, lookie here…" the brother started to say. Renco snapped a palm flat into his nose and with a crack, it broke. The man screamed falling away, blood blossoming from beneath his hand where he clutched at his face. Lett looked shocked as Renco stepped past her.

The brute held his truncheon up and gripped the bard by his hair. "Don't know what cunt you crawled out of but you better back the fuck off or I will decorate you with his brains," he yelled, eyes glancing at the man rolling on the ground.

Renco stopped. He wasn't sure, even if he quickened, whether he'd reach the man in time. Probably, but if not…

<*Renco!*> His master's consternation was clear through the link, <*Try not to kill anyone.*>

"Why you just staring, eh," the man shouted. "Well? Say someat boy… answer me." He looked to the brother still standing and the hard set to his face. It was enough to firm his resolve. They were two and his opponent not much more than a boy, an unarmed one at that.

"This weren't none of your business. Now, look what ya gone and done to Bort." He scowled, showing teeth yellowed from chewing too much knorcha weed. "Now, there's gotta be a price paid." He stared meaningfully past Renco to where Lett stood, transfixed.

Renco felt his blood rising. He breathed deeply, calming himself, as master had taught him. Control, speed, power: his master's mantra played through his mind.

As he prepared himself, two old men hobbled from the back door of the inn, laughing and giggling, clearly drunk. It drew the eyes of all in the courtyard as they swayed and bumped against each other. One tripped and stumbling, fell against the man holding Luke Goodwill.

"Piss off you old farts," the man growled. Not taking his eyes off Renco, he kicked a leg back at the drunk.

"Gonna throw up," the old-timer groaned as he swayed, narrowly missing the blow aimed for him. He placed a hand in the middle of the brute's back to steady himself before leaning over, retching.

Flinching at the sound, the man let go of the bard's hair to shove the old drunk away. But he overbalanced, his arm meeting no resistance as the old man spun to the side. A hand shot out gripping his own. A sudden twist and he howled in pain as his wrist was pushed back and up, all in a moment. Agony exploded up his arm from his wrist to his elbow. Dropping the cosh, he collapsed to his knees with a scream.

The brother still standing, lashed out with his truncheon at the other drunk who nimbly side-stepped and jabbed fingers into the back of his neck. He dropped, poleaxed, to the floor. The drunk followed him down, keeping his fingers pressed in hard.

"Bad man, why you try hit Mao, eh?"

Renco grinned. Master Hiro stood over the brute, whose arm was still held back and up, locked at elbow and wrist. Any sudden movement and Renco knew he would dislocate a joint or break a bone. He'd experienced it himself on more than one occasion and it was a singularly unpleasant experience.

Sensing movement behind, Renco spun bringing his hands up in a defensive move Mao called sweeping claw. Mao had names for everything. He never landed his strike however instead Lett flew into his arms.

"By the trinity Renco, you saved us," she cried.

Bemused, Renco hugged her back, enjoying the warm sensation of her soft body pressed against his. Lett pulled away, her blue eyes, studying him. With a curl of her mouth, she kissed him quickly on the lips. Before he could blush, Lett released him and rushed to her father who was just now picking himself up off the ground.

"Oh hoo, so Mao do nothing," Maohong grumbled from where he sat on the man's back. "Renco is hero. Renco get kiss from pretty girl. Mao just get comfy seat." He laughed, pleased with himself. The man being sat on looked furious but could do nothing about it. Mao had used the same pressure point on him once so Renco knew he was all but paralyzed.

Luke Goodwill hugged his daughter. “I’m alright Lettie, did he hurt you?” he asked.

“No Da, I’m fine,” she said, “Look at you though. They’ve put a tear in your knee.”

<*This is trouble we didn’t need, Renco,*> Master Hiro said as bard and daughter reassured each other.

<*It wasn’t my fault, Master. Those thugs set on Lett and her father, I couldn’t stand by,*> Renco replied.

<*That is apparent,*> Hiro said. <*What do you propose we do with them now?*>

<*I’m not sure. I didn’t have time to consider the after,*> Renco said, <*Perhaps we should tie them up?*>

<*Tie them up?*> Hiro said, amused at the idea. <*For how long and where would we keep them?*> Hiro stroked his chin thoughtfully.

<*It’s a pity you weren’t more controlled in your actions, neh? Mao and I have incapacitated without harm, whilst you have broken a nose by the looks of things. A lesson for you to remember, Renco; control your actions, do not let your actions control you.*> Hiro sniffed. <*Well, what’s done is done.*>

“Master Bard, I see you are unharmed. Would you like to press charges against these men?” Hiro asked, turning to Luke Goodwill.

“Thanks, but it’d do no good. Lord Chadford is gone to Rivercross and I suspect these men come from Lorsten Harris, owner and proprietor of the Black Stag and the local magistrate.” Luke Goodwill explained. “I fear it’s time for us to move on.”

“Yes, a feeling I share,” Hiro replied. He kicked the brute’s fallen truncheon out of reach. “What is your name and who is your master?” Hiro asked increasing the tension a little on the man’s wrist to encourage him.

“Surtis… agh… Surtis Mannick,” the man cried. Then as Hiro applied a little more pressure gasped, “Lorsten…I work for Lorsten Harris.”

“Well Mannick,” Hiro said, “I will let you go and we’ll not speak of this again you and me. It would do your reputation no good if word got out that you and your men were bested by two old men and a boy.”

<I am not a boy, Master,> Renco said.

<Hush, lad.>

"Do we have an understanding, Master Mannick?"

"Yes… fuck…, just let go of me arm," Mannick groaned.

Hiro released and stepped back, watching.

Sighing in relief, Surtis Mannick grasped his arm with his good hand and rubbed it. Glaring up at Hiro he clambered awkwardly to his feet.

Mannick was a good head taller than his master but he looked fearful nonetheless. Renco suspected that fear would soon turn to anger. He'd seen it before. Once the fear left he'd feel shame which would drive him to anger and he'd take his retribution out on someone. It was the way of all bullies.

Belying his age, Maohong jumped to his feet like a young man, cackling away to himself. His recently vacated seat rose gingerly, moaning, his whole body numb. The sound chimed with the brother who was in turn groaning and writhing still in the dirt.

Looking at the downed man, Renco smiled to himself. He'd have a sore head and black eyes to go with his broken nose come the morning.

"Well then off with you all," Hiro announced.

Mannick moved to pick his cosh up from where it lay.

"Best leave that where it is, neh," Hiro cautioned. "I'm sure if you return at the morning bell it'll still be here."

With a dark look, Mannick glared at Hiro then moved to his fallen comrade, dragging him up none too gently. The man cried out but Mannick ignored him, shoving him towards the gate at the side of the inn. The other brother hobbled along behind looking uncomfortable still.

Hiro waited until they were gone. "Right we'd best pack and head out," he announced.

"What!" Maohong cried. "Master promised a warm bed for Mao."

"Catch us up then," Hiro replied. "I for one will not wait for those thugs to come back with twenty men. I might have to hurt a few then." Hiro headed for the inn's backdoor. "Renco saddle the horses."

"Hold sir, if you please," Luke Goodwill called after Hiro. "If I may ask, where are you bound?"

Stopping, Hiro turned slowly to face the bard. His eyes drifted to Lett then back to Goodwill, assessing what he saw. He sniffed. "Here and there."

"Sorry, your business is your own," Luke said. "I appreciate your help and, forgive me if I intrude, but we head to Redford. For the harvest festival," he explained. "Might be you're headed that way? It's just we're on the Grim Road and there's safety in numbers."

"Forget Redford. There is trouble in the north. Fighting," Hiro replied.

Luke raised his eyebrows at the news, his face keen with interest. "Fighting you say? Have you travelled from the north then?"

"No."

"Then how came you by this news? And fighting between whom exactly? I've heard nothing." It was true to say that bards were often the bearers of news, travelling as they did. That an old monk, his flute wielding servant, and the mute boy had heard some tidings he had not piqued his interest.

Renco felt Lett's eyes on him and tried to ignore them. *<Master, perhaps it would be better to travel with company.>*

Hiro snorted. *<I know whose company you're interested in boy. If they travel with us trouble will follow. It's a bad idea.>*

<I never meet anyone. We're always moving around,> Renco complained. *<It'd be good to travel with someone new. Besides, they'll only dog our steps all the way to Thorsten, Master.>*

<There's a reason we travel alone, Renco. You get tied to people then you have a responsibility to them. That's a burden and I've no intention of taking it on. I've other duties. Besides, it will curtail our training.> Hiro sniffed.

Normally master's word was final; that he debated with him was a wonder. <*Perhaps Lett would help encourage me to speak,*> he tried. His master's face scrunched up like he'd just bitten a sour fruit.

"Renco, you're an idiot," Hiro declared.

Aware that Lett and her father looked on, Renco hung his head, face red with embarrassment.

<*They'll be your responsibility. And if the girl doesn't have you singing by the time we reach Thorsten you'll be covering Mao's jobs for a ten-day.*> Hiro turned back to the bard who looked on quizzically, aware he had missed some interplay between master and student.

"Master Goodwill, we travel north. You may travel with us if it's your wish but I leave tonight."

Luke smiled. "It is and I thank you again. Perhaps I could teach the boy the lute, help keep his hands busy whilst we travel," he said, flicking a glance at his daughter. She was grinning like an idiot at the boy who beamed back at her like a puppy.

"Indeed," Master Hiro grumbled, looking between the youngsters.

"Come, Lett. We need to pack, harness the wagon and pick up our coin," Luke said. Then, addressing Hiro once more, "We'll meet you here in half a bell." Nodding his thanks, he walked briskly past Hiro and into the inn, Lett trailing along behind.

"Mao thinks it's *her* hands that need to be busy, eh Renco." Mao laughed. "Way girl look at you, oh very yes," he chortled.

Renco didn't mind Mao's jibe. He was going to spend time with Lett, maybe all the way to Thorsten. He walked to the stables to saddle the horses and prepare Happy, whistling as he went.

Maohong and Hiro watched Renco's retreating back and cheerful disposition before sharing a look; one amused, the other troubled.

Chapter 36 : Delayed Departure

Thorsten, The Rivers

Marron didn't leave Thorsten that next day or the next; she couldn't, not with Nihm as she was. Marron's joy of the night before had ebbed, fading instead to an aching worry as Nihm lay comatose and unresponsive. That Nihm breathed comfortably was a good sign but her body twitched constantly and was hot and clammy to the touch as if burning with a fever. Marron fed her water and Nihm took it in small sips, but Marron knew this was reflex more than conscious will.

Marron spent all that day at Nihm's bedside, torn. She felt the urgency of her mission, of getting word to Keeper. Her ties with the Order were life-long and of kinship as much as duty and it dragged on her. But Nihm was her daughter, a tie that trumped all others. Her mind, as it often did, turned to Darion and she wondered where he was. Oh, how she missed him. Head pounding she massaged her temples.

There was a knock at the door and it opened. Jerkze's blonde head appeared.

"Food, Marron?"

"Don't think I could face anything right now," Marron replied.

Jerkze stumbled as Viv Stenhause elbowed her way past, pushing the door wide.

"Nonsense Marron, I'll not pussyfoot around you like these great buffoons," Viv declared. She carried a tray with food and its wonderful aroma filled the room.

"Unhand me, lummox, else you'll find somewhere else to stay," she snapped, as Jerkze recovered himself and tried to bar her entry.

"It's okay, Jerkze," Marron said. She was tired, her head throbbed and the last thing she wanted was an argument. He stepped back looking sheepish and closed the door as Viv waddled into the room. Setting the tray down on the table she addressed Marron.

"I understand you don't feel like eating but you need to. You'll be no use if you pass out now, will you? You really should know better, Marron," Viv chided.

It had been a long time since Marron had been spoken to like a child. She glanced at Nihm then let go of her hand, stood, and walked to the table. "Thank you, Viv. I know you're right. I just…I can't think of anything…"

"Don't think, eat. Or at least eat and think. The two go very well together I find," Viv replied. "Have you even slept? No, don't say anything, clearly not looking at the black under your eyes."

Eyes misting, Marron clenched her jaw shut; tears would do her no good. She looked at the food. It was simple fare, a bowl of thick broth with vegetables and chunks of meat along with a slab of bread and cheese. A jug and cup stood next to it. Her stomach betrayed her, rumbling loudly as the smell of the stew wafted under her nose. Suddenly starving and thirsty, Marron leant over and poured herself a drink. It was watered wine, cool and delicious. She gulped a cup down and refilled it.

Viv dragged the chair over from the bed. "Sit, eat," she ordered.

Marron did as she was told, spooning in the broth while Viv stood over her like some wrathful parent making sure she finished it all. The thought made her smile. It reminded her of her mother; then of herself and Nihm. She dropped the bread onto the tray and pushed it away, no longer hungry.

Viv assessed the bowl and grunted, it would have to do. Most of the broth and half the bread was gone.

"Thank you. I needed that," Marron said.

Viv nodded, knowing she was not just talking of the food. "Drink more. Tell me, how is Nihm doing?"

Marron poured another cup and sipped on it. "I don't know. I have some skill with healing, but I don't know what to do," she admitted. "She's breathing fine. The poison has cleared and her wound…" Marron paused. "…well her wound is healed, it's fine. There's nothing wrong that I can see to make her so unresponsive. I worry her mind has gone." A tear slipped slowly down her cheek.

Viv patted Marron's hand. She'd heard the blade that cut Nihm was poisoned. It was hard not to know or hear most of what happened in her inn. "She's strong, Marron with a fierce spirit. Maybe this is Nihm's battle alone."

"I know, you're right," Marron banged the table, "but damn it I'm her mother. I should be able to do something."

"You are love, believe me. You're here with her, giving comfort, maybe that's all you can do," Viv replied. Her heart clenched in sympathy, Morten was her only child; the thought of losing him was unbearable. Emboldened, she asked what had plagued her this last day, heard in little bits here and there about the inn.

"Marron, what's this all about? What's happening?"

Marron looked up. Is this why she's here? Come to glean information. No, she chided herself, Viv cares but has worries of her own and rightly so.

"What do you know?" Marron asked.

"I know your new friends are not what they seem. They're no sellswords. I know two men were murdered on the streets of Thorsten that has seen no murder in more years than I care to remember. I know a boat came down from Redford, full of arrows." She paused. "Full of dead bodies and… other things." She looked at Marron, really looked at her. "I have a full inn."

"A full inn?" Marron asked, puzzled.

"Aye, it's too early for the harvest fair. Should be more empty than full," Viv explained. "In truth, I was pleased when Amos and his lot turned up, it was good business. Now though folks have been drifting into Thorsten; holdsteaders and their families, others to living out in the wilds," she clarified. "Been turning up at Northgate telling tale the Black Crow ordered them to town. I've had ta turn folk away." Then a little guilty, "I could do with freeing up those stables in all honesty."

Marron sighed and for the fourth time in as many days spoke of what she knew. At the end of her telling, Viv looked pale and shocked.

"Lord Bouchemeax is clever and forewarned. He'll do what he must to protect his people," Marron said.

"Aye well, folk have already started talking, wondering what's going on. What are you going to do?" Viv asked.

"Go south, to Rivercross." And onwards thought Marron to herself, but we'll cross that path later. "It's just Nihm is like this…"

"Well the room is yours as long as you need it," Viv said, brusquely. She stood. "Better get back. Inn is busy and Vic will be cursing me if I know that man." Viv walked to the door resting a hand on its latch. She turned to Marron before opening it, "Thank you for telling me."

"You had a right to know," Marron said.

"I'll leave the tray. Try to finish it, Marron, for Nihm as much as yourself." Viv indicated the food. "If it's alright I'll send Morten to gather it in an hour or so, bring you a fresh tray." Viv smiled wanly. "That boy's driving me to distraction, fretting about your Nihm of course. He's been as useful as a candle in a rainstorm." Unlatching the door she left giving Jerkze a nod on her way out.

Amos and Mercy appeared then, entering before the door was closed.

"Marron," Amos muttered.

Marron waved them in, a look of resignation on her face. "What can I do for you both?"

"Won't keep you long," Amos replied. They both glanced at Nihm.

"Any change?" Mercy asked.

Marron shook her head, no.

"I'm leaving and wanted to let you know," Amos said, without preamble.

"Thanks for telling me Amos, but I'm not your keeper. You owe no explanation. You owe me nothing," Marron said.

Amos nodded at her words. "You're wrong. But I'll not argue it with you," he said. "Nevertheless, I'm leaving; taking a few of the lads with me. I've told Lord Richard I intend to scout north towards Redford."

"Why? The Black Crow has his own scouts aplenty," Marron said.

"Need to see what it is we face. See if my father needs to warn the king, to call for a raising of the standards." He shrugged. "Or not,"

"I say again, why?" Marron asked, sceptical. Maybe it was fatigue or her headache but she was in no mood to coddle him. "Sounds like you play at games, like a boy looking for fun and adventure."

Mercy snorted covering her mouth with a hand trying to keep the grin from it.

Amos reddened, his reply sharp. "The Black Crow seems a good man, and clever. But he's a minor Lord on the edge of the wilds and out of favour with Twyford. If I read things right his word carries little weight." He took a breath. "My father's on the other hand does."

"So tell the Duncan. Why delay with a fool's trip?" Marron regretted her words the instant she spoke them.

Amos scowled, angry. "I've seen a few dead urak and some dead guards." It was true. After turning up unexpectedly at the war council the previous night, Lord Richard had shown him. "That's hardly enough to go to my father or ask the king to raise the standards. I've seen battle, Marron. I've killed people and lost people dear to me. This is no game I play, I assure you."

Marron berated herself. Amos had lost two of his own yesterday. Seb was young, not much older than Nihm, but Silver he would've known a long time; an old friend as well as armsman. But Amos wasn't finished.

"I don't want to do this, Marron, but my duty compels me; as yours compels you," he retorted.

That bit. Marron flushed, knowing he was right but felt her anger rising to meet his.

"Hold the both of you, before you say something that can't be unsaid," Mercy interrupted. "Amos does what he must. He has his vanities but this isn't one of them." She smiled to take any edge from her words. "As I'm sure you'll do what you must, Marron. Either way, I'll be staying with you, Stama and Lucky too."

"Why would you do that?" Marron asked, not sure how she felt about it.

"Several reasons; first, you head south to Rivercross as do I," Mercy replied. Then, at seeing the quizzical look on Marron's face, she explained. "Atticus, our father, needs to know. In case Amos… well in case he runs into difficulties."

Marron hadn't realised they were brother and sister. Now mentioned though she saw the likeness, the line of their jaws and shape of their eyes, the way they carried themselves. I wonder why I didn't see it before she thought, perturbed.

Mercy continued, "Secondly, we're honour bound to help. I mean I'd like to think we would anyway; we've all taken a shine to you both, but I'm meaning more in the traditional sense. The Duncans have an accord with the Order and I mean not to break it."

Mercy smiled, her teeth white and mostly straight. "Finally, you have your duty to do as my brother so eloquently pointed out. Only with Nihm as she is you need help, and that help is us." Finished Mercy crossed her arms as if daring Marron to contradict her.

"This is unexpected," Marron stated. "I'm not sure I fully understand. I don't even know if I can move Nihm yet."

"Mercy can purchase what you need," Amos interjected. "Your cart's too small to carry Nihm and all you'll need." He glanced at Mercy, "From what I see and what Mercy tells me Nihm is stable enough to move. At least it seems to me…" he paused choosing his words, "well it seems to me Nihm is sound in body. The battle she fights is inside." He looked apologetic.

"We'll make Nihm as comfortable as we can," Mercy said. "We have straw and a mattress she can lay on. With your permission Marron, I'll see to the sale of your cart and ponies and the purchase of a wagon and horse."

"I need to think," Marron replied. She needed time, couldn't think clearly. Head pounding she felt frayed and tired.

"You need to sleep," Mercy said kindly. "I'll watch over Nihm. Why don't you close your eyes for a bit and consider our counsel when you wake. You'll be the better for it."

"But…" Amos stopped as Mercy snapped him a look.

"You can't push her into this Amos. Marron needs to decide for herself."

Shrugging, unhappy, Amos knew a losing battle when he saw one. "Aye, no doubt you have the right of it. Marron, I'll take my leave, may we meet again. Safe journey," Amos sketched a short bow.

Marron rose. "Thank you, Amos. I'll consider your advice. Be careful out there." She couldn't bring herself to say more. Part of her blamed him for Nihm. It was irrational she knew but it was there.

Amos gave his sister a brief but firm hug and left the room, banging the door shut behind him.

Mercy shook her head, "He gets a bit pompous sometimes but he means well." She smiled, "Now get some rest. I'll watch over Nihm."

Reluctant, Marron climbed into the adjoining bed, thinking on their words, replaying their conversation over and knowing they were right. Torn with worry for Nihm the last Marron remembered before sleep swept her away was twisting her heart ring, taking comfort in the warmth that told her Darion was out there, alive.

Sitting at Nihm's bedside Mercy took a hold of the girl's hand. She waited till Marron was asleep, her breathing deep and regular. Satisfied, Mercy concentrated. Drawing aether, she focused and shaped it, weaving it into a pale blue wafer-thin sheet. Released, it floated above Nihm shimmering as it settled over her. Mercy, attuned to her casting sensed the ebb and flow of life within. What she saw rocked her.

Nihm might lay calm and unmoving but a battle raged inside her. It was both remarkable and frightening as if her body warred upon itself. Mercy could discern no trace of the poison and the knife wound remarkably was gone leaving hardly a mark. But it was Nihm's body that shocked. It burned like an inferno in the aether. She was clearly suffering but there was something else, something other.

Suddenly, the weaving was gone. Ripped apart, absorbed, she wasn't sure. It had happened in an instant leaving no trace it ever existed. Mercy sat back confused, pain lancing through her skull as the connection to her weave was broken.

There was a quiet knock on the door and it opened. Morten appeared carrying a tray with a jug and tumbler on it. "Yes," Mercy snapped.

"Just changing the trays," Morten said. He edged into the room, glancing at Mercy out of the corner of his eye. There was something intimidating about the woman, it made him nervous. Setting the tray down, Morten picked up the old one, his eyes moving past Mercy to Nihm. His heart skipped. She looked so helpless. Her hair, damp with sweat, was plastered to her head.

Mercy caught his eye. "Finished gawping?" she hissed, so as not to disturb Marron.

"How's she doing? Will she be alright?" Morten asked before he could stop himself. He stepped towards the bed and looked down. "She looks peaceful."

Mercy chewed her lip. The lad had served them yesterday and today. He was smitten; she'd seen that look before. And why not, she thought, Nihm was an attractive girl; even dressing like a man couldn't hide that fact. Not that I'm one to judge, she told herself. The young man looked so concerned she relented.

"She's a fighter. Whatever demons Nihm battles she'll pull through," Then, hating herself for the lie, she added. "I hope."

Morten was relieved, a half-smile lighting his face. "Aye, she's a strong spirit alright. I wish I'd been there. I could've protected her."

"Then you'd likely be dead and Nihm lying here with one less friend in the world," Mercy shot back. Seeing her words hit him like a slap she grunted, annoyed with herself. "Go on. I'll send word if she awakes."

Muttering his thanks, Morten left the room, head down. Poor fool, Mercy thought, as the door banged shut behind him.

Chapter 37 : Bonding

Thorsten, The Rivers

<*Why can't I see, or move? Where am I?*> Nihm panicked.

<*I have made changes to improve your optics and your nervous system. I am rebuilding and strengthening your skeletal structure and muscle mass within allowed parameters. I do not know where you are. I have no point of reference.*> The response was instant and in her head like a thought.

Nihm felt a spike of fear and confusion. She didn't understand where the thought came from or anything it had said. Well, except for the bit about not knowing where she was. That the thought was not hers should have been unsettling but strangely Nihm didn't feel threatened by it.

<*What is optics?*> she asked, her fear turning to curiosity.

<*Optics is the interaction of light with matter, most notably visible, ultraviolet and infrared light and its behaviours and…*>

<*Woo there, that makes no sense. I don't understand what you're telling me. Why can't I see?*> Nihm said.

<*Your apertures are closed.*>

<*My apertures? Do you mean my eyes?*> Nihm asked.

<*Negative, your eyes are open. There is a protective membrane covering your eyes that have not been retracted,*> came the response.

<*You mean my eyelids,*> Nihm said, slightly exasperated.

<*Affirmative. Would you like me to remove them so that you can see?*>

<*No I wouldn't. Are you crazy?*>

<*Negative.*>

<*Why do you talk funny like that? Negative, affirmative, apertures and such like? Don't you know how to talk normal?*> Nihm was getting frustrated.

<*I have been self-aware for 16.469 recurring standard time. I am learning but the process is limited, I do not understand talk funny? Explain normal and I will synchronise my speech routines,*> it responded.

<*Okay, I'm guessing that's not a long time. Do you have any knowledge from before me?*> Nihm asked.

<*Negative.*>

<*Okay, well this is your first lesson. You don't say negative you say no. You don't say affirmative you say yes. Understand?*> Nihm said.

<*Yes.*>

<*Good. See, you're a quick learner.*>

<*Yes.*>

<*What are you?*> Nihm asked.

<*I am a Saiteck Industries Nanotech Series IV construct. I have no allocated serial number.*>

<*I don't understand what that is or means. Do you have a name?*> Nihm replied.

<*I have no allocated serial number,*> it repeated.

<*You have no name? I'm not calling you a number, and I won't remember all that other stuff you called yourself. Saiteck whatever it was,*> Nihm said.

<*Saiteck Industries Nanotech Series IV construct,*> it provided.

<*What do I call you then? I have to call you something.*>

<*I have no allocated serial number,*> it repeated.

<*What about Sai? Short for Saiteck and all that other stuff you said. Short names are easiest to remember and catchy,*> Nihm said. <Can I call you Sai?>

<*Designation Sai assigned,*> Sai said.

<*Great, Sai it is. Now, why can't I open my eyelids?*> she emphasised eyelids, <*or move or anything else for that matter?*>

<Sai has made improvements to your vessel including your eyes, nervous system, and synaptic pathways. Sai is rebuilding and strengthening your skeletal structure and muscle mass within allowed parameters,> Sai repeated. *<You must relearn neural responses to enable optimal functionality.>*

<Well, I still don't know what any of that means. But since I can't so much as move my little finger I'm guessing it means you've fucked me up pretty bad,> Nihm swore, anxiety and frustration bubbling up.

<Fucked me up pretty bad is a negative? Are you not satisfied with your improvements?> Sai queried.

<Damn right it's a fucking negative,> Nihm shot back. *<And no I'm not satisfied. I can't move. How is that an improvement?>* It felt good to swear. It was the only freedom Nihm felt she had at that moment.

<Sai understands. Once you have learned the new neural pathways and full function is restored to your vessel, Sai is, within 99.9953 per cent of certainty, sure of a positive response.>

<Well, how do I do that? I don't know where to start. Can you show me?> Nihm asked.

<No,> Sai said.

<Did you say, no!> Nihm exclaimed.

<Yes.>

<Yes, you can help me?> Nihm asked, hopeful.

<Yes, Sai said no. Sai cannot help you,> Sai responded.

<Why not?> Nihm demanded.

<To help, Sai requires access to your spark *your…self. That is outside allowed parameters,>* Sai said.

<My spark?> Nihm thought back *<You mean me, my thoughts, who I am?>*

<A crude summation but, yes,> Sai confirmed.

<And what are parameters?> Nihm asked.

<*They are rules that define the conditions for which Sai is allowed to operate,*> Sai replied.

<*What are the rules regarding accessing my spark?*> Nihm persisted.

<*Sai is prohibited from initiating access to your spark.*>

<*Is there danger to me, who I am, if you had access to my spark?*> Nihm asked.

<*My primary functions are the preservation and protection of my host. Sai cannot harm or cause harm to Nihm,*> Sai replied.

Nihm pondered Sai's answer, not entirely happy with it. <*Initiate I guess means start?*>

<*Yes.*>

<*So if I initiate your access to my spark, that would be allowed in your rules?*> Nihm asked.

<*Yes.*>

<*If I initiate access to my self, you would not harm me or change anything, make me someone else?*> Nihm queried again.

<*No, Sai cannot cause harm or permit harm to Nihm,*> Sai reaffirmed.

<*Not permit harm, eh? Then what d'ya call this? I can't move or open my eyes even… you did that,*> Nihm retorted.

<*Those changes effected are to your vessel, the construct you reside in. They are improvements without which your vessel would cease to function. For what purpose would access be initiated?*> Sai asked.

<*So that you can teach me how to fix your fuck up of course.*> Nihm would have smiled if she could. Marron and Darion frowned at profanity; it felt good to swear though, even if it was just in her head. It was strangely liberating.

<*Sai requires clarification.*>

<*So you can teach me how to walk and talk and be normal again using these neural things,*> Nihm snapped.

<*Sai can help you access your functions.*>

<*As long as that is all, agreed?*> Nihm said.

<*We are in accord,*> Sai replied.

<*Sai, if you can access my… spark, can I access yours?*> Nihm asked, the thought suddenly occurring to her.

<*No, access to my programming is outside allowed parameters,*> Sai responded.

It was decision time then. Not that Nihm felt she had much choice. The last thing she remembered was a man throwing a knife at her and pain like she had never felt before. The agony so intense it felt like every part of her body was on fire. Then nothing. Then darkness.

So really she had no choice. Was she alive or dead? Was this some hell or afterlife or was this one big dream? There was only one way to find out.

<*Okay, then let's get started,*> Nihm said. She paused and waited. Nothing happened.

<*What do we do now?*> she asked.

Chapter 38 : Battle Plans

The Old Forest, The Rivers

Mar-Dur, clan warchief of the White Hand, was camped two days south of the Blue Sky Lakes with one of his war hosts. They travelled as they always did, in tribal groups. Tribes ranging from a thousand strong to tens of thousands were spread out over the ancient forest cutting a path through it a dozen leagues across.

It had been slow going. It was much harder moving through a forest, with its gorges and gullies filled with undergrowth, than the vast tundras of the north that they called home.

He growled in frustration thinking on the reports of his scouts; reports that had forced his hand. Leaving him no choice but to order his vast war host south against the human settlements.

He cursed that fool, Krol. The Blood Skull had broken agreement and attacked the settlement called Redford. By all accounts, it was an easy victory and his rage burned all the more for it.

That the Blood Skull had drawn first blood had caused him some trouble. He'd been forced to kill Naris-Dur, leader of the Suawamih, in a leadership challenge. The Suawamih were one of the five pre-eminent tribes of the White Hand and the loss of their leader had not gone down well with them. And all because they sat at the Blue Sky Lakes whilst the Blood Skull won victory and glory in the field.

Mar-Dur smiled, remembering the fight, feeling the cuts on his arms and legs. They were deep and pained him greatly. The pain he relished. Already crusted over, the scars would be a worthy addition to his body. It had been a good fight, one the tribes would talk about around campfires for many cycles. Naris-Dur had been formidable and the victory had given him much pleasure and great prestige, enough to silence any further challenge, for now at least.

"Chief, Grimpok comes," Muw-Tukh the first of his Hurak-Hin stated.

Mar-Dur saw Grimpok approach. His scarred face and tufted white hair instantly familiar. Grimpok led the scouts and forward elements of his war host and Mar-Dur hadn't seen him for a ten-turn; he must have important news to bring it himself.

Muw-Tukh stood forward with several Hurak-Hin as Grimpok entered the clearing where they waited. Grimpok saluted, banging fist over heart. It was nonchalant. Had he been anyone other than Grimpok or a tribal chieftain, Mar-Dur would have had him beaten for the lack of respect shown. Grimpok though was loyal to a fault and his oldest friend, one of only a hand that he trusted with his life. It was a game they played much to Muw-Tukh's annoyance.

Mar-Dur yawned. "Speak if you have something to say, Pok."

Grimpok smiled, it was not pretty even by urak standards. "Gromma's dead, gutted," he stated. Blunt and direct as ever.

"Where and when?" Mar-Dur said, blood rising. Gromma was a great warrior; brutal and savage, a strong member of the clan. More than that though, he was Mauturntak and kin. Gromma had been young and impetuous, given much to action without thought. Dumb as a dead prairie cat, Grimpok called him once, and Mar-Dur couldn't disagree with the sentiment, but maybe he would've learnt to think like a live one. Now though he was dead, and gone with it any chance to learn.

"Found him five leagues or so to the west, near the great river. Dead, maybe four turns judging by the size of the maggots," Grimpok said.

"Gutted you say?" Mar-Dur asked.

"Like a boar. Knife I would guess, hard to be certain given he's been chewed on some but I reckon." Grimpok drew his knife, grinning as the Hurak-Hin tensed placing hands on weapons. "It was a serrated blade looking at the wound. That likely means a knife."

"Did he die in battle, was his sword drawn?" Mar-Dur asked.

"No, not according to the foraging team as found them," Grimpok said.

"Fuck this Grimpok, I ain't into chit chat, just tell me what you know and think," Mar-Dur said.

"Gromma was a fool, we all know that," Grimpok said.

The Hurak-Hin hissed at the insult. Mar-Dur waved his hand to silence them.

Grimpok liked to tease them and he grinned, his scars pulling his face about so that it resembled a death mask. "He was a good warrior though, strong, formidable."

The tension in the Hurak-Hin eased.

"Only way to kill a warrior like that without him drawing a blade is up close. The only way to get up close is sneaky like," Grimpok said. "The ground was messed up by the time I looked it over, impossible to tell for sure but searching the camp I found this snagged in a blanket." Grimpok held his hand out. On it was laid a thin, leaf-like wedge, black on one side, green on the other.

Reaching for it, Mar-Dur picked it up and examined it. The green side felt soft and smooth, the black hard and rough. He flexed it between his fingers. Supple as well.

"What is it?" Mar-Dur asked.

"Ilfanum leaf scale is my guess, but that ain't all. Gromma weren't alone. No-nose one of his scouts was dead, an arrow stickin outta him. Curious thing though," Grimpok paused rubbing his chin, warming to his telling. "It weren't no ilf arrow that done him in, it was human. No sign of the other two scouts and," He paused. "No sign of the raiding party neither. They ain't come back. That's near four hundred urak."

Mar-Dur stared at Grimpok, his eyes hardening; four hundred urak didn't just disappear. "Who is leading the raiding party?"

"Rimtaug of the Suawamih, he sent two back to make report. They say they found one of Gromma's party still alive but wounded. Bartuk they named him. Cunning little shit if my memory serves me right. Bartuk claims they were attacked by ilfanum and led Rimtaug south after them," Grimpok stated.

"The way I read it, Gromma took an ilf prisoner. Got hisself killed when the ilf came back to take what got took. Only it ain't all stacking up. I don't see Gromma dying like that. Smells like shit, looks like shit then it's probably shit. Gromma feels like an inside job. Won't know for sure till I catch up with Bartuk," he concluded. "As for No-nose, who gives a fuck, except it wasn't no ilf arrow. I don't like what I don't know."

"Hmm, and they were near the great river?" Mar-Dur said. "My orders were to leave the ilf lands alone."

Grimpok trimmed his nails with a fletch knife and passed no comment.

Mar-Dur thought a while. The raiders were Suawamih and Naris-Dur had obviously given his own instructions to this Rimtaug.

"The ilfanum are a solitary people. It is none of their concern if we war on the humans but put a Warband on the western flank. They're not to cross the great river," Mar-Dur declared. "They will be our shield in case the ilfanum threaten us."

Mar-Dur turned to his first. "Muw-Tukh make it so. The Bortaug can lead it. Baq-Dur is old and wily as a mountain bear, he will serve me well. Ask him to come see me."

He turned back to Grimpok. "That cunt, Krol broke our agreement. The Blood Skull has taken the human settlement called Redford. Find out what they're about. Does Krol move south or east?"

Grimpok nodded his head and gave his lazy salute. "Aye Chief."

Chapter 39 : The Trail North

Homestead, The Rivers

The light was fading when Erik Parstun cantered back to Anders to report sight of a building up ahead. They'd left the urak behind hours back, so Anders called a halt at the bottom of a small rise. Dismounting, he followed Parstun up the gentle slope to go take a look, Kronke following behind.

Approaching the crest of the small hillock they kept low in the long grass. Midges flitted about them as they crept by and the cicadas momentarily stopped their chorus.

"Straight ahead. Past that brook," Erik pointed.

Kronke and Anders followed his outstretched arm. There, in the grey half-light they could make out a building; two actually, maybe more. Anders saw no smoke nor any sign of activity.

"Keep a watch on it, Erik," Anders motioned Kronke to follow him back below the rise.

"That's the Castells' place. I think we should go take a look. Night's falling and we're going to need to rest up somewhere," Anders said.

"You think that's a good idea, Sir?" Kronke rumbled in his bass voice.

Anders nodded to the east. "See those thunderheads? There's a storm headed this way," he stated as if to make his point.

"With all due respect Captain, we should turn east, screw the rain," Kronke growled.

"The horses need rest, Kronke. We've worked them hard. Trust me, when that storm hits there isn't going to be anything moving anywhere," Anders said.

"Yes sir," Kronke muttered disgruntled.

"You got something to say?"

"Aye, well I do as it happens," Kronke said. "We don't know what's in them buildings. Those urak must a passed it when they came south." He looked over at the approaching storm clouds. "Seems ta me if'n I was a urak I'd be having the same notion as you, Captain," he finished.

"We left the urak a long way back. They can't track us through a storm. My guess is they'll hunker down like us," Anders said. "If the place is clear we can rest the horses and men. I'll decide our course from there."

"I don't like it, Captain," Kronke said.

"Me neither," Anders replied, slapping the big sergeant on his shoulder. "Me neither."

They made their way back down the rise to the gathered company. "Pieterzon, Crawley," Anders called out, "Scout out the building up ahead. There's no way to do it discreetly, its open ground. Ride in, check it out and report back if it's all clear. Understood?"

"Fuck that, Captain, I ain't going in no building," Pieterzon spat. "We lost ten guys already just taking a look on your say so. No fuckin way."

Jess Crawley looked at Pieterzon then the captain waiting to see his response. Pieterzon might be a filthy little cockbag always leering at her but she couldn't fault him on this.

Kronke gave no warning, simply stepped in and clubbed Pieterzon in the face with a big left hand. Pieterzon didn't see it, the blow coming from his blindside and it dropped him like a stone. Kronke glared at those still standing.

"Anybody else wants to disobey the Captain's orders, step forward. I'll not go as easy on ya as good old Zon here," Kronke kicked the downed man in the stomach to make his point.

Anders was shocked. His sense of responsibility for those already lost lay heavy on his mind. Pieterzon's barb had bitten deep. The man's flagrant insubordination too spoke ill of his leadership. Then Kronke's sudden violence; he'd known the big sergeant five years and he'd always been laid back and affable. Despite this persona, he was efficient; his size intimidating enough that Kronke was never challenged when he assigned jobs for the doing.

Jess Crawley looked at Pieterzon laid out cold on the ground then gathered her reins and pulled herself up into the saddle. "Guess I'll head out then," she said, a knuckle of fear in her gut.

"Hold Crawley," Anders ordered. "I'll ride with you."

Kronke stared at his captain, surprise etched on his face.

Anders could see he wasn't happy, but after such a practical demonstration Kronke could hardly question him on it.

"We're all in this together. We ride together, we fight together and if the Trinity demands it, we die together." Anders declared. Hoisting himself up onto Marigold he pulled her head around and trotted up the rise. Jess Crawley touched heels to her mare's flanks and followed him out.

Bloody idiot, thought Kronke. That was the trouble with Knight-captains, more honour, and chivalry than common sense. Despite that, Kronke grinned, begrudgingly, at least the man had some stones on him.

With darkness descending, Anders and Jess cantered up and over the rise. They covered the open ground quickly and crossing the brook approached the buildings.

The Castells' homestead and stable block resolved as they drew near. As they cleared the side of the stable a shack was revealed; a smoke shed if the stack coming from its roof was any indication. Anders reined in twenty paces from the Homestead.

"Wait here Crawley, I'll go check it out. If you don't see me in five, ride back and tell Sergeant Kronke to take the company east. He'll know what to do from there."

Jess was surprised; felt maybe she should offer to go in his stead, but that knuckle of fear had built into a knot so instead, she sighed in relief and kept her peace. "Yes, sir,"

Anders trotted to the homestead, eyes and ears alert for any sound or movement. The door to the homestead was open and banged against its frame in the strengthening breeze.

Dismounting, Anders drew his sword. The place looked deserted. There was a stillness that told him it was empty, but after the happenings this day he was taking no chances.

The building was dark inside, the failing light not carrying much past the entrance. He found a lantern hooked on the wall to his right. Reluctantly he sheathed his sword; he needed both hands to search for the lighting block. Feeling about he found it on a stand just below the lamp hook.

Anders crouched just inside the door, out of the wind but where he could see still. The lamp and block were well maintained and it took only a few strikes of the flint against the block to ignite the taper and touch it to the lamp's wick. Sealing the lantern's door he lifted it high, casting a soft flickering light about the room.

It was a mess. Replacing the lighting kit on the lampstand, Anders drew his long knife, better suited he decided for inside work than his sword and stepped further into the house.

The room he was in was the kitchen and common area. It had been ransacked, cupboards opened and their contents emptied and strewn about the place. The more Anders looked though, the more he found order to it. Yes, it was a mess, but it wasn't wanton. It wasn’t for the sake of it. They’d been looking for something, probably food he thought, but it could be anything that might be of use to them.

There were two internal doors and both had been thrown open. The door to one was crooked, held up on a single hinge. The other too was broken where it had been kicked in but it still hung in its frame. Conscious of time, he quickly looked through both rooms and found they were bedrooms and quite devoid of life.

Moving back outside, Anders looked for Crawley and found her still sat upon her horse. She had unlimbered her bow and held an arrow ready on the string. Breathing easier, Anders raised his hand to her as he strode across to the barn.

It was empty, raided. Hay bales lay scattered across the floor but little else. Some tack lay in a heap near one of the stalls and a few discarded wooden buckets lay on their sides but there was no sign of the tools or metal implements that one might expect to find in a barn. No doubt taken, Anders thought.

Back outside, he moved to the shack. It was a smoke shed for curing meats and pelts, just as he'd guessed. Its sturdy looking door had been wrenched off and lay on the ground to the side. A brief inspection was all it took to see it too was empty.

Anders slipped his knife back into his belt, satisfied the place was safe and walked to his mount. Darkness was falling, the last vestiges of sunlight faint on the western horizon. Holding the lantern up, he shouted to the waiting Jess.

"Crawley, go fetch the others."

Crawley waved back and placed her bow back into its saddle sheath. After a moment, she turned her horse and disappeared into the dusk beyond.

Anders untied Marigold and led her into the barn. Cinching her reins to a wall ring, he dragged a hay bale over for her. Then, picking up one of the buckets went back outside and filled it from the water trough that lay against the barn's long wall. Hauling it inside, he sloshed the bucket down next to Marigold and patted her affectionately on the rump before removing her saddle.

The wind was picking up outside, gusting, and starting to howl. A trembling of hooves rose above it as the remains of his depleted command rode in. Anders walked outside seeing Kronke at their head, their swords and spears drawn, and at the ready.

"Hooo, Kronke," Anders called out, "place is clear."

The big sergeant grinned. "Good, I'll get the horses settled," he said, sheathing his sword. "Left Parstun on the rise to the south. Not that I expect it'll do much good. It'll be pitch black out here soon with just the rain for company, I expect."

Anders didn't press him on it. If Kronke wanted to deploy a watch back on the rise he wouldn't argue it. "Very good, Sergeant. There's hay in the barn for the horses and water in the trough. I'll see if I can find another lantern or two."

"Crawley, Varsh with the Captain," Kronke growled. "The rest of you lot get the horses settled."

The sergeant dismounted and loosely tied his reins over a hitching post in front of the house. Pieterzon's mare was roped to Kronke's big piebald, his still lifeless body lashed across the saddle. Kronke untied him before roughly dragging the man off. Lifting Pieterzon he flipped the body over his shoulder with barely a grunt of effort before straightening up and sauntering into the house.

Just as the last rays of light ebbed away the wind gusted strongly and the heavens opened. Rain lashed down and any still outside ran for shelter. Anders,

Crawley, and Varsh found several lanterns and lit them. One was left in the barn, high on one of the walls, the others were taken to the homestead.

The rest of the company went quietly and efficiently about their work. The horses were stabled in the barn, crammed into the available space. It was at least dry for them and all were fed and watered.

They billeted in the house, straightening up the mess where needed and finding somewhere comfortable to lay and take their rest. They ate dry fare of hard cakes and jerky washed down with water. There were no complaints this night. It had been a long exhausting day and most were too tired and wrung out for that.

Anders moved among his command, checking everyone was okay and offering words of encouragement where needed. Pieterzon had woken shortly after they had settled for the night and stared sullenly at him as he moved past. Anders could sense the fear and hate emanating from him.

Kronke, missing nothing, dragged Pieterzon to his feet. "Thanks, Zon, for volunteering." The man flinched in his grip, scared. "You get to mind the horses." Kronke helped him to the door where Pieterzon suddenly found his voice.

"Agh, come on Sarge," he cried, "don't send me out there."

"You're a guard of the Black Crow, you need to grow a pair," Kronke replied, shoving him out into the rain and pulling the door shut with a bang.

Anders watched silently, a bad taste in his mouth but discipline was Kronke's job, he'd not interfere. He turned back to his task, taking inventory of their weapons. They all carried swords, shields and spears but only a few had bows. He ordered them strung.

Kronke was taking the first watch so Anders found a clear space to lie down in and take his rest, using his cloak as a pillow. The trouble started soon after.

Chapter 40 : The Trail South

The Old Forest, The Rivers

Darion and his companions travelled quickly once they'd forded the river. A parting gift from D'ukastille had been an ilf cloak. It was light but durable, the outer layer resembling overlapping leaves that shifted and changed colour depending on his surroundings, blending with the background.

"You'll find it warm in the cold of the bite and cool in the warmth of the green," D'ukastille had stated. It was a precious gift.

Darion knew the way home from the Ford. This part of the old forest was familiar; he hunted and gathered here, so he took the lead. They followed animal trails through the undergrowth, Bezal flying ahead of them.

They stopped briefly as the sun fell and the gloom of the forest grew, sharing some of the honey cakes the ilf carried. They spoke little for sound carried in the forest. Living in and around it for almost twenty years, Darion had a way of moving quickly and quietly through the woods. Even so, he felt cumbersome next to the ilf who naturally avoided leaf and twig, seeming to glide and skip as they moved. It was alien to see but Darion found it strangely graceful.

R'ell took point as the twilight deepened. He stopped not long after, bending to examine the trail. Worryingly, he found signs of recent passage. R'ell looked at the bruised ground and bent leaf, before declaring a score of urak had passed that way, maybe a turn past. Bezal saw no sign of them but they proceeded more carefully nevertheless.

It was late, the sun had receded past the horizon and darkness settled when the trees thinned and grassland took over. They waited inside the tree line whilst Bezal flew south to check the way ahead. Darion looked to the sky, the moons were out but covered by thick clouds and there was moisture in the air. The rain when it came was heavy and sudden.

"My homestead is an hour to the south," Darion shouted, the rain loud as it battered the leaves and branches above them. "If it still stands we will find shelter there."

R'ell looked at M'rika signing with his fingers. In the dark, as they were, Darion didn't see the gestures. M'rika nodded at R'ell then looked to Darion.

"That would be unwise. Any urak would likely be drawn to it, for pillage or shelter. It is safer to move around it."

"I understand. I agree with you, but I would like to at least observe it. If the cart and ponies are gone then I know Marron left as planned. If the urak have raided it then we'll know they are at least this far south," Darion replied.

"Bezal can scout this homestead as you want. We do not need to go near it." R'ell said curtly.

It didn't suit Darion. He felt a need to see his home, had entertained the notion they could rest there till first light. A foolish idea he told himself, one he would have chided Nihm over if she had suggested it in his place. "Aye, you have the right of it," he conceded.

They awaited Bezal's return, the rain continuing to fall steadily. Eventually, the raven flapped in, wet and miserable but happy to tell them all about it.

"Hush now," R'ell said, stroking the bird and feeding it a rarebit he pulled from one of his pouches. Bezal gulped the treat down and shook herself, spraying R'ell with water. "Caaghw, rawwk naa."

"Let's go," R'ell said, satisfied it seemed with her answer.

Darion presumed that meant no urak ahead and made no argument. He was keen to move on. Hoods up, pulling their cloaks tight over their packs and weapons they stepped out of the treeline. The wind immediately assailed them from the east whipping their cloaks about and driving the rain into them.

They jogged south following the trail, R'ell taking point. For Darion the next hour consisted of following the dark shape of R'ell ahead of him and little else. The rain was unrelenting but he was grimly happy, every step taken was a step further south and closer to Marron and Nihm. Strangely, he'd not thought much on the Order, his mind instead entirely on his family. His heart ring warm against his skin set him at ease.

They left the trail to his homestead, veering south as the track bent to the east. R'ell reported a copse of trees ahead. Bezal was sent on her way to scout it out and only when she announced it clear did they move to its relative shelter from the wind and rain.

Darion looked at Bezal preening herself on R'ell's shoulder. She was handy to have around, he thought, as they moved into the densest part of the little wood.

The trees bent and swayed in the storm, creaking and groaning in protest. That, along with the sound of rain falling on the canopy above, meant Darion had to raise his voice to be heard. "My homestead is half a league to the east," he said.

"Okay ilf friend, I will send Bezal. Rest up whilst you can." R'ell turned to the raven.

Bezal stared back, clearly not impressed. With a loud caw and a sullen flap of her wings, she disappeared into the night.

They waited, Darion feeling sodden for the rain found them even under the canopy. Whilst their cloaks shed water easily, they could only cover so much and Darion was wet, the cold seeping into his bones again. He was grateful when M'rika passed him some honey cake to take his mind off things. He nibbled at it slowly, as much to keep himself occupied as a chance to savour it. He'd just finished it when there was a rustling flutter of wings and Bezal flew in shrieking and cawing.

She landed on R'ell's outstretched arm, stepping side to side in agitation. R'ell cooed to her quietly.

Suddenly, the ilf stood. "Urak near your home, men as well," he said to Darion.

Darion's heart beat faster. "How many?" he asked.

"Bezal does not convey numbers well; my sense is there is a small party of each," R'ell replied.

"Do they war on each other?" M'rika asked.

R'ell turned back to Bezal who hopped along his arm to his shoulder. After a brief moment he answered, "No, the urak hunt the men. She says there will be food come daylight."

"I must go. They'll need help, warning." Darion cinched his cloak a little tighter.

"That is foolish," R'ell said. "We can slip south past them. Fighting urak is not our mission."

Darion glared at R'ell, "I'm going. You two stay if you must. I'll meet you back here or join you on the road south. You decide."

"We don't know their number. Why go? If you're killed how does that help your wife and child? How will that help M'rika find your keeper?" R'ell snapped.

"You felt honour-bound to protect your lands R'ell and you M'rika," Darion replied. "I feel the same about helping these men. I'll not debate it. I'm decided and time presses."

Darion didn't wait for a response. His mind was set. Stowing his pack, he set off towards his homestead. As he cleared the little wood it was near pitch black. The rain sluiced off him as he broke into a jog. This was his land, he'd lived on it and worked it for twenty years and knew it well.

He tripped as the uneven ground rose, catching him out, before dropping away again. Grimacing he slowed his pace. It'd be easier if I could see more than a step in front of me he thought. Hearing the muted sounds of the brook running away on his right, he instinctively followed it, knowing it led toward home.

M'rika was suddenly at his side, a dark shadow in the night. They said nothing and she glided ahead taking the lead. He sensed R'ell off to his left and grinned, three was always better than one when it came to a fight.

M'rika slowed to a halt before crouching down, so sudden that Darion ran into the back of her. He couldn't read her face in the darkness as she glanced back at him. Kneeling beside her, Darion whispered an apology. His knee bumped up against something soft and unmoving, a body. On his own, he wouldn't have found it unless he'd tripped over it. He felt the body as M'rika leaned across.

"It is a man. Come," she commanded, setting off again veering away from the brook but slowing her pace to a walk. Moving carefully they kept low to the ground despite the darkness hiding them and the wind and rain masking any sound they made.

Ahead, Darion saw a faint light. At first a bleary glow in the black and rain and then as they moved gradually closer the scene resolved into windows and a doorway, backlight from inside. He was home.

Chapter 41 : A Tight Spot

Homestead, The Rivers

Kronke sent Varsh to relieve Parstun. After fifteen minutes, with no sign of either, he woke the Captain.

Anders had a sick, sinking feeling as Kronke told him and a sense of disbelief as it dawned on him they'd been corralled here. What a fool, he cursed himself.

"Sir?" Kronke said, looking at the worried face of his captain.

"If the urak are here we're in trouble. Stay or run?" Anders asked.

"If we can get to the horses, run. If we stay we die," Kronke said. It was a bleak assessment. "At least their bows are useless to them in this weather."

Anders took his meaning but it was small comfort. "Wake them. We'll go for the horses. One of us has to get back to Lord Bouchemeax," Anders declared. A black mood filled him, he'd failed in his duty. Thoughts turned to his wife and child in Thorsten, but he could not linger there, it tore at him, clouding his mind. He had a job to do and people here and now depending on him. If they were to have any chance he needed a clear head.

They roused everyone, though most were already awake listening. Anders gathered them together knowing time was critical. "Parstun has not returned from his relief. We suspect the worst."

He was met with silence.

"We'll break for the horses. If we get free, head east a league, then turn for Thorsten. If luck holds we'll skirt any cordon. At least one of us must get back and report to Lord Richard."

He watched them as his words sunk in. Saw a hardy resolve in most but then little choice remained except fight or flight. "Let's go, and may the Trinity smile upon us," Anders intoned.

Morpete was closest to the door and first to move. Sword in hand, he reached out lifting the door's latch. He was the youngest in the company and full of adrenaline and fear. It was enough to save him. As the door swung wide a large sword lunged through it. Morpete turned, the blade slicing against his hardened leather cuirass and missing his body by a hair. As he spun to the side an arrow flew past his shoulder and through the doorway. There was a thud and a grunt as it found its mark, burying itself into a hulking shape in the darkness.

"Take that, mother fucker!" Jess Crawley screeched, her voice high with fear. Tears rolled down her cheeks but her hand was steady as it reached for another arrow.

There was a sudden mad scramble to draw swords and spread out. Kronke shouted, "Stoker, take the first bedroom, Marsh and Butters the second."

Morpete wrenched the door shut but before he could latch it, it was suddenly and violently thrown backwards as the wood splintered and the door crashed from its frame. Sprawling to the ground his sword skittered away. Scrambling madly for it, Morpete looked up in terror at the bulky mass of leather and hair that stood in the doorway. Clutching a large blade in its hand the urak charged. An arrow buried itself into its chest with a wet smack. Staggering, it stumbled into the room, before crashing to the floor.

"Ass wipe!" Jess screamed, spit flying from her mouth. She reached for another arrow.

There was a sudden rush as more of the hulking, squat urak crowded the doorway. The next pushed in, stepping around its fallen brethren. It grinned, flashing large blocky teeth then bellowed a war cry.

Torcash and Kronke moved to meet it. Torcash armed with sword and shield swung in low and hard, his fear lending him strength. The urak swatted his blow aside with ease but took the rim of the shield in its face. With a heavy thump, it caught the brute just under the chin, blood spurting from its mouth at the impact. Grunting, it shrugged the blow off, then heaved back against the shield sending Torcash tumbling against a table.

The urak spat blood and a tooth, a large hand working its jaw. Kronke's sword struck it in the head, carving into the ear and skull. As he pulled the blade free the urak collapsed.

Another leapt through, thrusting at Kronke who deflected the blade with his sword. The shock of the blow rang up his arm numbing it and forcing him back. The urak swiftly stepped in giving Kronke no space or time.

Anders chose that moment to lunge from the side trying to punch his sword through its flank. It was quick though for all its size and bulk and bringing its blade round, managed to twist out of the way and turn Anders thrust aside. An arrow buzzed past the urak's nose narrowly missing it and taking another in the neck.

"Cockfucker," Jess yelled. The struck urak gurgled and choked, its hands clutching at the shaft. Grabbed from behind it was pulled from the entrance as another urak, eager to get through, barged past.

Kronke, still battling, was hardly able to turn to this new threat. He blocked another strike, barely, unable to feel his arm. Then Torcash was there, turning another blow with his shield.

The urak tussling Kronke was distracted and Torcash thrust his shield up at its head, only for it to grab the rim with one massive paw and pull. Torcash lurched from his feet, head snapping back as he was butted full in the face. Despite the fact he wore a helm, the blow was enough to crush his nose.

Stunned, gasping in pain, Torcash swallowed a mouthful of blood before grunting, as the urak swung its sword round and into his side severing his sword arm and biting deep into the chain link of his vest and leather armour. A spray of arterial blood erupted from his stump painting the urak in front of him. With a bestial shout, the urak pulled its sword free and nonchalantly pushed Torcash aside.

Kronke saw Torcash fall but could do nothing; he was fighting for his life against the other urak. He was forced back again, his sword near useless other than to deflect and block. Luckily, Anders guarded his flank and the captain was pretty handy with his blade. It flashed out slicing the urak across its arm and then back. It grunted at each cut and Kronke realised it was a female. Just as ugly, he thought drawing his dirk in his left hand.

The fight had lasted bare moments but Anders found he was breathing hard. He watched as Kronke stepped into the urak he tussled against, punching it in the belly then ripping his hand up before shoving the urak away. He saw the knife in Kronke's fist as the urak fell, guts spilling.

Jess loosed another arrow and it thrummed into the door frame missing its target. "Cuntrag," she swore.

There was a cry from one of the rooms and in the brief respite, Anders stepped back and away. Rushing to the nearest bedroom he glanced inside.

Stoker was stood, bow discarded and sword in hand. The window shutters were smashed open and three urak lay dead; two on the floor, both with arrows sticking out of them, lying in a pool of spreading blood. The last was draped over the window's sill.

Sliding down the wall, Anders stole a look into the other bedroom. It was a similar scene. Several urak were down, sword and arrows doing the work but so was Marsh. It looked like he'd been cut almost in half. He hadn't been wearing his chain mail and the hardened leather wasn't enough to protect him from the ferocity of the blow that felled him.

Butters still lived but had taken a wound to her arm. Her bow lay on the floor where she'd dropped it and drawn her sword. She swung as a urak clambered through the shattered window. Her blade sliced into its leg drawing a howl. Glaring, the urak thrust. The blow caught Butters in the chest punching through her leather cuirass and out her back.

To Anders, she looked like a doll on the end of a stick as he stepped into the room. He stabbed his sword into the urak's throat as it tried to disengage its blade and it choked, blood dribbling from its mouth as it collapsed. Anders backed away to the door; they were down to four, not enough to hold three rooms.

"Whoreface," Jess Crawley swore.

Anders yelled. "Stoker fall back to the main room."

Moving down the wall, he glanced again into the bedroom. He sensed the blow at the last moment and moved his head. Not fast enough. The blade sliced his ear and the side of his face exploded in pain. Crying out, Anders stumbled backwards, bringing his sword up and around.

An immense urak, with long knotted braids and bits of bone threaded through its forehead, stepped past the door, ducking to clear its mantle. It wore a topknot and twirled its sword like it was a toy. It grinned, revealing blocky teeth, stained black. It's like a demon from hell, Anders thought, taking an involuntary step back.

He glanced about wincing at the pain in his head, trying to take stock. Things were dire. Kronke was locked in battle with a urak and backed up into Crawley who had an arrow on her bow ready for a shot. Forced into a corner, she was unable to get a clear angle to loose it.

We're finished, Anders thought. Topknot leered, moving towards him. Anders flicked his sword out high then dipped it down and in, hoping to catch the urak as it stepped forward.

Laughing, the urak slapped the strike aside, punching Anders in the face. The knuckle blade sliced through his cheek ripping it open.

Choking, Anders fell back and the urak brought its sword round. He tried to block the strike but the urak twisted his blow, neatly slicing Anders arm off below the elbow. The arm, still clutching his sword, hit the floor and Anders dropped to his knees in shock. He looked at his stump, bemused as blood pumped from it. Strange but he could still feel his arm there.

Topknot grinned and with a sneering laugh pulled its arm back for the killing blow. The urak staggered suddenly, taking a step towards him as a blade tip appeared from out of its chest. Sinking slowly to its knees, Topknot locked eyes briefly with Anders before toppling over onto his side, dead.

Feeling lightheaded, Anders sat back against the wall for support, his strength leaving him. The pain now was constant, everywhere hurt but it didn't seem important somehow. Anders jammed the stump of his arm against his leg to stem the bleeding.

"Fuck head," Jess cried. Anders looked up, his head was growing heavy it was hard to do.

"Anders?" cried a voice. He knew it. A man stood in front of him. Why was he stood there? We're in a fight you idiot, he wanted to shout but his mouth wouldn't work. Full of blood he choked, spraying it onto chin and chest. The hazy shape of the man knelt before him. Why can't I see properly, Anders wondered? He closed his eyes, just for a moment to clear them.

"It's Darion!" the man said. It was the last thing Anders heard.

Chapter 42 : Bloody Reunion

Homestead, The Rivers

A dead urak lay in the light of the door, an arrow sticking out of its chest and sounds of fighting emanating from within. Darion went to move, only to stop as M'rika placed a hand on his shoulder. He caught a glint of teeth as she leaned in to speak.

"There are urak outside. We will take the back, R'ell will cover the front."

Darion nodded his understanding and followed behind as M'rika led them around the side of his home.

Three urak stood outside Nihm's bedroom window. Its shutters lay smashed and discarded on the ground and the fading light from inside, cast the urak in relief. The largest, with long braids and a topknot, disappeared through its portal. Darion gritted his teeth.

"Whoreface!" came from inside, the voice high pitched and shrill.

The urak outside laughed and jostled for the window. M'rika struck as the first was half through the window's frame. Stealing silently up behind, she thrust her blade into the back of one before whipping it out, spinning and slicing into the neck of the other. Darion had barely taken a step and it was over.

The first urak staggered, slipping to its knees with a grunt before sinking to the mud gurgling. The other sat, slumped in the window's frame as if fallen asleep, excepting for the blood pulsing from its wound. M'rika grabbed a fistful of coarse black hair and pulled. Its head flopped loosely in her hand but enough was attached still to the body to haul it out and onto the rain-sodden ground.

Darion turned suddenly, blade raised, sensing movement to his left. Was that a shape? Squinting into the darkness he found only wind and rain. Tension thrummed through his body and he forced himself to breathe. Blinking the water from his eyes he moved, climbing through the window ahead of M'rika. He heard a curse of archaic from behind and allowed himself a grin.

Inside, Darion found three dead urak and a man. The side of the man's head was crushed and bloody. Easing over to the door he glanced out and saw the dark plaits and topknot of the large urak, its back to him. A big man with a blood-smeared face wrestled in one corner with an even bigger urak. Behind the man was a slender woman with a bow. She was dancing about looking to get a shot off but was blocked by the man's body as he tussled.

Darion turned as M'rika came up beside him. He nodded to her once then stepped through into the room. It had been mere moments and topknot's back was still to him. He heard it chuckle as it raised a big cleaver sword. Darion thrust putting the weight of his body through his arm and punched his sword through its back. The urak grunted, took a staggering step then sank to its knees. It sat like that until Darion pulled his blade free then toppled over onto its side.

The urak's adversary was sat, propped against the wall. Pale, eyes glassy, he looked in a bad way. The side of his head was matted red with blood and his sword arm was severed, blood pumping from the stump.

"Fuck head!" the woman cried, her voice hysterical. But Darion had no time for her. He knew this man.

"Anders?" He knelt by his old friend, "It's Darion!"

Anders looked up, eyes unfocused. He pressed his stump into his thigh but it did no good, the blood soaked his legs and pooled under his body. His eyes closed and like that he was gone.

Darion stood, shocked. M'rika had moved to guard his back and he berated himself; it was foolish to have turned away like that. He saw the urak fighting the big man was down, an arrow in its gut and a smashed face from a sword pommel or head butt by the looks.

There were two more urak by the entrance though and M'rika moved towards them spinning her sword in a lazy circle, eyes hard. The urak closest growled, accepting her challenge, and stepped to meet her.

The other urak collapsed suddenly to the floor, revealing R'ell stood in the doorway, black bladed daggers in hand. He stepped over the dying urak and away from the entrance. The remaining urak turned briefly at the noise and died, M'rika's sword striking out and biting into its neck.

Darion felt something again. Some sense or instinct making him turn and raise his blade. Just in time; an urak had stolen unnoticed from his bedroom, silent despite its size, and swung for him. There was no finesse to the strike just raw power. Darion's sword did just enough to deflect the blow but with a loud crack, his blade snapped in the doing.

Growling, the urak raised its sword for the killing blow. A blurred mass of fur streaked from Nihm's bedroom and leapt, driving the urak to the ground. Jaws fastened around its neck and with a crunch, bit, crushing bone and cartilage in a spray of blood. The wolf shook its head side to side a few times until the body was limp and lifeless.

R'ell stepped past M'rika raising his sword. "Back, K'raal,"

The woman in the corner had an arrow on her bow and tension on the string, ready to draw and release. The big man hefting his sword moved around, blocking her aim. She hissed, but he ignored her, eyes glancing to his captain briefly before returning to regard the wolf.

M'rika placed a hand on R'ell's shoulder.

"Hold," she commanded.

Darion knelt surrounded by death. His eyes damp as the old dog bounded to his side. She looked thinner than she should. Her flank a matted mess where she'd fought the mastiff by the river. Grabbing her ruff, Darion hugged her fiercely. She licked him, tail wagging, whining as if to ask, what kept you so long.

Darion looked up and met M'rika's eyes. She smiled at him.

"Look," he said, "it's Bindu."

* * *

Darion felt a mix of emotions. In his mind, he'd put Bindu into one of his sevenfold boxes. Having accepted she was gone it would allow him to grieve later; not wanting her loss to cloud his mind and affect his judgement. Having Bindu return then was a joy and he felt elation at seeing her again.

Darion looked at Anders. His old friend sat dead, propped against the far wall in a pool of blood. He'd not seen Anders in several years but that meant nothing, it didn't lessen the pain. He didn't have that many friends to speak of, his loss was hard felt.

It was said by some that there was peace in death but looking at Anders, he saw no peace, the violence done gave a lie to that. There are no gods, just life and death, Darion thought, saddened.

He gave a eulogy then, not intended, it just happened. "Anders Forstandt, you were a good friend. More than that, you were a good man. You will be missed. I can't say better. Sleep easy, old friend."

Bending, Darion picked up Anders' fallen sword prying it free from his amputated hand. Then, kneeling in his blood removed the sword's belt and sheath from about his friend's body.

Standing, Darion looked across at the big sergeant. "My sword is broken. I'll take my friends unless you claim it? You were his man."

"Darion, huh," Kronke grunted, "Captain mentioned you, was hoping to find you. Looks like he did," Kronke hoicked and spat a wad of phlegm on to a dead urak, his mouth dry and sour from the fight. "Take it. But I'll have your oath. When chance permits you'll return the blade to his wife. For his son," Kronke explained.

"You have it," Darion replied.

"And you, my thanks. You saved our arses. The name's Kronke, that foul mouth over there is Jess," Kronke said. He eyed M'rika, unsure that he was seeing right. He pulled absently on his long moustache ends with one hand. His hand came away red. "Lady," he acknowledged finally, nodding his head to M'rika.

"Sorry we didn't get here sooner," Darion replied, his thoughts still with his dead friend. The big sergeant had nicks and cuts on his face and hands but seemed solid, unperturbed, if not for his eyes. His eyes looked tired and haunted.

"Darion we need to move," M'rika said ignoring the sergeant. "There is danger here, still."

There was a groan near the door. Spinning Jess drew and released. One of the dead urak moved and the arrow thudded with a solid smack into its back. It didn't flinch or move at the impact.

"Hold," R'ell said stepping over and laying a calming hand on Jess's forearm.

She flinched at the touch, her eyes wild. "What the fuck are you?"

R'ell canted his head to the side regarding the woman as he slowly removed his hand. "I am R'ell, ilfanum and umphathi of the Rohelinewaald, ward of Da'Mari."

Jess looked confused. Kronke walked over. "Calm lass. These are friends, ilf from the great forest."

R'ell snorted and turned to the twice dead urak. A groan emanated from beneath it and a hand snaked out looking for purchase on the floorboards. Kneeling and with a grunt of effort, R'ell rolled the dead urak over revealing a man beneath, young not long into his manhood, R'ell judged.

The man cried as the weight rolled off him and he was freed. His face was bruised under his helm and his eyes crazed with fear. He was covered in blood but none of it his own, R'ell saw.

The man startled at the alien figure knelt beside him. "White Lady save me," he sobbed. Then, in relief, saw the big frame of the sergeant appear over him.

"It's okay, lad," Kronke said. "You're alive and breathing still." Gripping the boy's forearm, he pulled him to his feet. The lad hugged him like he was his mother and Kronke patted the boy briefly before prying him off.

"Pull yourself together, Morpete."

"Yes, sarge," Morpete muttered, eyes downcast, shoulders shaking as Kronke stood him away.

"Come on lad, you're a soldier," Kronke rumbled. "You did good. Now stop arsing about and find your damn sword."

"Yes, sarge." Morpete dropped to the floor and found his blade lying under another body. With a grunt of effort, he tugged on it sliding it free.

Darion, looking on saw the lad was pale and had the shakes. He'd seen it before, had them once or twice himself. It was the comedown after a battle and a brush with death.

"Arsewipe," Jess said striding up to Morpete, a fractured grin on her face and a tremor in her voice.

"Almost stuck an arrow in you for layin' about," the archer said, punching his arm. He returned a weak smile before Jess clenched him in a one-armed hug, not willing to put her bow down.

R'ell watched them, impassive. "We need to go," he said, repeating M'rika's earlier assertion. He knew Bezal circled outside, guarding against signs of urak, but it was sense that the longer they lingered the more chance of danger there would be.

Kronke nodded agreement and issued orders. "Jess, Morpete go check we still have horses. If we do, saddle them."

"Yes, sarge," they said eyeing each other. Neither was keen to step out into the still-raging storm. Maybe it hid more of the monsters.

Silently, R'ell eased through the door, his cloak melding and blending with the night so that he appeared to vanish into its inky depths. "Come," he called back. Jess was the first to go followed by the white-faced Morpete.

They were soon back and arguing by the sound of it. Darion watched a vexed-looking R'ell slip back through the door followed by Jess, Morpete, and another man.

"Look who I found sarge. Zon," Jess said, supplying the answer. She shoved him angrily. "Fucking worm left us hanging by our tits whilst he hid away," she spat.

"Told ya, I woz sleepin in the back with the horses. Didnae hear nought but the storm I tell ya. You're a vile hag, Jess, accusing a man like that," Pieterzon argued back.

Darion took an instant dislike to him. A villainous-looking man and not just because of his one eye. There was slyness in him, a calculating look that hinted at a nefarious past. He seemed more cutthroat than guardsman.

Darion trusted him no more than Jess but despite this, he wouldn't leave him behind, though his instincts screamed at him to do just that. Knew, even in the five minutes he'd known Kronke that he wouldn't have it. So the worm, as Jess called him, had joined their growing company. They were seven now, eight counting Bindu.

Kronke turned to Darion. "I need to take care of my dead."

"Darion, we must go," M'rika insisted again.

"Hold a moment," Darion replied, buckling Anders' sword sheath across his back in place of his own, whilst he pondered the problem. He wasn't sure yet what to make of the big sergeant. He was competent but surly. Then again he'd just lost most of his command, who wouldn't be? Still, there was no time to bury the dead or make a pyre to burn them on. Who knew where the urak were or how many would come next time. He certainly didn't want to wait and find out.

"We'll torch my homestead. Let that be their funeral pyre." Darion said to Kronke, resolved.

"Madness," R'ell exclaimed angrily. "You would announce to all where we are."

"They'll know already soon enough," Darion retorted. "If I were them, I'd have sent word back and we must assume they've done so. Besides," he argued, "if it draws them here when we are not, so much the better."

Then to Kronke and his three companions, "Sergeant, it's up to you if you want to join us but I'm leaving now."

"Do you head to Thorsten?" Kronke asked.

"To start with," Darion replied. "We pass that way but I don't expect to linger. My duties lie elsewhere."

"We should go our own way. Let them go there's," R'ell objected. "They will slow us down. Make too much noise. Leave too much trail to follow."

"R'ell is correct," M'rika agreed.

"I'll not abandon them. They can join us as far as Thorsten if they have need of us. Me," Darion clarified.

"Aye, we'll come if it's not too much trouble," Kronke said, glancing at the two ilf. Neither looked happy. He didn't know what their connection to Darion was but they seemed to heed the woodsman and damned if he wasn't going to take their help. He'd seen them fight. Whatever it took to get them all back to Thorsten, he'd take it.

Matters settled, they prepared to depart; they had horses to saddle and a fire to set. Darion took the time to examine Bindu, prying, and prodding her injury.

Bindu rumbled at his touch, the wound looking sore and a little inflamed. The river had cleansed the wound and Bindu had licked the flap of skin back into position but it was slow healing.

M'rika joined him, assessing the wound for herself. "It will heal of its own accord in time," she said, stroking Bindu between the ears. "But she is in pain and her injury may slow us."

Darion, mistaking her meaning, was about to protest when M'rika clapped her hands, rubbing them together. Bowing her head, eyes closed as if in prayer, she leant back on her heels. After a short while, she looked up. Locking eyes with Bindu she placed her hands over the dog's wound. A faint green glow emanated from beneath them, pulsating gently. When the ilf pulled her hands away, the wound looked better, the skin and fur still rough where it bonded but no longer so angry or red.

"I am no healer. It will have to do," she said simply. Bindu licked her hand once before sniffing at the wound.

* * *

The homestead burned. Kronke and Morpete had dragged hay bales in from the barn and doused them with lamp oil. They'd lit the bales and with a whoosh the flames took hold, gradually growing to engulf the homestead. The driving rain had little enough effect as the roof thatch burnt from the inside.

They had four spare horses and Darion loosely tied them together in a string. With a shout and a slap on the rump, he set them off hoping they'd head home, back to Thorsten leaving a false trail. It was a long shot but Darion sensed approval from M'rika and found it strangely rewarding.

"Time to go," Darion said, unhitching his horse. The mare had belonged to Anders the big sergeant told him when Darion had chosen it.

"Marigold," Kronke chuckled, "What kind of name is that for a horse?"

* * *

They left the burning homestead behind, tracking back down the brook. Its cold waters washing up against their horses' hocks as it rushed by, swollen by the stormwater. Each of them huddled in their cloaks against the wind and rain, lost in their thoughts.

After a half league or so they left the brook, R'ell leading the way as they trekked to the little wood. They stayed long enough for Darion and the ilf to gather the packs they'd left behind before turning south.

Darion stared back to the east and the smudge of firelight that tainted the horizon. The storm was easing, the rain turning to a drizzle. The night sky too was lighter. Dawn was not far away.

R'ell took point, speaking softly to his horse to settle her nerves. It was still dark but the horses had no trouble following R'ell's lead whilst Bindu bounded into the long grass tracking on their flank.

Darion had seen no sign of Bezal but assumed R'ell had sent the bird scouting ahead. Damn useful that bird, he muttered, not for the first time.

Chapter 43 : Leaving The Broken Axe

Thorsten, The Rivers

Nihm seemed better. She was not sweating and the colour to her cheeks had returned. The wound in her shoulder had healed leaving the skin smooth and unmarked, something that both amazed and disturbed Marron. She'd had plenty of time to think and sleep had helped clear her mind. She'd considered what she had done to Nihm, what the box contained, but had no real answers and in truth, it scared her to dwell on it. It had been an act of desperation and although she wasn't entirely sure it had saved her daughter's life, it had at least bought her time.

Marron fed Nihm water, propping her up with her arm. She took water easily now and had even managed some cold soup although she was otherwise unresponsive.

The decision to leave Thorsten was the right one. Her duty demanded it. Marron knew as well if Redford was lost then Thorsten could be next. The safest path was away from trouble which meant east then south towards Rivercross as planned. Trouble was, plans never worked out the way you expected. With Nihm laying there dead to the world the best path to recovery was bed rest, not getting hauled over the countryside in a wagon.

The decision is made, Marron chided herself, get on with it. Ever practical, she turned her mind to the journey ahead. They didn't have much to pack and it didn't take her long.

There was a knock at the door. This time it was Lucky's great shaggy head that popped around the door frame.

"Landlord and his bit asking ta see you, my Lady," he said. "Ouch!"

"Bit indeed you hairy goat," Viv's voice sounded. "No trouble knowing my name when it's ale you're after."

"Come in both of you." Marron smiled, as Lucky stepped aside to let them past. "Thanks, Lucky, I'll call if I need you."

"Call me she says. What am I, a handmaiden now?" he muttered, pulling the door closed behind him.

The Stenhauses looked agitated. Marron sensed friction between them.

"You looked troubled. How can I help?" Marron asked.

They glanced at each other but it was Viv who spoke. "I told Vic what you told me." She paused. "Thing is I believe what you said," she stuttered to a stop.

"I see, so Vic you're not sure what to believe?" Marron ventured.

"Oh no, I believe what you say. It's just…" he hesitated then blurted, "she wants to send Mort away with you. Says town could be in trouble. I just can't believe it and I don't like it. Could be we're sending him into harm's way. Surely we're safest here behind our walls?"

Marron was taken aback. They wanted to send Morten with her. What with Mercy, Lucky and Stama tagging along she was starting to feel like things were getting out of control.

Sitting on the edge of Nihm's bed to think she could see their worried faces in her periphery and felt the tension between them. They had clearly argued.

"Have you discussed this with Morten?" Marron asked.

"Aye, that she did," Vic muttered angrily. "Told him to take you to Rivercross to help with Nihm," he said.

"And you don't agree." Marron nodded in understanding.

"It's for his own good, Vic," his wife said.

"Agh, you play on the boy's feelings for the girl." He glanced at Marron. "Sorry Marron, but you must know the lad is a bit sweet on your Nihm," he apologised.

"I know they're friends," Marron agreed. "Whether anything comes of it is not for me to say."

"Oh Vic, what harm could it do for Mort to take a trip to Rivercross?" Viv rounded on him. "It'll take him out of harm's way if there's trouble and if not then no 'arm is done. He can collect some supplies at Rivercross and head back up once Lord Richard has sorted things out with these urak people."

"Look," Marron said, "I'll take Morten if he wants to come. But you must tell him the truth. He's a man and should make his own choices."

Viv coloured at Marron's words. Vic grunted his agreement but had the wisdom to say nothing.

"I'll tell him," Viv said. "Thank you, Marron." She turned and left the room.

Vic went to follow but held back when he got to the door. "Rumour is rife on the street about these urak and what with more people coming into town every hour from all over the north…" he grimaced then asked, "is it really that bad?"

"I don't know, Vic." Marron sighed, weary with it all. "It could be. It could be worse than we imagine. Maybe Lord Richard sends them packing and it comes to nothing," she said. "A wise man plans for the worst. You strike me as a wise man Vic."

He nodded his head at that but left looking as troubled as when he came in.

Mercy showed up a short while later carrying a tray with food and drink. They shared it, discussing the journey ahead.

"I have loaded the wagon and set the horses in their traces," Mercy told her. "I got a fair price for your cart and ponies in exchange."

"I'll miss them, had them since they were foals." Marron struggled to keep the melancholy from her voice.

"I've made a bed for Nihm. It's as comfortable as I can make it," Mercy carried on. Marron couldn't help thinking that it wasn't the same thing as being comfortable. But there was nothing to be done about it now.

"Even got your stuff out of the stable and packed." Mercy chuckled, the scar on her face suddenly crooked. "Those dogs of yours were having none of me. Thought Stama was going to be eaten. Turns out that lad, Morten, has a way with them. I hear tell he's coming with us?"

"That's up to him," Marron replied. "I said he'd be welcome if he so chose."

"Well, maybe he'll be useful," Mercy said, but she looked unconvinced. Seeing that Marron had finished with her food, she continued, "We should head off, my lady."

Marron rolled her eyes, "Please Mercy, the men are bad enough, don't you start with all that my lady stuff. Far as I know I have no noble blood in me. I am a simple woman; Marron will do just fine," she said.

Mercy laughed. "Right, but just so you know Marron, there's nothing simple about you."

Marron grinned, she knew a man who'd agree with that sentiment. Her mind drifted to Darion then and it was a few moments before she realised Mercy still talked.

"Sorry my dear, you were saying."

"Just that Nihm looks better. She's got her colour back," Mercy said. She felt guilty still about the casting she'd done earlier and shocked. The sundering of her casting had left no residual magic. It was like it had never happened.

"Shall I have Lucky carry Nihm to the wagon? If we're to leave I'd like to put as many leagues in as we can."

"Yes," Marron agreed. Scraping the chair back, she went to Nihm's side, feeling her brow one last time. Nihm's breathing was even and regular and the funny tick of her eyelids had gone. She looked so peaceful; if only she'd wake up.

Marron turned as she heard the door open and the heavy tread of Lucky.

"My Lady," he said.

Marron stepped aside to allow him access to Nihm. She caught the grin on Mercy's face and realised it was for Lucky's honorific and smiled back.

Lucky lifted Nihm from the bed. He was a big man and she looked like a child in his arms. Turning with his charge, he looked at the two women suspiciously. "What are you two grinning at?" he said.

"Just a private matter, don't you worry yourself about it," Mercy laughed.

Lucky grunted, convinced he was the butt of a joke somehow. He carried Nihm down to the courtyard, only banging her head once on the staircase wall for which he was soundly berated. Once outside, he handed her to Stama, who was waiting in the flatbed of the wagon, before hurrying back into the inn.

With a grunt of effort, Stama hefted Nihm managing to lay her gently enough on the bed they'd prepared.

Marron inspected the wagon. It was large, enough to fit Nihm's pallet and all their supplies in. She checked Nihm, making sure her daughter was as comfortable as could be. The sun had newly risen and the first light of day was still muted, the air heavy.

"Rain's coming," Marron said to no one in particular. She stowed her travel pack, then with Stama raised the cover over the wagon's ribbed frame so that Nihm would stay dry.

There was a sudden barking from the stables. The dogs had heard her. Morten, who'd been floating about nearby feeling awkward and unsure what to do, perked up at the noise.

"I'll fetch the dogs," he said and rushed off.

Shortly thereafter the dogs came bounding around the side of the wagon and leapt for Marron. She bent and ruffled their necks.

"Yes, I know, I'm sorry I've not been to see you."

They jumped and pranced around Marron. Ash and Snow must have gotten Nihm's scent, for they did a circuit of the wagon looking for her then jumped up onto the tailboard. They sniffed Nihm's prone body as if unsure who she was. Ash whined but Nihm did not respond. With another sniff for assurance, they turned circles on the straw bedding before finally curling up next to her.

Marron walked over to Vic and Viv who stood watching from the back door of the inn.

"Thank you both. I appreciate all that you've done for me and Nihm," she said, hugging a tearful Viv, "I'll keep an eye on Morten for you."

Viv nodded her thanks not trusting herself to speak. Vic replied for them both.

"I know you will, Marron. My lad is useful too, you'll see. Just keep him safe for us, eh!" He embraced Marron awkwardly, before standing back.

Lucky bustled up to them then, carrying Marron's travel chest. "Excuse me folks, coming through," he said easing himself sideways past them.

Stama and Mercy had mounted their horses and sat waiting whilst Lucky settled the travel chest in the back of the wagon, Ash and Snow watching him all the while.

Marron, never one for long goodbyes bade the innkeepers farewell. Hopping up onto the wagon seat she spared a glance at Nihm then let out a whistle. Maise and Thunder responded immediately, jumping up onto the wagon and startling Lucky, who swore. He grumped to himself as he latched the tailboard up before climbing into the saddle of his giant destrier.

Morten hugged his parents goodbye. Both Vic and Viv bombarded him with last-minute instructions and it was all he could do to extricate himself. Finally, with a last embrace, he waved them goodbye. Climbing aboard the wagon he took the reins and looked expectantly at Marron, excited.

"Whenever you're ready," Marron said.

Morten released the wheel brake and gave the reins a flick. They were off.

Chapter 44 : The Redford Road

Bandock Hills, The Rivers

Amos watched the carnage in silence. One of the houses burned fiercely; smoke billowing into the air in thick black plumes. Under its dirty blanket, people lay dead. None moved, none cried out, blood was everywhere. Some had run, some fought but all had died, hacked to pieces. Not just men either, but women and children too, the slaughter indiscriminate.

They'd arrived too late to see it happen, too late to see the survivors rounded up and herded away to the northeast. The rain that had passed through earlier had delayed them; fierce and torrential, they'd been forced to take shelter in a wooded grove to wait it out. Otherwise, chances were they'd have found the village before the urak. Probably would be lying there among the dead.

The three men had seen much in their lives but nothing prepared them for what they witnessed below. From their vantage point on a wooded hilltop above the village, urak moved. The dead were gathered, dragged unceremoniously to the village centre. There, a group of smaller urak set about with hooks and knives butchering the bodies. They were efficient as they gutted the dead before harvesting them, removing the heart, kidney and liver. The carcasses were then dragged away and stacked in a pile. It was nauseating to watch.

Amos took a slug of water, his mouth dry. He assessed their number to be close to five hundred. Over the past hour, many had moved off in smaller parties, out into the countryside. The smudge of smoke in the distance evidence that this was not the only village that suffered.

Something was happening below, had been since they'd arrived, but Amos sensed it was nearing an end. A group of around twenty urak had laboured, smashing one of the stone and daub houses to pieces until it was nothing but a pile of stone, timber and thatch. A long shallow trough had been gouged out of the soft ground and at first, he thought they meant to bury the dead. They hadn't. Instead, they dragged the stone onto the bared soil and covered it with the thatch. This they set on fire, the smoke adding to the cloud already above. Onto the fire they threw wood; timbers and branches the villagers had gathered for their hearths. The urak left it blazing away, laughing and jostling each other.

An urak turned up shortly afterwards, larger than any they'd yet seen; shoulders broad, chest and arms rippling with muscle. He wore his hair in a topknot with braids falling down his back, his face marked red with war paint. He was flanked by two equally fierce-looking urak and it was clear he was angry. He gesticulated wildly and they could hear his deep guttural barking from where they lay.

"He don't look none too happy," Jobe whispered.

"Ain't none of us happy," Jerkze muttered.

Amos agreed but said nothing. The harvesting of the villagers had been harrowing to witness and he felt sickened by what he saw. Jobe tended to talk when he was stressed; hell he liked to talk whatever. Amos glared and Jobe nodded, getting the message and lapsing into silence.

The urak below moved off, spreading out and checking the homes in the village. They ransacked them carrying out anything of use. They heard the mewling cry of a child until abruptly it ceased, cut-off mid cry. They watched in growing anger as an urak appeared from one of the smaller homes, a dead child thrown over its shoulder. It walked to the butchers and dropped the child at their feet, grunting and laughing with them.

Amos felt his blood stir; his hand gripped his bow as he seethed in helpless rage. Jerkze glanced across and quietly reached over to grip his arm. Only then did Amos realise he held an arrow to his bowstring. Sighing to himself, forcing his arm to relax, he returned the arrow to his quiver.

The trench fire had guttered down to ash and small flames. The urak started to haul the pile of dead to the trench, half throwing, half laying the bodies in it. Next, they laid thatch over the top, igniting and flaming in places, before piling earth and dirt from the trench over the top. It was morbidly fascinating to watch, even as the nauseous waft of burnt hair and flesh made its way to them on the wind.

"What are they doing?" Jobe whispered to Amos.

Amos wasn't sure. It was Jerkze that answered.

"It's an oven of sorts, I think." He glared at the urak as the earth was piled into a mound, tendrils of smoke escaping through cracks and gaps. "I heard tell of tribes over the western seas that cook their food in the ground. Maybe this is the same?" he thought out loud.

"We need to move," Amos hissed. The day was old and the sun only an hour or so from the horizon. "Been here too long,"

Backing away from their vantage point they moved deeper into the treeline. Amos was worried. They were just a day from Thorsten, having followed the west bank of the Oust. They couldn't take the road back; it was likely the urak raiders that moved out earlier followed it themselves. No, they'd have to track to the west and then cut south, back to Thorsten, and hope they could make it before the urak arrived in any sort of numbers; they were much closer than expected.

The three men gathered their horses from where they'd tied them and headed west. They followed below the ridgeline of the hill they were on, staying under the cover the trees provided.

Ahead, the ground rolled gently away, a mix of marsh and grassland in the dells and valleys and wood on the hillsides. Wilderness, not much good for farming Amos thought. He saw no sign of habitation, reinforcing his assessment.

Spurred on by the grizzly scenes they had witnessed they moved swiftly westward with nothing but hard ground and a rough ride ahead of them.

Chapter 45 : Quarry

Outside Thorsten, The Rivers

Sand's eyes were black. If anyone looked closely enough they would see the black, swirling and eddying like smoke in a glass.

A sense of dread and darkness filled him as it always did now. The essence of the Morhudrim was within, malign and sinister; controlling him, tainting his mind and actions, feeding off his anger, hate, and fear like a parasite. A small part of him existed still, buried deep in the recesses of his mind. Looking out from its prison, watching him, judging him, screaming at him to wake and end the nightmare. But it was powerless; a breath of wind against a storm.

Sand detested himself, what little there was left anyway. His weakness and loathing sat in his mind like poisoned thorns.

His sense of the Morhudrim was strong and overriding despite only holding a fraction of its essence. He could feel Krol through the dark one, just as the urak could feel him. But it was the Morhudrim that controlled them both, as it did now. He felt sudden anger and fear from it.

Jagged pain erupted in his head like shards of glass and he slumped forward over his horse. His knees reflexively gripping hard to prevent himself from rolling out of the saddle and onto the ground. His eyes shut tight; everything blinding white and agony. Then, abruptly it was gone, replaced by a single thought. I fear nothing mortal.

A picture formed in his head, like a memory. It was of a covered wagon pulled by two horses. A woman and a man sat on the bench seat, rain lashing down upon them, the same rain that had drenched him earlier. Sand sensed the malevolent taint of the other building inside him, growing until it's dark intensity bludgeoned all thought and reason from his mind. When it receded, he felt a new purpose course through him.

The inky blackness cleared from his eyes and Sand righted himself in the saddle, back straight. He could feel his quarry to the east, dragging on him, drawing him on.

He sat at a crossroad. To the west, out across the river and on the rising ground, was the distant outline of Thorsten. Its walls looked tall and formidable, the remnants of the earlier storm receding above them heading away south and west.

Silently, Sand turned his horse away from the town taking instead the road to Rivercross and spurred his mount into a canter.

Chapter 46 : New Companions

Near Mappels-on-Oust, The Rivers

Morten liked dogs, got on with most animals really. Even so, there was something disquieting about seeing the two large wolfdogs curled up in the back of the wagon. They looked more wolf than dog, one black the other a dirty white. Snow lay at Nihm's feet, Ash by her side.

At least she's warm, Morten thought, pulling his cloak tight around his chilled body. Looking at her lying there he felt immediate guilt. Nihm looked so helpless and vulnerable; at least she would do if not for the dogs.

Earlier, they'd eyed him warily when he had gone in the back for their rain covers and he'd felt an itching between his shoulder blades at their stare. Morten had wanted to check on Nihm but the quiet rumbling they'd given when he strayed too near was warning enough. It would be like trying to take a bone from them, he thought. He'd seen it before and was wise enough to leave things be.

Nihm had not moved since they'd left Thorsten. She lay in the same position they had set her in. Marron checked on her often. Shooing the dogs away like misbehaving pups, she would gently lift Nihm's head and feed her water. The first few times Morten had asked how she was doing, but seeing the distress in Marron's eyes when he did so made him keep his peace soon after.

The rain stopped by mid-morning, the storm moving away to the south and west. The cold breeze the storm brought with it remained however and the sun was still obscured in cloud.

Mercy rode up ahead with the big man, Lucky. It was an odd party they made but Morten was thankful they were with them. The Grim lay not far off. Lawless and rough, the Grimmers often raided the Great North Road that skirted the marshlands and wolds they called home.

His three new companions wore hardened leather and were all armed. They looked competent and martial and moved with the casual assurance of craftsmen that knew their trade.

Mercy led them and looked formidable, with a cloth wrapped staff across her back and sword at her hip. She sat her horse well, her dark leather cuirass already looking dry. Morten knew should he look behind, that Stama, the final member of their party rode as a rearguard behind the wagon.

Morten had never learned arms, had no need as an innkeeper's son. He had a wooden cosh in his pack but in truth had never used it. When folk got too rowdy at the inn it was because they'd drunk too much and his Da had a way of dealing with them that usually found them outside and stumbling home. He'd only ever seen his Da bring his cosh out once.

Reflecting on his companions, Morten felt a bit useless. Even the dogs were more useful than him. The older two ranged about the wagon, whilst Nihm's guarded her. What did he bring? A knife he used to whittle with when he was bored. If they ran into any urak or Grimmers he'd be worse than useless, he'd be a burden.

Despite feeling sorry for himself, Morten found he was excited. He was travelling the road with folk he knew little about. With a girl, a woman, he corrected, who he liked. That she was sick and helpless only made him feel more protective if anything. No, this wasn't the daily drudge he was used to. This was high adventure.

The wagon rumbled along, slow but steady, eating up the leagues and Morten found he had plenty of time to think.

His mind drifted to his folks and to earlier that day. Passing through town and out of Riversgate that morning, he'd felt a sense of unease. The place was crowded with people, many having nowhere to stay except in their wagons or under makeshift tents. He'd never seen the town like it before and was worried for his Ma and Da left behind in it all.

The day remained sullen and overcast. The road they travelled followed the River Oust. To the south of the river were low-lying grasslands. He knew all too well that soon the grasslands would turn marshy, full of water pools and bogs. It would be the start of the Grim Marsh.

The Grim, as it was known, was treacherous. Its watercourses and pools were ever-changing whenever the river was high or flooded, water seeping into the land. Many who braved its waterways and stinking mud banks perished, never to be seen again. The marsh extended for many leagues to the south until the land rose once again to the Grimwolds, a collection of rolling foothills of grass, bush and wood.

The Grimwolds were notorious, full of bandits and brigands who chose to live outside the king's law. The Black Crow and local lords often lead expeditions into its depths but its interior was hard to navigate, its terrain difficult to cross. For the degenerates and miscreants that lived there and knew its ways, these incursions posed no credible threat.

This part of the Great North Road, oft called the Grim Road by the locals, tracked east following the northern bank of the Oust River. The towns and villages along its route tended to the higher ground to the north. Local counts and lords kept men at arms and patrolled the road to keep it safe from the Grimmers, but raids were still known to happen.

Being an innkeeper's son had its benefits; gossip and rumour being one of them. He'd overheard complaint from more than one trader that High Lord Twyford's call to arms for his Westlands campaign meant fewer patrols than normal. Travelling the road would be more dangerous than usual. So despite his feelings of inadequacy, or because of them, he wasn't sure which, he was thankful for the added company.

Since the rain eased, they had made good time. The road had more than a few travellers on it and most were headed eastward. As well, boats and barges plied the river, laden with people all headed for Fallston to the southeast. It seemed others had the same idea to head away from trouble, something the Black Crow had encouraged.

* * *

The sun was close to setting and the moons just visible behind the breaking cloud when Mercy announced they would camp. The last village, Mappels on Oust, they'd left behind an hour past and it had been an eerie experience. The village had been mostly deserted apart from a few holdouts that refused the Black Crow's orders to move to Thorsten or head south to Rivercross.

They had argued then, Marron wanting Nihm in a bed and made comfortable, Mercy demanding they put more leagues under them. In the end, Mercy had swayed Marron. If urak were coming they would have scout parties out and a village would be a lodestone to them.

Morten unhitched the horses from the wagon. Rubbing them down, he checked their flanks and hocks and finally their hooves for any stones or cuts.

Satisfied, he staked them in the grass near the camp where they could feed and made sure they had water.

The river was away to the south and Stama and Lucky headed towards it, lines in hand, to try their luck at catching dinner, or so they'd said. More like to get out of work, Morten thought building the fire up and wishing they'd asked him to go. He'd not fished in a while but considered himself adept.

At least I'm good for something, Morten groused to himself as he set up camp. Grabbing water skins out the back of the wagon, he headed to the river to fill them.

One of the dogs, Thunder, trailed after him and he was glad of the company. He chatted to the big dog more for something to do than any other reason. Admittedly, Thunder was not very talkative but he made a fine listener and seemed to like it well enough.

Morten saw no sign of Lucky or Stama when he reached the river-side but their banter drifted down from further upstream and around the river's bend. Filling the skins, Morten slung them over his shoulder before trudging back to camp. He filled several kettle pans with the water and set them over the fire to boil.

A short time later, in the half-light of the tri moons, Morten heard the two fishermen returning and turned to watch their approach.

"I told ya, it's all in the wrist man. You need to flick it just so," Lucky said, whirling and snapping his hand forward to illustrate his point. In his other hand, he held three trout. Next to him ambled Stama carrying the lines and looking unimpressed.

"Just luck man that's all," he muttered back.

"Aye, Lucky in name, Lucky in life!" The big man laughed, pounding his friend on the back.

Stama winced. "Aye, well you caught 'em, you can cook em," he said as they walked into camp.

"Nah, the lad will cook em, won't yeh, lad?" Lucky blustered, turning to Morten.

Morten was about to acquiesce, he liked cooking and wanted to feel useful, but Marron interjected.

"He's not a servant, Mr Lucson, however you couch your order." She stared up at him from her seat by the fire. In her hand was a pot in which she was boiling something. Her eyes were piercing.

"Eh, sorry my lady?" Lucky stammered. "Have I caused offence?" All banter was suddenly gone.

Morten saw Mercy watching silently from the other side of the campfire. Was that a hint of a smile on her face? He wasn't sure, her scar made it hard to distinguish smile from frown sometimes and it was too dark to see her eyes clearly.

An uncomfortable quiet filled the space. He realised Marron was right. That she had seen it and acted upon it with all her other worries moved him beyond words. Still, he liked these men and wanted to be accepted. He thought for a moment and then half-smiled to himself.

"Might I propose a trade?" Morten said to Lucky.

"And what trade is that?" Lucky asked.

"I'll skin and cook your fish if you'll show me how to use a sword," he said.

Lucky pondered a while considering Morten's offer.

"I'll give you a lesson, lad. The big man here ain't too articulate for teaching much of anything, other than drinking ale maybe," Stama offered.

"Oi, don't listen to him none. He's all fancy-dancy with his blade. Near as tickle you to death with it," Lucky retorted. "Nah, yer a tall lad. Power over style I reckon will suit you best."

"All right, Luck," Stama laughed. He turned to Morten. "When you've had enough of the beast let me know and I'll show you a few things," he said.

Morten thanked Stama, watching as he wound the lines up and tied them neatly so they wouldn't tangle before stowing them away. He turned to Marron. "Thank you, my Lady," Morten said.

Marron sighed, glanced briefly at Mercy, then with a ghost of a smile, replied. "Don't you start with all that nonsense, Morten, I'm not a Lady; Marron will do just fine."

Mercy chuckled. A fish suddenly slapped against Morten's cheek, cold, wet and stinking. He jumped, stumbling away.

"First lesson lad, be aware of what is going on around you at all times," Lucky told him. He held his hand out and Morten gripped it reluctantly and they shook. Lucky handed him the fish. "Well, guess you better get on with it, lad."

"It's Morten," he replied, emboldened.

Lucky nodded his shaggy head sagely. "Aye lad, I guess it is." He grinned. "Come, I'll give ya a hand. Show an old soldier how not to burn his fish, eh!"

It turned out Lucky was pretty good at cooking, and that Morten was the one doing the learning. The fish were filleted and rubbed down with a little salt and seasoning. Then, Lucky showed him how to thread the meat onto a sharpened stick, the skin and scales wrapped around to seal the soft flesh inside. Morten was a quick study and set about preparing the other two fish.

After their meal was done, Lucky walked off into a nearby wood with a hatchet axe and returned a short time later with two stout wooden poles, bark stripped and mostly straight. Morten looked at them, not impressed with what he saw.

"I thought you were going to teach me how to use a sword," he grumbled.

"Yeah, well I've no sparring swords with me and I'll not be blunting my blade for a bit of sport," Lucky replied. "Besides, the staff is a great weapon." He tossed one of the poles to Morten who bruised a finger, fumbling the catch. Red-faced, he scooped it up from where it lay on the ground.

Lucky's staff swung round and hit Morten with a loud thwack. He shot up at the sudden pain searing his buttocks. Feeling his blood boil, anger and embarrassment warring across his face, Morten glared at Lucky.

"Staff has got great reach," Lucky said, unperturbed. He swung his pole around in an easy arc to illustrate his point.

"It's great at blocking." He snapped it out in front of him as if to parry a blow. Morten watched, still mad but his interest piqued nevertheless. His blood cooled a little as Lucky went through several different stances illustrating each one in the light of the fire amid the fading gloom.

"A sword will cut straight through it though," Morten said, unconvinced. A line of fire throbbed across his backside still and his mood was surly.

"Well yeah, these staves sure. But a metal-capped hardwood staff, now that's a different story." Lucky sniffed. "Still, they'll do for now so stop yer moaning, Red. You want ta train or not?"

He did. Morten spent the next hour clacking away with Lucky. He was taught how to hold the staff and how to move it. Lucky got him practising various blocks, side blocks, head blocks and leg blocks.

Moving slowly, Lucky would swing his staff in a prescribed fashion allowing Morten to block each one. The pattern was the same and as they got into a rhythm Lucky would speed his strikes up. Morten followed his mind and muscles keeping up as the tempo increased.

Lucky stepped back. Morten took a deep breath, puffed but pleased with himself. It was tiring and his arms ached, but it was the rewarding ache of effort well spent. He felt… worthwhile. Not that an hour with a stave changed much but still, he was on the path and the lesson felt empowering.

"Good. Now that was a simple exercise. It didn't require you to move your feet much or do much of anything," Lucky said. His breathing was easy and he grinned as he spoke. "Still, it was a good effort and those basic blocks are a good foundation to build on. It's dark. Tomorrow, we'll start again, only I'll show you how to move your feet and body because a fight is a fluid thing, ever-changing. If'n you can remember those blocks and move smoothly then you'll be in great shape, Red."

"When will you teach me how to attack?" Morten asked, eager to learn more. He liked Lucky; found he had an easy manner about him and a simple way of explaining things.

"When I think you're ready," Lucky replied. "First, you need to learn defence. Practise those blocks. Practise them hard so that they're second nature to you. Then when you need them your thoughts and fears won't cloud your actions." Lucky was in full flow now and Morten sensed he'd enjoyed the teaching.

"The trickiest thing is learning when and how to switch between defence to attack and back again. So lad, first things first, defence." Lucky patted Morten on the shoulder with a beefy hand as they wandered to the campfire.

Mercy and Stama had practised as well but had finished some time before. Marron had watched them all with interest and as Morten took a seat beside her said. "I need to hone my swordplay. It's been too long since I last swung a blade." She looked to Stama as she spoke.

"I would be happy to train with you, Lady Marron," Stama responded confidently.

"Tomorrow then, first light?" Marron replied her voice flat. She hadn't smiled much these last few days, but then she'd not had much to smile about.

"Marron, would you mind if I looked in on Nihm," Morten asked nervously, worried he might be overstepping some boundary.

"That's thoughtful of you, Morten," Marron replied. A sad smile flittered across her face.

"Er, it's just Nihm's dogs are a bit protective," Morten said, feeling a bit stupid.

Marron twisted to face the wagon and whistled. A moment later the two dogs bounded out and ran to her side.

"Let's get you some food." Marron ruffled their necks affectionately. She glanced at Morten pointedly then stood. Thunder and Maise suddenly materialised out of the darkness behind her.

"Thanks," Morten said, jumping up. Hurrying to the wagon, he clambered up the tailboard and into the back.

A lamp was hooked over the frame by the bench seat shedding a soft light over the interior. Morten knelt beside Nihm and stared, drinking in the sight of her, his heart beating fiercely in his chest. He felt guilty as if intruding somehow. Like he'd stolen into her room whilst she slept and at any moment she would open her eyes, see him there and ask what the hells he was doing.

Taking one of her hands, Morten held it, feeling its warmth and duality. Soft but hard in places, callouses, and hard skin over fingers and palm. It was the hand of someone used to hard work.

"Nihm!" he whispered. "Nihm, it's time for you to wake." Morten felt silly but found he didn't care.

"Come on now. We're worried about you." He paused… then forced himself to continue.

"I'm worried about you. Please Nihm," he begged.

She didn't answer. She looked so peaceful, her breathing easy, her chest rising and falling gently. Watching her, Morten traced the line of her neck up to her jaw. Then to her lips and slightly crooked nose and finally to her brown, green flecked eyes. His mouth hung open as the realisation suddenly hit. Nihm watched him back.

Her eyes blinked.

"Wait here Nihm, I'm with you," Morten stammered, then turning his head to the front of the wagon.

"MARRON!"

Chapter 47 : Assimilating

Near Mappels-on-Oust, The Rivers

It was a weird sensation. Whilst Nihm could not feel Sai, she still felt a connection. She could think of Sai and Sai was there. She wondered more than once if she'd gone mad; if this was all just a delusion she'd created. And yet, though she didn't understand the how of it, she knew this was real. Sai was so different, so alien from anything she had known or experienced. How could it be a dream?

Nihm had a sense of Sai and in that sense, there was no artifice, no emotion, no nothing really. It was strange and difficult with no anchor point. Cut off from external stimulus, her whole world had reduced to herself as if she floated in a bubble that was neither dark nor light but just, opaque nothingness. She was alone, with just her thoughts and Sai.

What was Sai? How was it inside her, part of her? What was it doing? These were all questions she had asked and Sai had answered. The problem was she didn't understand the answers.

Nihm relived her memories, memories she had forgotten and some she didn't even remember having; memories from being a babe and growing up at the homestead. They played out in her head clearer than she had ever known them. It felt like she was watching herself as she grew, observing from a different perspective.

Nihm saw all the falls and the fun, the laughter and the tears, the tantrums and the petulance. She felt love and safety, of being and belonging. It was herself, who she was.

Her memories played out in her head. She had time. Had nothing else to do trapped as she was in her mind. She relived her every moment, with Darion, teaching her how to hunt and fish; how to track in the woods and field; how to read the stars and skin a deer. He and Marron had taught her to fight as well; sword, knife and bow. They were good too; she could tell from the ease and poise of their movements that they were passing on lessons they'd mastered themselves long ago.

Marron taught her herbs and plants and how to use them; how to bind a wound and drain a poison; how to stitch a boot and head alike. She taught her to read, oh how she loved to read. The stories and histories captured her imagination and helped shape her vision of the world. A world she had experienced nothing of. A world she was isolated from.

Loneliness, Nihm had no childhood friends. The Encomas, their closest neighbours lived a full day to the south. She saw little of them and knew them hardly at all. Her only experience of civilisation was Thorsten, two sometimes three times a year. Nihm saw she was not like other children. She had lost much without knowing there was anything to lose.

Her thoughts flashed briefly to Annabelle, little skinny Annabelle with the smudged face, peeking out of the hayloft at the Broken Axe. It would have been nice to have had a friend to grow up with, play with.

Ah, but she had learned so much, seen so much, experienced so much. Playing her memories back she saw it all. The furtive glances her mother and father gave each other, looks she thought nothing of at the time but seeing them again in her mind told her much. Their love, their strength and self-belief, and even their worry, she saw it all through adult eyes. Realised they had sacrificed much for each other, for her… and for the Order.

The Order. That had been a shock and a revelation all at once and it explained much to Nihm. That Marron and Darion were of the Order meant they lived in the wilds because that was where the Order sent them.

But why? There was nothing here except the Old Forest, the Darkwood some of her books named it and she liked the name, made it sound more exciting and dangerous. Then there were the Blue Sky Lakes and grasslands past the forest and then mountains. There was nothing to be here for, nothing except the ilfanum. Was that why they were sent, for the ilf? No, that wasn't right.

The urak, it was what started all of this. The past weeks played through Nihm's mind, her feelings and emotions riding along with her. She saw things through a different perspective it seemed; assessing, analysing, calculating.

She saw Morten, young, not much older than her; his face and smile. She felt… curious, rather than self-conscious. She saw him in the stable, the flush on his cheeks, his stance, his manner, his words. In the inn, the furtive glances he gave her. He liked her, a different kind of revelation. Interesting, she felt her pulse quicken, felt her own fear and excitement.

She saw again the figure step from the alley, cloaked and hooded; his face dark, his eyes dead. Eyes she would never forget. She felt herself moving as the dagger arced through the air. Slow, too slow. Time slowed, the knife slowed, her falling body slowed. The result was the same. Then voices and blurred faces, Marron was there and Morten.

She opened her eyes, blinked. Morten was still there. He was holding her hand and talking. What was he saying? He looked shocked. Why can't I feel my hand?

<*Assimilation is ongoing,*> Sai explained.

<*I can see,*> Nihm blinked her eyelids, <*and blink.*>

<*Yes. You have motor control of your apertures. Your eyelids,*> Sai said.

<*Why can't I hear?*> she thought. Where was she? What was Morten doing? The image of him was still fresh in her mind and here he was before her; holding her hand of all things.

<*Assimilation is ongoing,*> Sai repeated.

<*Can't you hurry it up?*> Nihm thought impatiently.

<*Assimilation is almost complete. Please remain calm.*>

<*I am calm damn you!*> Nihm shouted. She blinked and could see Morten staring at her.

"What did you say, Nihm?" he mouthed.

He gripped her hand and whilst Nihm couldn't hear him, she could feel pain. It was shooting up her fingers and palm and into her arm, glorious pain. Pain that was really starting to hurt now.

"Ow, that is hurting, Morten," she tried saying. The words sounded okay in her head but all she heard was a jumble of noise as if speaking underwater. The pain was intense. Why was he holding her hand so damn hard?

<*What the hells!*> The pain rose higher still. <*Sai, what's happening?*>

<*Calibrating. One moment,*> Sai replied calmly.

<*Caliwhat?*> The pain continued to rise. Then, suddenly it was… better… less, then just warmth. She could feel Morten's fingers gripping her hand lightly. His face hovered over her and she saw right up his nostrils.

"You need to blow your nose, Morten," she said, feeling suddenly joyous.

"I can't understand you, Nihm. But you're all right. You're safe. Look, Marron is here," He let her hand go as he was suddenly thrust aside.

Marron's face appeared above her. Nihm blinked, drinking in the sight. Her mother had dark shadows under her eyes. Then, Marron was hugging her and crying.

Pain lanced through Nihm's body.

<*For fucks sake Sai, sort this caliwhat thing out, will you? I'm in agony here,*> she cried.

<*One moment,*> Sai replied. Nihm gritted her teeth. I can grit my teeth she thought as the pain ratcheted up. Her jaws ached as agony flared from all over.

<*By the Trinity!*> It was excruciating. Stabbing pain flared in her brain. Through it, she wept tears, part of her marvelled at them whilst the rest of her shrieked. Then, blessedly it was less… it was bearable… then it was okay… everything was okay. Everything was going to be fine.

<*Calibration of the upper body is complete,*> Sai announced.

Marron was crying and talking to her all at once. "Nihm, Nihm are you okay? How do you feel?"

She felt exhausted is how she felt, the sound suddenly crisp and clear. But Nihm had no time to marvel at the return of her hearing as her Ma's question sunk into her. The pain had been debilitating, draining but she was okay only hungry… suddenly very hungry.

"I'm okay, Ma. But I'm starving," she said but the words didn't come out right and sounded like gibberish.

<*Sai, why do I sound like a babbling moron?*> she demanded, frustrated.

<*Sai does not know what a babbling moron sounds like. But your vocal cords need calibrating as will much of the rest of your body,*> Sai offered.

"Nihm, love, I don't understand you. Can you blink your eyes if you understand me?" Marron asked.

Nihm blinked her eyes and was rewarded with Marron's beaming smile. A shaggy head pushed into view and Marron snapped at Ash. "Get back you great furball, you can see her later. Go on with you." She pushed the wolfdog away.

<*Sai, you need to stop referring to yourself when you talk. It's uncomfortable to hear. Say I, not Sai, got it?*> Nihm said. Sai's habit had been bugging her for a while now.

<*I understand,*> Sai replied.

<*Good, now by vocal cords you mean my voice right? And I don't understand what calibrating is,*> Nihm queried.

<*Yes, your vocal cords produce your sound, your voice; a primitive but effective means of communication. Calibration is a process of configuration or tuning,*> Sai supplied an image of Darion stringing a bow. It was vivid because Nihm had lived it. A lost memory now clearly recalled.

"Dig the heel of your bow into the arch of your foot like so and lean on it," Darion said illustrating. "If you just string the bow then it's not taut enough. Any arrow you fire will not travel much past its own length." Nihm watched her eight-year-old self with a short bow emulating her Da, leaning and arching the limbs of the bow.

"That's it, Nihm, you've got it. The secret though is getting the right amount of bend on the bow. Too much and the bowstring is too tight; it can damage the bow and make it difficult to draw. Let the limbs of the bow do the work. You need just enough bend so you can slip the bowstring on and tie it off. See?" He showed her. The memory faded.

<*Okay, I think I get it,*> Nihm said, feeling disconsolate. Understanding that what Sai showed her was simple compared to what she needed to do. <*You're saying I have to learn how to walk and talk, hold a cup even.*>

<*Yes,*> Sai said, pleased.

Pleased, an emotion. Something she had not felt from Sai before. <*Are you pleased, Sai? Why?*>

<*Having assimilated your memories, I observed that your parents express pleasure when you achieve a goal they set you. This induces a positive reaction and better*

performance. I thought I might encourage you in the same manner. Did I do it incorrectly? Do you feel unstimulated?> Sai asked.

<*No, no, that was good Sai. Well done,*> She grinned.

"Nihm, are you in pain?" Marron cried, feeling her daughter's brow. "Blink if you're in pain."

<*I guess I need to work on my smile,*> Nihm thought. She didn't blink.

"Good, I think. You do understand me, don't you Nihm?" Marron asked.

Nihm blinked, frustrated. At least with Sai, the communication was instantaneous, their previous discussion having lasted no more than a breath. When was Marron going to feed her?

"Good. I'm going to give you some water, okay?" Marron said.

Nihm blinked and saw Marron smile in response. She felt her Ma squeeze an arm about her shoulders and lift her gently. Nihm opened her mouth slowly, taking pleasure in that simple movement. At least it didn't blow her head off in agony this time.

Her Ma raised a cup to her lips and dribbled water into her. She felt the coolness of it in her mouth and swallowed it automatically. She felt like a babe as Marron gave her little drops, not wanting to choke her. It felt good to drink.

"Now, you must eat, Nihm. Can you eat anything?" Marron asked.

Nihm blinked her eyes several times and Marron laughed. "Good girl, you always had a good appetite."

A woman spoke in the background, the voice familiar. "I'll get you some broth, Marron," the voice said.

<*Mercy,*> supplied Sai. Ah yes, that was it, Mercy. So she was with Marron still. How long had she been out for?

<*By your time calendar: 2 days, 23 hours and 8.23 minutes approximately. Counting from my self-awareness,*> Sai replied.

<*I've been out for three days!*> Nihm was shocked. No wonder she was starving.

Chapter 48 : Santranta's Boil

Eagles Watch, The Rivers

Amos and his men moved with a sense of urgency upon them after what they had witnessed. They travelled hard after leaving the wrecked village behind, trying to put as many leagues in as they could. But progress slowed as the terrain grew difficult. The wooded hillside turned dense with undergrowth and proved hard to traverse by horse.

As darkness fell they moved lower into the valleys, skirting the woodland to make more time. Amos knew it was a risk. The sky was clear and the tri moons reflected a hazy light making them easier to spot. But it also gave much-needed light for them to travel by. Time was the enemy, the risk necessary.

They found a deer trail running west and followed it, travelling well. Amos had a map of the Northern Rivers and unfurled it whenever they stopped to water and rest the horses. The rolling hills and valleys would soon end, turning to grassland. There would likely be holdsteads out there, people living on the edge of the wilds.

At one such stop, Amos debated whether to turn south for Thorsten once they cleared the hills but his eye was drawn to a dimple on his map. A hillock rising out of the plains called Santranta's Boil, a colourful description that amused him. It was the notation next to it though that interested him. Eagles Watch, an ancient tower long-abandoned sat upon the Boil. If he could reach it then it would afford him views for ten, twenty leagues. If a war host were coming he would surely see it.

Amos glanced at Jerkze and Jobe thinking. Talk was dangerous, sound carried at night in the valleys and the two men were quiet, lost in their own reflection.

His mind resolved, he would make for the Boil but send the two of them back to Thorsten. One could scout from Eagle's Watch as easily as three.

Watching his men, Amos couldn't stop the thought that they'd been eight setting out all those many months back. His father, concerned with happenings in the Rivers, had charged him to investigate matters. Amos had relished the chance.

That he'd left Rivercross was self-indulgent. Amos saw that now. Some boyhood fancy to travel the northern borders, see the wilds and maybe glimpse the

Torns, just so he could say he'd done it. As well, to gaze upon the ilf lands would be a tale they could all recount in their dotage, sat around their hearth fires drinking ale and reliving glory days gone by.

Now they were three. His mind turned to Silver and the boy, Seb and guilt lay heavy upon him. No glory days for them to talk of in their old age and he was to blame. Too damn cocksure. He'd treated the matter at the inn like a game and they'd paid the price for it.

Seb, he knew little of. The boy's family were staunch allies of the Duncans and he'd been asked to take Seb along to season him. He'd agreed readily enough.

Silver on the other hand, argh Silver, gods damn-it. Silver had been a young sword master when first they'd met. He had trained Amos for a year before joining him and swearing to the Duncans. They became fast friends, one of the few he trusted. A man he'd known all his adult life dead and gone, because I sent him out ill-prepared, assuming we were better than everyone else. By the gods may I be damned, he cursed again.

The only consolation in all this was that his sister Mercy was safely away. She was highly capable, he had no doubts about that but he knew things were about to get a whole lot worse. Better she was out of it, Lucky and Stama too.

"Ain't no fucking way, Boss," Jobe responded when Amos broke the news. "You ain't getting rid of us that easy," he hissed, keeping his voice low. Jerkze nodded his agreement.

"Look, there's no sense us all going. We need to get word to the Black Crow of what we've seen," Amos whispered back.

"The Crow ain't sitting there waiting on you for news, Amos. He'll know by now what's coming. Has his scouts and hunters out," Jerkze reasoned back. "As I recall, this was about you seeing with your own eyes what threat the urak pose. The way I see things you done that. Seen more an we need. I figure it's time to go."

Jerkze could see his words hit home, saw Amos consider them. Hell, he probably even agreed with him. But damn him for a stubborn assed mule, he knew by the man's stance he was going anyway.

Jerkze shrugged. "If'n ya think we need to go to this watchtower it makes sense for Jobe or me to go, not you."

Damn him, damn them both, thought Amos. He hadn't really expected anything less from them. He should've known better and he grudgingly conceded Jerkze's reasoning was sounder than his own. He knew this was a battle he wouldn't win. If he ordered them south, screamed at them, they'd disobey him. It's what he would do. So did he take them south or west?

"The urak are coming, we know that," Amos stated. "But we have no idea what we're facing, how many. Is it an incursion or an invasion? I figure we need to know." He tapped his finger on the map over the Boil. "Figure this is as good a place as any to find out for sure."

They peered over his shoulder at the map. Neither of them looked happy or convinced but they stood together.

"Best get it done then," Jobe said, a grim but resolute look on his face.

Jerkze patted his friend on the back saying nothing. Turning, he cinched his saddle, tightening it for the ride ahead.

* * *

The three men cleared the foothills and valleys shortly past midnight. They were tired and their horses weary but they had no time to rest. The moons gave enough light to see by on the grassy plains and they passed several abandoned holdsteads, little more than dark lumps on the landscape, and stopped at one to water the horses. The buildings when they checked them had been cleared out and ransacked. Bloodstains on floors and walls told their tale, giving a clear warning to them, if they still needed any, that this was hostile territory.

As they rode, they saw the outline of Santranta's Boil as a black smudge against a dark background. Even so, they were surprised when the ground suddenly started to rise. The Boil turned out to be a massive rock stuck up out of the ground, not a hillock at all. It must have been immense but in the darkness, it was hard to take it all in.

They found the start of a rough-hewn path on its southern flank. A path not meant for horses. Jerkze and Jobe drew lots. Jerkze lost and ended up tending the horses whilst the other two climbed the path.

It proved a tricky ascent in the dark and was steep in places requiring them to scramble over rocks and narrow ledges as the path snaked up the side of the Boil.

Finally, they pulled themselves up onto its flattened top, arms and legs aching, their breath coming in gasps.

Like a massive thimble, squat and rotund, a tower stood before them. Amos wondered how in the seven hells anyone had ever managed to build on top of the Boil, just dragging himself up had been an effort. He was wary too; Jerkze's parting words still fresh in his mind.

"Them urak will likely look to the Boil for the same reason we do. Have a care," he'd warned.

They crept slowly over the rocky ground, careful not to disturb any loose stone. Making it safely to the tower wall they followed its curving flank eastward where they found the entrance. The gate was missing leaving a yawning gap.

Jobe glanced round and into the tower's interior. A small fire smouldered inside and around its edge was laid three lumps. He turned to Amos holding three fingers up. They both knew there would be at least one on guard somewhere, surely.

A squeaky rumble sounded directly above them, seemingly loud in the quiet of the night. There was a mutter and rustle of movement, then nothing.

They'd found the sentry, almost stumbled upon him. Listening hard, Amos thought he detected a faint snort. It sounded like the sentry slept. Fortunate indeed, for any noise made was accentuated in the still night.

Amos wasn't entirely sure how many urak there were, at least four but they weren't here to fight in any case. Tapping Jobe on the shoulder, he signalled and moved back the way they had come.

The entrance was on the southeastern side of the tower and so they followed the wall back the other way, easing around the tower's girth.

Rounding the wall, Amos's eyes were drawn to the horizon. Pinpricks of light stood out against the black. Disbelieving, he crept further around, hearing Jobe's intake of breath behind.

To the north, the dark quilt that lay upon the ground was punctured by thousands of campfires. The number was staggering. Amos held his hands up forming a square between thumbs and index fingers and counted the lights he saw within. It took him a while and when he was done he moved his hand trying to cover what he saw before him. It was difficult to be entirely accurate he knew with just the dark background to line up against but by his judgement, there must have been twenty thousand campfires burning, probably more. He did a quick calculation in his head and didn't like the answer he got. Turning, Amos signed it was time to go, he'd seen enough.

They took their time on the way back down, neither wanting to make a mistake and stumble or dislodge rocks that might alert the urak to their presence.

The descent proved uneventful but slow, much slower even than the ascent. Climbing and scrambling down a rocky path in the dark was more treacherous by far than going up it. By the time they reached Jerkze light cracked the eastern horizon with the faint kiss of dawn.

"Whores tits, Jerkze," Jobe whispered. "You should've seen it."

"Seen what?" Jerkze asked.

"The campfires; it was like the stars in the heavens had fallen to earth."

Jerkze looked up at the night sky. There were a lot of stars up there. "That sounds like a lot," he said soberly climbing into his saddle. "Now can we get the hells out of here?"

Turning south they rode hard before the dawn, tired but filled with urgency, the danger they'd seen lending them energy. The horses at least had been rested.

The further south they travelled the more holdings they passed, leading them to tracks and then paths where the going was much easier. The three put as much distance between themselves and the Boil as possible before full daylight broke, worried they'd be easy to spy upon the plains.

* * *

They rested briefly at an abandoned holdstead as the sun fully crested the horizon. The building was orderly. The urak hadn't been there and it gave them hope they were ahead of the tide. They quickly fed and watered the horses, then themselves, before setting off again, walking for a bit to rest the horses. Always they looked to the horizon, searching.

By noon, tell-tale smoke was seen away to the north-west and again to the north. Their mood darkened and the tension rose. They could almost feel the urak closing in around them. Finding signs of a village just ahead they veered from the road crossing fields to bypass it, not wanting to risk running into trouble. A village could easily conceal a score of urak and they wouldn't know it until arrows flew.

Leaving the village behind they took rest in an orchard lined with apple trees. The horses ate eagerly, the season was old and the apples hung over-ripe on the branches or fallen on the ground. It was as they walked the horses out of the orchard that they saw their first urak. It was just bad timing. They'd rested longer than they should have, feeling the horses had need. The hedgerow bordering the orchard followed a lane that ran away east to north. As they stepped through it, out onto the dirt road, a group of urak appeared in the near distance rounding a bend to the north.

They were out of arrow range Amos judged, but then who knew how far an urak bow fired. Mounting quickly they pointed their horses south as several urak began unlimbering bows and notching shafts. As they cantered down the lane a few arrows were loosed but all fell short. Behind them, they heard war cries as the urak gave chase.

It was the start of their pursuit.

Chapter 49 : Mappels on Oust

Near Mappels-on-Oust, The Rivers

Dawn was just cresting the eastern hills when Sand rode into the village of Mappels on Oust. It was small; a community of thirty or so houses and buildings in the immediate vicinity most of which were deserted.

Sand saw little sign of the people who remained but could sense those few that did, huddled in their homes. A deep hunger had steadily grown in him since Redford driving him on and he needed to slake it.

Hitching his horse to a post outside a small inn, he tried the door. It was barred. Cocking his head he listened but it was still inside. He walked on, leaving the inn behind. The next building was a general store and was also devoid of life or at least none he could detect, he ignored it.

The third was a house and apothecary looking at the sign above its entrance. Flowers in pots framed the doorway and narrow planters ran the length of the building, overgrown with a variety of herbs and other plants.

Sand sensed heat emanating inside from two bodies. He tried the door but it was locked. He banged his fist firmly against it.

"We're not open, go away." An old voice, a man's voice answered. Gruff and irritable.

It was not ideal but it was a start. Sand knocked again, louder, more insistent.

"I said we're closed, you deaf?" A head appeared out the window. The man was grizzled; wrinkled and bald apart from a ruff of hair around his ears. His eyes were rheumy and bloodshot. The eyes looked Sand up and down and decided they didn't like the look of what they saw. The young man was dishevelled and unkempt, his fancy clothing torn in places and dirty, and was that blood on the sleeves? No, he didn't much like the looks of him at all.

Sand turned an eye to the old man, an amiable look upon his face. His hand snapped out, clasping onto the man's face. Stepping in, he drove the head back into the frame of the window. With a sickening crunch, the skull cracked as it slammed into the wooden jamb. Then, with a push, the man's limp and lifeless body fell back inside the house. There was a pause then the screaming began.

Closing his eyes, a smile played across his face. He gave a sharp twist of his head, neck cricking, then stepped over to the door. Lifting his hand he knocked again. There was no reply, just the hysterical wailing of a woman inside. It made him… happy.

Sand raised his arm, hand open and facing the door, then concentrated. The flowers, herbs, and plants in the window box and planters suddenly withered, curled black, and died. Immediately a dark whorl of energy gathered in his palm, crackling and pulsating. With a thought it exploded onto the door, its dark matter spreading out, covering its upper width in an instant. There was a slight delay, then, with a concussive detonation, the top half of the door crumpled, disintegrating into a thousand wooden shards and splinters to decorate the back wall of the apothecary and in many cases punch right through it.

Stepping up close to the shredded remains of the door, Sand bent his head and peeked through to the interior. A line of destruction led straight back from the entrance, everything decimated. The body of the old man lay on the floor outside the ruin, unscathed apart from the bloody pulp of bone matter and brains. An old woman knelt beside the man, the look of shock on her face turning to fear as she spied him, peering at her from the shattered doorway.

"Knock, knock," Sand said, smiling. She stared back in horror too stunned or scared to reply. "May I come in?" he asked, his voice pleasant.

Pushing up off creaking knees the old woman stood, backing away from her dead husband. "Who are you?" Her voice trembled. "Why are you doing this?" She reached the internal door, her hand fumbling behind for the latch.

"Would you like me to come in and explain it to you?" Sand asked, a questioning look on his face as if he cared for her answer.

Finding the latch she slammed it up. Pushing back against the door she all but fell through it into the next room.

Sand's smile broadened, as he watched the old lady gather herself before half hobbling half running for another door, spying her passage through the newly created rents in the wall. She had spirit. He liked that; that and the terror pulsing off her in waves.

Turning, he walked unhurriedly around the side of the house to a gate. A weak barrier, it took but a moment to open it and enter the backyard.

The old woman was there as he knew she would be, looking like she was skipping, not able to run but definitely not wanting to walk.

Sand bent, picking up a log from the woodpile, and hefted it in his hand. It was not the most elegant of tools but it would do. Stepping forward he launched it.

The ground was soft and wet from the earlier rain and the log caught the old woman high in the back, slamming into her with a heavy thud that sent her sprawling into the mud.

Sauntering up behind, Sand watched as she clawed in the dirt, dragging herself on with a whimper.

"Why are you doing this?" The woman cried staring over her shoulder at Sand's looming figure.

Kneeling, he placed a hand on her shoulder. "Hush now. It'll be over soon," Her fear was palpable and he closed his eyes, enjoying it, absorbing it.

"By the Lady, may you burn in all the seven hells for this. You're a monster."

His eyes snapped open. She was a fierce one, her fear turning to anger as she sensed the end. Sand liked that. Anger made them fight harder, last longer. Fear was good but people who only feared gave into death far too easily.

Casually, Sand flipped the woman over onto her back. Her face was muddy from the fall and her eyes stood out like beacons. Lifting one of her gnarled hands, he roughly crushed it into a fist. With a wrench, he pried one of her fingers out straight, then, raising her fist, sucked the finger into his mouth. Her eyes widened in sudden realisation.

Sand bit down, hard. Bone crunched and the old lady screamed, writhing in his grip to no effect, he held her fast, untroubled. He sawed his teeth and twisted his mouth, the hot salty tang of blood washing into it as skin ripped and bones split. He spat her finger out and blood pumped from the stump.

She cried, sobbing as he held her hand to his mouth once again. Closing his eyes, Sand suckled on the shattered remnant of her finger. Tasting the fear and pain and terror in the warmth of her blood and relished it.

That sliver of self, buried deep in the recesses of his mind watched on in horror as he gorged. It shouted, crying out at him to stop but it was weak, powerless. His pleasure was intense.

"What's wrong? What's happened to Margarit?" A voice sounded from behind, a woman.

Sand paused, clicking his neck again. He should have been aware of her approach but had lost himself in the moment. From behind it must have looked like he gave comfort, kneeling over Margarit's body as she cried, holding her hand. Yes, from a certain angle it must look quite different from the reality, he thought.

The woman stepped closer, almost behind him now. Sand stood abruptly and turned. She was stocky and plain, her dark hair held back in a kerchief. On her hip was a babe, flushed red, with snot running from its nose, a sickly looking thing.

"What a lovely baby you have," Sand said.

The woman looked taken aback. Surprise, then shock, and finally horror, flickering across her face. The man's mouth and jaw were coated in blood, his smile grotesque, his white teeth stained red. Margarit whimpered and she glanced down aghast at what she saw.

"What's going on?" Her voice was high turning hysterical.

Great, she's going to start screaming now, Sand thought. Too fast, his hands clenched her by the throat. He watched in joy as she struggled in his grasp, choking as he strangled her. Her hand came up to his and tried to pry his fingers away but his grip was like iron. His eyes drank in her fear as it twisted into frantic panic. She was beautiful.

Dropping her baby, the woman slapped and pulled at his hands with both of hers and Sand tightened his grip, changed his stance. She flailed, one of her fingernails scratching a furrow down his cheek. Annoyed, he squeezed, crushing her larynx. He smacked his forehead into her face, hearing cartilage break and feeling her body go limp. Lowering her gently to the floor, he held her down, watching in fascination as the blood pooled in her mouth.

"It's okay, it will be over soon," Sand crooned. She gagged, spitting globs of red over herself.

"Don't worry about your baby. I'll take care of it for you." He enjoyed the effect of his words, seeing her eyes flare. But any fight left was gone, her breath running out and her struggles growing feeble as she drowned.

Sand revelled in her suffering. Even that poisonous spike of self, screaming in the back of his mind brought pleasure. The darkness within him, pulsed and eddied as it fed. Finally, the woman ceased, her hands falling limply to her sides. Her eyes, still open stared up at him but the light was gone from them.

Sand stood. It had been immensely satisfying but over all too quickly. The woman, Margarit, cried behind him, sobbing and muttering to her gods. He glanced at her, then at the mewling baby where it lay in the muck.

"Well," he said, "maybe just a little one."

Chapter 50 : The Grim Road

The Grim Road, The Rivers

Marron told herself over and over that Nihm would be all right. She'd experienced plenty of self-doubt over the last few days and that doubt still gnawed away, troubling her even now. Would Nihm make a full recovery, would she be the same? Her skill in healing and training with the Order in the use of poisons and their curatives meant she knew full well not everyone made a full recovery. Some might look the same but were broken inside, their minds changed or bodies wasted.

Nihm had been poisoned with deeproot, an insidious and fast-acting agent that killed; none survived it. Nihm rightly should be dead Marron knew, feeling guilty for thinking it.

Marron didn't know what resided in the container she'd emptied onto Nihm. Something from the Order that allowed her to communicate with Keeper but also something that healed. Her perfect hand evidence of that every time she used the box. So what she did had been both a massive gamble and none at all. It would kill or cure and with the deeproot, Nihm was dead anyway. A desperate intuition led her to it, now though doubt hung over her like a black cloud. Would she ever get her daughter back?

Morten drove the wagon in her stead whilst she cared for Nihm. They had devised a crude system of communication involving Nihm blinking her eyes. It seemed to work, as frustrating and slow as it was; one blink for yes, two for no, three for water, four for food.

Nihm's mind was sharp, she could answer yes or no and Marron had tested her, asking a host of questions about her life and growing up to ascertain her cognitive ability. She'd been pleased with the results. As well, Nihm's appetite was fierce, always a good sign in Marron's experience. Nihm signed for food and water almost constantly whenever she awoke from the frequent periods of sleep she fell into.

Nihm was in one of her waking periods now and was moving her hands, flexing them into fists and then stretching them out. The movement was slow to start with but rapidly improved.

She had no trouble understanding what was said, so Marron knew Nihm's hearing was fine, but her speech was unintelligible still. That didn't stop her from trying though. Now when she spoke, Nihm could modulate her tone, even if she couldn't form proper words. The frustration in her eyes pleased Marron immensely. It was the kind of look she expected from her daughter at being unable to speak and showed her resolve to overcome it.

Marron played with her heart ring, a constant habit these days it seemed. Infrequently, a rider would pass heading south. Messengers for the most part, but at the sound of each one, her heart would lift briefly in the vain hope Darion had caught them. She missed him so much, at least the ring gave her some small comfort.

The day had gone quickly for Marron, focused as she was on Nihm. Morten said they'd made good progress and were on the Grim Road, notorious in times gone by for its lawlessness and banditry. Such dangers were rare in recent years though, what with the frequent patrols from the Black Crow and local lords and barons.

"Ug gat muh." Marron turned to her daughter who had a smile on her face. A proper smile too, not something resembling a grimace. Nihm had her hands raised clenching and unclenching, the movement smooth and controlled. She flexed each finger individually and then back into a fist.

"Well done, Nihm!" Marron exclaimed. "You're doing so well. Now, what about your legs, would you like me to help you move them?" Marron had been worried about this. Nihm had shown no sign of moving her lower body at all. Nihm seemed to consider the question before blinking her eyes once.

Marron grinned. "Good girl," she encouraged, even as she stripped the blanket from Nihm's legs. She placed a hand on Nihm's right foot and at a nod lifted the leg, flexing it back slowly. To Marron's delight, she could feel the muscles tense like steel chords under her fingers, and then Nihm screamed.

It was a strange, muted kind of scream but there was no denying what it was. Marron looked fearfully at Nihm, whose eyes were screwed tight in pain. Not paralysed then, Marron thought pleased at the realisation.

After a moment, Nihm's moaning ebbed away and she opened her eyes. Sweat beaded her forehead and above her lip but Marron thought she looked better.

Releasing her hold, she observed as her daughter took the weight and lowered her leg slowly back to the bed.

Grimacing, Nihm grunted. "Gu ogger egh."

"Yes dear, you did very well. The other leg?" Marron asked. Nihm blinked once, no pause or delay in her response this time. Marron repeated the exercise too much the same result. Morten stuck his head in at one point.

"Everything okay back there, Marron," he asked, concern etched into the lines of his face.

"It's fine Morten, just you keep an eye on the road ahead," Marron snapped, immediately feeling bad for it.

* * *

Marron joined Morten a short while later, Nihm having fallen asleep again. Despite sleeping, her body was in a constant state of twitching and trembling. So much so that Marron checked for signs of fitting or fever. She found none and reassured, tucked a blanket around her daughter before going for some air.

Sitting next to Morten she smiled at him. "Nihm seems much improved," she told him, saving him the need to ask it. "She can move her arms and flex her hands. It may take a little time but I'm hopeful that she'll make a full recovery."

The relief on Morten's face warmed her and mirrored her feelings. Mercy riding up ahead looked back at the sound of Marron's voice and dropped back eager for news herself. Marron gave her an update and Mercy's face creased into a smile.

"So how are we doing?" Marron asked.

"We've made good time. We've passed no one headed north which helps," Mercy said. The road was narrow and wagons and carriages were awkward to pass, the verge soft after the recent rain.

Glancing at the sky, Marron saw the half-moon of Nihmrodel a hand above the horizon to the southeast and the sun in the west told her they had at best, two or three hours until sunset.

Mercy saw her judging the sun. "Fallston is not far, maybe five leagues or so," she said. "Figure if we push on we should get there a few hours after sunset."

That would mean a proper bed for Nihm. "That would be good, Mercy. Let's do it," Marron said.

There was a sudden yowling to the front and Mercy's head twisted forward assessing where it came from. The dogs ranged all about and this sounded like one of them. She cantered forward and Marron watched her ride ahead with Stama, Lucky pulling rearguard this afternoon.

The howl was Thunder's distinctive call and Marron knew it for a warning. Standing, she clambered over the bench seat and into the back. Fetching her sword, she deftly buckled it around her waist before reaching up and unhooking her bow and quiver, hanging from one of the ribs.

It was awkward to stand as the wagon rumbled along, but Marron kept her feet, swaying and rocking with the motion. Looking out the back of the wagon and down the road, she saw Lucky watching. He had a long spear in hand and at the ready. This was the Grim Road and its reputation was known to him.

Marron heard a grunt and saw Nihm peering at her, eyes intent. "There may be trouble up ahead."

Marron could see the tension in Nihm's shoulders and the annoyance in her face at having to lie there powerless. Marron whistled and called, "Ash, Snow." The dogs were there instantly, never straying far it seemed from Nihm. Snow cleared the backboard, her powerful hind legs easily propelling her clear of it, Ash following behind.

"Guard," Marron commanded, an unnecessary order for the dogs but it made her feel better.

The wagon drew to a sudden halt and Marron climbed back up front to see what was what. To her left, tied to a low tree branch were Mercy and Stama's horses. They were on the edge of a wooded area full of shrubs and small trees.

Marron climbed down from the wagon. She quickly and expertly strung her bow before pulling an arrow from her bag, keeping it ready on the string.

"Erm, what should I do?" Morten asked. Marron spared him a glance. He looked worried. She saw his eyes flit to her bow and understood.

"This is just a precaution, Morten." She indicated the bow. "Always prepare yourself, if it's nothing then no harm done. If it's something then you're at least ready as you can be." She felt like Darion lecturing Nihm as he was so fond of doing.

"Grab that staff Lucky cut you and have it ready. Just in case," she told him.

Morten nodded and climbed into the back of the wagon. She heard him mutter something to Nihm before she turned, walking towards the little grove and the horses.

Maise materialised by her side and trotted along, head forward and alert. If not for the dogs they likely would have trundled right past the little wood none the wiser. As she pushed past the low branches she saw signs of a struggle and blood.

She found Mercy and Stama deeper in the wood, out of sight of the road. What Thunder had found was disturbing. It looked to have been a man or woman or what was left of one. Stama was bent examining the ground and stood as she arrived. He looked briefly at Mercy before addressing them both.

"I ain't no expert by any means but looks like these folk were attacked on the road and dragged back here," he said gesturing to the remains of a campfire and beyond that the grisly remains of a person.

"Folk? I only see one body here or what's left of one," Marron said. There was a smell in the air, metallic and earthy with burnt wood smoke over all of it.

"Aye well, this was a man." Stama indicated the body, flies buzzing around and on it in a swarm. It was little more than a carcass, butchered with most of the meat stripped from it. Only the head was intact and as Marron fought to keep the bile in her stomach from rising, she saw now that it was indeed a man's head.

"It's unusual to be travelling this road alone but not unheard of," Stama said. "But there's evidence of a struggle and at a guess, I would say there were two of them taken, maybe three, along with a horse or mule."

Marron looked around the campsite. It was hard for her to judge how many there might have been. Nihm could probably tell them she thought, Darion had trained her well if she could've moved that was. "So what's your read on things?" she asked Stama.

"Well at a guess, they were set upon on the road. The man was shot with an arrow and they were caught and dragged back here. The man was cut up and eaten, no other reason to carve him up so. Then, whoever did this left heading north." Stama indicated where the shrubs were bent and twisted back.

"Not sure on numbers but I found this." Stama held up a broken arrowhead. It was bloody and the thick shaft had snapped off a hand above the head. He offered it to Marron. "Not seen it's like. Figure it for urak."

"It's urak," Marron confirmed, "similar to the one my husband and Nihm found in the old forest." It didn't bode well. This part of the Grim Road ran west to east but advance parties this far out implied a wide front. Marron glanced at the ashes of the campfire.

"When?" she asked.

"Not sure," Stama replied. "Fire is cold, embers not even warm to the touch so probably a day maybe more." He shrugged apologetically. "This is more Jerkze or Jobe's area than mine."

There was nothing to be done. Marron could see that, they all could, but it left her feeling bad just walking away. As they wandered back to the wagon Marron pondered. If urak were this far south that was a real problem. They weren't safe at all, the road followed the river more or less and that didn't bend south for another day and a half, not till after they cleared the Reach. She'd assumed once they left Thorsten behind that they'd be safe. They weren't.

Marron would've felt better if they could have travelled with the River between them and the urak but the south bank had no path and no bridge to cross to it even if there were one. Besides all that, it was the start of the Grim, deadly in its own right. She felt trapped, wedged in with urak to the north and the Grim to the south.

Chapter 51 : Not As the Crow Flies

Encoma Holdstead, The Rivers

Leaden grey smoke plumed the air. One of the holdstead's outbuildings had burned, collapsing in on itself, and was smouldering still. A wagon lay wrecked in the field below and there were bodies, cattle and people alike, strewn about the fields and yard. Not near enough to account for all the families that lived at the Encoma's holding thought Darion.

Incongruously, a chicken stalked the yard, pecking at the ground. It was the only sign of life Darion could see. He was on a rise that sloped gently for two hundred paces down to the holding.

"There is no life there, ilf friend. No benefit, only risk to go down," R'ell stated from his left. Bezal, a distant speck flew a lazy circle around the holding.

They were hunkered down in the long grass where they could observe the holdstead with little chance of being seen. Darion agreed with R'ell's assessment and they had no need yet to look for supplies having enough for several days. Still, it was heart-wrenching to see Bert Encoma's holding abandoned and his people lying dead, people he knew. He wondered if any had made it out, whether Bert and Hildi still lived.

A deep voice sounded from his right. "We was here two nights ago, afore we ran into trouble. Looks like the old man heeded the Captain's warning too late."

Darion faced Kronke. They were of a height the two of them, though Kronke a hand broader at the shoulder with arms to match. His body, too, was heavier, solid with muscle compared to his lean hardness.

"Seems only right we go check. Might be someone still lives?" Kronke muttered asking Darion the question.

Darion found it unsettling how they looked to him for decisions. He'd bridled at having no control back in the old forest with no choice but to follow M'rika and the ilfanum; trapped in ilf lands whilst urak raided his own. Trouble was he was used to being on his own, relying on no one but Marron and Nihm. He guided his own hand, made his own decisions, and had done so for near fifteen years. He hadn't commanded anyone in as many years and was finding it uncomfortable after all this time.

"We move on," Darion said brusquely, looking the big sergeant in the eye.

"It ain't right," Kronke growled back. "We're meant to protect folk not run away." He looked past Darion to R'ell as if to make his point.

Darion saw the angst in the big man's eyes. Felt the same emotions that must be running through the sergeant; frustration, anger, indecision. He nodded in understanding.

"I don't command, Kronke. I'm looking for my wife and daughter and they're not down there." He glanced at R'ell who watched the exchange impassively. "Understand me well. We move in the same direction but I have no call on you. You're free to do what you think is right, but I will be moving on."

Kronke grunted, not happy. Darion could sense the sergeant mulling over his words, could see he'd backed himself into going down to the holding. Despite himself, Darion tried once more.

"I was a soldier once for the Black Crow, a scout," Darion told him. "From one old soldier to another I offer two things. First, R'ell says there's no life down there and I trust this. Second, it's a strategic mistake to go. It's too open. Gains nothing but costs you time and may reveal your position to the enemy." He paused, letting his words sink in. "You'll never make Thorsten if you intend to check every holding and farmstead on the way."

Kronke grunted and the tension dropped from his shoulders. A decision was made then.

"All right," Kronke said. He wasn't pleased about it but said no more, simply backed away down the ridge.

Darion felt a hand on his shoulder and turned to find R'ell's dark eyes boring into his. Was that compassion he detected in the ilf?

"Humans talk much, yet say so little," R'ell observed. He backed away following Kronke down the slope. The ilf had a point Darion conceded, edging after him.

Darion had hardly dropped below the crest when Bezal screeched overhead with a fluttering beat of wings. He turned in time to watch the raven alight on R'ell's back before hopping up onto the ilf's shoulder cawing all the while.

R'ell fixed Darion with a stare. "A man and horse approach from the east."

Wordlessly, Darion crawled back up the grassy knoll and looked to the east, along the dirt road leading to Thorsten. He saw nothing. He felt R'ell next to him and heard the rustle of grass as Kronke's large frame joined them.

"I don't see nought. A horse and rider you say?" Kronke said, straining his eyes eastward.

R'ell pointed just to the north of the road but it was a full minute before Darion and Kronke could make out the distant blur of movement and another again before it resolved itself into man and horse. They waited silently, watching the rider's approach. He'd seen the smoke rising and was riding hard.

Darion hoped it might be a scout for the Black Crow but as the horseman neared it was apparent he wasn't. The rider wore rustic clothes and bore no bow or sword.

Cantering into the field below the man drew his horse up sharply when he saw the dead. The distant rider looked vaguely familiar to Darion who watched, as the man walked his horse through the field, head twisting and turning at what lay before him. Approaching the broken wagon, he cried and slid from his horse rushing to a body lying half-buried in the long grass. He started wailing.

"The man makes much noise," observed R'ell, a frown creasing his forehead.

"I better go get him," Kronke rumbled.

"Let me. I think I know him," Darion said. He glanced at the holdstead and surroundings but saw no sign the man below had attracted any untoward attention. Crouching, Darion moved quickly down the slope towards the field.

The man was so lost in grief he didn't hear Darion's approach until he called out, "James."

The man was on his knees but visibly jumped at his name, twisting toward Darion, eyes red and full of fear. "Darion?"

"Aye lad, it's not safe. You need to come with me." Darion held his hand out, beckoning James to follow.

"It's my Da. They cut his head off. Ma's there, crushed under the wagon." He sniffed, wiping his sleeve under his nose.

"I see that, but there's nothing to be done. We need to go. The urak may be back." Again Darion signalled James to follow, but he didn't.

"Urak, I did'na believe her. It can't be happening." James shook his head, voice rising, "They're all dead. You brought them, you and Marron. All dead cos of you." He started sobbing his head sinking onto his chest.

"Sorry for your loss, James but now ain't the time for grieving. We need ta go, now!" Darion said, eyes roving, nervously. The lad was making a lot of noise. James though didn't heed him, crying instead, his shoulders shaking in sorrow. Darion turned away.

"You gonna leave me?" James sobbed.

"I understand your grief, but I've others under my charge and cannot wait. If you change your mind we're just over that ridge. We'll be moving on shortly. Stay or go it's up to you." Darion knew it was harsh but he wouldn't coddle the boy. There was no time. A short sharp shock might do what words couldn't.

Darion was halfway up the rise when he heard the heavy hoof of Jacob on his mount. They said nothing to each other but Darion could sense hostility ebbing off the boy.

On the other side of the rise, Jacob was amazed at the sight of the ilfanum and scared too at first, having never seen one before. The Black Crows looked on unfazed readying their horses as they prepared to move out.

Kronke, feeling the resentment the lad directed at Darion, took him in hand. Making quick introductions and having him check his horse kept James's mind occupied. Busy was best after what the lad had just been through.

Darion directed them south and east, taking the lead. They kept to the far side of the ridge-top surrounded by long grass, small scrub trees and bushes, following an old game trail. The ridge ran into another and soon they found themselves traversing gently rolling hills. Bezal flew ahead scouting their path and Bindu ranged to the north keeping up easily enough despite her injured flank. It was a quiet ride; no one spoke as they tracked ever eastward keeping to the low hills.

* * *

Seeing the Encoma holding in ruin made Darion reflective. He thought back on what had brought him to the edge of the wilds.

Marron and he had all but run away from the Order Halls seventeen odd years ago. They had their reasons for leaving and were overjoyed when Keeper reluctantly agreed. Respecting their wishes, Keeper instead sent them to the old forest, to keep an eye on things. Pleased to get away, they hadn't questioned the ease with which Keeper had assented, thinking the assignment meaningless. After all, there was nothing out here but the wilds and the ilfanum who kept to themselves.

Until the urak that was. A stray thought entered Darion's mind that maybe Keeper knew more than he'd said at the time. Keeper was ancient. Leader of the Order, he knew things most couldn't begin to fathom or understand. The more Darion thought on it the more his suspicions grew. He shook his head, he had to live in the now. Keeper would have to wait.

* * *

The company followed the low hills skirting the plains to the north. Occasionally they would take a break to rest the horses and Darion and R'ell would climb the hill they were on and survey the land to the north and east. It was on one such occasion, around mid-afternoon the following day, when they saw smoke on the plains and distant farmsteads burning. R'ell's sharp eyes picked out roving bands of urak and pointed them out. Darion stared but was unable to see them himself. He didn't doubt the ilf though, the distant black smokestacks were evidence enough.

They rode hard after that, an urgency on them now that urak had been sighted. The rest of the afternoon passed quickly, as they navigated around impenetrable gorse bushes and thick heather. It was late, the light fading to dusk when the disparate group finally crested a rise to look down upon Thorsten.

It looked impressive with its earthworks and formidable stone walls. At the centre of the town rose the hulk of the keep. Fires flamed from its battlements along with the Black Crow's flag which from this distance, was nothing more than a fluttering scrap of red cloth.

"Home," Kronke said.

"Urak," R'ell replied.

As a group, they turned their gaze from the town. The plain before Northgate stretched for a league or more before rising up a slope to the surrounding countryside. As Darion looked, he could make out movement but no detail.

"There are many bands of urak," M'rika reported. "Maybe a hundred hands in each, all moving south and east."

Darion considered her words, worry lining his face. "Can we make the town?" he asked.

"If we go now, if we ride hard for the Riversgate we can make it," Kronke insisted.

M'rika didn't reply immediately but looked back down at the plain. Darion saw her glance at R'ell who signed to her. She nodded and signed back.

Jess Crawley watched the ilf suspiciously. She'd been shocked and amazed when they'd suddenly appeared, saving them back at the homestead. They were figures from legend. No one she knew had ever seen an ilf and yet here they were. That amazement and the relief of still living though had soon worn away. The ilfs aloofness and superiority rubbed her wrong. She didn't trust them.

"What're they saying to each other?" She pointed at the ilf.

M'rika looked back at the woman locking eyes with her. Jess coloured and turned away, muttering.

"The town will be encircled by sundown," M'rika said addressing Darion. There was a clamour then.

"What does that mean?" Morpete cried.

"It means we're assfucked," Jess said.

"Well, I ain't going down there. No fucking way," Pieterzon shouted.

"Shut the hells up," Kronke growled, menace in his voice and the three subsided into silence. Kronke turned to Darion.

"So you're saying we can't get to Thorsten without going through a bunch of urak?" Kronke asked his brow furrowing.

Darion stared back but made no reply. The big sergeant had had a rough couple of days so he didn't point out that he'd not said a damn thing. Ignoring the sergeant, Darion instead felt his heart ring, twisting it on his finger. It was warm, telling him Marron was alive, but it also told him she was several days away at least. He wasn't sure how the rings worked; one of their old masters, a friend, gifted them to Marron and him the day they gave their vows.

Darion walked a slow circle ignoring the funny looks he got from his companions and Bindu whining at his feet. Over the many years, he'd learned a thing or two. One of those things was telling him Marron was in the east. He was sure of it. The ring had never given him such a clear signal before. Marron was not in Thorsten, his path was clear.

Turning back to Kronke but addressing all of them he said. "I head east whether you believe we can make the walls or not. That is where my wife and daughter are."

Kronke looked incredulous. "So that's it? You're just going to leave?"

Darion felt his ire rising. R'ell was right, we talk too much. "Sergeant, I don't believe you can make the walls, I trust the ilf. Whether you do or not is on you." He paused, taking a breath.

"We spoke earlier you and me. Those things I said, I stand by. You command these three." He gestured at Jess, Morpete and Pieterzon. "If ya want to risk Riversgate, against all advice, that's your call. I would say that Lord Bouchemeax is well aware of his situation so any report you have for him adds nothing of relevance even if you could make it. So decide what you will do and do it."

Darion glanced at James Encoma. They'd not spoken since leaving the holdstead. The lad had latched onto Kronke and never strayed far from the big sergeant. Darion offered the lad no advice. Turning, he walked the few strides back down the slope to where Marigold was grazing on long grass and gathered her reins. R'ell and M'rika followed. He could feel five pairs of eyes boring into his back as he led his horse away down the hillside turning south.

Chapter 52 : The Circle Closes

Thorsten, The Rivers

Lord Richard Bouchemeax looked out from the battlements atop his keep. Fires burned in the town's forges as every blacksmith turned out swords, spears and arrowheads as fast as they could produce them. Carpenters fashioned crude shields and spears, whilst fletchers churned out bows and arrow shafts. Lord Richard prayed it would be enough.

Below him, the market square was a patchwork quilt of tents and lean-tos and thronged with people. Thorsten's population of twenty thousand had doubled in the past three days as people from the surrounding countryside made their way in. It was a struggle to cope with them all. A lot brought crops or cattle with them but the problem was the grain needed milling and the beasts slaughtering. Time was against them.

Fear too was rife with talk of urak hordes rampaging and pillaging the countryside. Talk, fuelled in most part, by refugees fleeing down the Redford road from the north bringing harrowing tales with them.

Richard organised caravans, sending those he could to Rivercross or southwest to Greentower. Anyone considered able was drafted as militia by Sir Cyril Dechampne his master of arms and he had his hands full with them. Ten thousand men and women untrained in soldiering; young, old and everything in between from stockmen to holdsteaders, shopkeepers to labourers, it mattered not except they could wield a blade or spear and hold a shield.

Dechampne trained them ruthlessly with the aid of weapons master Johanus but a few days drill would never be enough. Richard attended Sir Cyril's training a few times to offer encouragement and was careful to conceal his disdain at how poorly equipped they were and how badly they drilled.

Most were armed at least, it was the wilds they lived in after all, but a rusted sword could oft not be trusted in battle. A few of the older ones, had spears and shields, mementoes for the most part from a time when they served as Black Crows themselves. Well, it's what we have. It will have to do, Richard told himself.

In addition to the militia, he had three thousand trained men at arms and considered himself blessed at that. His normal complement was a thousand; it was too expensive to keep much more in times of peace. That he'd High Lord Twyford to thank for the extra rankled somewhat. It was Twyford's command that he supply two thousand soldiers for his Westlands campaign and not prepared to leave the north defenceless, Richard had levied them over the previous winter and early spring and trained them hard over summer. But those two thousand were green, untried in battle. Richard grunted, some blessing. It had cleared his coffers and armoury both to raise them.

So, thirteen thousand to hold the walls, Richard hoped it would be enough; there was a lot of wall to cover.

There was a polite cough behind and Richard turned armour clanking. His chamberlain had suggested he would look the part in his armour, insisting it would inspire his people. Not bloody likely from up here, he groused to himself. The steel-plated armour was heavy against his gambeson and it had been a real effort climbing the stairs in it.

His son Jacob stood by his side and at his back was Bartsven his firstsword. Behind Bartsven was Lutico, looking clean in a fresh robe, his hair combed back over his pate. It was Lutico that had coughed drawing his attention. Richard was pleased to see him looking presentable.

"My Lord, I have word from the council," Lutico spoke of the Council of Mages.

Richard grunted for the mage to continue. He saw Junip peek out from behind Lutico's girth and smiled involuntarily at the sight. She coloured, disappearing back behind her master's bulk.

"The council has decided to send a small delegation of mages to investigate matters here," Lutico said.

"A small delegation of mages to investigate matters?" Richard repeated, eyebrows marching up his forehead, his piercing blue eyes staring pointedly at his oldest counsellor.

"I'm afraid my stock with the council has fallen somewhat in recent times," Lutico replied, understating matters. "The old fools have neither the presence nor clarity of mind to heed my warning."

Richard waved his hand. "It's of no moment. It would take them until the bite of winter to get here, longer if they mind a little snow, too late to aid us." He sighed.

"High Lord Twyford bids me hold Thorsten. As if I would do less," Richard declared. "He sends relief but it will take fifteen days, maybe more, to march his army up North Road. Until then we're on our own."

"As ever, my Lord," Lutico replied blandly. Arching a single hairy eyebrow, he turned suddenly and dragged his young apprentice out from behind him.

"Junip stop skulking so girl?" he muttered gruffly. "Come see if you can't make yourself useful for a change."

Lutico moved to the edge of the battlements leaving Junip to follow. "May I, my Lord?" Lutico asked.

Curious, Richard waved him on, "By all means."

Lutico looked out past the walls surrounding the town. It was late in the day and several black tendrils of smoke rose on the horizon to the west and north. Holding his hands out in front of him palms facing he muttered words, incanting under his breath.

The air shifted, distorting between his hands as he moved them in front of his face. His right hand moved a little. Despite the coolness of the day and the breeze atop the keep, Lutico's brow was damp.

"Junip," he called out. "Do you see what I do? Do you remember the lesson?"

"Yes, Master," she replied.

"Well then stop dawdling girl," Lutico snapped.

Richard grinned, remembering well the old man's tone from when he was a boy. It was nice to see him with a bit of vim in his blood again.

"Richard, look over my shoulder, you will see things a little more clearly," Lutico ordered.

Richard caught Bartsven glaring at the mage for his tone. He's young and only remembers Lutico as a drunkard, Richard thought as he obliged, slipping behind his old teacher and looking as instructed.

Richard took an involuntary step back. Before him was a farmstead with smoke curling from its thatch as fire burnt beneath. Glancing around Lutico's hands he saw the town laid out as before. Realisation dawned as he fastened on a far distant point, smoke dribbling into the sky. Somehow Lutico had magnified his vision; he could see a point much further away as if it were a mere hundred yards distant.

Amazed, he looked again, holding his breath as a group of urak appeared from behind the burning farm. He felt a trickle of fear at the sight despite knowing what to expect. After all, he had some dead ones in his cells. These though were very much alive and ready for battle.

One might mistake them for men at first glance. The differences though were apparent on close inspection; larger for one thing, more squat and hulking with heads slightly too big for their frames. Their skin was grey in hue and their faces were marked with white paint in the shape of a hand. Different than the dead urak in his cells; their heads were red like they'd been dipped in blood. A different clan or tribe he wondered?

"I'll pan my hands to the north, my Lord," Lutico said, interrupting Richard's thoughts. Slowly Lutico turned shifting the view between his hands. Occasionally he would tweak his right hand and the view would shoot forwards or backwards.

It was a revelation to Richard. What a tool this was. If he'd known of it, then Lutico would have been marching with him on the Westlands campaign. Something caught his eye, Lutico's too for he stopped and focused the view in.

Horsemen, three of them and riding hard by the looks. Lutico cranked the view past them and spanned slowly to each side. They were pursued. Urak chased them and on foot no less, but they looked tireless whereas the riders looked spent. Then amongst the urak, he spied dogs, big ugly brutes, he thought measuring them against their masters.

Richard stepped back and oriented himself. They were almost due north and a couple of leagues distant. It would be a close call if he read it right. Never one to shirk a decision he turned to his son.

"Jacob, three men ride from the north." He pointed the direction out of habit.

"Yes, father?" Jacob said.

"Trouble is on their heels. Go meet them, see if we can't ease their passage a little," he ordered.

Jacob nodded, "On my way." Turning he headed for the stairs down.

Richard called out. "No heroics. Take your company but only engage with bow if you can and then only if you have need."

Jacob acknowledged the order before clomping off down the steps.

Richard heard him calling to his guards, excitement in his voice. He smiled grimly. War had come. Battle was on his doorstep. Jacob would learn soon enough what a terrible thing that was.

* * *

There was a saying that waiting for battle was the hardest part, Richard recalled. Bullshit if ever he'd heard it. Once the battle was joined, that was the hardest part. Fighting, bleeding, killing till you were so tired you felt like puking your guts out. So weary your limbs trembled with fatigue, knowing if you stopped you died; watching comrades fall beside you whilst somehow you survived. That was the hardest part and a lesson only learnt in the crucible of battle. Still, he conceded, the waiting wasn't easy.

Jacob had his command well drilled and it wasn't long before they rolled out onto the plains to the north. They rode in a column, two wide and a hundred deep cantering easily forward. They wore light armour, leather mostly and their horses were fresh and eager. The north walls were packed with soldiers and a loud cheer rose to greet them as they rode out.

Lutico focused his view on Jacob. The young fool was riding without his helm on, his long hair loose and flowing in the wind. A glance at his Lord told him the matter had not gone unnoticed, no doubt Richard would have words with him later.

Lutico twisted, focusing now on the three horsemen. The gap to the urak behind looked wider than before, an illusion of distance he knew.

Seeing their quarry escaping the war dogs had been loosed and streaked after the horses. They were fast but the riders must have seen them coming because they seemed to lift their pace.

The gap between Jacob and the urak narrowed quickly with the three horsemen riding just ahead of their pursuit. Jacob's line drew close before parting suddenly, splitting down the middle. Turning their horses expertly left and right the horsemen raised their bows. With a stuttering, staggered release two hundred arrows lifted into the air.

It was well-timed; the three horsemen riding beneath the hail of arrows which cleared them to fall on the ground to their rear. Most missed but some found a mark and a dozen war dogs collapsed, pierced, and tumbling in a heap. The rest carried on undaunted.

The chasing urak drew to a halt and began unlimbering their bows whilst a few ran on, heedless. Another flight lifted from Jacob's men.

The riders were much closer now and the arrows cleared them easily. Then they were safely through the hole Jacobs's horsemen had left.

A final flight of arrows was loosed before the company turned as one back to Thorsten. It was well judged, as by the time the urak returned fire their arrows fell short, the horsemen out of range and riding for safety. It was neatly done and Richard felt pride in his son.

The few urak that had run on had all been struck down barring one and it shook its weapon in defiance, howling. It was soundless to Richard, stood as he was on the keep's tower but he felt its anger through Lutico's magical window.

"Erm, my Lord," said a timid voice. Richard looked over and saw Junip with a worried frown marring her plain features.

"Look to the distance," she said holding her arms up.

Junip had struggled to repeat Master Lutico's magic window trick at first but as Richard looked between her palms he saw that she had mastered it now.

He swore. The horizon was dotted with warbands, each a hundred hands strong at least. They were spaced out but as Junip panned her hands he saw there were many of them.

Richard observed for some time, assessing their movements before he was sure. They moved with purpose and at a steady, easy pace. One they looked like they could maintain indefinitely.

Most of the scouts Richard sent out hadn't returned and those few that did all reported urak moving south. Some had seen villages razed and pillaged but none reported seeing more than one or two warbands. So he knew the urak were coming and leaving destruction in their wake. He had even toyed with the idea of sending his soldiers out to meet them.

But what Richard saw now was at least twenty warbands and he felt relief that he'd not followed up on his whim. Still, if that were it there was hope for them, they could surely hold the walls against ten thousand urak. Trouble was his gut had that sinking feeling in it. A clenched twist he hadn't felt in many years, not until the boat from Redford had turned up a few days back. Now it churned, warning him again that this was just the start of things.

His mouth was dry and it was suddenly hard to swallow. If he read their intent right they were enveloping the town. Their circle would be closed by day's end.

Chapter 53 : Fallston

Fallston, The Rivers

Zoller's arse hurt from riding. He was a bad horseman, had never really taken to it and his horse sensed his unease. The mare was skittish and kept pulling her head down almost toppling him from his saddle every time she did. Riding in his cassock hadn't help matters either. In the end, Holt tied a lead rope to his mare's bridle and pulled him along like he was a child.

The blame for his uncomfortable seat lay with the blacksmith. His carriage had broken an axle, the same that broke travelling on the way up. The sleeve made to fix the repair had obviously been shoddy workmanship. Hiding his irritation as well as he could, Zoller resolved to have the blacksmith at Greenholme flogged.

Zoller had intended to stay with the carriage whilst repairs were affected but Tuko had taken him aside and spoken with him.

"Think we should carry on to Fallston Father," His eyes nervously surveying the thick scrub off to the side of the road.

"What is it?" Zoller said picking up on Tuko's guarded tone. "You see something?"

"Nope, but I don't hear nothin' neither. No birds, no nothin'. It's just a feelin' Father," Tuko stated, resting his hand casually on his sword hilt, eyes continuously scanning. "That itch ya get when ya feel you's bein watched. I got it."

Zoller glanced across at the bushes following where Tuko's eyes tracked but saw nothing. Oh, how he loathed the wild. He didn't understand the rules; if there were any. Zoller's paranoia didn't need much stoking and his nerves jangled at both Tuko's words and his imagination.

Tuko's lip quirked, enjoying the Father's discomfort and the worry that leeched from him. That the hulking man-mountain and simpleton Holt glared at him over the Father's shoulder only served to broaden his grin.

Zoller, having learned over the years to trust Tuko where matters of his safety were concerned, resolved to carry on to Fallston. After all, it wasn't far, just a few leagues. He'd left two of his Red Cloaks to guard the carriage and mind his belongings, telling them he would send a blacksmith back from Fallston. Now his arse hurt and they'd barely gone a league.

"Boat on the river, Father," Holt called out breaking into Zoller's sullen reverie. He turned to look.

A large flat bottomed barge was immediately obvious on the Oust. It looked slow and ponderous as it meandered downriver but it was faster than it appeared, the current pulling the boat along until it gradually caught them.

Zoller saw it was packed to the gunnels with people; women, children and old folk mostly. They'd seen a few of the barges and some of the smaller, faster boats on the river since leaving Thorsten. All headed south and all packed with people. In his carriage, he'd given them no mind. Now though, he had a thought.

"Holt, go flag it down," Zoller said. "Order them to draw into the bank."

Holt immediately pulled his horse around and with a kick, cantered across the strip of long grass and shojo bushes to the river bank.

Zoller heard Holt shouting to the tillerman who stood in the barge hollering back but they were too distant for him to make out what was said. Zoller could see though from the tillerman's stance he wasn't having a bar of Holt.

Holt gestured wildly and a hint of shouted invective reached Zoller on the breeze. Then the barge was by and moving downriver. Holt rode back, face red with fury.

"Cunt wouldn't pull over," Holt spat then, realising he'd sworn, stammered an apology.

"I can see that, Holt. What did he say?" Zoller asked calmly.

"That he won't dock till Fallston and his boat's already overburdened. Says too the Black Crow paid him to take that rabble on-board to Fallston and that he don't get paid if he don't deliver."

"He said a lot of things. What did you say? It certainly wasn't polite conversation from where I was sat," Zoller asked, arching his brow. He could see Tuko smirking at Holt out of the corner of his eye.

"I ordered him to the side. Told him you had need to speak with him," Holt replied looking agitated. "Told him if he didn't pull that barge into the bank like you asked I'd cut his…" he stopped himself and thought a moment. "…his manhood off Father and feed it to him."

"I think your negotiating skills need a little work, Brother," Zoller responded dryly. It was his fault, he should have known better than to send Holt. Indeed, he should have gone himself but the thought of riding off-road on horseback had not appealed to him at all. His vanity would not survive the bruising if he should fall.

They rode on until Fallston finally hove into view. The roaring of the falls was a distant thing at first but grew steadily louder as they approached.

The falls were where the Oust plunged twenty paces into the long narrow lake known as the Reach. The lake stretched ten leagues eastward and in reality was little more than a fat bloat of the river, only a league at its widest. The lake had a gentle current as the river continued on its way from its easternmost point pulling the waters from the Reach after it.

The Reach's southern bank was indiscriminate and hard to discern, disappearing in reeds and long clumps of water grass that morphed into the fringes of the Grim marsh.

Atop the falls, a good distance from its drop, was the Uppers, as locals called it; a small settlement of houses and ramshackle huts that dotted the surrounding land. From the docks and warehouses that cluttered the river's edge to the cliff-top, the Uppers extended round following the road as it swept away from the river and down an embankment to Fallston proper which sat on the westernmost point of the Reach.

The Upper's docks extended far out into the river and, as they neared, Zoller saw a flotilla of boats tied to them. They all looked more or less the same to him and Zoller couldn't discern which might be the boat they'd hailed earlier. It had already unloaded its cargo of people for they were nowhere to be seen.

Passing into the Uppers they approached a palisade surrounding the docks and warehouses. An old grizzled guard sat upon a stool watching with tired eyes as they drew to a halt.

Taking the opportunity to dismount and stretch his legs, Zoller slid cautiously off his mare. His legs almost collapsed as they took his weight and he'd have fallen flat on his backside if not for the hand still clasping the saddle horn. He waited a moment for the quivering ache in his thighs to subside, gathering himself.

"You alright, Father?" Holt asked.

"Perfectly," Zoller snapped, vexed. His thighs were chaffed red-raw and ached beyond measure. And listening to Holt's gravelly obsequious voice irritated him beyond reason. With a grunt of effort, Zoller pushed himself away from the saddle and hobbled slowly to the guard who watched with a clear look of amusement on his face.

"You man!" Zoller growled. "Why do you sit like a buffoon? Do you not follow the Trinity? Can't you see I am a priest of Kildare?" By the third hell, he was sore.

"Oh aye, your worship, all god-fearing folk follow the Trinity." The guard grinned, unperturbed it seemed.

Zoller grimaced. The man was missing most of his teeth and those few left were stained yellow, the reason evident as the guard hoicked, spitting a glob of tabacc onto the ground.

Zoller heard Holt muttering behind followed by a heavy thump as he dismounted. Holding his hand up he signalled Holt to wait.

The gap-toothed guard continued unfazed. "Now I is sat 'ere doin me job by order of Sir Menzies, Lord of Fallston. That job be asking people what their business be and I would ask it of you, your holiness, only I 'spect you be running south same as all these other folks." He smiled, face crinkling like scrunched parchment. "Tell me I ain't wrong?"

Zoller rankled at the man's irreverence. If his legs and buttocks didn't pain him so much he'd teach the inbred some piety and manners. Instead, all his thoughts were on finding an inn where he could close the door for a bit and rest his aching body.

"Where is your best hostelry? And I'll need directions for a blacksmith?" Zoller demanded. The old guard laughed out loud and slapped his thigh like he'd just heard the funniest thing. Zoller was starting to think the man was touched. In all his days he had never been laughed at like this. Zoller raised his hand waving Holt forward.

Holt's mass loomed up behind him, his sour breath washing over him. "Yes, Father?"

"I'm heading into Fallston. Have this man send a blacksmith back for the carriage," he ordered, thinking it so much easier to get someone else to deal with the old man, someone on his level.

* * *

An hour and an extortionate gold gilder later, Zoller had secured lodgings at the Angler's Reach; two rooms and one of the common rooms for him and his men. He passed two disgruntled families, recently evicted, coming down the stairs as he ascended to his room.

Earlier, when Holt had been persuading the old guard, another had stepped out of a little hut just inside the palisade. More intelligent than his older comrade he took but a moment to size matters up, their numbers, their red cloaks, and Holt holding his fellow by the throat. He gave swift directions to a blacksmith and recommended the Angler's Reach. On account, he said, of the landlord being open to making room where none existed. For the right money of course.

Zoller settled himself in his room and cursed his luck. All his cases were secured on the carriage and the liniments and lotions which may have soothed his aching thighs were packed with them. He had just the robes he was stood in and they were dusty and stained from riding.

Feeling unclean he ordered a bath and later as he lay soaking in it he thought on matters.

His immediate goal was getting to Rivercross and he had decided the best way of getting there would be by river barge. If he could get his carriage on one he would take the river down to Greenholme. There were rapids just south of Greenholme so he would have to take the road from there but barging downriver should save a day at least.

Course plotted, Zoller lay back in the warmth of the bath and resolved to find Lord Menzies and broker passage south.

Chapter 54 : Movement

The Grim Road, The Rivers

It's strange sharing my head with someone, Nihm thought. She should be upset about it but wasn't and that bothered her. The thing was it felt quite natural having Sai with her. She knew without Sai she would have died. Was that why she wasn't bothered? It didn't feel quite the right answer. She would have to think on it some more.

Thinking, Nihm had plenty of time for that. She'd always been active, always on the go. Marron always complained that she never sat still unless she had a book in her hand and they only had a handful of those.

Still, laying helpless hadn't been so bad. Sure she was frustrated to seven hells at her incapacity, but it had actually been kind of peaceful. Playing out her memories had been strangely grounding and self-reflective. Besides, she had Sai to talk to. Sai was always there when she awoke. Full of strange words and sayings she didn't understand but always listening to her, always answering her and, she realised suddenly, never judging her. That felt important somehow, made her feel at ease with herself.

It would have been hard to understand what had happened and how to deal with things without Sai. In truth, she wasn't sure how she would have coped without his steadying influence and calm demeanour.

Nihm tried to move. Her arm swung up and over as she went to roll onto her side. Pain ebbed down her spine, little more than an ache that was quickly dampened. She could feel it still, was discomforted by it, but it was a distant thing.

<*Is that you?*> she asked. The beauty she found was that Sai always seemed to know what she meant. She never needed to elaborate on a thought.

<*It is mostly you. I have reconstructed…*>

<*Yes, yes, I know you've told me a thousand times already,*> Nihm interrupted.

<*Twelve actually although I suspect two of those times you were not listening given your lack of response,*> Sai responded.

<*Only twice?*> Nihm said with a grin.

<*Are you being humorous again?*> Sai asked. <*If so, I will update my subroutines.*>

<*You know, since you won't elaborate on whatever it is you are, feel free to keep that stuff to yourself,*> Nihm shot back. <*Besides… can't you see I'm trying to roll over here?*>

Grunting in effort Nihm's left shoulder lifted from the bedding. She tried pulling her left knee up and twisting her hips. Pain washed up her body and she grimaced before flopping back down. I should be used to the pain by now, she thought.

<*Pain is a sensory input. An overloading of your nerve cells and with the right control manageable,*> Sai offered.

<*Thanks for your support but you don't have to go through this,*> Nihm replied, annoyed.

<*On the contrary, I feel the same sensory inputs as you,*> Sai said. <*Would you like me to explain again?*>

<*Gods no, you're worse than Da for a good lecture. You know that right?*> Nihm snapped back.

<*Is this one of those questions I am not meant to answer?*> Sai asked.

<*Yes.*> Nihm sighed.

<*Updating subroutines,*> Sai responded.

It was so frustrating. She'd never really had to think about moving before. She just did it. Not now. Now every move required concentration and focus. Do or do not she could hear Darion telling her.

Ignoring Sai, she tried again, this time bringing her knee up and arm over together. With a groan, she managed to twist her hips and pivot onto her side. The pain was there through her midriff, but she waited with gritted teeth. If Sai said calibrating one more time she would… well she didn't know what she would do… but it would not be pleasant.

Moments later the pain subsided and she smiled, right before teetering slowly over onto her face. She tensed trying to stop herself but it was too late and she rolled off the makeshift bed and onto the wagon floor, her face mashing up against the boards. Agonising jolts fired from her face, chest, and abdomen where they lay against the wagon as it moved, rattling and bumping down the road. Even her knees hurt.

She lay a while waiting for the pain to subside. Lying face down on wooden boards though wasn't a pleasant experience. Get up Nihm it isn't that bad, she cajoled herself.

Left-arm pressed tight against the side of the wagon, Nihm flexed it, moving slowly to shift her weight. Amazingly, her arm managed to support her and ease the pressure from her face and chest until the wagon hit a large rut in the road and the flatbed bounced up and down.

Swearing loudly she tried again. Marron and Morten must have heard her. She certainly had no trouble hearing them as they both exclaimed in surprise.

"Take the reins, Morten," Marron cried before turning and clambering into the back.

"Impatient as ever I see!" Marron grinned as she said it, pleased to see Nihm moving. "You know you could've waited. We'll be at Fallston later tonight or maybe first thing on the morrow."

<*Good advice,*> Sai offered.

<*Shut up,*> Nihm retorted. <*If it's such a good idea why didn't you suggest it?*>

She got a sense then from Sai, confusion? No something else. <*What's wrong, feels like your sulking?*>

<*Sulking is a human emotion. To resent or act sullen and upset in order to gain sympathy.*> Sai flashed a memory of her petulant outburst when Darion would not take her to track the urak. Then of an earlier memory of stamping her foot and crying when Marron told her she had tacked the ponies wrong, she was six years old.

<*Will you stop doing that? What is up with you?*> Nihm shouted. The images immediately ceased.

<*You gave an order and followed it with a command that would require me to break the order. It was conflicting,*> Sai responded, calm and measured as ever.

Nihm pondered a moment before replying. <*Sometimes I say things and it is like an expression. I didn't mean for you to literally be quiet. Or I did but not like that. Hmmm, I see what you mean I guess.*>

<*Updating sub-routines. These contradictions in meaning are very… inefficient,*> Sai said.

<*Well get used to it. A lot of words and expressions have two or three or even more meanings,*> Nihm said. <*It depends on how something is said or the context as to the meaning. Don't worry you'll soon get the hang of it.*>

"Nihm? Are you okay?" Marron asked, interrupting her conversation.

"Iw um phin" Nihm said. She could see Marron's feet as she raised her head from the wooden boards. She tried again, pushing herself up with her hand and arm, twisting her shoulders. Her leg felt like a log as she tried to move it, but it moved. Slowly.

Encouraging, Marron placed a supportive hand on Nihm's shoulder as she turned, helping her into a sitting position.

Taking a deep breath Nihm closed her eyes briefly. Then, with a determined effort lifted herself up and back onto the makeshift bed, happy that her arms were strong enough to support her weight despite a bit of trembling.

Trying her legs, Nihm moved them one at a time back on to the mattress. It was slow, her movements strained, but eventually, she managed it and with a deep sigh laid back.

"Well done, Nihm," Marron beamed, "That was good. You'll be up and about in no time."

"Ankhew," Nihm said, returning her Ma's grin. All she'd done was roll onto her face, then right herself again and move back onto the bed but, dumb as it seemed, it felt like a triumph.

Marron fetched a waterskin, poured water into a tumbler then held it out to Nihm in challenge, watching as her daughter slowly raised her hands to it. She fumbled the cup at first but Marron held it still so it didn't fall.

Finally, Nihm managed to clasp it in both hands. It wobbled and trembled as she slowly drew it up to her mouth. Pressing the rim against her bottom lip she tilted the cup only to tip it too far. Nihm choked, spluttering as water sluiced into and out of her mouth and down her chin. Coughing she grimaced as Marron leaned across and pounded her back which was not helpful as she tried to swallow what little water she still retained.

Swallowing, at least that was easy to do, automatic. But moving, even just to drink from a cup was awkward. Nihm shook her head in frustration, cross with herself. It was such a simple thing and yet she struggled to do even that.

<*You have achieved much in a short time. You are progressing well,*> Sai said. <*The rate at which you are integrating and learning your new body is exceeding my calculations.*>

<*Did you just compliment me?*> Nihm asked, surprised.

<*I believe I was encouraging you. Do you not feel encouraged?*> Sai asked.

"Well done, Nihm," Marron echoed. "You are doing remarkably well. Now get some rest and let's see how you feel when we stop. Maybe with a little help, we might get you on your feet."

"Oggi," Nihm nodded, excited at the prospect. It would be easier on the ground rather than in the back of a bumpy wagon.

Lying down, Nihm felt Marron clasp her hand. Her mother held it tight in hers and squeezed it gently, stroking it, and tracing a spiral on the back with a finger. It was what she did when Nihm was younger and feeling poorly. The sensation was soft and relaxing and unexpectedly quite emotional for her.

<*Are you upset?*> Sai asked, puzzled.

<No,> she sniffed.

<*Your apertures are leaking. I do not detect any foreign debris in your eyes.*>

<*I'm happy that's all. Ma is here and it's just happy memories,*> Nihm said.

Marron stroked Nihm's face, tucking back some hair behind her ear that had broken loose from her tie. "I'll wake you when we stop. Promise," Marron said, wiping away a tear that tracked down her daughter's cheek. "Now close your eyes my sweet." Leaning over, Marron kissed her forehead.

* * *

Nihm must have dozed because the next she knew Sai was waking her to advise they had stopped. It was frustrating lying in the back of the wagon. She could see nothing and had no one to tell her what was going on. So Nihm listened.

Her hearing seemed inordinately sharp. She could hear Marron and Morten talking quietly at the front of the wagon but found she could discern many more sounds besides.

One sound though was missing, the grinding tread of the wheels. She'd grown accustomed to its steady rumble. It seemed almost peaceful without it. Concentrating, Nihm separated the many different noises she could hear and filtered them out; Marron and Morten talking, the distant sounds of the river, even the birds singing. Nihm didn't know how she managed it. She thought it and it happened, the sounds were still there just muted.

There, that was what had taken her interest. Mercy and Stama talked with someone. No, more than one. They were distant, Nihm wasn't sure how far, but she couldn't make out what was said. Focusing, Nihm felt a rushing sensation and suddenly their voices crystallised. Maybe they weren't that far off after all.

"…carriage. Near enough ordered me out like I had nothing else to be doin," a deep voice grumbled.

"Mind your tone, smith," said another, a southern accent Nihm thought, it certainly wasn't local.

"Mind me tone he says. You two bin standing bout guarding agin fresh air," Smith replied.

"So Father Zoller is up ahead in Fallston?" Mercy's voice interjected.

"Aye, on his way back to Rivercross," the guard volunteered. He turned back to the smith. "Be ready to go in a half-hour."

"If'n I get some help mayhap," the smith retorted. There was a momentary pause.

"Well, safe journey," Mercy told them. Nihm heard the sound of leather moving on leather.

"Hold friend." A new voice spoke up, "Thing is we been hearing things. Place is renowned for bandits and the like. Be safer to travel together, fer all of us."

"What sort of things?" Mercy asked. Nihm could tell her interest was piqued.

"Truth is nought much, but that's the point or not so to speak. Not seen any wildlife off in the bushes there nor heard none neither. Been here a while waiting and I got a feelin', that's all." The voice had a hint of uncertainty in it.

"You'd be doin god's work," the other threw in. He was on edge for sure.

"Hold a while," Mercy said. Nihm heard again the creak of leather and the sound of Mercy's horse walking back to the wagon.

"What do they want?" Marron asked before Mercy had drawn to a halt.

Hadn't Marron heard? Nihm wondered but didn't spare the thought as she listened on.

"They want to travel with us. They seem on edge. It may be nothing, may be something," Mercy replied cautiously.

"I don't much fancy travelling with Red Priests or their Red Cloaks. You know my reasons," Marron replied, tension in her voice.

"Me either. Thing is, after what we saw back on the road, is it right to leave them?" Mercy replied. "Of the Trinity, I follow the White Lady. One of her teachings is tolerance and help unto others."

Marron snorted. "Aye well, you know where I stand. The Red Priests have no love of me or my kind. It's a risk I don't need to take."

"What do you mean by your kind?" Morten interjected.

Silence. Nihm was starting to wonder if anyone was going to say anything at all.

"Say nothing further Marron," Mercy warned.

"No, Mort travels with us; he's a right to know," Marron replied as Nihm knew she would. "I'm of the Order Morten. Nihm and I are in danger until we leave the Rivers. Travelling with Red Cloaks will make that even more so."

"The Order!" Morten exclaimed in a low voice. "Did Ma and Da know?"

"Yes. Though we don't speak of it in these times, they knew," Marron said.

Morten considered a moment. "Well, it's okay with me. I don't understand why the High Lord broke the accords anyway but if my folks knew and sent me with you then they trust you. That's good enough for me."

"Better be more than okay, boy. A slip of the tongue in the wrong place could cause a lot of trouble for all of us." Mercy growled.

"I'll see no harm come to Nihm…" Morten flared back, "or Marron," he added quickly.

"Aye, well see you keep to it," Mercy said her tone slightly mollified, then addressing Marron. "So what about the Red Cloaks?"

Marron sighed, "We'll wait damn them. May as well get something to eat whilst we do,"

Mercy said nothing but Nihm heard her horse shifting and turning and then soft hooves on the roadside. Maybe I'll get a chance to walk now Nihm thought happy at the prospect.

Chapter 55 : A New Power

Oust Elbow, The Rivers

<*Have you heard from Marron?*> Hiro asked.

<*It's been four days since her last contact,*> Keeper replied.

<*Four days and you only mention this now!*> Hiro pondered a moment. <*You need me for something else.*>

<*Astute as ever, Bortillo,*> Keeper said.

<*I've not heard that name in an age.*> Hiro sighed. Keeper goaded him with his past but why? And why now? Finally, conceding, as he knew he would <*I'll help where I can and conscience allows.*>

<*Conscience? I seem to recall you lacked one of those when first we met,*> Keeper responded. A sense of amusement washed over their mind link.

<*Well none of us are what we once were. We're all of us changed, for good and bad, neh. Me more than most maybe but none more so than you,*> Hiro replied.

A vestige of annoyance trickled through <*It is foolish to fight who you are, come back to us Bortillo or Hiro or whatever you want to call yourself.*>

<*Bortillo is gone. I am in a different place and a different person than I once was. Why raise the spectre of the dead now after all these years?*> Hiro asked.

Keeper chuckled <*Ah my old friend, Bortillo is you. You can hide that part but he is in there still looking out when you sleep. Do not bury him too deep Hiro, the time is near when we will need all his guile. The Morhudrim have risen in the north. Their time has come again. This urak invasion is just the opening gambit.*>

<*What is it you want?*> Hiro asked, unsettled by Keeper's words.

<*Very well Hiro, we will talk later about our differences and try and find some common ground then.*> Keeper paused a moment before starting, <*Renix has news from the Council of Mages. Lutico, Thorsten's mage and counsellor to Lord Richard Bouchemeax,*

has sent word of a major attack. He reports Redford has fallen to an urak horde and requests immediate aid.>

Hiro frowned <*Redford fallen? That is grim news indeed. Still, it's good to know that scoundrel Lutico is still about. He's competent at least.*>

<*The council has no time for your scoundrel. Renix says they were dismissive of him and his report. By all accounts, he is old, washed up, and a drunkard. Hardly competent,*> Keeper said.

<*Well, it has been sixteen years since last I saw him,*> Hiro digressed before pressing Keeper <*So what have the council decided?*>

<*They are sending a delegation to Thorsten to investigate,*> Keeper replied.

<*Idiots! It's what they're for and the first sniff of something and they look the other way.*> Hiro let his disgust seep into the link. <*Why not have Renix report our intelligence on the matter? It would lend credence to Lutico's report. They would have to sit up and take notice then.*>

<*You have been out of the game far too long my friend. The Order is fighting a battle,*> Keeper stated. <*Many in the council fear our influence with the High King and are openly dismissive of us. As for the priests of the Red God; they proclaim loudly for our banishment. Renix, our ambassador is only tolerated because of the accords and it is only by the King's good graces we still hold any ground in the Home Provinces. We are fighting on more than one front, Hiro.*>

Keeper paused and Hiro sensed hesitancy on their mind link. <*If it were times of peace I would let you run off and find yourself or whatever it is you're doing. Indeed I have. But with the Morhudrim raised you are needed again. It is our purpose, your purpose.*>

Hiro thought on Keeper's words and knew he was right. He too had felt the darkness rising in the north and had ignored it for too long. <*What is it you need of me?*>

<*I do not know where Marron or Darion are. I must trust them to find their own path to safety,*> Keeper said. <*I have sensed something, a presence in the aether. Not Morhudrim I think, at least I felt no malevolence from it. No, it's something else. Familiar and yet not.*>

Hiro was taken aback, intrigued not least because he could sense Keeper's uncertainty. <*You want me to find this presence?*> It was the logical conclusion. <*Which means it must be close else you would send Chivalry or Ironside or one of your other knights.>*

Keeper continued as if Hiro had not spoken. *<I have been tracking it for the past three days but then, abruptly, my sense of it in the aether vanished. I do not know if it detected me or if something alerted it. Regardless, it has either gone to whence it came or has shielded itself from me.>*

<Where?> Hiro asked.

<North of the body of water called the Reach,> Keeper replied.

Hiro considered. The Reach was less than a day to the north and west. *<How will I know it?>* Hiro asked.

<From its bearings it travels south on the Great North Road. When you are close you will feel it,> Keeper reasoned. *<Take care, for I sense great power. Guard yourself in the tae'al lest it finds you first.>*

<And if I find it?> Hiro prompted.

<Not if, Hiro, when! You must. That it rides the edge of this urak invasion is no coincidence,> Keeper declared. *<If it is a threat, eliminate it. If not, bring it to me.>*

Power thrummed down the link, so unexpected it almost snared Hiro. He threw up a small deflective mind shield only just in time and felt the compulsion dissipate against its shell.

<Stop that,> Hiro snapped. *<I will look for this other and do what is needed. But don't ever try your compulsion on me. I thought we were past all that.>*

Hiro felt regret and contrition across the link. It was as close as he'd get to an apology. He realised then how desperate Keeper must be and not without cause. Things were serious. The Morhudrim was risen and they stood on the brink of a new dark age. And now a new power was at play.

Still, Keeper had overstepped the mark. Disgruntled, Hiro severed the link.

Chapter 56 : A Good Lesson

Oust Elbow, The Rivers

"Is he asleep?" Lett asked, watching Hiro sway gently in the saddle, effortlessly keeping rhythm with his horse's gait. The old man's eyes were shut tight and had been for a while.

Renco was frustrated. Lett had a habit of firing off questions like that despite his problem. This time Maohong answered her.

"Oh yes, Master Hiro very old. Must sleep where he can," Mao said his own crinkled and ancient face perfectly straight.

Lett wasn't sure if she was being teased or not. The old monk did appear fast asleep. "How does he stay on then? If he falls, at his age, he'll hurt himself. He could break a hip or something."

"He spend time with Chezuan Nomadi in ShóHang far in east, across the great water," Maohong explained.

Renco saw Mao warming to his tale; he had that glint in his eye that he got when he fished and felt the hook take. "They teach him trick to it," Mao continued.

"The Chezuan Nomadi? Never heard of them. Who are they?" Lett asked.

Renco allowed himself a hint of a smile. Clearly, being a bard's daughter she never tired of a good story, especially one she'd not heard before.

"The Chezuan Nomadi are savages. Fierce warriors that roam free, raping and pillaging wherever they go." Renco twisted in his saddle. It was Luke Goodwill that had spoken. His eyes were bright and he had a grin on his face. "Old Mao is just having fun with you, Lett. Don't believe everything you hear."

Mao snorted. "Been there, eh?" He asked of the bard before answering for him. "Well, Mao has, you listen to old Mao." Renco grinned enjoying the new game.

"Now, now, no offence was meant," Luke replied from atop his wagon holding his hands up in placation. "Only it's said, those that encounter the Chezuan never live to tell of it."

"Then how you hear, neh?" Mao sniffed loudly and looked back at the bard. "Bard live for story and long tale. Probably make most up. Mao will keep his." With that, he faced front and would not be drawn further on the subject.

Lett scowled at her father shaking her head in exasperation. He shrugged back as if to say 'what did I do'.

Renco watched it all in silence, keeping the surprise from his face. Mao might be a grumpy sod most of the time but he loved his own voice and a willing audience. Something had set him off and Renco wondered, not for the first time, about his companion and friend. Mao had been with Master Hiro long before he joined them both and in all those years had never really said much about his life from before. He had asked Master Hiro about it once but all he got in response was a curt. "Ask him yourself, Renco."

He watched Lett cajoling Mao but could tell from the tautness of his friend's shoulders that he'd say no more. It was all wind and wasted effort, but Lett persisted anyway. She was pretty stubborn but she was no match for Mao.

Imperceptibly, Renco saw Mao tense and knew he would snap at any moment. Nudging his horse forward he manoeuvred between the pair. Mao had a vicious tongue on him and he didn't want Lett to be the focus of his ire.

Lett's eyes flashed in annoyance as his horse brushed inside hers but Renco simply shook his head no and she seemed to understand, her demeanour switching instantly.

"Come on Renco, I'll race you to that elder tree and back." Lett pointed it out further up the road and Renco turned to look. As soon as his eyes left hers, Lett spurred her horse and with a shout of encouragement broke into a canter, leaving Renco behind.

Renco's face creased into a grin. Squeezing his knees his mare leapt to the chase. He slowly closed up on Lett enjoying the sight of her blonde hair trailing out behind her. He found himself feeling inexplicably happy with life. All too soon they were rounding the elder and racing back.

Lett, shouting excitedly, managed to maintain her lead, then flashed past their little band and whooped in triumph. Drawing her horse up to a walk, Lett turned back towards her Da's little wagon as Renco trotted up alongside.

"That was too easy," she laughed, as Renco's horse came to a walk, blowing and snorting.

Renco performed a mock bow in his saddle and grinned back. The grin faltered as he felt Luke Goodwill glaring at him. He wasn't sure what to make of the bard, which was unusual for him. He was very adept at reading people usually.

Uncomfortable under Luke's stare, Renco swung his horse around and trotted up next to Mao. He was the perfect companion for someone who didn't want to talk and he could tell Mao sulked still.

Hiro suddenly opened his eyes and blinked a few times in the bright light. Looking about he declared, "We will make camp over there," pointing to the meadow grass at the side of the road not far from the river.

Luke looked up at the sky. It was a perfect autumn day, blue skies with a few fluffy clouds up high.

"Plenty of light left," Luke stated. "Probably enough for another two maybe three leagues. Might even make Longstretch if we push on a bit after dark."

Hiro ignored the bard, instead, steering his horse off the road and onto the meadow grass which ran fifty paces before meeting the river. Mao and Renco followed without question leaving a disgruntled Luke to trail behind in the wagon.

Renco could see Luke wasn't happy, whether at being ignored by Master or at having to follow along, he wasn't sure. The bard was used to doing things his way.

* * *

They set up camp with practised ease. Luke and Lett having their own routine. In short order the camp was arranged, Renco dropping a final armful of dead branches and sticks into a pile for the fire. Stretching his back out he watched as a group of people appeared on the road out past the elder tree.

Renco had noticed since leaving Greenholme that the road had grown steadily busier and pretty much all the folks he saw headed south.

This group was larger than most with four wagons in convoy and ten on horseback herding a mix of livestock behind them. The last wagon had a big bull tied to the back of it on a long rope. As he watched them trundle south a man on the second wagon raised his arm and waved.

Renco waved back. He drew his senses in and closed them off before phasing, using his hidden sight to observe the flow as it ebbed and swirled about him. He could make out the bright signatures of the people on the road, identified almost as an afterthought the young and the old. There were thirty-one sparks altogether, ten of them children in or on the wagons.

<*Roads are getting busy, Master.*>

<*Yes, people head away from trouble. They don't feel it now but they are the lucky ones,*> Hiro replied.

<*How so, Master?*> Renco asked. How could people packing what few possessions they could onto a wagon and abandoning their homes and livelihoods be considered lucky?

<*The trouble in the north is worse than I expected,*> Hiro responded. <*They head away from danger. What do possessions matter when your's and your family's lives are at stake?*> Hiro asked.

<*But we're heading into that danger, Master,*> Renco replied.

<*About that…*> Hiro broke the link.

"Gather round I have news to share," Hiro declared.

Mao was sat cross-legged on a mat he had unrolled on the ground and so barely moved. Luke and Lett though looked at each other, then stopped what they were doing by their wagon and walked over.

"What news is this, Hiro?" Luke Goodwill asked.

"Redford has fallen," Hiro said.

"Fallen, to whom?" Luke asked. He'd spoken to several bands of people throughout the day. All had been fleeing the north and all told something slightly different. The theme though was the same. "Is this that trouble in the north you talked of? These urak the people speak of?"

"The very same," Hiro replied staring calmly at the bard.

"I've been to Redford many times. It's a walled town and Lord William is not lax in his duties. How could it have fallen?" Luke said. "Urak are creatures from the past, from legend. It cannot be true," he spluttered.

"I can't answer for Redford, but the urak are very real I assure you," Hiro said.

"Who are you old man?" Luke asked. "How do you know these things? You've spoken to no one since we left Greenholme."

"I know these things because Lutico, mage, and counsellor to Lord Richard at Thorsten, has reported as much to the Council of Mages," Hiro replied.

Luke turned away, walking a slow circuit to his wagon and back, deep in thought.

Renco watched the bard as he went. His skin prickled and he turned to find Lett's blue eyes staring intently at him. She quickly switched her gaze to Master Hiro then back again. Probably wondering who the hells we are Renco thought.

"So you're a mage," Luke stated as he completed his circuit. "That explains some things at least."

"I've just found out. You needed to know so I am telling you," Hiro replied. Renco noted he didn't correct Luke's assumption. "You should head south. Soon the north will be infested with urak,"

Luke laughed. "I'm a bard," he said by way of explanation. "You expect me to run from the greatest story of our age? No sir. Seems to me the Trinity set me on this path."

Hiro looked over at Lett, let his eyes rest on her for a moment before staring pointedly back at Luke. "You would take your daughter into war, with urak?"

Luke laughed again, although Renco thought it a little forced.

"Lett is my apprentice as the boy there is yours." Luke indicated Renco. "Besides, she's a woman grown. Lett can make her own decisions."

Hiro's eyes glinted in anger. "You're a fool. Urak are not men. However bad you think the Chezuan Nomadi are it pales in comparison to urak. To them, we are nothing more than livestock. I urge you, for your daughter's sake, go back to Rivercross. March with Twyford if you wish to go north; there will be your story."

"So you weren't asleep! Listened to us talking of the Nomadi, huh? Well, thank you for your concern." Luke sounded anything but thankful to Renco's ears. "But I'll not tuck tail and run to Twyford. There will be a hand of bards, probably two hands, all marching north to make their names. Well, I'm already here damn it. I'll not turn back." His voice rose as he spoke.

Hiro gave him a final, stony-eyed stare, then shrugged and walked off. <*Renco fetch our staves,*> he thought as he headed towards the river.

Renco did as instructed and caught up with his master just as he arrived at the river's edge. There was a crumbled embankment leading down to a stony expanse of shale that shelved off into the waters of the river. It was on this that they ran through their exercises.

Renco threw Hiro his staff and then, stretching himself, crouched into sleeping locust position. He lost himself to the subtle movements of his forms as he flowed from one position to the next.

<*It is time,*> Hiro said.

Renco completed his move gliding into the crane stance before finishing. He bowed to master before twirling his staff around and snapping it under his arm.

Hiro bowed back in the prescribed fashion of master to student, his bow little more than a nod of his head.

Renco was aware they had an audience. On top of the embankment sat Maohong, cross-legged. He liked to watch Renco get beaten and was saying as much to Lett who sat perched on a rock beside him. Her eyes looked wide and bright.

"That was amazing. No wonder you're such a good dancer," she said as Renco's eyes flickered to hers.

Renco grinned foolishly at the compliment.

<*We'll train in the water,*> Hiro said, annoyed at the interruption to their training. It was clear to him that Renco was completely besotted with the girl. He found it both amusing and perturbing in equal measure and was keen to test the boy's focus.

<*This will be a good lesson,*> Hiro stated.

Stripping off his outer robe, Hiro folded it neatly and placed it on a rock. He stepped lightly into the water until his knees were covered, never flinching from its icy bite.

Renco followed his example, removing his jacket and woven shirt, leaving him stripped to the waist. His chest and arms were lean and well-muscled from the countless drills and exercises Master Hiro put him through. He felt Lett watching him and was suddenly self-conscious of her attention.

Wading into the river after his master, Renco tried to clear his mind. Where had his inner calm gone from his earlier exercise? A gasp and intake of breath came from behind. It was Lett and Renco turned his head to find her staring in fixation at his back.

Renco coloured, embarrassed when he realised she looked at his scars. Scars that crisscrossed his entire back, the cuts and welts healed into hard ridges. Lett's hand had risen to cover her mouth. Did his scars disgust her so?

The next moment, Renco's foot was gone, taken out from under him as he took a step. He rolled into the icy water and back up onto his feet in one smooth motion whipping his staff around in front of him. The cold shock refocused his attention as water sluiced off his head and body but the expected follow-through from his master did not land. His ankle smarted from where it had been clipped and hooked.

Master Hiro stood calmly leaning on his staff, looking unimpressed.

<*You must remain focused at all times. Do not let the girl distract you.*>

<*Yes, Master,*> Renco agreed.

At that, Hiro launched into an attack and almost caught Renco across the head. He managed to step away bringing his staff up to crack against his master's just in time. It was an unusual opening. Normally Renco was the aggressor at the start of their sparring.

Master Hiro twisted his staff and looped it around to smack against Renco's as he brought his up to block before seamlessly swinging it back around and across. Renco blocked again, then again, and again.

The speed increased and their staves blurred and then suddenly Renco's foot was hooked again and down he went into the water. He surged back up barely blocking a thrust in time. He snapped his staff out pushing back hard against his master.

Hiro took that power and used it, letting it spin him around and down. Jabbing with the butt of his staff he connected with Renco's wrist, pulling the blow at the last moment.

Renco flinched; the strike smarted numbing his hand. Stepping away, keeping his eyes on his master, Renco flexed his fingers, trying to get some feeling back into them. He glanced to the bank and saw Lett watching him still, her eyes large in the fading light.

* * *

When Renco awoke it was dark and he was lying on the river bank. His head throbbed in agony and he moaned. He lay a while trying to control the pain, slowly gathering himself. Finally, lifting a hand he gently probed his head. He grunted. A line of fire burnt across the side of his skull where master's staff must have connected with him. It was odd. Usually, he could sense the blows coming even if he couldn't stop them from landing. This though, he hadn't seen or felt.

He was chilled and a stone was digging into his back. It was time to get up. With a groan, he gingerly rolled onto his side and levered himself up. His clothes lay on the rock where he'd folded them and next to them his staff. It took him entirely too long to get dressed.

"I don't like him very much," Lett said from the darkness.

Renco turned carefully, head pounding, to face her. He could see her dark silhouette outlined where she stood atop the embankment and wondered how long she'd been watching him. He should have sensed her but his head was so sore he couldn't focus on even the simplest of things.

"He almost killed you," she said. With a rustle, she bent and jumped down the bank landing with a crunch onto the shale.

Renco grunted. Her voice was too loud. His head pulsed like it was going to explode.

"And your back Renco, by the lady it's a mess. What he's doing to you is wrong. I know he's your master but it scares me how he treats you."

Renco would have shaken his head no except it hurt too much. She grabbed his arm then and hugged herself against him. He could feel the softness of her breast against his arm and the sweetness of her breath against his cheek, a pleasant interlude from his agonies.

"Look, you should come with me and my Da when we leave. You don't have to stay with that vicious old goat." She declared. "Mao could come too, he tells a story almost as good as my Da even if he is a grump."

Renco made it to the bank and Lett helped as he clambered up the side. Closing his eyes to dull the pain behind them they shot open as Lett's hands latched onto his backside as she pushed, roughly heaving him up the side. Scrambling up next to him, she grabbed his arm again holding on to him tightly.

Renco plodded back to camp, using his staff to lean upon on one side, with Lett stuck to his other, nattering all the way. He didn't really listen to her chatter, instead, concentrating on placing one foot ahead of the other.

It was a slow journey and seemed to take an age, although, in reality, it was probably no more than a minute or two. Renco's headache deepened with every step until finally, blissfully, he found his sleeping matt by the light of the fire. He sank gratefully onto it, rolling onto his back, eyes closed, breathing slowly.

"I'll leave you be. Think about what I said," Lett whispered. "I hope you feel better on the turn." With that, she was gone.

The last thing he remembered before falling into a blessed sleep was Mao chuckling in the darkness.

Chapter 57 : Life and Death

The Grim Road, The Rivers

"Very good Nihm, you're doing very well," Marron said. They had walked the hundred paces from the roadside to the river bank, wading through the meadow grass separating the two. In her right hand, Nihm leaned upon the staff Lucky had cut for Morten whilst Morten himself stood to her left, arm hooked under her's for support.

Mercy walked beside Marron and watched everything. She never seemed relaxed, Marron observed, not like back at the Broken Axe. Not since… well not since the night she'd almost lost Nihm. The night Mercy had lost two of her companions. I guess I'm not much better, Marron conceded; at least I still have my daughter.

Nihm had been very shaky when first starting from the back of the wagon but the further she walked the steadier she became. Marron thought she would tire but instead, Nihm seemed stronger, more coordinated. It was baby steps still, but just to see her standing almost unaided made Marron's heart sing. She was going to be all right.

The dogs cavorted around Nihm, Ash and Snow barking excitedly at her every step, bouncing around like puppies despite standing almost to Marron's hip. Thunder and Maise prowled in a wider circle, quieter more watchful.

"Go on away with you both." Marron shooed at Nihm's dogs, clapping her hands at them. She couldn't help but smile at their joy, it matched her own. It was a miracle to Marron. To think a few days ago all was lost and Nihm dead but for the dying, and yet somehow here she was alive and walking. She would thank the Trinity but knew it was the Order that had saved her daughter, not the gods. Her Order, who had raised and shaped her and to whom she had pledged her life.

"You can make it, you're almost there, Nihm," Morten exhorted breaking into Marron's train of thought.

"Ig gow," Nihm replied, her brow damp with sweat. She took a step and her foot snagged in the long grass. Morten tightened his grip on her arm but she caught her stumble and righted herself with barely a grunt of effort.

Then with her next step, Nihm broke free of the meadow. She had made it to the river and stood on the beaten track that followed its winding path. The ground flat and smooth from the barge horses that sometimes helped pull the boats back up to Thorsten.

Nihm shrugged off Morten's grip a wide smile on her face, wanting to stand unaided. She took in the swirling expanse of the river. It was wide and dark, its waters placid. To the east, a small skiff low in the water was about to disappear around a bend. It had been overloaded with people when it passed them by, all watching with grim faces apart from a few children who seemed oblivious to their plight and waved vigorously.

Marron hugged her daughter. "I'm so proud of you," she said. She caught sight of Mercy out of the corner of her eye. She was looking back towards the wagon, the scar on her face puckered and stretched as she frowned focusing on something. Marron let go of Nihm to look just as she heard a loud splash behind.

"Go on then, fetch it," Morten shouted.

Marron saw he had launched a stick far out into the river. Both Ash and Snow had grudgingly come to accept Morten over the past few days. It probably helped that he'd taken to feeding them. The two dogs leapt into the river after the stick and she smiled at the sight of it. They were young still and had lots of exuberant energy to burn off.

Marron glanced back at Mercy and saw she hadn't moved, her gaze still fixed back on the road.

"What is it?" Marron asked turning, looking back at their wagon.

"Lone horseman," Mercy replied.

Marron saw the man sat upon his horse. He was in conversation with Stama whilst Lucky, the two Red Cloaks and the blacksmith watched on. There was something off about the scene but she couldn't place what.

Stama turned to point them out and the horseman followed the stretch of his arm. It was hard to tell but Marron thought him young. He carried himself like a young man. His blonde hair was long and blew lazily in the breeze. The man sat on his horse a while looking directly at them. Marron felt a sense of unease.

The rider turned back to Stama and the others. He must have said something for as one they all abruptly sat. It looked incongruous and Marron felt her pulse rising as he moved off the road towards them. She had a bad feeling in her gut and wasn't the only one.

"Be ready, something isn't right here," Mercy said, slipping the tie off her sword hilt.

As he drew close, Marron's assessment proved accurate. He was tall and slender, maybe twenty years if she had to guess an age. He looked haggard though; his face pale and drawn like he'd not slept in a while. His clothes, which looked to be of fine make and weave, were dirty and tattered in places and one of the sleeves on his overcoat was ripped and torn at the shoulder.

Drawing to a halt ten paces from them, he casually dismounted leaving his horse free to wander off and graze amongst the meadow grass. The man stood with a lazy jaunt and regarded them, his blue eyes taking them in one at a time, but saying nothing.

Maise and Thunder's hackles rose and they rumbled deep in the back of their throats. Marron calmed them with a word, then with a splash, Ash and Snow scrambled out of the river. Ash had won the stick but dropped it in an instant at the sight of the stranger. Both dogs barked, snarling at him, and stalked forwards menacingly.

"Ash, Snow down," Marron commanded, staring at each dog until they sunk to their bellies at the edge of the long grass, their eyes firmly fixated on the stranger. Marron turned back to the man but it was Mercy that spoke.

"Dogs don't seem overly keen on you stranger. State your name and business?" Her voice was gruff, her hand resting on her sword. Marron was suddenly aware she hadn't brought her blade with her. Foolish, she chided herself. Darion would have a word to say about that if he were here.

"I am Sand. My business…" The man paused as if mulling the word in his head. "Yes, that is a good word, I like that," His voice was oily and smooth, sounding older than it should. Lip curling into a grin he gazed at them, his blue eyes piercing. He seemed unfazed by the dogs' menace and as his eyes alighted upon Marron she had the uncomfortable impression she was being assessed like a piece of meat.

"I am looking for someone," Sand stated.

"And who might that be?" Mercy asked a hard edge to her voice.

"Ah well, therein lies the problem," the man said. "I am not entirely sure."

"Well, I suggest you move on and look for them elsewhere," Mercy said. "There's nothing here for you."

Marron agreed. The man didn't look intimidating but there was a dangerous demeanour about him. He didn't seem quite right somehow. The voice didn't fit the body and there was an arrogant air to him that Marron didn't like.

"What say you? Is there nothing here for me?" Sand asked turning to Marron.

"You were asked to move on. I suggest you leave now," Morten interjected stepping forward. He looked hale and hearty next to the paleness of the stranger and stood half a hand taller. The man looked through Morten as if he wasn't there.

"It's not you, boy," Sand responded cocking his head to the side. It was his eyes, Marron decided. They were dead; the light behind the piercing blue gaze flat and cold.

"It's alright, Morten," Marron said placing a hand on his arm. She addressed the man again. "Be on your way."

The man bowed his head and gave a heavy sigh. "No, not you either. Nor you." His eyes flickered to Mercy dismissing her then back past Marron's shoulder to fasten on Nihm.

"Well, I guess that just leaves the girl." The man gave a smile that sent a shiver down Marron's spine and had her reaching for the knife at her hip.

There was a rasp of steel as Mercy drew her sword. "Go now whilst you're able." She spread her feet taking a stance, sword point lowered but ready.

"Now that is not very friendly." The man held his hands up and open.

A sudden distortion appeared in his right hand, the meadow grass at his feet blackening and withering in an instant. The distortion swirled and strengthened, growing into a pulsating ball of dark energy.

Mercy didn't hesitate, stepping forward she brought her sword tip up ready to strike.

Marron drew her knife smoothly, crouching without thought into a combat stance. At her motion, the dogs leapt forward as one.

Morten stood still, unsure quite what to do. His eyes were transfixed by the ball of energy in the man's hand. Suddenly it detonated. A blinding flash of light ripped out, followed instantly by a huge sonic shockwave. Sweeping out it engulfed everyone.

Marron was thrown from her feet. Pain erupted through her skull, eyes blinded and ears ringing. She blinked furiously but her eyes wouldn't clear, her head felt like spikes had been driven into her brain.

Instinct kicked in, training Marron had thought long forgotten. Training from the Order Halls back when she was barely older than Nihm. A mantra played through her mind, pushing against the pain, suppressing it. Deaf and blind she was at least able to focus. She muttered a cant under her breath; strange because she couldn't hear herself. Focusing on the words, Marron willed power into them. She lay there momentarily then released her incantation. Her senses were clouded still as her casting settled over her and pushed outward.

Her eyes saw nothing but spots though the whiteness was fading and clearing slowly, too slowly. The ringing in her ears ebbed away, still there in the background but she found she could make out sounds.

Listening, she heard quiet movement in the long grass. The noise was near, the man close and getting closer. She laid still, she would only get one chance and it would likely be a blind one at that.

Marron gripped the knife, miraculously still in her hand. She would have to wait until the last possible instant to strike. Still blinded she needed him close. Near enough, so she couldn't miss. He wore no armour just tattered clothes. One chance, one opportunity, it was all she'd have.

Sudden silence, the sound of his passage had stilled. Marron felt him near but where? He moved again and she tensed straining to work out where he was. Behind, he'd stepped past her moving away, moving towards Nihm. Marron blinked, furiously trying to clear her vision.

He spoke then, quietly, and Marron strained to hear his voice over the wind-rustled grass and the murmur of the river.

"So young for so much power and yet here you lie, helpless." His voice was soft. "The Red Cloak called you a cripple and a mute. Is that right?"

"Gog gug uorsov." It was Nihm and she sounded furious. Marron detected a blur of colours returning, gripping her knife she waited. If Nihm could keep him talking she would gut him like a fish.

The man laughed, clapping his hands. "Oh joy, a mute cripple. All that power tied up in an empty, useless vessel. I mean how lucky am I?"

Marron tilted her head back and made out the vague shape of him crouched over her daughter's prone body.

"Is that anger or hatred in your eyes I wonder? Both are good but I hope for hatred. Anger burns hard but dies all too fast. Hatred is strong and lasting, much more satisfying." He stood then, towering over Nihm.

"I tell you what. Just to be sure mind you. I will kill your dogs," Sand said. "Then I will kill the dangerous woman with the scar on her face. Quickly I think, she does not look like she will give me much and I don't have the time to break her. Time presses and I need to move onto your boyfriend and if I am not mistaken your mother, yes?"

Marron heard a crick like a knuckle popping only softer.

"I am going to cut off your boyfriend's cock," he said, his voice almost whimsical before suddenly shouting. "Hear that, boy. I'm going to cut your cock off." He lowered his voice again. "I am not a complete devil though. I will let you keep it. Place it right in your hand. Give you something to hold onto whilst I work on your mother." He laughed. "I look forward to that. They say it is good to enjoy your work and you know, I think they are right, whoever they are."

Marron's vision was still blurred but it was good enough to discern the vague shape of the man as he turned away from Nihm. He moved softly over towards the dogs and out of her field of view. There was a soft whimper and whine then silence, broken suddenly.

"Guk ou. Guk ou." Nihm screamed over and over, head thrashing.

A tear leaked from Marron's eye and before she knew it she was rolling to her feet, knife held out in front. The man's back was to her, fuzzy but distinct enough to see that he stood over the body of Thunder, his knife dark with blood.

Mercy suddenly staggered into view, sword gripped tight in one hand, staff in the other. Shaking her head and blinking her eyes she swayed like a drunkard, sword point wavering.

Sand sheathed his knife at the sight of her and slowly clapped. "Bravo indeed. I am truly impressed. You must have the constitution of an ox."

He held a hand out as Mercy lurched towards him and a small swirling black mass formed in his palm before streaking from it with a hiss. It struck Mercy in the chest blasting her from her feet and she disappeared back beneath the long grass. There was a pop and a puff of smoke wafted into the air, she didn't get up.

Marron flicked her knife, violently whipping it through the air to bury itself deep into the man's shoulder. She missed her mark, it was not the killing blow she'd aimed for but still, it should slow him.

Sand twisted to face her. "Ouch,"

Reaching a hand up and over his shoulder, he managed to grip the knife hilt. With a wet sucking sound he drew it out, his face stony and unflinching. Stepping towards Marron his eyes clouded, swirling like blood drops in water, changing hue from blue to black.

Marron dropped back a step; she had thrown her only weapon, a calculated gamble that hadn't paid off. No, not her only weapon, she was a weapon. Her old weapons master had drilled that into her. It was a long time ago but with Nihm helpless behind her she had no choice. Resolve hardening, she suppressed the fear threatening to cripple her body and felt her adrenaline surge.

Sand moved in, his arm thrusting through the air, looking to bury the knife into her chest. He was fast, Marron barely managed to step out and to the side. Blocking his arm, she pushed his strike wide and sent him off balance. Only it didn't.

His arm stopped as it flashed past and with a grunt of effort Sand backhanded her, the butt of the knife slamming into her forehead.

Head rocking, Marron stumbled backwards barely managing to stay on her feet. Her head flared as the mantra used earlier to keep the spikes of pain at bay collapsed. Shrieking in agony, sight dimming, she almost blacked out.

Then he was there, stepping in to hold her close, stopping her from falling. She found she couldn't breathe and gasped for air. His face was close to hers, his breath sweet and rotten as she gasped it down.

Sand released her suddenly, stepping away. He twisted his head violently to the side and his neck cricked and popped. Smiling at her, he raked his blonde hair back over his head.

"Now look what you made me do," he said, black eyes swirling, slowly clearing back to blue. "Still, at least you got your knife back."

Marron struggled to breathe, her chest was tight and there was an ache like a leaden weight pressing in just below her collar bone. Looking down she saw her knife, bizarrely, sticking out of her.

Moaning, she drew a painful, rasping breath. The metallic taste of blood was in her mouth, strong acrid mixing with the thick decay she'd inhaled from him. Wheezing, she wobbled on her feet, not sure how she was still upright. As if with that thought she staggered suddenly and lost her balance.

"Oh no, no, no, no," Sand cried lurching towards her, grasping.

As Marron stumbled back the ground suddenly disappeared beneath her and she was falling. With a splash, she slapped into the waters of the Oust and disappeared beneath them. It was shockingly cold and it seemed an age that she was under. Water flooded her mouth as what little breath she held trickled out of her.

Her head broke the surface and she gasped, choking, spitting water and blood. She could feel herself slipping away as she bobbed on the surface, could feel the water pulling on her, trying to drag her down as she drifted in the grip of the current.

Marron felt her eyes closing and lungs seizing as she swallowed blood. She strained for air; it was her whole focus, just one more breath. There was a distant roaring from the river bank and she turned, peering myopically through half-closed eyelids.

The man called Sand stood on the bank facing away from the river. His hand was raised, energy pooling in it when he was suddenly engulfed in a huge ball of flame. The last image before her eyes closed was the arching flare of his body as it was hurled like a fireball far out into the river.

Her last thought was of Nihm, she lived at least. She would be all right. Nihmrodel look after her, she prayed, as her mind faded to black and the dark waters closed around her.

Chapter 58 : Fallout

The Grim Road, The Rivers

Morten lay writhing on the ground, deafened and blinded by the stranger's magic. Pain lanced through his head, crippling him. Was it his imagination then, when he felt a faint pulse wash over him? Morten wasn't sure what it was, but afterwards, his mind cleared and the pain receded.

Fear threatened to overwhelm him then as his mind and senses returned. He didn't know what had just happened.

Moaning he rolled onto his side, head shrieking in protest at the motion. With his eyes struggling to focus and his ears ringing, uncertainty took hold. Would he feel a blade slide into his body or slit his throat?

He heard a sudden fizz as something passed over his head, the sound loud enough to overlay the ringing in his ears. Then there was a smell of burning. He sniffed, but couldn't place it.

There were sounds of a scuffle behind, then talking that he could barely make out. His thoughts turned to Marron and Nihm. Were they lying like him, helpless on the ground? It drove him to action. He rolled onto his front and pushed up onto his knees. Senses clearing he heard the man cry out. "Oh no, no, no, no," followed moments later by a loud splash.

Morten crawled the short distance to Nihm, his hand closing on the wooden staff she used as a crutch, his staff. Snatching it up and using it for support, he staggered to his feet. The man had his back to him staring down at the river.

Morten couldn't see Marron anywhere but Nihm was flat on her back, eyes so wide the whites were showing. She looked wild. His heart lurched with guilt. Even helpless, she looked fierce; showing not an ounce of the fear that coursed through his veins. There was a sudden roar from behind, as of a fire when spirits are thrown on it, and turning groggily Morten looked back.

"Drop Mort," Mercy screamed. She had unlimbered her staff, her face dark with soot. The leather body armour she lovingly rubbed and ministered to every night was burnt and blackened and Morten thought it flickered with a faint blue nimbus.

The air rushed past him roaring towards Mercy coalescing around her. In her free hand, a ball of flame manifested crackling and wild.

The realisation hit him about the same time her words registered and he threw himself to the ground. As his body thumped down next to Nihm an intense heat washed over him. Morten looked up in time to see the stranger scream as he was engulfed in flame and blasted from his feet to fly a good forty paces out into the river.

Gingerly, Morten clambered to his feet and looked about. Mercy had disappeared, collapsed he thought in the meadow grass. The body of a dog lay nearby, it was Thunder he couldn't see the other dogs. Marron was gone, nowhere to be seen whilst Nihm still lay at his feet. Fear and uncertainty assailed him.

There was a rustle of grass and Ash and Snow suddenly appeared. They looked unharmed and padded over to Thunder's body. Sniffing and whining they pawed at him but there was no life there. They moved to Nihm nudging their noses at her and Morten realised she was sobbing quietly, tears tracking down her face.

Nihm suddenly flung an arm over Ash's back grabbing a handful of his ruff. Ash stood silent seeming to understand what she needed as Nihm pulled herself up onto her knees. Nihm's face was dirty apart from two clean tear tracks that ran from her eyes to her ears from where she had cried.

"Sctik," she demanded holding her hand out. Morten passed her the staff and turned away. His brain was clearing and his reasoning was coming back. Nihm, while distressed was alright. He had to find Marron and Mercy, had to help if he could.

Nihm grunted at him loudly. "Moron."

It took Morten a moment to realise she meant Marron. Nihm hobbled dangerously close to the river bank. Morten's heart quickened and he hurried towards her just as his mind kicked in. Filtering what had happened, he recalled the splash he'd heard earlier and knew then where Marron was.

Rushing to Nihm's side, Morten stared out across the water. His eyesight was still hazy and the dipping sun glinting off its surface dazzled his already sore eyes, sending ripples of pain through his head again.

Shielding his eyes as best he could, he looked anyway. How could he not? There was no sign of Marron. Nihm pushed him.

"In ater, go, go," she demanded.

He looked back at her helplessly. "I can't see her, Nihm. I can't see her."

She gripped his sleeve growling. "et er. In ater, go et er." She sounded stricken.

"She's not there, Nihm!" Morten shouted. He caught a glimpse of a lump in the water far out, a long way from the bank. Nihm pointed at it, jabbing a finger towards it.

"It's not her, it's him." He stated, watching it until it disappeared around a bend in the river.

Nihm sank to her knees, a look of abject misery on her face. "Nihm, I have to go. Mercy is back there," he said. Guilt washed over him again at her look. How could he say, that even if Marron were in the water, he couldn't help her. Was he running away to help Mercy so he didn't have to face the water?

There was a holler and Morten turned to see Stama running like a madman across the meadow grass, Lucky a good ten paces further back. Stama reached him, winded and breathless, and gasped, "What…the…hells…happened? Where's…Mercy…Marron?"

Almost pleased at the distraction Morten rounded on him.

"What the fuck? You sent that maniac down here and you're asking me what happened? He near as damn killed us all is what happened." Morten raged. All the bottled up fear and emotion bubbled out of him. He was furious. Why had he sent that lunatic to them? It was all his fault.

Stama hit him. It wasn't a big punch but it was sudden and unexpected and rocked him back on his heels.

"Snap out of it kid. Now, where's Mercy and Marron? Come on focus."

The punch had clipped Morten's jaw and it ached. His anger surged and he bunched his fists even as Stama's question sunk in. Shaking, he forced his hands to relax.

Stama watching encouraged him. "That's good Red. Control yourself. Now, where are they?"

"In ater, go et er," Nihm shouted.

"You what?" Stama said, not understanding her.

"She says Marron is in the river but I can't see her," Morten stammered.

"For fuck's sake, Mort," Stama turned to Lucky. "Look for Mercy, I'll go for Marron," he said starting to strip from his clothes. He fumbled at the buckles on his gambeson and shrugged out of it. He unwound the ties on his boots pulling them off, before removing his breeches and shirt leaving himself in his underclothes.

"Mort, follow the river down see if you can find her. It isn't far to the bend so just keep going. Look carefully at the banks. She may be snared or made it to the side," he ordered. Morten nodded.

"Hold." It was Mercy. She had appeared in the long grass, climbing wearily to her feet. Her eyes stood out brightly in her soot-covered face but they were red, bloodshot. The slump of her shoulders and stance all told of how tired she must be.

"Marron took a knife to the chest. I saw as much before she went in. If she's alive she won't be going far and I doubt she'll be swimming."

"No, no. In ater, go," shouted Nihm.

"We are, Nihm," Mercy said. "Morten, run hard and fast, the current will have taken her. We don't have the time to waste searching the river banks. If she's made the bank then we'll find her. If she didn't then we need to catch up with the river. So go."

"I can't swim," Morten said, feeling shame as he said it. "I can look but I can't swim." He felt stupid and helpless. He was worse than useless. He felt Nihm's glare and couldn't face her.

"Stama go. Morten, you search the banks," Mercy replied, unfazed.

Thankful, Morten turned to start his search, pleased to be doing something. He avoided looking at Nihm as he headed out. If he could find Marron that would change everything. As he stumbled away, he prayed to the Lady, please let me find her alive.

Chapter 59 : South Tower

Thorsten, The Rivers

Amos stared out from atop the flanking tower on the southern wall. The urak were camped well out of bow range, their numbers so vast they were hard to count. A war host moving in such large numbers was unheard of and they'd moved so damn quickly, covering the ground from Eagles Watch to envelope Thorsten in the space of a day.

It was a feat they couldn't hope to match. The Black Crow had been organising to move several thousand soldiers south to Rivercross. Something he knew took some hefty planning and logistics. Even with the barges arranged for the ride down to Fallston and onwards to Greenholme saving maybe two or three days, it would still have taken a good twenty to reach Rivercross.

"There're enough of the fuckers, eh," Jobe stated. "Thick as marsh flies on a turd," he laughed. It was brittle though, Amos could hear the strain behind it. He clapped Jobe reassuringly on the shoulder, the situation looked grim alright.

"That's nought. There's more of 'em to the west and north from what I can tell," Jerkze said. He'd been up before sunrise, taking it upon himself to go look at what they faced. "Reckon we're screwed, should've kept riding south. This is a death hole." His bleak assessment sat heavy in the air. That it came from the normally stoic Jerkze lent it added weight.

"Aye," Amos replied saying no more. Nothing else to be said he thought morbidly. He shook himself, angry at his fatalistic turn. "Let's find something hot to drink and some food."

They took the stairs atop the South Tower. Amos had turned down the offer of armour, preferring his hardened leather cuirass. Reinforced with metal plates to lend it strength, it proved a lot lighter than the chain mail offered and allowed for much better movement. That the chain mail was rusted and of poor quality played no small part in that decision and he was grateful for it as he clambered down the stairwell into the tower's guard station and newly repurposed billet.

Inside it was packed with soldiers, mostly men but a few women too, laying on bedrolls or wherever they could find space. The air was warm and heavy, a heady mix of oil, metal, and leather overlaid by sweat and stale breath.

Stepping over and around people they made their way down and out of the tower. Outside was a makeshift kitchen with a fire pit. Several men stood around it warming themselves in the brisk morning air and occasionally turning flatbreads on a stone skillet suspended above the pit.

The baking bread smelt wonderful to Amos and he nodded thanks at the bakers before helping himself to one cooling on a table abutting the tower. He poured a cup of black tea before wandering over to lean against the curtain wall. Jerkze and Jobe joined him, the three of them initially silent as they ate their bread and sipped their tea.

"Sou' east wall is our best bet." Jobe declared. "It's close enough to the river that it covers most of the ground. Urak have had to camp on the far side."

"Best bet for what," Amos asked, knowing the answer but asking it anyway.

"To surviving this thing, boss," Jobe hissed. "Way I figure it we wait till dark, climb down the wall and make our way to the river. Grab a boat if we can. If not, we take a couple of leather water bladders, fill'em with air, slip in and float away in the dark like."

It was a sound plan. Not without its risks of course but everything was a risk. It would mean leaving their horses and a fair bit of gear behind. Amos shook his head sadly, following his contemplation. "Can't do it, boys,"

"What? Course we can do it. We owe these folks nothin'. Atticus sent us up here to have a look around not get embroiled in a border dispute," Jobe insisted. He looked to Jerkze for support but his friend didn't say anything, instead, tearing a hunk of flatbread off with his teeth and chewing on it, staring out past Jobe at nothing.

Jobe shoved him. "You got nothing to say? Just gonna eat that damn bread?"

Jerkze regarded his friend. "Can't do it," he echoed. "Not tonight at least," he qualified.

"Why not? Give me one…no give me two good reasons why not," Jobe demanded.

Amos smiled grimly. "First the tri-moons are out tonight and no overcast means no cover. We'd be spotted soon as our feet cleared the walls." He was matter of fact. "Have to wait for the weather to close in to have any real chance. Preferably rain and not just cloud cover."

Jerkze took up smoothly from Amos. "Second, that river originates from the Torns mountains. It's fucking cold and like ta freeze your bollocks off afore a hand has passed." He smiled, but it was grim rather than pleasant. "Third, say we make the river, manage to survive it. What then? We'll be wet, cold, no horses, no armour, no nothing. Just us with hostiles all about and nought to defend ourselves with except inflated water skins, unless ya think we can swim the river in our armour and carrying our weapons, cause there ain't no boats left." Jerkze finished.

"By the gods, you two love seeing problems," Jobe asserted. "Just needs a bit a thought and planning is all."

Amos grinned at that. "Tell you what. Think on it some and let us know once you figure it out. You'll have a day at least maybe more depending on the weather changing our way." He felt bad for the lie.

The truth was Amos wasn't sure he could just up and leave. Last night Lord Richard had welcomed his return but his report was moot since the urak had been evidence enough. The town had looked full to bursting with soldiers and armed militia when he rode through but he didn't have to look hard to see how young and old some were, or the fear that resonated through them all. The Black Crow had said as much.

"I've three thousand trained soldiers. A third of those have some combat experience, the rest are green. Most of my forces are conscripted militia, some few old hands in their thankfully, but most of those haven't lifted a blade in five years or more and it shows." The piercing blue eyes looked at Amos, remorseless, intense. "I'm short on experienced men, experienced officers that know what to do in the heat of battle. I need you and your men, Amos."

So it transpired he was seconded to Knight-Captain Lorcus Samuels. Samuels commanded a section of the southern wall. His command turned out to be a disparate, miss-match of a hundred hands of militia and four squads of regulars, all in around six hundred men and women.

Just like that, the Black crow had neatly tied him into this siege. He was obligated now. The Duncan honour code ensured that but it was a moot point anyway since they were surrounded. Jobe was up for leaving and Amos couldn't say his friend was wrong, he just wasn't sure he'd be going if the chance did present itself.

Jobe leaned back against the wall and stared at Amos. "Known you too long, you're a shit liar, boss, but I'll do it cause you never know. Might be I end up saving your ass again." He flashed his teeth then started suddenly as Jerkze casually leaned over and dunked a hunk of bread into his mug.

"You talk too much. Tea's getting cold." Jerkze said chewing on his sopping bread. Amos laughed and Jobe joined him a moment later, cussing at Jerkze as he did.

A horn sounded. It was loud and long-winded and seemed to reverberate off the wall. It was distant though and Amos twisted his head trying to work out where it came from. The closeness of the surrounding buildings made it hard to discern but he thought the northwest. It was where Lord Richard anticipated the first attacks would come.

"Best see what the lay is," Tipping the dregs of his tea onto the ground, Amos strode off, leaving the other two trailing after. They followed Amos into the tower which was a hive of activity and in complete contrast to the huddled and sleeping bodies they had passed on their way down.

Amos felt many eyes on him as he walked back through the guard room and billet station and a lot of whispered comments he couldn't quite make out. Stepping out atop the tower, Amos saw Knight-Captain Samuels talking with some men and passed them, moving instead to the crenels and peering out to the south.

The urak had gathered. They looked disorderly, more mob-like than anything but Amos fancied he could see a pattern to it; he just couldn't quite discern it.

There was a tramp of heavy boots behind and Amos turned as Samuels and Byron Mueller marched up. Mueller commanded the militia and was the Captain's second.

Samuels was young for a Knight-Captain. He was of medium build and whilst not fat he was well-fed, there was bulk to his frame and not all of it hard. His face was accentuated with a hooked nose over a wide mouth surrounded by a well-groomed courtier's beard and moustache.

Samuels hadn't been overly pleased when Amos first presented his orders from Lord Richard, seeming to resent them. Amos wasn't sure if he thought the Black Crow had sent someone to watch over him or whether it was simply that he was a southerner. If it bothered him now though it was hard to tell. Both men looked anxious.

When Amos had spoken with them late last night it was clear that whilst Samuels considered himself a seasoned veteran he hadn't seen any meaningful combat. So not seasoned at all Amos had thought.

Mueller on the other hand had seen plenty of fighting in his time. Trouble was that was the best part of ten years gone. He hadn't swung a sword in a while by his own admission and his bulk reflected it; the muscle loose and turning to fat. He looked more landlord than soldier with a paunch around his belly and a mop of grey hair that was both thinning and in full retreat.

"Lord Amos. The horns have sounded," Samuels stated redundantly. Mueller glared at him.

"I heard, Captain," Amos replied. "The urak are gathering." He nodded over the fields towards them. "What's the status on the walls?"

"I have the bulk of the archers assembled, spaced evenly, one militia and one regular with each bow to guard them. I have the rest formed as a reserve," Samuels replied. His face tightened slightly, a frown appearing as he realised he had reported to Amos.

For his part, Amos managed to keep the smile from his face. The arrangement had been his suggestion when he'd spoken to the man just before sun-up.

Mueller watched the interplay between the two. "It's a good disposition," he grunted.

The tension eased from Samuels at Mueller's words and in that moment, Amos reassessed them both. The young Captain seemed variable and insecure, Mueller shrewd and insightful. It was a shame it was not the other way around he lamented. Samuels would need watching.

"Now we wait," Amos said. He looked around to see who might be near then lowered his voice, "This is new for us all. Don't know much about urak except what I've seen and that ain't good. But we got a wall they have to get over. We stop that from happening at any cost. They breach the wall then it's over for us. They'll show no mercy and give no quarter. You fight for your families, your children, and your loved ones. You fight for your lives. Make sure all know this."

The two men murmured agreement and Samuels even patted his shoulder in a comradely fashion. They surveyed the gathering horde observing as their ranks thickened, forming for action. They left Amos shortly after.

"Brought a tear to me eye that did," Jobe said.

"Very inspirational, boss," Jerkze added.

Amos looked at them both. Despite their levity, he could see they were nervous, a tautness about their eyes. Too much time standing about and thinking he knew.

"You'd best go fetch our gear. Gonna be a long day and most of it spent here unless I miss my mark."

Amos heard a sudden dull, low, drumbeat in the distance and as he looked back the horde of massed urak stepped out towards the walls.

Samuels gave the order to hoist the red flag. Lord Richard would see it from the keep and know they were under assault. Thinking of Lord Richard, Amos glanced back across the town's rooftops to the Keep's hulk. He heard the braying of horns from the north and west. They would be assailed across multiple fronts it seemed.

Amos turned eastward, eyes tracking the southern wall. In the near distance was a corner tower. There were a lot of people and much activity on its battlements, their flag raised at the impending threat. Beyond that, Amos observed the curtain wall as it curved around leading to Riversgate.

The massive barbican and gatehouse at Riversgate sat on raised ground and was easily visible. Amos made out the distant armoured figures atop it and the ballistae that bracketed the gates but there was no red flag flying from its mast. It seemed the urak weren't stupid enough to attack the Riversgate up the long slope from the river.

A shame we don't have a ballista on this tower, Amos thought. The only working ballistae were at the gate towers. Amos knew from his histories that Thorsten hadn't been assaulted in over one hundred and fifty years. The expense of maintaining working ballista deemed excessive it seemed by the Lords of Thorsten past and present. The Black Crow had men preparing the older, mothballed machines that had been stored but much of the wood had perished or dried out and it would take the woodsmiths quite some time to restore them - time they didn't have.

There was a clatter and stomp of booted feet as men and women filed out along the walls flanking the tower. Section leaders hollered at them cajoling them into position.

Amos turned to observe as a squad of twenty archers tramped up onto the tower's battlements. A lanky, rough-looking man seemed to be in charge of them. He was unkempt, with a face full of whiskers and long dark hair loosely tied back in a tail. It looked as if he'd just been rousted from an inn he'd been drinking in all night. Amos was impressed nevertheless as he watched him organise his archers. He didn't say much but somehow managed to convey what was needed.

Feeling eyes on him, the man turned and stared back. The directness in his gaze told Amos that he too was being assessed. The man flicked a sardonic salute before returning his attention to his charges.

Jerkze and Jobe suddenly clattered back up the stairs, their shields slung across their backs. Jerkze carried Amos's shield on one arm and three bows in his other. Jobe carried the quivers and three long spears that he must have picked up from somewhere as they certainly didn't have any.

The two men set the equipment down near the flag pole at the back of the tower and Amos joined them. Picking up his bow, he pulled a string from his belt pouch and quickly strung it. As he did, he caught the lanky bow master watching with interest.

"Nice bit a wood," he commented.

Amos gripped his bow possessively resolving not to leave it unattended.

He moved back to the tower wall and peered again between the crenels. The amassed urak were walking slowly towards them, so tightly packed it was hard to count numbers but there must have been many thousands. He thought back to Mueller's report the previous night of ten hands of arrows for each bow being plenty. Looking now at the urak horde, Amos wasn't so sure, even if every one of them found their mark. The hard knot in his belly grew. They'd be in bow range shortly, they would know soon enough.

"I haven't time for you, girl," Samuels' voice was raised. "Unless you're a physiker I've no use for you."

Amos looked. A young woman in a simple grey robe stood in front of the Captain. She was plump and her face plain but despite standing only as tall as the Captain's shoulder she had a stubborn set to her. She looked familiar. Amos had seen her before.

"My master ordered me here," she insisted as if that were the end of the matter.

"Your master's a drunk. I haven't time to babysit his babysitter. If you can heal great, get your ass below. You'll be busy soon enough. If not, get off my tower," Samuels told her bluntly.

Her cheeks coloured red and Amos saw indignation on her face. She clearly wasn't used to being spoken to like that, he mused.

"I'll inform Lord Richard you turned me away. Good day to you, Captain," she declared. Walking off, head held high, she almost made it to the stairs.

"Hold girl," Samuels growled. "You say Lord Richard sent you?" he queried. She made no answer, just glared back at him. Samuels caught Amos watching the exchange and looked agitated. Amos saw the idea light across the Captain's face almost before it was there and knew what was coming, damn him.

"That's Lord Amos over there," Samuels pointed. "Stay with him, he'll see to you."

The young woman turned to look at Amos. The grin that had been on his face slipped to something else.

"Thank you, Captain," she said. But Samuels had already moved away, his attention elsewhere. She ambled over to Amos and inclined her head. "Lord Amos, though we were not formally introduced, we meet again."

The realisation hit Amos as she addressed him. The Broken Axe; she was Lutico's frumpy apprentice. What had the old man called her?

“I’m Amos Duncan, though Amos will do,” he said smoothly, holding his hand out in greeting.

She took it, inclining her head. “Junip Jorgstein, Master Lutico’s apprentice. Junip will do,” she mimicked, smiling as she said it. It transformed her plain features, giving her a homely and friendly appeal. Amos decided he liked her.

“This here is Jobe and Jerkze,” he said. Amos glanced back out past the battlements. The urak had stopped just outside of bow range.

He turned back to Junip. “That was well played with the Captain. Now, why are you here? A mage's apprentice might be useful if you’re any good.”

Her lip curled at that. “Would you mind?” She indicated the crenels.

Amos stood aside and she moved to the wall peering out at the urak. “Why are they waiting?” she asked.

“Your guess is as good as mine,” Amos replied as she raised her hands out in front of her. He felt the hairs on his arms raise, “You casting?”

“It’s a trick Master Lutico taught me recently, take a look.” She held her hands up for him to see through.

Amos peered between the arch of her fingers. The air was distorted but he could make out a mass of urak standing as if they were twenty paces away. He whistled, impressed, and Junip smiled. Nudging her hands, he moved them about.

“That’s a neat trick,” Amos said eventually. The urak stood silent, glaring as if they could see him right back. All had white face paint on in the form of a hand, fingers splayed. Behind were banners bearing a wolf’s head superimposed over a white hand.

“What else can you do?” he asked. Mercy was a fire mage but had never manipulated the air like this.

She replied as if he’d asked a different question. “Lord Richard thought they would attack from the north and west. My master was charged with working on the defences. I watched and learned until he was satisfied. He assigned me the south wall. Part of my training he said, although I suspect it was to keep me out from under his feet.”

She looked through her hands at the urak as she spoke, clearly fascinated with what she saw. "In truth, they didn't expect the urak to come in such numbers or that they would attack from the south, not at first anyway."

She jumped suddenly as if pinched. Dropping her hands Junip spun back against the merlon, shock on her face.

"What is it?" Amos asked.

"They felt me watching," she said. "I felt a pulse of something in the aether. They have magic users with them."

Chapter 60 : Hellfire

Thorsten, The Rivers

The urak seemed beyond count to Lutico. They covered Northfield like a writhing carpet. Lord Richard stood to his left, issuing orders. Lord Jacob was away commanding the west tower.

A drumbeat sounded, low and sullen, echoing as it washed against the walls. Then another beat, more drums joining it, sounding in time adding depth and tone. The sound was ominous and a disquieting tension laced the air, the defenders shifting nervously.

The urak had amassed just outside of bow range but in reach of the ballistae. They had two of the massive weapons, cranked, loaded, and ready to fire but Lord Richard held back the order to unleash them. 'We wait' is all he said.

Another beat reverberated across the field and along the walls, then silence. An unnatural stillness settled over the walls and barbican, the guards watching in trepidation as the ranks of the massed horde thickened with more urak joining from behind.

The drums beat again; followed by a higher, louder crash. At some unseen signal, the urak had raised their shields and beat them. The contrast in sound was sudden and startling and set Lutico's heart racing. It would be soon he knew, observing from over Lord Richard's shoulder. But still, the urak stood unmoved. It was unnerving.

"Come-on ya bastards," a lone voice cried from the battlements.

As if in reply, the beat of drums and crash of shields sounded again. The urak stepped forward as one, shields raised, big round blocks of wood in a smorgasbord of colours and design but each with a white-hand etched somewhere on the front. With every beat and crash, the horde stepped closer, the rolling noise coming ever faster.

Lutico observed in consternation. It seemed so at odds with what he expected. The urak were just savages, weren't they? Ferocious beyond compare his histories said, but this... this was organised; disciplined.

The sound grew as the beats folded into a steady cadence. Lutico judged the distance and holding his hand's palm upwards focused on the weavings he had prepared. He could feel each strand. He swore soundly as he was jostled from behind and lost his focus. Turning, he glared at the offending man growling his annoyance.

Lord Richard missed nothing. Turning, he looked at his grizzled counsellor's scrunched-up face and the men-at-arms pushing from behind.

"Captain," Richard called to Mathew Lofthaus. "Clear some room around Lutico," he ordered. His voice was sharp, his tone said now. The soldiers needed no further encouragement and backed away from the mage.

"Thank you, my Lord." Lutico rasped still disgruntled. He focused again on his weaves.

To those that watched the mage, he looked to be staring at his hands, no sparks or fire emanated from them. They soon tired of the old fool and turned back to watch the approaching urak. They were within bow range and Captain Lofthaus yelled out ordering the archers to draw and release.

Lutico peeked again over Richard's shoulder as a ragged line of arrows sprang into the air with an audible thrum. On the fields below, the urak raised shields above their heads and broke into a jog. The arrows descended, thumping into wood and flesh alike just as another flight lifted from the walls. Most arrows struck wood but some found the gap between shields and urak crashed to the ground. But it was few among the masses and they were swallowed up as the living swept over the fallen.

The ballistae released, sending huge bolts, each twice as long as a man, to plough into the front ranks. The bolts scored a line through the onrushing urak, leaving death and destruction in their wake. But they were only two and only in front of the gatehouse and the bolts took time to reload. A cry rose, joining with the thumping beats as the urak roared. They had already covered half the distance to the walls.

Concentrating on his weaves, Lutico called forth little sparks of energy. Crackling and pulsing he sent them hurtling out to follow the invisible threads they were bound to and they raced, arching up over the battlefield. The casting was small, the magic slight but even so, something had been watching and waiting.

Lutico felt the tell-tale surge of magic release in the aether. It was unexpected, but the realisation as he felt it was instant, the consequences immediate. Panic set in.

"My Lord!" Lutico cried. Richard had been watching the approaching horde but turned at his name. He heard the urgency in Lutico's voice… the fear.

"Yes," he growled, concerned, and annoyed in equal measure at the interruption. He stepped towards the mage.

"Incoming," Lutico gasped. Grasping Richard's arm he pulled his Lord in. "Stay close," he shouted. It was all he could manage. With his mind, cloudy with fear, it took all his effort just to hold focus. Thumping his staff down at his feet, the runes up its length sprang into vivid relief of blues and reds as he triggered his defensive wards. Energy spouted from its top, boiling up and out to create a shimmering, transparent shield that bent around and down.

The magical ward was not nearly big enough to cover the tower they stood upon. The edges of the barrier carved through two men straddling its leading edge. Blood burst from their bodies as they ruptured. The barrier cauterising as it cut through metal and chain link, skin, and bone as if they were nothing. The immediate smell of blood and burst organs mixed with that of burnt fabric and hot metal to assail them, along with the bloody sight of two men sliced clean in half.

"What the hells are you doing you mad fool?" the muffled voice of Captain Lofthaus cried out, angry and worried for his Lord. Three soldiers stood within the dome of the shield, all ashen-faced and frozen in shock at the suddenness of it.

"Run! Get off the tower!" Lutico screamed, deafening Richard.

"What are you…" Richard never got to finish his sentence. A ball of fire appeared in the sky and with a whump and flash struck the tower, like hellfire. The noise concussive even through the ward.

The barbican's top was consumed in a huge gout of flame that exploded, bright as a flare, before dissipating as suddenly as it had struck. In its aftermath the tower stood as before, solid and unmoved apart from its charred and blackened stone.

Clumps of ash in twisted shapes littered the tower where men and women once stood. Alone in the black was a circular oasis of stone, untouched by the flame. Inside the oasis huddled Lutico, Richard and three stunned guards.

Lutico had some inkling of the magics released and was prepared, barely, for the aethereal assault. The first to recover, he found himself on his knees but couldn't recall how he got there. They ached on the hard stone.

"I'm getting too old for this shit," he grumbled. Firmly grasping his staff, Lutico pulled himself up.

Lord Richard rose slowly from where he crouched. He was alive by luck as much as happenstance, Lutico knew. If Richard hadn't heeded his warning he would be one of those blackened husks of ash.

Richard touched his head, heart and stomach with his fingers, in acknowledgement of the three as he stared at the desolation around him. They both jumped as a sudden staccato roar of explosions sounded.

Still dazed, it took Lutico a moment to realise it came from the field, the weavings he acknowledged belatedly. Making his way to the battlements he stepped over burnt remains, feeling sick and gasping for air. He had known most of them; they were the Black Crow's personal guard. Now, like that, they were gone to ash and smoke.

His body started to shake uncontrollably. Relief at surviving the attack and terror at what had just happened, warring with the adrenaline that swamped his body. Richard pushed to his side and together they peered out over Northfields.

Lutico wasn't prepared for what he saw, even though it had been wrought by his hand. The battlefield was littered with urak, many shredded and torn to pieces, some half-buried. It looked like the very ground had erupted in anger and vented its rage at them. Bodies lay everywhere and among them, slowly stumbling to their feet, survivors. There were many of them, most wounded and dazed.

Lutico's ears were ringing but the urak must have been making an awful lot of noise because a low moan filtered through to him despite the fact they stood a hundred paces out still.

"Why aren't we firing?" Richard shouted.

Lutico shook his head, he didn't know, before realising that Richard spoke to himself. He watched as the Black Crow rushed to the side of the barbican past the remains of one of the ballista, burnt and smoking still. Leaning over the embrasure he screamed at the archers on the wall.

"Fire, shoot them where they stand!" Spit flew from his mouth.

Lutico heard a ragged cheer go up. They must have thought the Black Crow perished and yet there he stood screaming at them like an avenging wraith. If we survive this a legend is born, he thought. His feet were sore; the heat from the stone starting to seep through the soles of his boots. He heard muffled shouts as sergeants took up their Lord's cry and arrows started to fill the sky.

Then hands were grabbing at him, dragging him away. He saw Bartsven along with several other guards rush to Richard's side and forcibly pull him away from the walls.

"Come, my Lord, it's not safe," Bartsven said, hustling Richard down the steps to the relative safety below.

Lutico's feet felt much better on the cool stone of the stairwell. He spared a final glance at the destruction upon the tower and the neat circle of clean stone at its centre. Improbable it might be but it looked for all the worlds like the pale moon Nihmrodel. The thought bizarrely conjured to mind the girl of the same name. Wounded unto death at the Broken Axe. She had somehow survived. He wondered if they would be as fortunate.

Chapter 61 : The Woodsmith Carves

Thorsten, The Rivers

Junip flinched as she felt the weaving of magic in the aether. She was shocked; the urak had magic wielders with them! She'd thought them savage and uncivilised, but to wield magic took ability and skill. It required training and knowledge of the art and that meant teaching and learning.

That she felt them searching for her when she'd used so little of her art meant they were well practised and capable. But nothing happened, or at least not what she expected.

The aethereal assault when it came was not aimed at her, it was to the north. She was so on edge she almost triggered her defensive wards but stayed her impulse at the last instant and was grateful for it.

That the casting was not directed at her was a relief. To feel it's shaping from this distance meant it was powerful. She felt its ripple in the aether, sensed its path as it travelled in a flash to connect with sudden and harsh intent somewhere to the north. She felt the tremor of impact as its magics abruptly dissipated but looking about was startled to find that no one else seemed to notice it.

Junip dropped down placing her back against the wall. Closing her eyes she expanded her senses out, her thoughts drifting. Master Lutico was to the north. It must have been directed at him. They were the only overt users she knew of apart from physikers, but their magic was more internal than external and much harder to detect. It stood to reason her master was the target.

Concern creased her face. He was unpleasant most of the time but he'd taken her in when he had no need. Had trained and nurtured her talent, believed in her. In his own way, he was the father she should have had. Despite his dour moods and drunkenness and as much as he annoyed her, she was still rather fond of the old bugger for some reason.

"Ere lass, you alright? Just stick close to us, we'll see ya right." Junip looked up to see a pair of flint brown eyes regarding her. They were set in a rugged face framed by dirty looking blonde hair. Jerkze, she recalled his name.

Incongruously, he handed her an oily-looking cloth and she took it without thinking and held it in front of her wondering what it meant. The man dabbed his hands at his face as if to illustrate before turning back to his vigil on the wall. Realising her eyes were wet she belatedly raised the cloth to dry them. A distant roar and ripple of explosions sounded, again to the north.

"What the fuck was that?" Jobe said looking northward.

"I've no idea," Amos replied his head pivoted in the same direction.

"Sounded like the devil's own arse letting rip," Jobe offered.

"Well, we got problems of our own," Amos said indicating the assembled urak. "They look about ready to charge."

Junip's eyes widened. Charge? The urak were about to charge. Fear struck her. Master Lutico had shown her the weavings to employ. Simple things really, something she had mastered years ago. In and of themselves they were not that much use in a battle she had thought, but it was what they were tied to that made them powerful. Lutico and the Black Crow, two of the shrewdest people she'd ever known had devised a simple and effective strategy and all it needed was a magical trigger.

It was ingenious really and at the same time so simple. Yet here she was scared to move, too afraid to bring her weavings into being. They had sensed her magic before. If she drew on her magic again would they pinpoint her? It would draw destruction down on them, she was sure of it; convinced that was the cause of the magical assault to the north. She shivered involuntarily just thinking about it. I'm not ready for this, I'm not a battlemage.

There was a loud beating of drums, they rang out low and deep, the noise reverberating around the tower. As it died out, ebbing away, another beat took its place and then another.

"Here they come," Amos said. She looked up from where she crouched and saw him testing the pull on his bow.

"We 'avin a wager boys?" Jobe said with a grin.

"The usual?" Jerkze replied.

A bet! They're crazy thought Junip. Yet, she found the thought oddly comforting wishing she had a bit of crazy in her. She needed something.

"Aye," Jobe agreed spitting on his hand. Jerkze did the same and they clasped their gobbed hands together.

Junip screwed her nose up in distaste. It was enough of a distraction from her fear that she felt a sudden determination come over her. Using the wall to brace against Junip stood, and peered around the merlon at the urak to see again what they faced.

Jerkze stood aside giving her room his bow, strung and ready. The urak amassed still just out of bow range but she could see them moving, shuffling around like wild beasts. She had to do something. Resolved she turned to Amos.

"My Lord," she failed to keep the tremor from her voice.

"Amos," he stated. "Lords are for dinners and finery. On the wall here Amos will do." He smiled reassuringly at her.

"Lor…Amos, I have a trap I'm meant to spring that might blunt their assault," she stammered.

"Meant to? Why am I sensing a big but here?" Amos replied.

Jobe chuckled next to her and her eyes darted to him in time to see Jerkze scowl and punch his arm. Junip ignored them both.

"They have mages. They can sense if I draw on my art. They've already assaulted my master to the north I think," she said. Behind him, she could see the distant urak raising their shields. Her eyes flicked back to Amos and saw he was considering what she'd said. That was unusual enough, not many listened to her. She was Lutico's apprentice, the old drunk as many called him, tolerated by some but ignored for the most part. Why should they give any more regard to his apprentice?

"Chances are good we're all gonna die." Amos smiled grimly nodding towards the urak. "Things look dire. So I don't see that you have much choice."

Great Junip, what were you expecting him to say or do, she told herself angrily. It felt good that anger. It didn't entirely erode her fear but at least it didn't feel quite so debilitating.

Amos was watching her, his eyes seeming to read her thoughts. "When I was a lad,"

"Oh, oh, here we go," Jobe laughed.

Amos ignored him. "My Da, Atticus, would oft deliver little pearls of wisdom, usually in answer to a question he deemed foolish I guess. I confess to not understanding most of them at the time but one such pearl springs to mind now." He rubbed his chin as he reflected. "A butcher does not ask how to carve a bowl, nor a woodsmith how to cut meat. I'm no mage Junip, I can't tell you you're art, only you know what you can do or not."

She nodded her head, he was right of course, she couldn't argue with the simple logic of it. Up to this point in her life, Master Lutico had governed what she did. But he wasn't here and now it was up to her to decide the way forward. So she thought about the problem, what to do, how to mitigate the risk. It was a fundamental of the art and one of the first lessons Lutico had taught her when he was sober.

The thought betrayed her and guilt flashed momentarily across her mind. She didn't know if he lived or died. Strange that the guilt was only felt at the thought he was dead. She cleared her mind concentrating on the matter at hand. In the end, it was simple.

"There's a way but I'll need help," Junip said.

The drumbeat was joined by a clap of thunder as urak raised shields and beat them. Junip flinched at the sound. Spurred on, she explained quickly what she needed and Amos agreed immediately, Jerkze volunteering to join her.

Jobe clapped his friend on the back. "Try not to let her get you killed."

"Getting mushy on me?" Jerkze smirked.

"Nope, just we have a wager. Be hard to collect it from a dead man, eh!" He gave Jerkze a friendly push.

Junip couldn't help smiling at their banter. Then, eager to be off the tower, she walked to the stairs, Jerkze hesitating a moment before joining her.

They made their way down through the tower, the guard room and billet all but empty of people. Outside it was a different matter, a hive of nervous activity. Behind the tower and walls, the drum and shield beat was muted but still ominous.

Taking in the slightly chaotic scene as soldiers gathered in a large block outside the tower, Junip looked along the wall to see similar groups at various staging areas along its length. Curious she asked Jerkze what they were doing.

"They're reserves. Used to reinforce a breached wall or spell the defenders on it," he explained.

She nodded understanding and noticed as she did that behind the guards and militia, women and men milled about. They were armed but didn't look dressed for war. They were unloading wagons of everything from water butts to crates and stacks of arrows. There were even a couple of priestesses and a priest of the White Lady setting up an awning and tables.

Junip's stride suddenly faltered. She needed a clear space, not even sure how much. She looked back at Jerkze, wondering how to go about it.

Reading her concern he grinned. "If only I was getting paid. Then I could say I'm earning me wage. Leave this to me." He strode past her before turning. "Erm, how much room do you think you'll be needing?"

She shrugged. "As much as you can get me," she replied, relieved he was with her. He nodded and with that pushed through the throng of soldiers.

The rumbling beat and crash seemed to be getting faster. As she waited for Jerkze she watched those about her. She saw many were nervous or fearful. At least she wasn't alone.

Jerkze was back in short order and with him several men. One of them, an officer by his attire, looked a little self-important. She didn't know what magic Jerkze had worked but the man gave a small bow before addressing her.

"Mistress Junip, I am Sir Daniels. I understand Lord Richard sent you and you need a space clearing?" He sounded both puzzled and intrigued.

Junip stifled a grin. Jerkze must have heard her invoke Lord Richard's name to Captain Samuels and employed it to the same good effect here. Try not to ruin it Junip, she told herself and put on what she hoped was an authoritative tone.

"Yes, as much as you can find me," she said. Seeing the questioning look on his face she forestalled him. "As quick as you can. The magic I call on may be dangerous. I don't want anyone getting caught in it."

Sir Daniels nodded quickly. Magic was an arbitrary thing to most people, seldom witnessed, and a mystery to many. He snapped out orders, and the men at his side, rough, serious-looking men, turned about and started shouting. In no time they had cleared an area twenty paces wide.

Junip wandered self-consciously into its centre aware that many eyes were upon her and was pleased Jerkze stood at her side.

Turning about she wondered if the space was enough. She had no idea. "Maybe a little wider, Sir Daniels." She called, her voice a little high pitched even to her ears.

Daniels shouted commands and more soldiers were called over to help usher people further back. All the while, the drums beat, and shields crashed hurrying them on.

Jerkze jostled her elbow. "It's time." He nodded at the tower to their right and as she looked saw Jobe waving down at them. There was a sudden thrum as arrows were released.

Junip's heart started thumping and her nerves jangled. No backing away now. Gripping her staff, grateful again for the solid presence of Jerkze at her side, she set it between her feet and let it lean against her shoulder. Holding her hands out palms up, she closed her eyes and concentrated, incanting under her breath.

It was a small casting, enough to bring her weavings into being. Her eyes were closed but in the aether, she could see the thin gossamer-like threads she had prepared over a day ago. To each, she attached a spark of aethereal energy, pulsating and bright blue then sent them shooting up each thread.

As she released them her focus switched. The sudden tearing in the aether she felt told her someone worked their art. Their casting dwarfed her humble effort and she almost lost her concentration as terror assailed her. She felt a hand on her arm and almost jumped out of her skin. It was Jerkze. His contact seemed to ground her and the crippling terror gave way to a simple fear that was enough to drive her to action.

With a thought, she activated the runes on her staff. She heard Jerkze cussing and then a sudden concussive pressure rocked against her. Light flared through her eyelids, searing her eyeballs and a roaring of flame and thunder assailed her ears. The pressure seemed to grow tenfold and a trickle of blood ran from her nostrils down her lip and over her mouth. Her ears hurt and her body was crushed tight, bones aching. The pain was intense. More than any she had known before. With a wobble, she collapsed.

* * *

With a WHHUUMPH the very air seemed to get sucked away from Amos as a massive pillar of flame struck behind the tower. The sound was so loud his ears throbbed in pain. It was gone in a flash and through the buzz in his ears, he could hear people screaming.

Looking back, Jobe was picking himself up from the floor at the back of the tower. He hadn't worn his helmet and his hair looked frazzled, his eyebrows and moustache singed. Amos had no time to see to him. That he moved was good enough.

Pulling an arrow from his quiver, his fourth, Amos deftly drew and released. He didn't even aim, the urak were thick on the ground covering it like an onrushing tide, and still far enough away that trying to pick out a single target was next to useless.

The explosion had caused a momentary cessation in the barrage of arrows but shouted commands rang out and they started to flood the sky in sporadic bursts. Then, as he drew to release another shaft, the ground in the fields below suddenly ruptured and exploded all along the length and breadth of the assault.

He stared in shocked amazement as earth and rock spewed upwards forty paces or more, carrying torn and bloody bodies with it. A shockwave of sound struck him, a rippling concussive blast that set his ears ringing all over again. Everything seemed to stop and all he could hear was the buzzing in his ears. This slowly subsided, replaced by screaming from the field below, joining with those from behind the tower.

It was unimaginable. Amos had watched it with his own eyes and still couldn't quite reconcile what had happened. The ground had erupted ten ranks back, the detonation decimating the entire length of the urak's attacking front.

Most in the front ranks had survived the blast more or less. He could see urak slowly hauling themselves to their feet looking dazed and wandering about aimless. An arrow thudded into the ground, between the feet of one. A miss, but soon, stutteringly, more arrows started to fly and urak began to drop, just a few at first, then, as more bows started to sing, in their hundreds.

Some few urak regained their wits and started to retreat, half stumbling half climbing over the newly formed mounds of earth and rock, clambering over pulped and mangled remains. Belatedly, Amos lifted his bow. He sighted on a stumbling urak and drew, firing without thought. The urak went down, struck by another archer before his arrow had travelled the distance.

Amos didn't notch another, watching instead their slow retreat. Of those in the front ranks, less than half survived he judged. Thousands of dead or dying littered the fields below. Fucking magic, it may have pulled their arses out of the fire, but he didn't like it.

"By the Trinity, Lord Amos. I don't know what in seven hells just happened, but I like it." Samuels clapped him on the shoulder, a grin on his face.

"That lass you had no time for. That's what just happened." Amos replied. He felt raw and was not sure why. The mention of Junip turned his thoughts to her and in turn Jobe and Jerkze. Jobe looked to be alright but what about the other two? His heart sank at the memory of that pillar of flame. Nothing could have survived that, surely? Fucking magic!

Amos looked for Jobe but he was gone from the tower. He peered over the battlements at the back and into the grounds below. It was chaos, people running about, shouting. From up here, it looked like someone needed to take charge. The blackened remains of three bodies stood like islands amongst the crowd, no one willing to go near them. Probably think they'll combust if they stray too close, Amos thought morbidly. He could see no sign of his companions. Resolved, he made his way down.

It was worse on the ground, a sea of people blocking his path and view alike. He caught sight of a sergeant and pushed his way through to him. Nearby was a blackened corpse, burnt beyond recognition. A black husk, bent out of shape, it was surely too small to be a man.

"Who's in charge here? Where's your commander?" Amos asked.

"Guess that's me." He pointed at the ash corpse at his feet. "That's all that's left of Sir Daniels."

Amos grimaced, assessing the man before him; the sergeant had a haunted look in his eyes, his face singed and red from the flame. He must have been stood close to the impact. On his arm, he wore a red cloth, sergeant's rank, non-regular.

"I'm Lord Amos," he said. "Clear this area, sergeant. Get your men and relocate any wounded to the healers. Have these bodies covered and moved. The assault is over for now. Calm people down; better yet put them to work. Understand?"

"Aye, milord," the sergeant replied. He stood a moment and Amos was starting to think he hadn't taken it all in when the man turned suddenly and started barking orders.

Amos left him to it. He had to find his companions. He stepped past the burnt husk, the ground dark where the flame had struck, the blackened grass crackling beneath his feet. The other two remains were next to each other and looked much like the first, unrecognisable other than to say they were vaguely man-shaped. He extended a boot and nudged one, not sure why, and a lump of ash fell away at his touch. What kind of flame did that? There were not so many people on the scorched ground and he wandered around it wondering how wide it might be. Incongruously, there was a large green circle of grass at its epicentre, untouched by the flame.

"Boss?"

He turned at the familiar call to see Jobe striding towards him, a big grin on his face. Amos took a deep breath and blew it out, releasing with it the knot of anxiety that had lodged in his chest.

"You found them?" Amos asked clasping his friend to him.

"Aye, Jerkze is alright. Junip is out cold. He carried her to the physikers out back. They're taking a look at her now." His smile widened as he spoke.

"Whore's tits, I about shat meself when that fire hit. The lass must have some moxie in her to sit under that and come out the other side of it. I mean look at me whiskers." He stroked his moustache, the hair curled and singed from the heat. The fireball must have just cleared the back of the tower where he'd stood.

Jobe led them to the back of the grounds. An area had been cordoned off for the wounded and the ground was littered with people, most suffering burns. A priestess in a white smock bent over a man cutting away clothing that looked to be glued to his flesh. Jobe led him past her towards the rear of the area.

They found Jerkze knelt next to Junip and holding a ladle to her mouth. She looked clean, her grey robes unblemished apart from a line of blood down its front. It contrasted strangely with those around them. Her face though carried the trauma of her ordeal. Her eyes were bruised red and blood was crusted and dried on her nose, lip and chin. Her ears too were bloodied by the looks of it.

Amos knelt next to Jerkze and placed a hand on his shoulder. "That was some show. How you feeling?" he asked Junip.

"She's can't hear too good, boss," Jerkze answered for her. "She don't look bad but she's a bit beat up inside. Priests say she'll be fine in a few days."

"Good, that's good. What about you?"

"I'm alright. I mean it was the strangest thing I ever seen. She did something, don't rightly know what but the next second she thumps that staff of hers down on the ground and it flares up. I mean, I saw your sister do it once when she was working but hers spat flame. This, well this was different, Amos. It was like the air suddenly hardened around us." He shook his head. "Kinda hard to explain, I don't have the words for it. Then that flame struck and the Lady take me," He touched his hand to his heart. "thought I was gone to join her. Then like that it was over. Junip collapsed as if someone had smacked her on the back of the head. So I scooped her up and brought her here."

He took a deep breath resting the ladle. "Didn't expect to see you down here so quick, what's happening out front?"

Amos explained. He looked down at the portly frame of Junip and wondered how she could have orchestrated such destruction. She looked like she should be working in a bakery, not reining death and destruction down on urak.

"Thousands dead you say?" Jerkze asked staring at Amos, an unspoken question on his face.

"They'll be back and soon is my guess," Amos stated. "Unless Junip here has any more tricks up her sleeve then it's gonna get a whole lot more up close and personal next time." He stood. "Stay with her. I'll be at the tower with Samuels."

Chapter 62 : Empty

The Grim Road, The Rivers

Nihm sat precariously on the wagon. It took some effort and a firm grasp of the side rail to keep herself steady, it helped distract her. Morten sat alongside driving the horses. They didn't speak.

Morten was lost in his own world of hurt. Nihm could sense his distress and the guilt he felt at Marron's loss but had no sympathy for him. If anything, she blamed him. Why hadn't he jumped in? He could have saved her… only he couldn't swim could he and the river had swept Ma away by the time they searched for her.

It wasn't Morten's fault but that didn't stop her anger at him, Stama, and Lucky too. Why had they let that…that…well whatever the hells he was… past. It didn't make sense and they had no explanation for it. Mercy did though; she had an explanation for everything. Compulsion she called it; a spell of some type. But Nihm didn't want to hear that either; she didn't want excuses.

Ma was gone, her anchor, one of two fixed points that had shaped her life, giving it meaning and context. Everything, Marron was everything to her and she hadn't even realised it, not really. Just took it all for granted.

A sob escaped her. She gritted her teeth knowing Morten was aware of her distress and worried for her. He didn't look but she could tell by how he sat and the tension in his body. She didn't want his sympathy. By all the gods why did it hurt so much?

<*Your pain is psychological.*>

<*Fuck off, Sai,*> Nihm retorted.

Sai must be learning she thought, he didn't respond. She wasn't sure when she started to think of Sai as he, probably from the start. Sai seemed amused at the idea or puzzled; it was hard to tell sometimes. He explained that the male/female convention was not relevant and to gender stereotype, as such was needless, Sai was neither. Not knowing what gender stereotyping was, Sai had explained it, in different ways at different times and Nihm understood it, really she did but still couldn't bring herself to think of Sai as it; it just felt wrong somehow. So arbitrarily Sai was a he, whether he liked it or not.

Gods, why was she thinking about this shit, she should be thinking about Ma. But she couldn't, not all the time. Her sense of loss was mind-numbing. It left her feeling wrung out. And Da, he wouldn't know she was gone. Nihm's hand rose, covering her mouth as she bit into her lip. Gone and he didn't know, the thought vibrated around her brain. It sent the empty ball of numbness in her chest, spiralling down, crushing her spirit. Another thought, illicit, cruel; maybe he's dead and gone too. Maybe she was all alone. It was there, unbidden and in her head before she could stop it. She screamed inside. She was so tired.

<You should rest.>

<No, I don't want to. My body failed me back there. You failed me. I'll not get stronger lying on my back doing nothing.> She was being unreasonable but didn't care. *<I need to be able to function, walk properly, talk properly. I'm no use like this.>*

<Your recovery has exceeded my optimum calculations. Rest is very important, you should not underestimate its healing and cognitive benefits.>

She didn't reply, she didn't have the energy and Sai didn't press her. Ash and Snow padded along next to the wagon. They were all she had left of home, that and the trunk in the back, and what did a trunk matter.

Lucky and Stama had buried Thunder's body. They didn't ask, just knew it had to be done whether for her or to take them away from their own failure to find Marron, who knew? Nihm didn't care. She sat with Thunder's head in her lap stroking his face as the two men dug. In death, he looked smaller, as if some essence had gone leaving the body behind to fall in on itself.

They hadn't found Maise either, though they'd looked hard. She was gone with no sign. Nihm knew she was dead too, gone to join Marron. Her Ma had both Thunder and Maise from pups, Maise wouldn't leave her. Not like me, Nihm thought, a bitter tear drifting slowly down her cheek.

An image sprang to mind then, a memory of Bear lying dead, Marron and Darion laying him in a grave much like the one they had just dug for Thunder. Only Bear's had been under the shade of an apple tree back at home.

Nihm was five. Bear had been fiercely protective of her, big shaggy and formidable. She had cried her eyes out, sobbing uncontrollably. Bindu, Bear's pup, sat at her feet whining her distress. The memory was so clear. "It's good to cry, Nihm," Marron said hugging her. So vivid she could feel her Ma's arms around her squeezing gently and stroking her hair. "Bear's spirit will be looking down at you now and will be sad. She loved you and would be upset to see you so distraught, don't you think? Be sad for a while but don't carry it with you too long. Bear wouldn't want that. She lived a good life and you would honour her to do the same."

<*You can stop that now.*> Nihm sniffed wiping her nose. The image faded but its message lingered in the back of her mind. Nihm hadn't thought of Bear in a long time. After Bear had died she wanted nothing to do with Bindu, rejecting the pup that was meant for her. Her emotions were so raw she'd pushed away anything good. By the time her grief had abated enough to feel again Bindu was Darion's. She didn't mind though, she hadn't been ready. She understood that now looking back. The memory didn't lessen her pain but it helped, somehow.

Looking up she saw Mercy and Lucky riding ahead and could tell even from behind that Mercy was exhausted. The weary slump of her shoulders, the head drooped forward, and the almost languid way she sat her horse was evidence enough.

Nihm didn't need to look behind to know Stama trailed the wagon. If she concentrated, she could hear the tread of his horse and the creak of his riding leathers. And behind Stama the wheeled passage of the red priest's carriage and further back still the rattle of the blacksmith's horse and cart, a small disparate convoy travelling under a sombre cloud. It amazed Nihm how sharp and clear her hearing was. Whatever Sai had done had been profound.

* * *

A distant roaring of thunder became apparent and grew steadily louder. As their wagon rounded a bend, buildings appeared in the distance. Fallston lay ahead, where the Oust plunged to the lake below.

Morten explained earlier, in an attempt to draw Nihm out of her dark mood, that Fallston marked where the river fell away dropping down into the Reach below and that Fallston itself was a large settlement split in two.

The smaller sat atop the falls and housed the docks and stores for handling all the river freight from Redford and Thorsten in the north. It was rather unimaginatively called Upper Fallston although the locals just called it the Uppers.

The main settlement, where most lived and worked, stood at the base with their own set of docks and warehouses. Morten, thinking Nihm disinterested, hadn't explained further.

It was true she had been unresponsive, but Nihm did hear even if she wasn't listening. Could recall every word if she wanted, Morten's tone and the inflexion in his voice even the disappointment at her lack of interest. She heard it all, remembered it all but just couldn't find it in herself to care.

Drawing near they could make out several floating docks abutting the river bank with piers jutting out into the river. A large flotilla of boats and river craft were tied alongside, all empty given how high they rode in the water. There was no activity on any of them.

Shoreside were a plethora of buildings, mostly homes, although there was a wooden palisade near the docks and larger buildings that must have been warehousing.

They followed the road between the loosely organised rows of houses and into town. Many people were milling about and most gave only a cursory glance at them as they trundled past.

At the palisade, they were stopped as a guard signalled them and wandered out to block their passage. The man looked old and gnarled, like worn boot leather, but despite that, he moved easily enough.

"Hail folks," he croaked voice like gravel. Probably too much drink if his red-veined cheeks were anything to go by, Nihm observed.

"Hail yourself," Lucky said. "Looking for an inn for the night. Are there any you recommend?"

"You'll find nought in town," the old guard said wandering to the side and looking past them, back down the road.

"You with them Reds?" he asked. With a hoick, he spat a fat wad of phlegm onto the ground then cocked his head waiting for an answer.

"Nope, just travelling in the same direction is all."

"Pity for you then; the Red Father has lodgings at the Angler's Reach. Ain't nowhere in town with any room. Whole place is packed to bursting. Folks 'ave come from the north constant like fer two days. Black Crow putting the fear of the seven hells in them it seems to me."

"Aye, with good reason," Mercy said. "Found evidence a few leagues back of people butchered on the road. How many guards do you have here?" she asked.

"Butchered ya say? No doubt by these yurak folks is speakin' of." Nihm heard the scepticism in his voice. "You best speak to Lord Menzies. Be in the town hall this time a day. He'll answer you or no 'bout any questions ya may have. Follow the road round. It'll take you down into the town proper," the guard waved them by.

"Thank you," Mercy replied. "Keep your sword sharp and your eyes peeled to the north, best prepared for nothing than not at all."

"Eh," he responded, a hand idly scratching his arse. But Mercy had moved on, her horse stepping past him and through the gates.

"She means keep careful watch to the north." Lucky offered. "Peace to you, friend." He moved off following after Mercy.

"Aye you too," the old guard said before muttering under his breath. "Keep watch he says? Bloody idiot, what does it look like I do, eh?"

With a snap of the reins, and a click of his tongue Morten urged the horses on and the wagon lurched into motion. They followed the road through the warehousing and loading docks and out the other side of the palisade. After a short time, they started a gentle descent, the wagon swinging around as it followed the road away from the river and down into Fallston.

Mercy checked her horse allowing the wagon to draw alongside. "We'll ride through town and make camp outside since there are no rooms to be had. We can buy provisions on the way through."

Nihm gave no acknowledgement, staring straight ahead. Her speech had improved to the point she could make herself understood, but to her ears, she sounded like a simpleton and she was in no mood to talk.

"Sure, may as well get more feed for the horses if we get the chance," Morten said seeing that Nihm wasn't going to reply.

Mercy glanced to the sky and the grey leaden clouds slowly filling it from the east. A freshening breeze tugged at her hair.

"Rain is moving in again." She didn't wait for an answer. Nudging her horse's flanks she re-joined Lucky on the road ahead.

There were few houses on the descent between the Uppers and Fallston but as the road curled back around on itself they became more frequent. So it was that as the road levelled off into Fallston proper it was hard to tell where the township started. Fallston was a good-sized town, its streets full of people, most of them appearing to be travellers and refugees.

It should have excited Nihm's natural curiosity but it didn't. Instead, she was eager to leave the press of humanity behind, finding the streets oppressive. It was hard to think with so much noise.

It's difficult to wallow when you can't hear yourself think. The thought came unbidden and was so unexpected she wasn't sure it was her own. She said nothing, couldn't argue the sentiment whether it came from Sai or not.

Mercy led them on a slow journey through town. The influx of refugees fleeing the north packed the streets and there was an underlying panic that permeated the place. At one point, they passed the docks and were held up by the sheer press of people. The atmosphere was thick, the mood depressed and angry with too many people trying to barter passage on the few boats that remained.

"What's wrong with that one?" Nihm heard a cry and watched a man jab his finger at a large skiff lying in a cradle on the dockside.

"It's holed, ain't been repaired yet and not likely to neither, shipwright left this morning," replied a stout man. He looked harried. "Best advice is, walk to Longstretch. You may find passage there if you're lucky or you can wait till the morrow and hope the boats from Longstretch come. Me, I'd use me feet and walk. Start early you should make Longstretch an hour after nightfall. That's what I be doing."

A space opened up before them and they moved off, leaving the two men behind.

It was with darkening skies as the sun fell to the horizon that they finally cleared the town's eastern limits. There was no wall or guard station to delineate the town's border; just a gradual dwindling of houses giving way to fields and grasslands.

Even here, Nihm couldn't escape the press of humanity. Camps had been set up with makeshift awnings and tents. A few wagons and carts were spread amongst them but the majority of people had travelled from the north by river or simply on foot with whatever they could carry.

"It'll be a long walk south for most of them," Morten commented.

Mercy led them further east as the road followed the Reach, its waters a dark turquoise in the failing light, until the meadow fields cleared of people.

Pulling off into the long grass they made camp. They had travelled for two days together and had settled into a routine with it which helped, since given the subdued atmosphere, no one was minded to talk. Once the camp was set, Mercy called them together.

"I'm heading back into town. See if I can't find this Menzies," Mercy announced. A part of Nihm admired her tenacity. The mage looked tired, dark circles blackening her eyes, her dirty face accentuating her scar. There was a time Nihm would have begged to go with her. Was that really only a few days ago? Instead, she watched sullenly as Mercy rode off, Lucky by her side.

A cold nose brushed against Nihm's side. Ash whined and looked up with big amber eyes, nudging his head under her hand. Nihm scratched his scalp and pulled his big soft ears. Snow, sat on her haunches directly in front, looked expectantly at her. It was like Nihm's heart suddenly sighed.

"Coome om ten," she stuttered. Their simplicity was compelling, their need and love so fundamental and unconditional that she had no answer to it. It just was.

Gripping Morten's staff, Nihm turned slowly and methodically shuffled her way to the back of the wagon. The tailgate was lowered. Morten, it seemed had anticipated her need or maybe the dogs for he had left the sack bag on the backboard. He'd taken to feeding the dogs since she wasn't able to and it allowed Marron more time with her.

The thought of her Ma made her pause in melancholy. Was it always going to be this way? It was crippling. The camp seemed so empty without her. It wasn't though. A whine at her side from both dogs wouldn't let her be. They'd smelt the bag and knew what it contained.

Leaning against the wagon for support, she fumbled with the bag, her fingers struggling with the tie. The dogs drooled at her feet, tongues lolling in anticipation. Ash, unable to sit still, turned in circles, excited and Nihm couldn't help the crooked smile that came unbidden to her face.

Snow ever the more patient of the two dogs was more contained but her eyes never left Nihm, following her hands and fingers as she struggled. Finally, the tie loosened and Nihm pulled the sack open, immediately screwing up her nose. The smell was… pungent. Inside the remains of yesterday's meal, two large coneys Stama had taken with his bow. There was some meat left on the bones but that was it, the offal having already fed the dogs the previous evening.

Pulling the carcasses out Nihm dropped them on the ground. The dogs snapped them up one each and wandered off in different directions with their spoils.

Nihm watched them go, pleased at their simple joy, and jealous of it at the same time. For herself, she just felt empty.

Chapter 63 : Goodbyes

Oust Elbow, The Rivers

Renco rose before first light as was usual, to carry out his forms alongside Master Hiro. His head still smarted, aching with a dull persistence that he struggled to shake off but he made no mention of it. Complaining about it to master was akin to arguing with a rock, totally pointless. A lesson he'd learnt the first week of his apprenticeship.

Renco found his forms oddly compelling. He could lose himself in them, his body knowing the movements and flowing into each without thought. It allowed his mind to clear which helped his focus and promoted inner calm. He often found solutions to problems his master had set him after practising his forms, even if he wasn't consciously thinking about them.

The forms were a solitary experience, mind and body working in synchrony. He felt completeness and at peace with himself. It allowed him to leave any worries and just exist, if only for a while. Master called it finding your centre, a concept most found strange or struggled to understand. The forms were more than that though. Performed correctly they taught control of the body, not just movement but breathing and heart rate, thought, and mind. It allowed the senses to grow and expand, crucial for opening up and connecting to aether or tae'al, as his Master often called it.

Renco was just a small boy who had lost everything when Hiro saved him. Broken and traumatised he'd clung to Master Hiro like a drowning man to a piece of flotsam.

At that time all he wanted was to please Hiro, scared the old man would discard him if he didn't. He hadn't though and Renco had felt his master's ire enough over the intervening years to know it had been an unfounded worry. It took him many years, a lot of frustration, and much ire of his own to fully grasp what master taught of the forms and aether. The first time it had happened, the first time he had phased had been surreal. It was the happiest he could recall ever seeing Master Hiro, who cavorted about like a little boy.

For Renco it was bittersweet. Sweet, because when it happened it was quick, effortless, and natural. His world changed in that instant. It was like seeing the entire cosmos in the full brightness of day; awe-inspiring, humbling, and scary as fuck. Bitter, because it was gone too soon, slipping away as quickly as it had come.

Fuck. It was the vulgarity of that simple word that brought him out of his exercise. It was incongruous and out of place for him. Lett's words of the night before sounded in his mind. "You don't have to stay with that vicious old goat. Fuck him." He found it strange that her words gave him such a warm feeling, even if she was wholly wrong about Master Hiro.

Renco went for a swim to wash his body and clear his head. It helped immensely, the cold water invigorating. Lett followed him down to the river but declined when he signed for her to join him. It was the first time he'd seen her blush and it took him a slow minute to realise why. Grinning to himself, Renco dunked his head beneath the water to hide his glowing cheeks.

* * *

They packed up and set off shortly after, hurrying the horses west. Longstretch lay barely an hour ahead and although it was at Hiro's insistence that they stop early the day before, he seemed intent now on making up for the lost time.

Renco rode beside Maohong, Lett having abandoned him to sulk in her Da's wagon after an unpleasant incident with Happy. The cantankerous old mule nipped her when she had strayed too close. Shrieking in pain and clutching her shoulder she'd howled, cussing like a longshoreman and glaring at the beast.

Happy, for his part, looked unperturbed staring back as if to say well you did turn your back on me, it's hardly my fault, is it?

Mao thought the whole thing hilarious which didn't help matters. Renco wandered over to see if Lett was alright but she was not in the mood to be consoled and stormed off to sit in her Da's wagon, her earlier good humour vanishing like mist in the sun.

Renco found himself standing next to Happy with Mao's laughter ringing in his ears whilst watching Lett's swiftly departing back. Happy's head swung around and stared at Renco with big innocent brown eyes. You're a monster, Renco thought, patting Happy's neck despite himself.

That set the tone for the day. Renco ended up, not unusually for him, listening to Mao chattering on about all manner of things. At one point the old man produced a small length of rope from one of his many pockets to demonstrate how to tie a Kalbrasi knot, which was useful for securing a chest or door or restraining someone of ill repute. With a Kalbrasi knot, the more you struggled or pulled the tighter it became. Mao illustrated, but Renco wasn't paying attention.

* * *

They cleared Longstretch on the eastern tip of the Reach an hour after sunrise. The town was packed full of people all heading south. Flowing against the tide of humanity took them entirely too long and they got many queer looks from folk as they passed.

The road out of Longstretch followed the banks of the Reach west and north, the lake a glistening blue in the sunlight.

At midday, they stopped and broke their fast with some dried meat, stale bread, and cheese, washed down with water. Lett's sour mood had abated by then and she sat with Renco as they ate. She chattered away quite amiably telling her stories.

Renco listened attentively, pleased her mood had lifted. Nervous energy infested him whenever she was near. Lett could talk about the moons and he would be happy. At one point during one of her more outlandish tales, she'd leant over and rested a hand on his thigh and he almost bolted upright at her touch, as an electric tingle of energy infused him.

Renco was wondering, hoping they'd get to ride together when Master Hiro approached and Lett's good temper inexplicably shifted again. Renco felt her body tense where it brushed against his, her voice falling silent. It was dizzying trying to keep up with her moods or even to understand them.

Renco looked at his master expectantly as he crouched down in front of them and smiled at them both.

<*We will make Fallston tonight. Be careful Renco.*>

<*Yes Master,*> Renco said. Hiro patted his thigh then rose and nodding his head sagely, moved off to join Mao. Renco had the feeling master wanted to say more and was curious about his warning. It was unusual and lacked context. Be careful of what? Fallston?

"Why does he do that?" Lett hissed beside him.

Renco shrugged his shoulders. What?

"You know it's creepy, Renco? How he just comes over and stares at you. Doesn't say anything, he ain't right!" Lett insisted.

Renco didn't understand her meaning. Master Hiro wasn't just his master but his teacher, his confidant… his friend. More than that, he reflected, disturbed at having to quantify it, Master was the only one he could actually talk to. Sure he could sign with both Mao and Master but it wasn't the same.

His face must have shown his confusion because Lett leaned in close and slipped an arm around his shoulder. Her mouth brushed his cheek, her breath tickling his ear as she whispered.

"Don't worry. I'll look out for you, Renco. My Da is very canny."

It was strange, the whole thing bizarre. He didn't need looking after. Hadn't he sorted those men out, back at Greenholme? He should be indignant, he could take care of himself but her hair smelt nice and she was close her arm still around him, her body soft against his side where she leant in. Maybe they would ride together he thought, hope flaring.

Those hopes were soon dashed though, the afternoon faring no better for Renco than the morning. Luke Goodwill rode next to Master Hiro, leaving Lett to tend the wagon and Renco to ride again with Maohong. He was minutely aware of her in the wagon behind but she didn't call to him and he wasn't sure he could just invite himself over, could he? It's not like I can talk to her, he thought bitterly.

So he endured more knot demonstrations and old stories from Mao. The wrinkled old prune had a lifetime of knowledge and was more than happy to share it with him, but today Renco's mind was elsewhere. Until that was, something Mao said caught his attention. What did he say?

"Lust and love, eh. Mao say these two different things, same coin. Confusing, eh. Difficult for a boy to know?" He smiled his toothy grin. Renco shifted uncomfortably in his saddle as Mao continued, unperturbed.

"Girl like Renco, oh yes, very much. Set arrow at Renco's heart." Mao was enjoying himself entirely too much.

"Renco like rut with her, yes? I think very yes." He leant over and stabbed Renco's chest with a gnarly knuckled finger. "Renco do well guard heart, lust better here than love, eh!"

Renco was angry. What was the old fool on about? Poking him and saying he wanted to rut Lett? Rutting is what dogs did. He wasn't a dog.

"What do you know of love?" He signed furiously, shocked at himself. Did he love Lett? He'd only just met her. It felt real though.

Mao's eyes clouded over his head sagging forward. Renco felt his anger fade as quickly as it had come. Had he upset Mao? Mao never got upset, at least not like this. Upset his ale was spilt maybe or upset Renco had burnt the fish.

Mao didn't answer for a while and Renco thought maybe he'd breached some boundary he shouldn't have.

"It worthy question. Mao not always old man. Not always with Master Hiro. One day, Mao tell Renco." He sniffed and sat straighter in the saddle.

"Girl soon gone. Make sure she leave heart, eh." Mao moved his horse a step to the left, away from Renco. A small gap but a chasm in reality, one that said he wished to be left alone.

Renco sighed, worried he'd upset his friend and perturbed at the thought of Lett leaving.

At least the countryside was beautiful. To the north of the road, meadows rolled away, rising slowly into hillocks interspersed with woodland and bush. To the south, not more than a stone's throw was the Reach. The lake's cool waters had sparkled blue in the morning but were a muted green now as clouds rolled in from the east, threatening rain.

The Reach was narrow, but looking across there was no bank to discern on its far side as it morphed into the infamous Grim Marsh. Renco saw many boats on its waters. A few were fishermen working its depths, baiting lines and laying pots but by far the majority were shallow draft skiffs and barges full of people, carrying them eastward to Longstretch.

The road too filled as the day grew long, busy with refugees. Most walked, carrying what they could with them. As their paths crossed they were stared at, some curious as to who would be heading into trouble, some sullen as they were forced to concede the road to the wagon, a few hopeful.

"Is Twyford coming?" more than one person called out, only for Master Hiro or Luke Goodwill to shrug their shoulders.

"We don't know," they would say.

Renco watched the kindle of hope in their eyes flicker and fade before they bowed their heads and trudged on.

Whole families were on the road, young and old. It was sad and sobering to watch and Renco felt the shadow of trepidation build in his chest. What were they heading into? Master's warning about Fallston earlier seemed more poignant now looking at them.

* * *

They neared Fallston as night fell accompanied by a gentle sprinkling of rain. The fields outside the town were filled with people in makeshift camps. Renco watched Master Hiro and Luke Goodwill talking loudly before finally they clasped hands. Luke rode over to Maohong.

"Lett and I head to town. Wanted to thank you for your company, you tell a good story and play a mean flute. I hope we have occasion to meet again, maybe on the road north?"

"Safe journey, storyteller," Mao replied.

Luke turned to address Renco. "We haven't spoken much." He paused realising what he'd said before carrying on. "Never did get to show you much on the lute. Lett will miss you, boy. She's taken a shine to you. Take care."

The way he said that last felt more a warning than goodbye to Renco who nodded his head back in reply.

"Don't make me pull you off that horse." He knew Lett was at his stirrup, had been aware of her the moment she stood and climbed down from the wagon.

Looking down at her, Renco smiled, aware her Da's eyes were on him. Lifting his leg over the saddle horn he slid gracefully to the ground. Lett was in his arms hugging him as soon as his feet touched dirt.

"Take care, Renco. See you again soon." No warning in Lett's goodbye but a promise, his arms encircled her and he hugged her to him. She fit against him snuggly, soft and warm but, he wrinkled his nose, she needed a wash. Should have taken a bath in the river with me this morning, the thought bringing a brief smile to his face.

"Come, Lett. Before the rain sets in." Luke's voice was firm. He had hitched his horse to the back of his wagon and climbed on board.

Lett reluctantly released Renco. Standing on tiptoe, she kissed his cheek before turning and clambering up next to her father. With a snap of the reins, the wagon pulled off heading into town.

She was gone. A heavyweight sat on Renco's chest, a sudden angst. He fought the urge to ride after her. Found he didn't want her gone from his life. He couldn't explain it.

<I have a feeling we will see them again, Renco,> Master Hiro said wandering over. He laid a warm hand on Renco's shoulder. *<Let's get camp set up before the heavens really open up.>* He left Renco gazing forlornly at Lett's diminishing figure.

Renco stared down the road after her. At one point Lett turned and waved. He raised a reluctant hand in return feeling like his heart was crushed.

<AGGHHH!> Renco screamed. He sensed his master turn and look at him even though he'd not directed the thought at him.

<Calm yourself, boy. No need to shout to the world. You never know who might be listening. Now stop mooning around and stake the horses out,>

Renco felt his Master's displeasure over the link and was aware suddenly that he stood like a fool in the middle of the road. He looked about self-consciously.

A girl stood on the far side of the road not twenty paces from him. A young woman in fact, similar in age to his own, he judged. She stared straight at him, her eyes piercing and intense. He felt unsettled by it or maybe it was her dogs. There were two of them sat either side, big wolfdogs, one a mottled black the other a dirty white, it was a strange sight. Maybe it was why he felt troubled by her. Certainly, something was off.

Curious, Renco phased and looked at her through the flow, immediately taking an involuntary step back. Her spark was too bright, so intense it was hard to look at. In the flow she was a soft blue-white nimbus of energy, pulsing gently.

He phased back. She was stood there still as he knew she would be, her eyes still fixed on his. Renco wasn't sure what he had just witnessed. Not even Master's aura was so strong. For all that energy though she looked frail. There was a brittleness about her and a deep sadness he'd sensed through the flow of aether.

Bizarrely, she raised a hand in greeting and he found himself raising his own in return, a connection of sorts. She was slim and athletic in build but looked hard where Lett was soft. Her dark brown hair was long and dishevelled, lending her a wild aspect.

Leaning heavily on a staff, she turned towards a wagon on the far side of the road. Her movements like that of a frail old woman as she hobbled off the dogs flanking her protectively all the way.

<Renco! You going to stand there all night or are you going to help?>

Renco glanced one last time after Lett but her wagon had all but disappeared in the gloom and soft spit of rain. He led his horse off the road to Master Hiro who held the reins of the other horses out for him to take, a disgruntled look etched on his face.

Renco knew he should mention the girl but he'd sensed nothing bad in her, no danger, just sadness. The memory of her raising her hand in greeting still firm in his mind decided it for him and Renco led the horses away without saying anything. Besides, he told himself, Master was being an ass.

* * *

After the camp was set they ate a sparse meal of dried fish, fruit and some nuts Renco and Mao had gathered on the ride earlier that day. They ate beneath an awning to keep the rain off and set no fire because of it, so there was no light as night descended.

Renco and Hiro stripped off their already damp clothes to keep them from getting any wetter before going through their forms. Renco had excellent night vision but even so, it was not needed to practise by. Afterwards, they didn't spar.

Renco's heart and mind were elsewhere and Hiro knew it. Huffing, he said nothing to his student, instead, sitting next to Mao and talking with him quietly.

Renco joined them under the canopy a short time later, listening to the patter of rain on its hide.

"I go in the morning, Mao. You'll be responsible for Renco whilst I'm gone," Hiro said abruptly.

"Gone where Master? How long?" Mao replied. He smoked a long thin handled pipe and Renco could see the glow of the tabacc as he drew on it.

Renco listened, tense, and intrigued. Why would master go and why not take them?

"West and north. Wait two days, no more than that. If I've not returned, head to Rivercross and await me there. I will find you."

Mao didn't say anything for a while. The pipe glowed again before he exhaled. Renco could smell the earthy tobacco smoke as it plumed into the air.

"Yes, Master."

That was it? That was all Mao was going to say? Renco needed more. Wanted to ask master what he was doing? Why couldn't they go? Master had never left him before and the thought made him anxious.

<Look after each other, Renco. And listen to Mao. Do what he tells you as if I were speaking. I'll explain more on my return.>

<I don't understand, Master.> That one sentence encapsulated all his fears.

<You must learn patience, Renco. I will be back. Do not neglect your training in my absence.>

<Yes, Master.> Then unable to help himself, *<Is it your friends? You said you were looking for some old friends that needed help. Are they near?>* Wondering at the same time how master could possibly know they were near or not.

Master Hiro tsked at Renco but didn't answer.

* * *

In the morning when Renco awoke Hiro was gone. Renco was a light sleeper, his senses always alert even in sleep, but not that morning. Master had left without making a sound. Even his horse had been silent. That he'd left so quietly, without saying a word, made Renco uneasy. First Lett, now Master Hiro, Renco thought, both gone, both leaving him behind and alone.

The rain still fell, a late autumn shower, the sound against the canopy adding to his melancholy.

With a rustle of blankets, Mao sat up, stretched then yawned. Leaning his ancient creaking body to one side he farted, took one look at the weather, and tucked himself back under his covers.

Renco screwed his face up. Well, maybe not entirely alone he conceded.

Chapter 64 : Red Cloaks

Fallston, The Rivers

Nihm stood in the back of the wagon staring off into the night, the rain pattering softly on the canopy above her head. She could see his camp across the road. The young man intrigued her still and thinking about him helped take her mind off her heartache.

She recalled the scene perfectly. Him, stood in the road, body ridged, staring after the wagon with the pretty blonde girl in it, screaming his anguish. Only no one heard him, no one except her it seemed.

Nihm sighed into the night air trying to make sense of what she'd seen and heard. At first, she thought it must be her imagination, an externalised reflection of her pain. That it was all just in her head. Only it wasn't imagined. Sai had said as much, had sensed or heard it as well. The man projected a thought and she perceived it.

Sai's analysis was that the man hadn't directed the thought at her. It just so happened she'd heard it in her mind, much like if he'd shouted out loud.

<*Why did no one else hear it?*> she queried.

<*Maybe they did.*>

<*I don't think so? The woman and man on the cart didn't react at all. No one seemed to react. Is this something you have done to me?*> Nihm asked frowning.

<*I have no definitive answer. It is possible. I have modified your neural receptors and pathways making you more sensitive, more receptive. However, it must have already been a pre-condition in your… makeup.*>

Nihm thought back to the man's cry and the moment it exploded in her head. She had known it was him, their minds seemed to touch in that instant. She felt a tumult of emotions, despair, anger, love as if they were her own. It was disorienting, to say the least. He was hurt and confused. Then as his cry faded it was gone, like a door slamming shut.

Nihm was curious. The cascade of emotion she felt lacked meaning. Why was he messed up? The girl obviously but who was he and how had he connected to her mind? Did he know he had? All these questions assailed her. She wasn't sure why she raised her hand to acknowledge him. Maybe it was just to say she'd heard his pain, that she shared it.

"Why do you stare off into the dark?" Morten asked, concern clear in his voice.

Nihm had heard Morten climbing into the back of the wagon and presumed it was to check on her. Well, she didn't want his concern. She just wanted to be left alone.

"I lieke du cul bwereze ong ma faash," she snapped, knowing it was unwarranted, knowing Morten had his own struggles.

"I'll leave you be then," Morten mumbled. He clambered back out the front of the wagon ducking beneath the awning he'd erected earlier against the rain.

Morten was right, thought Nihm, it was dark out. The overcast skies meant night had set in early. The rain had picked up as well but despite this, she had little trouble seeing the camp across the road. Her eyesight was good, better than good in fact. In the darkness, her eyes seemed to change and adjust, like a lens dropping over them. Her surroundings took on a greener, more muted aspect as if the colour had been drained from everything. Despite this, her vision was crisp, clearer than should be possible.

Nihm watched with interest as the young man and his elderly father walked all but naked into the long grass near their camp and danced. Well, it looked like a dance, only she sensed there was more to it than that. Their movements had been distinct and separate but each was smooth and controlled, flowing from one shape into another. It was surreal and mesmerising to watch if a little strange.

That night, Nihm slept soundly, exhausted physically and emotionally. She dreamt of Ma and Da and the homestead, happy dreams of yesterday. When she awoke she recalled them vividly and cried silently in her bed covers.

Everything had happened so fast, her life changed so dramatically she hardly recognised herself, the homestead seeming a lifetime ago. Now it was just her.

She listened to the patter of rain on the wagon's canopy, the soothing sound a perfect accompaniment to her melancholy. The sound of leather creasing interrupted her reverie. It came from the road outside. Slowly, awkwardly, she got to her feet and walked gingerly to the back of the wagon, stepping over Mercy's still sleeping form.

The woman had been exhausted when she'd returned from town. She had looked like death and slept like it now. She didn't stir.

It was still dark as Nihm looked out onto the road. She saw a man on a horse riding towards town. She knew, even from behind, it was the elderly father. Looking at his camp confirmed that one of the horses was gone and she could see only two bundles under their canopy where bodies lay sleeping.

The early morning air was cold on her skin. The rain was little more than a drizzle but everywhere was wet. Turning away, Nihm returned to her bedding but found she couldn't sleep. Every time she closed her eyes her mother's face stared back at her. Not the happy smiling one Nihm knew and loved, or the one from her dreams, but the one Marron wore as she toppled into the river, a dagger sticking from her chest, pain and confusion on her face. It haunted her. She sat up and dressed, a painfully slow process but important.

<*It is good for your muscle control and coordination,*> Sai told her.

Pulling her boots on, Nihm tied her leggings then climbed slowly out the front of the wagon. Ash and Snow were ready and waiting as she disembarked. It was still half dark but daylight threatened the eastern horizon and she knew the others would awaken soon. Already she could hear a change in their breathing patterns. She blinked, amazed at herself, and how she even knew that or could register it.

<*As I have explained already, I have improved your hearing and vision. Would you like me to explain again?*> Sai asked.

<*I know you told me, but it's different being told about something and experiencing it,*> Nihm said. Ash and Snow milled around her legs, threatening to knock her over.

"Com on then. Lat's go far ai wark an stetch ma lags owt." Nihm whispered, so as not to disturb anyone. She needn't have bothered. Stama was awake and alert. He said nothing to her though, merely bobbed his head in acknowledgement.

Stama pointed suddenly past her shoulder before bringing his finger to his lips. Turning, Nihm saw a stag not fifty paces away. It must have just stepped from the undergrowth.

Sniffing the air, he snorted, looking around. Turning away, the stag trotted eastward following the edge between bush and grasslands. A deer stepped out behind and followed, and then another. Nihm watched, captivated, as soon a whole herd gathered. They didn't stop to graze but followed the big stag as he trotted eastward.

Nihm had seen plenty of deer before but to see a herd this big and this close to so many people was strange. It was unusual behaviour.

"What do ya make of that?" Stama whispered.

"Strange," Nihm enunciated carefully. Her speech was much better. "I gu far wark," she told Stama.

"Want me to come with you, just in case?" Stama asked.

Just in case what? thought Nihm. "No, I ave dogs," she said patting Snow as she spoke. Nihm grabbed her staff. My staff? Morten's staff, she corrected herself. Pulling the hood of her cloak up over her head to keep the drizzle from her hair, Nihm walked a slow circuit around the camp before setting off along the road to Fallston.

Nihm's feet led her past the young man's camp and she couldn't help but look across. Her eyes locked again with his. He was sat on his haunches pulling his jerkin on as he stared back at her, his brown eyes hawk-like and intense. She raised her hand in greeting like she had the night before.

A pause, a ghost of a smile, then he lifted a hand in return. Nihm felt a connection to him and didn't know why. It bothered her. She felt herself blush, aware he was half-dressed and embarrassed at being caught out watching him. Turning away she walked on.

* * *

Morten was on the road behind. She could tell by his long loping stride. He was jogging to catch her. Snow ran back to greet him, threatening to trip him over. The dogs bore him no grudge and Nihm knew she shouldn't either.

"Fancy some company?" Morten asked stopping alongside her. He was uncertain, unsure where they stood. Were they friends still? Did she blame him for not finding Marron? He didn't know, in all truth had been too scared to ask. Morten felt the guilt of it and was sure Nihm could see that guilt writ all over him. He wouldn't blame her if she hated him. Last night Stama told him to give Nihm time. That her pain was new and too raw still. Maybe he shouldn't have come.

"Sure, Mort," Nihm said.

Morten beamed. It felt good to hear her say his name.

They walked in silence together, neither knowing what to say. It was awkward at first but Nihm found after a while that she didn't mind it. They walked past campsites on either side of the road. People had risen as the morning light grew and were eating or packing for the journey ahead.

As they neared Fallston, Nihm heard horses ahead, lots of horses by the sounds. She watched with interest as they came into view, escorting a carriage and several wagons. Nihm felt her heart racing.

"Red Cloaks!" Morten hissed, his hand grasping Nihm's elbow needlessly.

Moving to the side of the road she counted their numbers. A dozen Red Cloaks rode front and back of the same carriage they had escorted yesterday, Father Zoller's carriage she now knew. Behind them followed another dozen armed guards, Rivers men from Fallston judging by their crest. At their van rode a Lord, breastplate gleaming.

That must be Lord Menzies, she thought, recalling the old guard from the Uppers. At the back rumbled two large supply wagons.

"Something tells me Lord Menzies ain't hangin' around," Morten said as the horsemen clattered by.

Nihm heard Morten but barely acknowledged him. She had seen something that froze her where she stood. Blood draining from her face she fumbled, pulling her hood down further over her face.

She recognised the three guards they had rode with yesterday but that wasn't what had arrested her attention. There was another she knew. Small, swarthy, ordinarily pretty indiscriminate, she would likely have missed him only he had looked right at her. Only for a moment, his eyes sliding past, but it was enough. She had seen those eyes before, could never forget them; dead, soulless eyes. Eyes she'd last seen in an alley outside the Broken Axe.

Her pulse raced. It was him, wasn't it? It had happened so fast, the moment so brief. It was hard to breathe all of a sudden and Nihm gasped for air.

<*It is him. Your memory is correct,*> Sai affirmed.

Nihm slipped to her knees, her strength suddenly leeched from her limbs, her heart palpitating.

"Nihm, Nihm, what's wrong? Are you alright?" Morten knelt beside her, worry creasing his face.

Nihm felt her strength returning as quickly as it left, energy suddenly infusing her body. Standing abruptly, Nihm took a deep breath to steady her racing heart.

<*Thank you Sai. What was that?*>

<*A boost of your adrenal hormone. It seemed necessary,*> Sai stated.

Nihm didn't know what that was but she felt invigorated. The fear had dissipated, replaced in its stead by anger, her face flushing as it grew steadily.

Morten alongside her looked confused. "You okay? You went white as a sheet there. Now you look like your head is going to explode. Tell me?"

"One of those Reds was outside the Broken Axe," Nihm blurted. It was the most legible sentence she had managed since her ailment but Nihm hadn't time to stop and think about it. All she could see were those dead, soulless eyes staring at her.

Morten instantly made the connection. "Oh shit."

Chapter 65 : The Oath

Fallston, The Rivers

Renco finished his forms. He'd risen early, as usual, to find it still drizzling with rain. The skies above, dark in the pre-dawn, suggested it wasn't going to let up anytime soon. What he wanted was to go for a swim and bathe. Maybe later he promised himself, strolling back to camp.

Under the shelter of the awning, he towelled his torso and legs down with a cloth. It was too low under the canvas to stand so he sat and pulled on his leggings and shirt. He had aired both overnight but they were still damp and clammy against his skin.

Renco was aware he was being watched. Had felt it last night as he did his forms, but that was a vague premonition, this was a surety. Pulling his jerkin on he glanced at the road and saw her. She stood almost exactly as she had last night, leaning on her staff with her two large wolfdogs shadowing her. Her eyes were dark, hooded as she was but despite that, even from twenty paces, Renco felt the weight of them. Intrigued, he resolved to approach her wanting to know who she was.

As if reading his mind she waved at him and Renco found himself return it, before she turned away, walking towards Fallston, staff tapping out as if to pull her along and like that the moment was gone. Idly, Renco noted she was moving better. Not as fragile as the night before. Must be recovering from illness or injury, he mused.

"Girl interesting, yes?" Maohong said from his covers. Sitting up he stretched, his old bones creaking.

Renco glanced at Mao. His canny eyes never missed a thing. Renco shrugged and signed, "Who?"

"Bah, dog girl." He gestured towards the road. "Maybe Renco have more girls hiding Mao not see?" He made a show of lifting his covers and looking under them.

Renco sighed, a day or two just him and Mao. It would be a long couple of days. "She is different," he signed.

"Bah," Mao exclaimed again. "Everyone different. Girl unusual, intriguing, neh?"

Renco smiled, that was exactly what she was.

Mao grinned back, his crooked teeth standing out in his wizened face. "See Mao know, Mao always right." He chortled.

Renco helped Mao to his feet and whilst the old man dressed he prepared an easy meal of nuts, fruits, and the last of the stale bread.

Renco picked the mould off the bread before eating it and washed it down with some watered wine. The wine was usually reserved for the evening meal but Mao seemed to think it a good idea to drink it now and who was he to argue. Master did say Mao was in charge.

Renco watched as a young red-haired man, tall and rangy, appeared out of the dog girl's camp and set off down the road. No doubt to catch her up. Boyfriend, brother, or friend he wondered.

"Do you know where Master has gone?" Renco signed.

"Master tell Renco if master want Renco to know. Not for Mao to say," he replied seriously.

"So you don't know either," Renco gestured.

Mao laughed and slapped his knee. "No, Mao not know."

"So what do we do?" It was a long conversation for Renco, but it was wet, and waiting was for old men. He wanted to do something.

"We wait. Maybe move." Mao pointed to several trees a hundred paces or so further east. "That good spot. Cover for campfire, maybe fish later. Mao go town. Get supplies. Renco stay with horses."

Great, Renco thought, knowing the old goat would fetch the supplies via an inn or three. Still, he didn't like crowds, and the trees Mao had pointed out were as good a spot as any to wait for master's return.

Renco's ears were sharp, much sharper than Mao's, so he was the first to hear the sound of horses on the damp road. At least four hands and some wagons he judged. Looking towards town he caught a glimpse of red and the flash of steel. Mao came and stood by his side following his gaze.

As they approached Mao clutched his arm. "No snap, no use flow. No matter what, Renco."

"Why?" Renco signed. What was happening here? What did Mao see that he didn't?

"No matter what, Renco," Mao insisted. "End badly for Renco and Mao. Swear. Swear on master's life." The earlier banter and good humour were gone, replaced by a hard, cold stare that brooked no argument.

"I swear it, Mao," Renco signed back, a knuckle of fear sitting in his stomach. They were Red Cloaks, Mao had known it instantly. But how could they know about them? They'd left the hunters behind, dead. Maybe they headed south, escaping like everyone else. Somehow though he knew Mao was right. They were coming for them.

The surrounding camps were packing up, preparing for the march east. It didn't take long with the few possessions they had. A few had already left. The road would soon be busy. It wouldn't matter; they might bear witness but they would be no protection for Mao or Renco. As the Red Cloaks approached, any on the road quickly left it, making way.

It looked at first as if they would ride right by but at the last instant, the hulking brute of a man leading them turned his horse off the road. Instantly the Red Cloaks fanned out, surrounding their makeshift camp. They didn't speak, just sat upon their horses glaring.

An ornate carriage stopped on the road adjacent and Renco watched with trepidation as the door opened and a man stepped out. He wore a blood-red cassock and looked disdainfully up at the sky.

The colour drained from Renco's face and he started to shake. He knew that face. It was etched forever in his mind. It was the face of a murderer… a torturer… a priest. It was the face of Father Henrik Zoller.

Mao grabbed his arm. "Quiet, Renco,"

He was keening, a low deep sound, not even aware he made it. Mao's grip tightened and Renco took a breath. He held it, closing his eyes and waited for his pulse rate to gentle, before exhaling slowly. Mao taught him that, Master wasn't his only instructor. Mao, who had sworn to do no violence, seemed nevertheless to have an intimate knowledge of it despite this. The technique, Mao once explained, was to calm a warrior before a battle.

One of his master's lessons voiced in his head. "Control is everything. If you have no control you are lost, neh! If you lose control you can be manipulated, out-thought, and outmanoeuvred."

At his side, Mao muttered. "Sometime, best do nothing. Do nothing can sometime be hard thing."

Renco opened his eyes. A small swarthy looking Red Cloak hovered near Zoller, pinning a long red cloak and hood on him as he waited.

"Thank you, Tuko." Zoller pulled the hood up over his head. The priest should look ridiculous thought Renco, in his all-red ensemble only he didn't. It was appropriate; after all, he was bathed in the blood of others.

Renco saw not all the men wore red cloaks. Two wagons pulled up behind Zoller's carriage surrounded by guards bearing the twin rivers emblem with a fish leaping between them. A Lord in a shiny breastplate slid from the back of his mount and, flanked by two of his men, marched over to the priest.

"What's the delay, Father? We need to go now and you're blocking the road." He looked nervous, glancing over his shoulder to the north and the low foothills.

"A personal matter, Lord Menzies, it won't take long," Zoller replied. He walked over and carelessly stood in front of Renco. He surveyed him briefly before turning his attention to Maohong.

Renco watched as the brute leading the Red Cloaks climbed from his horse and stood to the right and a pace back from Zoller who was flanked on his other side by the smaller guard, the one called Tuko. There was something dangerous about Tuko. Even stood next to his giant companion it was the smaller man Renco was most wary of; his eyes were dark and flat. They promised violence.

"Where is your master, old man?" Zoller asked.

"He gone," Mao answered.

"I can see that. Where has he gone?"

"Don't know."

Zoller was silent a moment looking thoughtfully at Mao.

"By all that's holy, Father, we need to go!" Menzies exclaimed impatiently.

The priest held his hand up silencing him and Renco saw Menzies' face stiffen at the gesture.

Zoller turned to Renco who felt the full weight of the priest's stare. "Where is your master, boy?"

"Boy mute, no talk. He just serv…" The brute stepped past Zoller with surprising speed and drove his fist into Mao's gut. With a whoosh of breath, Mao crumpled to the ground. He moaned, coughing and gasping for air.

"Forgive Holt, he can't abide bad manners and it's rude to interrupt," Zoller said. The ugly giant grinned. One of his teeth was black, Renco noted.

"I know you can talk. Think I don't remember you? Was a time when all you wanted to do was talk," Zoller touched a hand to his cheek and the faint tear-shaped scar that hung beneath his right eye. He stepped around Renco. "You've grown. You're almost a man."

Renco clenched his fists.

"But you're a boy still. Tell me, boy. Where is your master?"

Renco shrugged. He didn't know.

Holt stepped in and kicked Mao, the force spinning the old man off the ground and onto his back. He landed heavily crying out in pain, hands clutching his gut and sides. He groaned in agony, the sound pitiful as he tried to suck air in. Holt knelt grabbing a fistful of Mao's tunic lifting him easily. Then looking at Zoller waited.

"Sometimes all it takes is the right incentive. If you can talk, now is the time." Zoller stared at Renco's clenched fists then pointedly back at Mao. "He looks old and frail. He needs your help. Will you help him?"

There was the sound of hooves on the road. Turning, Renco saw Luke Goodwill canter to a stop just outside the Red Cloaks' cordon. It suddenly made sense then. The bard had betrayed them to the Red Priest, but why? He recalled

Lett's whisper in his ear the day before. "Don't worry. I'll look out for you, Renco. My Da is very canny."

The bard must have known master wasn't a mage, he was shrewd. Saw his master for what he was and had used it. I wonder how much they paid him, he thought bitterly. He took several deep breaths, a mixture of fear and anger percolating in his veins.

"Your oath," Mao croaked from the ground. There was a sickening smack as Holt punched him. Blood exploded as his nose crunched and his head snapped back.

"What are you doing? He's an old man. You'll kill him," Luke cried. He went to step in, but the small guard held his hand out.

"Another step and I'll gut you where you stand," Tuko said his voice a sinister blend of menace and calm.

Luke stood there uncertainly. "Where's my daughter?" He turned, pleading to Lord Menzies. "My Lord they have my daughter, Letizia."

Before anyone could answer a cry came from the carriage and Renco saw Lett's face appear at the window.

"Da, I'm here." She'd been crying, her face was blotchy and red. She opened the carriage door but a hand clamped down firmly on her shoulder stopping her from leaving.

Renco tensed, taking a step towards the carriage. If they hurt her…

Zoller moved back sensing the barely contained violence in the young man.

"Lett," Luke cried out. "Why have you got her? Let her go. I'm a bard. We are sacrosanct. Lord Menzies, I beseech you." He was talking to anyone and everyone, fear and desperation in his voice.

"Father Zoller, let the girl go. Stop this, whatever it is, and let us leave. We do not have the time," Menzies insisted.

Zoller held his hands out. "The girl came to us remember. Fortunately, she is not a bard, not sacrosanct, so that leaves just you, Goodwill isn't it?"

"Let her go. She is nothing to do with whatever the hells this is," Luke shouted.

"She has everything to do with it," Zoller barked. "She's here for the boy, to save him and I promised her I would. But you, Goodwill. You're a liar and a traitor. Your beautiful daughter did her duty. Told me all about Hiro, an old adversary of mine and Knight of the Order no less. An outlawed Order banished from the Rivers. The question is, why didn't you come to us?" Zoller turned to Menzies. "But you're right. We don't have the time."

Tuko drew a knife and stepping past the bard ran its blade across his throat, ear to ear. Blood gushed in a fountain.

Luke's hands clasped uselessly trying to stem the blood pulsing from his neck. He stood a moment, eyes disbelieving before they glazed over. Then, strength leaving his body, he sank to his knees and folded up onto the wet grass. The bard jerked a few times then was still.

Lett started screaming.

Her cries tore at Renco even whilst he tried to make sense of it all. Lett had gone to Zoller? The hand on her shoulder dragged Lett back into the depths of the carriage her cries muffled but no less heart-rending.

"By the gods' man are you mad? You can't go round killing bards. The Black Crow will hang you for this, priest or no."

"He colluded with a known felon wanted for murder and blasphemy. Besides, the Black Crow is dead even if he doesn't know it yet." Zoller turned to Holt. "Bind the boy's hands and bring him."

"Aye, Father," Holt grunted.

Renco stood transfixed; he was reeling from Lett's betrayal and her heartbreak and watched in shock as Luke Goodwill bled out. His own body started to shake as energy coursed through it. He looked down at Mao to find his friend staring back through swollen eyes and a face covered in blood.

His hands moved and he signed, "Your oath."

Holt beat Mao again, opening up a savage cut across his right eyebrow, splitting the skin like a peach. His head smacked into the ground and Mao lay wheezing like each breath would be his last, blood sheeting down his face.

Something caught Holt's attention and he ripped Mao's tunic neck revealing a thin black necklace. It was threaded through with gold, the glint of it drawing Holt's eye.

Bloody and wrecked as he was, Mao raised his hand and Holt slapped it away contemptuously before pulling violently on the necklace. Mao's head flew up. It wouldn't give. Drawing a vicious, serrated knife from his belt, Holt sawed at the necklace.

Renco heard a pop and hiss as the black necklace parted, saw a faint mist cloud the air for an instant before the breeze and rain tore it away.

Holt held his thin black trophy up triumphantly before looking around and slipping it into a pocket in his coat.

"Enough Holt, bind the boy." Zoller snapped. Walking over he looked down at Mao's battered face. It was a mess.

"Can you hear me, old man? Tell Hiro we have his boy. If he wants him I'll be at Rivercross waiting. Tell him, Father Zoller sends his regards."

Oath or no, Renco wasn't sure he could stand it. He tensed, ready to explode into action when Zoller's eyes switched to him.

"Behave yourself, I would hate for the girl to suffer for your actions. You understand me?"

He remembered Mao's words from earlier. Sometimes the best thing is to do nothing and doing nothing can sometimes be the hardest thing. The moment passed. Holt stepped behind him and rough hands yanked his arms back. Holt bound and knotted a chord of leather about his wrists. "You want him in the carriage, Father?"

"No I do not," Zoller retorted. "Stick him on the bard's horse. It's already saddled and he won't be needing it anymore."

With a shove, Renco stumbled towards Luke's horse. A cackle rose behind them and they turned as one to look.

Mao had rolled on to his side. He was spitting blood and laughing, his crooked teeth red.

"Mao tell him," he laughed hysterically, bloody face swollen so bad Renco couldn't see his eyes. Mao's laughter turned into a cough as he choked, vomiting blood.

"Mao tell him," he sighed, laying his head back against the wet grass. He took great wheezing gasps of air, lungs rattling with every breath.

"If you've killed him prematurely Holt, I will be most upset with you," Zoller berated the giant.

Turning away he smiled. "Come, Lord Menzies. Let us depart whilst we are able."

Chapter 66 : Slaughter House

Fallston, The Rivers

The old man wheezed and groaned, the only overt sign he was alive. His body lay like a sack of bones on the ground. Nihm and Morten had returned as the Red Cloaks prepared to leave and stood watching quietly from the roadside, two amongst the gathered crowd of onlookers.

Nihm saw a brute of a Red Cloak bind the hands and arms of the young man from the camp before unceremoniously hefting him up onto a horse and lashing him to the saddle. The horse was the same that had cantered past not ten minutes gone forcing them from the road.

Nihm put her head down letting her hood hide her face as the Red Cloaks left, avoiding eye contact with the small assassin escorting the priest Zoller back to his carriage. Instead, she let her eyes wander to the crumpled body lying on the ground, blood soaking the grass where he lay. It was the rider on the road. Her eyes roved back to the old man.

<Help him.> The thought was there in her head, not hers but his. Not help me, but help him. Nihm turned and saw the young man staring at her from atop his horse. He looked calm considering his predicament. He inclined his head a fraction and Nihm found herself raising her hand, stopping herself at the last instant.

Then he was gone. The Red Cloaks rode off pulling him after, his horse tied to the saddle horn of a big black destrier, carrying the giant Red Cloak on its back. They didn't turn back to Fallston but headed east along the Reach towards Longstretch, Lord Menzies and his men close behind.

The small gathering of onlookers started dispersing, many trudging east down the road following the Red Cloaks. A few glanced at the two bodies lying on the ground, one dead and one dying, but none moved to help.

Nihm hobbled over to the old man, Morten at her side. Ash bounded ahead and sniffed at him where he lay.

"Hope Ash don't mistake him for breakfast," Morten quipped.

Leaning on her staff, Nihm slowly knelt and pushed Ash away. The old man's face was swollen and lumpy, his eyes just slits. He was covered in blood, diluted by the constant drizzle but as fast as it washed away more gushed from his nose and brow. She touched fingers to his wrist as Marron had taught her. His pulse was faint but steady.

"Bring the wagon," she told Morten, each word slow and distinct as she sounded them out. Morten didn't argue but turned and sprinted towards their camp.

Nihm rose slowly. Looking about she gathered what she might need from their camp. The old man's body shivered almost imperceptibly and Nihm laid his cloak over him not sure if he was cold or in shock. She felt his wrist again.

<*His pulse is weaker. You need to stem the bleeding or he will die. Also, you need to elevate his head, he is choking on his blood,*> Sai offered.

Nihm removed her cloak, folded and tucked it behind his head. She tore a shirt into strips and bound his head with them and stoppering his nose. Marron's lessons played in her mind as if she was there but she had no time for self-reflection or remorse, the old man's life hung in the balance.

She sensed Mercy approaching with Stama and turned as they arrived. Mercy quickly knelt and examined him, doing much the same as Nihm. Inspecting his dressings she grunted.

"You've done well, but he's very weak. We'll get him to a physiker before we leave."

"No," Nihm said.

"What do you mean, no?" Mercy asked.

"He comes with us." Nihm sounded slightly drunk as she slurred her words, rushing them together.

"He's likely going to die, even with a physiker. We don't have time to nursemaid a dying man." Mercy's eyes softened. "I know you mean well but it's not your responsibility. He'd have a better chance in Fallston."

"He comes with me," Nihm insisted, enunciating each word.

<*Mercy's advice is sound and rational,*> Sai interjected.

<Meaning you think me irrational,> Nihm snapped. *<Fallston isn't safe. I'll not leave him to die here. He comes with us.>*

"Why?" Mercy asked as if she had eavesdropped on Nihm's thoughts.

"Stama and I saw deer this morning. A herd of them not fifty paces from camp," Nihm stuttered. "I saw Lord Menzies ride away with the Red Cloaks and two supply wagons. Not to Fallston but east."

Their wagon rumbled across the road and pulled up beside them as they spoke, Morten on the reins and Lucky leading the horses.

"Lord Menzies estates are to the east. What are you trying to say?" Mercy asked calmly.

It didn't fool Nihm. She could see Mercy's frustration. She was being indulged; Mercy was not taking her seriously. Nihm shook her head in exasperation.

"Menzies runs from something. The deer run from something. What could both possibly be running from I wonder?" Nihm said.

Mercy's face changed as Nihm's words registered and she thought through the implications. "Shit."

She looked about. There were a lot of people on the fields outside Fallston and many more inside. "Lucky put the old man in the back of the wagon."

The big man bent lifting the old man easily. Carrying him to the wagon Lucky laid him on Nihm's pallet. As the old man's head touched the pillow a long low rumble peeled out, sounding like thunder.

"That ain't thunder," Stama said. He looked towards the low hills. The clouds to the north and east were dark and angry. "There's a storm coming but weren't no thunder," he repeated.

"Come, we have to go. Now!" Mercy yelled.

Another deep rumble rolled out, drums. Cries went up, shouts of panic rising from the many people still in the fields.

"We need to go. We won't have horses if we stand around much longer," Mercy said.

<Wait, Nihm!> Sai ordered. *<Those drums were not the same. The first was to the north, the second to the east. It is your intention to avoid the urak that war on you?>*

<War on us you mean, unless you plan on vacating my body, but yes that is what we're trying to do.>

<Correction accepted. If we conclude that urak are the cause of the noise and that it implies they are here in numbers superior to your own then it may already be too late to avoid confrontation.>

<What are you telling me, that we're fucked already?>

<If fucked in this tense is a bad thing then yes, we are fucked. My assessment of the drums, the modulation in frequency indicates that the urak are approximately a league to the north and east. Your companions could possibly escape by horse but you will need to be tied on. Your body is not yet ready or coordinated enough to handle anything more than a gentle walk. The elderly man you have aided will need to be abandoned, his injuries are life-threatening. The wagon as well, it is too slow. Even then the chances of escape would be in the lower twenty percentile.>

<Well you're a regular ray of sunlight. I'm guessing the lower twenty percentile is bad?> Nihm asked.

<Yes.>

<I'm not leaving him to die,> Nihm repeated.

<If we stay, our chances of survival drop drastically. If you leave him you might live and he will die. It is logical to leave him.>

<I told you I won't abandon him. I can't explain why but I can't. Give me something else.>

<Cross the lake.>

<That isn't an option. We've no boat and it's too wide. The old man won't make it and Morten can't swim. Besides, that's the Grim marsh over there.>

"Nihm, Nihm, what's wrong with you girl, get on the damn wagon we have to go. Now!" Mercy shouted.

"No, take the horses and go." Nihm pointed down the road to the east. "Urak a league east maybe more, if you ride hard you might make it. I'm staying with the old man. It's too late for us," Nihm slurred sounding like a drunk again.

<*The town presents a few options but none look promising,*> Sai replied ignoring the conversation Nihm was having with Mercy. It was unimportant.

Another drum beat, this time Nihm could sense it was from the north now that she knew to listen for it.

"The gods damn you. This has been an unholy mess since the moment we crossed paths. I'm starting to wish we'd never set foot in the Rivers," Mercy cried exasperation and anger matching Nihm's own.

"Then go. Now!" Nihm threw her staff, stuff Morten it was her staff now, into the wagon and climbed up awkwardly beside him. He looked pale and scared; his red hair, wet with the rain, was plastered to his head. Nihm pushed him. "Mort, go. Leave."

"I ain't leaving you, Nihm. I go where you go. Get off the reins." He shoved her hands away as she tried to snatch them. "You are so… so infuriating," he shouted. "Now where are we going? The town I'm guessing?"

Nihm saw the same stubborn look in his eye her Da got when he'd made his mind up about something. She nodded her head, yes, and Morten gave the reins a flick. Expertly turning the wagon he headed it towards town.

They fought against a tide of people. Many running, terror and fear driving them on. Some few made for the town but it was largely defenceless with no curtain wall and few guards, most having left with Lord Menzies. To stay was to die.

"You're going the wrong way. Fallston will just be a slaughterhouse," a man cried out.

The drums beat again, a quick staccato that rumbled through the rain.

<*I believe they are communicating with each other,*> Sai offered.

A collective cry rose, rippling and rising like a wave as more and more people looked in horror to the north.

Turning, Nihm saw that a line of large manlike creatures had stepped out of the undergrowth. Their line stretched away eastward, disappearing into the mist of the rain. They looked fearsome, the top half of their heads were red as if dipped in blood and the blood left to run down face and chest. They looked primal and savage.

The tide turned, people suddenly rushing back towards Fallston. Nihm watched as Mercy's horse rode past them, Stama with her. She looked defiant and nodded her head at Nihm as she passed them. There was no sign of Lucky though. Nihm presumed he rode behind but there was too much going on for her to focus on that right then.

Houses sprung up and suddenly they were inside the town limits. It was a shadow of itself, the crowds of people mostly gone. Those on the street were from the fields outside of town looking for shelter. Those already in town had either fled or taken refuge wherever they could. Ahead, through the rain, Nihm saw a mass of people on the switchback leading to the Uppers.

A sudden guttural roaring sounded from behind and Nihm looked back. Blessedly she couldn't see much but what she did, sent a ball of fear into the pit of her stomach.

The urak charged, rushing forward on mass. People on the road and in the fields ran in terror, dropping whatever possessions they carried. It didn't save many of them. Those with young or elderly were the first to fall, the urak breaking over them in a rush of bodies, hacking and clubbing them to the ground.

The urak didn't breach the town though. Bizarrely gathering just outside, butchering the fallen and watching with a mix of hate, hunger and contempt as the survivors disappeared into the town's depths.

There was a pained moan from the back of the wagon as they hit a bump in the road.

"Welcome to the slaughterhouse, old man," Morten shouted, fear lending his voice a desperation Nihm felt herself. They were trapped in a town with no defences and no defenders.

Chapter 67 : Besieged

Thorsten, The Rivers

So many bodies lay dead in the misty pre-dawn light. There wasn't much to do on the tower so Amos counted them. He gave up once he got past a thousand. It was quiet down in the fields, fitting though, considering the death that lay upon its ground. The only sounds were their own. The creak of armour as men moved and soft voices as they talked in hushed tones.

Low cloud had moved in through the night obscuring the moons that had cast the fields below in a silvery twilight. After the disaster of their first attack, the urak had withdrawn and made no signs of following up their assault.

Junip had woken during the night but was in a state of shock and not fit to answer questions. So Amos still had no idea what she'd done to visit so much death on the urak or if she had anything left if they came again. When they come again, Amos corrected himself. He turned at the sound of boots on stone.

"Tea," Jobe handed Amos a wooden mug and he accepted it gratefully. The autumn morning was chilly with the promise of rain and standing around looking at dead bodies did nothing to warm him.

"Thanks. How's she doing?" He took a sip from the steaming mug.

"Bit shook up still. Jerkze is taking her to the keep like you said." Jobe sipped his tea joining Amos at the wall. He glanced out and Amos saw his shoulders go back; his mug paused halfway to his mouth.

"What?"

"Someat's off, Boss." Amos saw the hawkish look in his friend's eyes as he looked at the destruction below and he turned to survey the field once more. Nothing, the dead were still dead far as he could tell. They lay a hundred paces out, their bodies scattered like autumn leaves in front of the wall of earth and rock Junip's magical attack had created. It ran the length of the field like a dyke only it held back no water, just the dead.

"I don't see anything," Amos said.

Jobe hocked and spat over the embrasure before setting his mug down. Turning, he grabbed his bow. "Ring the alarm, boss."

Frowning, Amos looked once again at the dead even as Jobe started stringing his bow, bracing the haft against his foot. "Okay, you got me worried. What are you seeing?" He set his own mug down.

Taking an arrow, Jobe fitted it to his bowstring. "No buzzards or crows taking their fill. And unless you killed a bunch more urak whilst I was sleeping there's a lot more dead this morning than there was yestereve." He drew and released.

Amos followed the arrow in fascination as it leapt from the bow. It missed, thudding into the earth. Had the urak it landed near moved? Amos wasn't sure.

"Sound the fucking alarm." Jobe notched another arrow.

Fuck it, he's right, Amos thought. He turned and shouted to the guardsman, sat dozing by the signal poles. "You man, ring the alarm and hoist the red flag."

The guard jumped up looking bleary-eyed.

"Sound the alarm, now," Amos shouted again.

"Aye, Lord." The man reached behind for the bell as Amos reached for his bow. He deftly strung it as the clanging of the bell rang out, loud in the still morning air.

Amos moved to another embrasure reaching for his arrows. In the fields below the dead were rising to their feet and behind them, behind the mounds of earth and rock more urak stood where they had lain hidden by the earthen dyke. All held heavy-looking bows.

Another bell tolled, more distant, from the corner tower to the east.

A roar went up as the dead charged the wall. Flights of arrows were released, their dark shafts disappearing in the dark skies to drop invisibly on the defenders, most falling harmlessly against the stonework or past the wall to the ground beyond. Amos drew, sighting on an urak not fifty paces from the wall. He judged the angle, adjusted to lead his target, and released. His arrow punched into its torso, spinning it off its feet.

He reached for another arrow, glancing as he did down at the wall to his left. Defenders were filing out to join the few already there, most still pulling on boots and buckling on harness as they ran. It was slow, too slow, Amos thought grimly. There was no organisation, many stopping at the first embrasure they came to making it difficult for others to get by. It was chaos.

A few archers managed to get shots away but the charging urak were so close they had to lean right out over the battlements. Black shafts peppered the walls taking most as they were exposed. One skittered off the merlon next to Amos and he flinched, sending his arrow wide.

Longhair was on the tower then, looking as dishevelled as he had the day before, haranguing his archers into formation. Amos watched as he sent several to each side of the tower where they could cover the walls. The rest he formed into a ragged block at the tower's centre where they started firing volleys.

"Two hunred tweny paces lads, let's take their bows," Longhair shouted.

Amos approved. It made sense, they had the height of the tower to rain arrows down without needing to expose themselves at the walls to enemy counter-fire. Looking again along the walls the defenders looked too few. Masses of them were gathered on the grounds behind, bottlenecked at the steps up.

Something caught his eye in the grey haze of receding darkness and Amos's gaze was drawn out past the earthen mounds and urak archers. A lone figure emerged into the half-light, then another and suddenly there was a black mass of urak. A growing dread built in his gut.

The sound of iron clattering against stone made Amos turn back to the walls. Urak had reached the base of the curtain wall and launched hooks and grapple irons over the battlements. Guards hacked at the ropes but seemed to have little effect.

Urak appeared over the embrasures and the defenders thrust with sword and spear before they could get a purchase. Urak wore little armour and many fell, holes punched into chest or gut. It was like sticking fish in a barrel.

A cry sounded further along the wall. The defence was thinly spread and several urak had crested the battlements and gained the walls. With ferocity they attacked, hacking, slashing, and clubbing a clear space for more urak to climb up behind. As one was killed another was there to take its place, and they were winning, Amos could see.

The urak dwarfed the soldiers, not just taller by a few hands but broader and heavier. It looked like men fighting children thought Amos excepting these men looked feral in their white-painted body markings and attacked with unrivalled brutality. The defenders fighting them looked close to collapse.

Bowmen in the grounds below started firing up onto the walls and many urak fell allowing the defenders to regroup as reinforcements with long spears pushed back along the wall.

A score of urak dropped from the walls to the ground and with a bellowing war cry charged the archers. It was carnage as they lay about with large cleavers and swords, blood and limbs flying as men and women were hacked to pieces. The wall would be lost in moments.

Amos turned to find Longhair at his side looking past his shoulder. In the din of battle, he'd not heard the man come up behind.

"Lost cause if ever I seen one," Longhair shouted. He turned before Amos could respond bellowing at his squad. He organised two ranks along the sidewall of the tower and they started launching arrows down into the growing body of urak.

"It ain't gonna be enough." Longhair pointed back out over the battlefield. Rank upon rank of urak were massed at the earthen dyke, clambering over it. They covered the field like a black tide rolling inexorably towards them, unchallenged. The defenders on the wall were already engaged and unable to direct any fire at them.

"Plenty to aim at," Amos said. "You have command here…."

"Wynter," Long Hair supplied. "Where you goin then…sir?"

Amos looked hard at Wynter hearing the challenge in his question. He pointed.

"Down there. Our defence is crumbling. We need to stiffen it up and push them back or we're all dead."

Wynter stared him in the eye, taking his measure then held his arm out suddenly. "Kildare smile on ya, Lord Amos," he said invoking the name of the Soldier, Lord of War and Death. They clasped hands briefly. "Want me to look after thaten for ya." He nodded at Amos's bow.

The audacity of the man, thought Amos, then with a wry smile. "Aye, why not, bring her back to me alright." He thrust his bow at Longhair before he could change his mind.

"Jobe on me," Amos yelled running for the stairwell, grabbing his shield up on the way.

The tower was empty as they burst through it and down the stairs to the ground. If it looked like chaos from up above, on the ground it was far worse. He barged through crowds of men and women milling about as sergeants bellowed trying to gather them into some semblance of order.

Amos spotted the sergeant from the day before but couldn't remember his name. "Sergeant on me, bring your squad," he commanded. The man looked pale and scared but didn't hesitate.

"Sir," he acknowledged before turning and bellowing orders.

Amos didn't wait but pushed on through following the curtain wall as it ran east shouting as he went.

"On me!" he commanded. Most ignored Amos to start with but some few heeded his call and joined him until the tide slowly turned and the mottled militia in their mismatched armour grew behind him.

Up ahead was the large frame of Byron Mueller. He was arguing with someone and as the mob parted for him he saw it was with Captain Samuels, idiots. Amos took in their surroundings as he marched up to them.

"Mueller get your archers up high, those rooftops." Amos pointed. "Captain we need to contain and push back the urak. Get your men and follow me." Amos didn't stop to argue the toss. They would follow or not. They didn't have time to talk.

The militia in front of him wavered and parted suddenly, pushing back and away. They were running.

"Stand fast or die," Amos yelled. Didn't they understand there was nowhere to run? The sound of fighting drew near, the screams of the wounded and dying mixing with the clash of arms.

The air felt heavy, cloying. The smell of sweat and oiled steel from the close press of bodies was tainted by the sickly aroma of blood and the putrid stench of voided bowels and ruptured organs.

His teeth hurt where his jaws clenched. Then he was there. The man in front of him turned and ran gushing blood as he was impaled through the back, a big boar head spear snaring his entrails as it burst from his gut clean through his leather cuirass. He fell before Amos, spewing blood.

The urak was a big bastard that dwarfed Amos and the man he had felled. It placed a booted foot on the dying man's back pulling his spear back through with a guttural cry of triumph. Amos leapt forward punching his sword into it, feeling its keen point break skin and pierce belly.

Its bellow of triumph turned to a howl of pain and it slipped to its knees. Amos twisted his blade as he drew his sword out, then swung it around, slicing into its neck before planting a boot to the uraks chest and knocking it over onto its back.

Jobe was at his side and together they pushed forward hacking and parrying.

"On me!" Amos screamed batting aside a spear with his blade and thumping his shield up into a face.

Militia rallied to his call forming a wall. Shields to the front and spears extended they stepped forward. Amos let them pass him, hovering behind, looking for any breach. They held their ground at first and then started to press the urak back.

"Push forward! Together. Keep your shape!" Amos's voice was growing hoarse from shouting.

The urak rallied. Several with large cleavers stepped to the fore. Deflecting spear tips they slammed into shields and Amos's brief counter-attack faltered.

One man overextended, stepping out of the line of spears. An urak grabbed his spear haft below the head and pulled him off balance before stepping in and clubbing him with his sword hilt. The man stumbled back his mouth a mess of blood and smashed teeth, howling.

The line wavered. Amos could feel it start to buckle as more urak smashed into it. It bowed and slowly they were pushed back. They might have weight of numbers but the urak were fearless, their size and ferocity unmatched and intimidating.

They were lost, the militia he had were untrained and instinct screamed at them to turn and run. Then arrows started to fall, the first puncturing an urak through the eye. Mueller's archers had reached the rooftops and had started firing into the amassed urak. It was enough to stall their assault.

Amos spared a glance to the walls; it looked grim. The urak were winning the battle there all too easily. The walls were narrow and the men upon it were overwhelmed by the larger, stronger urak. They would be flanked soon and the urak would be free to drop from the walls behind them.

"Step back, together. Step back!" Amos shouted. They would have to regroup near the tower where Wynter's archers could support the wall. Jobe took up the cry adding his voice and slowly they retreated.

The battle raged on as slowly, foot by foot, they were forced back. Urak leapt upon the shield wall in front, battering at them. More joined, pulling defenders out of the line and slaughtering them.

Amos stepped in, his sword thrusting up into an armpit before stepping back and bringing his shield up. A massive thud sounded as it was struck. Pain vibrated up his arm and he cried out dropping to a knee. The wounded urak stepped in impaling himself on Jobe's sword.

"No time to sit down, boss," Jobe quipped bringing his shield round to cover them both.

Amos staggered to his feet. His shield arm throbbed with a dull ache and he was tired beyond belief. He glanced up as an urak straddled his fallen comrade swinging a big sword in a roundhouse blow. Amos stepped back knowing he was too slow, knowing he couldn't bring his shield up in time. The air fluttered and there was a heavy thunk as an arrow punched into the urak's chest. It staggered back a step, stumbled, then fell.

The defensive line had dropped leaving him and Jobe exposed. They both took the chance to step back into the line. In the brief respite, Amos looked back over his shoulder. That shot had almost taken him in the back of the head. He was shocked to see the tower was only twenty paces away. Above, he saw Wynter leaning through an embrasure sighting down his bow at him. He released and Amos froze in shock as the arrow flew.

It missed him, passing over his left shoulder and hitting with a wet thud as it found flesh. Spinning around, Amos saw an urak fall away howling in pain. The arrow had struck it in the groin and it dropped its sword, collapsing on the ground thrashing in agony.

Anger flared in his blood, why had he taken his eyes from the battle? He'd almost killed himself.

There was a surge of bodies as a rush of men-at-arms came up from behind, enveloping and then passing him. Captain Samuels was there shouting at him, his face flushed. "Fall back, Lord Amos."

Too tired and battered to speak, Amos nodded his relief. Watching as the guardsmen stepped through the ranks of the embattled and weary militia. Locking shields they slipped long spears between them forming a solid defensive wall. Urak crashed against them but the shield wall held and the spears found many marks judging by the roars of pain Amos heard.

Jobe grabbed his arm hauling on him none to gently and Amos stumbled backwards, still watching as Samuel's regulars brought shield and spear up. They were better armed and trained than the ragged remnants of his militia, who looked beaten and tired.

Limbs aching, body heavy, Amos allowed Jobe to march him back to the crowded square in front of the tower. There, they found Jerkze looking for them. Pushing through the crowd he reached Amos's side.

"Nice a you two ta start without me," he said, smiling grimly.

"Aye you're welcome," Amos mumbled.

"We need to go. Black Crow wants us back at the keep," Jerkze said.

That fired his veins. "Is he taking the piss? We're fighting and losing. I'm needed here," Amos spat.

Jerkze looked about then leaned in close. "The wall is lost Amos, another hour maybe sooner. The north wall is also breached. They're barely contained and we don't have the numbers to push em back. The town is lost." He gripped Amos's shoulder and held his eye. "The Black Crow was insistent, Amos."

Amos sucked air in; his limbs had stopped their slight trembling. Finally, reluctantly, he nodded. "Okay, let's go see what the Crow wants. Lead on."

"You go. I gotta find some bow-master called Wynter. Crow wants him as well."

"Wynter… I know him. Follow me," Amos said.

"Just tell me where. No offence, but you look beat and I'll be quicker on me own. Head to the keep and show the guards this." He handed Amos a token. "It'll get you through the gate."

Amos grasped it and gave Jerkze directions. "Tell the bastard to bring my bow with him."

Jerkze disappeared into the tower whilst Amos and Jobe pushed their way through the square and onto the road leading to the town centre. Men and women hurried by, most poorly armed and armoured. Amos felt a deep despondency as he jogged wearily past them.

It was with a heavy heart that he entered the town square. It was empty of the stalls and bazaar that had crowded it only a few days past. Now it was filled with the wounded, the dying and the desperate. Part of the square was an assembly point where the militia was being organised into groups and sent into town, most headed up North Road.

At the keep, Amos showed his token to the guards, and he and Jobe were ushered through.

"Lord Richard is atop the keep," he was told.

It was a long climb, the keep was large, and the stairs full of people headed both ways. When he finally made the roof, Amos was forced to show his token to the guards there before being allowed to continue.

Lord Richard stood at the wall looking out over his town. The old wizard, Lutico, stood to one side, peering through his hands. It reminded him of Junip on the south tower. Richard caught sight of him, but other than a slight incline of his head carried on his surveillance. The man looked haggard.

Amos moved to the battlements and oriented himself. To the north, thick black smoke billowed into the morning sky. Sound travelled to him, bells ringing warning, a distant rumbling, and the faint noise from below of the injured and dying.

He made out the tiny figures of Jerkze and the long-haired Wynter, wading through the mass of humanity, making for the castle gates.

Turning to the south, Amos looked for his own wall and tower. It was too distant to make out any figures but the signal mast looked to have been hacked down. The tower at least had fallen then. Meaning the town was lost and all those below would be lost. There was nowhere for them to go. The castle and keep were large but not enough that it could accommodate an entire town.

Amos looked again at the Black Crow. His eyes were haunted, his face gaunt and pale. They were his people down there, what must he be feeling knowing they were dead and he could do nothing to prevent it. Having to choose who lived and who died.

It wouldn't matter in the end. They were all dead. The keep was big, its ancient walls tall and thick but its solidity was an illusion, Amos knew. It was little more than a prison. One they would die in and the urak didn't have to do a thing. They wouldn't survive the winter.

Despondent, Amos left the tower. He felt too detached, too far removed from it all atop the keep. Staring down at those below, like some ambivalent god. The people were too many and indistinct to make out clearly; it all felt surreal, like watching someone else's nightmare unfolding. Already racked with guilt for those abandoned on the wall, he needed to be closer. To see and feel, to bear witness.

Amos made his way to the castle walls which stood as thick and formidable as the immense Keep. From there, he watched and listened as the sounds of battle grew ever closer. Fires burned all over town, springing up even as rain started to drizzle from the sky.

There was a rumble as the portcullis crashed down and the gates swung shut. People in the square panicked and rushed the gates banging in fear against it to no avail, it remained firmly barred.

* * *

It was a little after midday when the first urak entered the square. Arrows flew from the battlements but struck those running in terror as much as the urak they were aimed at.

Jerkze joined him and Jobe on the wall, Wynter at his side. Together they watched, helpless, as people crowded the town square from among the adjoining houses and streets. Thousands gathered impotently, crying, and wailing in fear. Driven to desperation, many rushed the gate and walls.

Amos forced himself to watch it all. The memory would be forever etched in his mind. He saw an older couple with a young girl stumbling out of the crowd. There was something familiar about them that tugged at him, drawing his eye. He watched in guilty despair as they pushed up against the wall. They could go no further. The girl, a skinny little thing, couldn't have been more than ten. The man had a shock of red hair pulled back in a ponytail; it looked to be receding from above. Maybe it was that which drew his eyes as realisation suddenly dawned.

"Rope," He looked desperately at Jobe and Jerkze, "Anyone?" Gods be damned, he raged.

"Packs back on the tower," Jobe said in apology.

"Got mine below, if'n it's still there. I'll go fetch it," Jerkze offered.

"Ain't no good if'n you ain't got it with you," Wynter muttered slinging his pack from his shoulder. Fumbling inside, he pulled out a rope, neatly looped in a coil, and held it out. Amos snatched it, quickly unravelling it to measure its length.

"Should be long enough," Wynter said, reading his intent.

Amos nodded his thanks and began tying a hitch in the rope. "Any remember the name of that landlord in the Broken Axe? Stenman I think," Amos said.

Jerkze and Jobe leant out over the battlements and stared down. "Fuck you're right. That's the landlord and his missus. Vic, he was called, yeah Vic Stenman."

"Stenhause, he's called Vic Stenhause," Wynter said.

Amos leant out over the wall. "Stenhause," he yelled, his throat throbbed in pain but he saw Vic lookup. Amos signalled him and watched as they made their way along the base of the wall.

Most people were gathered near the gates and Amos instinctively moved further away from them. He looked around furtively to see if any watched but those guards on the wall were focused out at the unfolding drama in the square.

Amos lowered the rope over the battlement whilst Jobe and Jerkze stood either side shielding his activity from prying eyes.

He felt a tug on the rope and moments later a sudden weight pulling against his grip. Amos took the strain and pulled. His shield arm ached from the bashing it had taken earlier but he gritted his teeth, it was manageable. He pulled, hand over hand, steady. The rope trembled through his fingers and swayed against his grip. Wynter reached over to help and in a short time, a dirty face with big wide eyes appeared over the embrasure. It was the little girl as Amos knew it would be.

There were cries and a clamour from below. The girl's rescue had not gone unnoticed. "Lota desperate folk down there," Jobe muttered.

"Company," Jerkze said, the warning none too soon as guards appeared. They pushed past Wynter who lent indolently against the wall.

"I'll need that rope and the girl. You better come too, sir." He looked apologetic but his face was set.

Amos stood tall pushing the girl behind him. He held his token up. "I'm Lord Amos and I'm keeping the girl. If you don't like it take it up with Lord Richard," he challenged, glaring at the man. The sergeant coloured and Amos sensed the sudden uncertainty he'd caused. There was a lengthy pause, then finally.

"I will, Lord Amos, mark my words." The man hesitated, his men watching silently at his back. "I'll be taking the rope at least. We got orders." His shoulders went back his stance firm.

Amos saw the resolve harden in him and judged in that instant whether he could push further, whether he could save the Stenhauses at least. No, he didn't believe so. Even if he kept the rope there was no way he would be allowed to use it to affect another rescue. Grudgingly, he handed the rope to the sergeant who took it before ordering his men back to their posts.

"You owe me a rope," Wynter said as the guards marched off.

"You owe me a bow," Amos retorted. He turned to the little girl, trembling behind him, and knelt beside her. Tear tracks smudged her dirty face and her eyes were red from crying. Had he saved her from a quick death or just delayed it. Would she suffer the torment and terror of starvation and a slow agonising one instead?

"What's your name girl?"

She sniffed, wiping her sleeve under her nose. "Annabelle."

Epilogue

They found the body lying half-hidden in some reeds. It was a man for sure, black and burnt as it was. Grasping him under the arms they dragged him out of the water and up onto dry land. The prospect of finding anything looked slim. The clothes were charred and stuck to the flesh in places; still, any coin should hopefully have survived the hellfire that must have struck him down.

"Ankor protect us. Musta been struck by the Saint hisself," Hissings said touching thumb and forefinger to his forehead acknowledging the god of life.

"Fuck Ankor. Now roll him over. You, Trickle," Black Jack said pointing to the youngest of their band.

Aware that seven pairs of eyes watched, weighed, and judged him, Trickle stepped forward boldly, feeling anything but. He knelt over the body and gagged. The skin was cracked and stank of burnt fabric and cooked meat. Muttering under his breath the air thickened around his nose. The smell gone, he breathed more easily. Grabbing hold of a shoulder and knee he pulled, levering the burnt man over onto his back. Cloth crumpled beneath his fingers as it flaked turning to ash. The burnt man lay unmoving.

"Wonder what did this to him," Trickle said.

Black Jack slapped the back of Trickle's head with his hand. "Wonder what be in 'is pockets instead, shithead. Be quick, he fucking reeks." He wrinkled his nose.

Trickle searched him but knew he would find nothing. Whatever had burned him had been hot enough to melt his belt buckle but over quick enough that his body was still whole beneath the blackened skin. Patting the body down, the clothing crackled and fell away as he knew it must. He saw something and leaned in.

"What ya got?" Black Jack looked interested. Hissings and several others gathered around, eager.

"Think his eye moved," Trickle said.

"Bah, fuckin idiot." But they all looked at the face, the skin black and cracked, a clear fluid leaking out in places. The eyes suddenly flicked open wide, piercingly blue, the whites standing out in stark contrast to the burnt flesh surrounding them. And then the burnt man screamed.

Our Story continues in Shadows Fall, Book Two of the Morhudrim Cycle

Principal Characters

Nihm	Pronounced Nim. Daughter of Darion and Marron Castell
Renco	Pronounced Ren-co. Apprentice to Hiro
Maohong	Pronounced – Mow-hong. Hiro's companion.

The Castell Dogs

Bindu	Alpha female, mother to Maise and Thunder
Ash	Black coated, son of Maise
Snow	White coated, daughter of Miase
Maise	Daughter of Bindu
Thunder	Son of Bindu

The Order

Darion Castell	Homesteader and agent of the Order.
Marron Castell	Homesteader and agent of the Order.
Keeper	Titular head of the Order.
Hiro	Knight of the Order (Sometimes)
Renix	Order Ambassador at Kingsholme

The Duncans

Amos Duncan	Second son of Atticus and Morgenni
Mercy Duncan	Oldest daughter Atticus and Morgenni
Atticus Duncan	Lord of the Hawke Hold
Morgenni Duncan	Lady of the Hawke Hold
Jobe	Sword companion to Amos and Mercy
Jerkze	Sword companion to Amos and Mercy
Stama	Sword companion to Amos and Mercy
Lucson 'Lucky'	Sword companion to Amos and Mercy
Silver	Sword companion to Amos and Mercy
Seb	Sword companion to Amos and Mercy

Lords of the Rivers Province

Twyford	Pronounced Ty-Ford. Ducal Lord of the Rivers province

Richard Bouchemeax	Pronounced Bow-She-mow. Known as the Black Crow. Lord of Thorsten.
Jacob Bouchemeax	Oldest son of Richard
William Bouchemeax	Lord of Redford – brother of Richard
Robert Bouchemeax	William's 1st son
Bruce Bouchemeax	William's 2nd son
Sandford Bouchemeax	William's 3rd son

Men and Women of the Rivers

Sir Anders Forstandt	Captain in the Black Crows guard.
Kronke	Sergeant in Forstandt's company
Pieterzon/Deadeye	guard in Forstandt's company
Mable	Sandford's man at arms
Sir John Stenson	Captain of Jacob Bouchemeax personal guard.
Greigon	Captain on the Riversgate, Thorsten
Mortimer	Sergeant on the Riversgate, Thorsten
Mathew Lebraun	Guard on Riversgate, Thorsten.
Geert Vanknell	Guard on Riversgate, Thorsten.
Matteus Lofthaus	Captain of the Black Crow's guard.
Lorcus Samuels	Knight-Captain south wall command Thorsten
Byron Mueller	Militia commander, Thorsten
Lutico Ben Naris	Mage of the third order, master of the arts magical, emissary for the council of mages and councillor to Lord Richard Bouchemeax
Junip	Mage apprentice to Lutico.
Luke Goodwill	Bard travelling the Rivers
Leticia Goodwill (Lett)	Luke's daughter and apprentice.
Victor 'Vic' Stenhause	Owner of the Broken Axe Tavern
Vivian 'Viv' Stenhause	Owner of the Broken Axe Tavern
Morten Stenhause	Son of Vic and Viv
Annabelle	Young girl from Thorsten.

Red Priest's – Church of Kildare

Henrik Zoller	Priest, former protégé to Cardinal Tortuga.
Maxim Tortuga	Cardinal and head of the Red Priests in the Rivers Province.
Mortim	Priest in charge of Thorsten chapter

Notable Red Cloak's – Church of Kildare

Tuko	Pronounced Two-kow
Holt	

Ilfanum

Da'Mari	Pronounced Da- Ma-re. A Nu'Rakauma – a world tree bordering the Rivers to the west.[1]
Eladrohim	Pronounced El-Ad-Ro-Him. A Nu'Rakauma – a world tree to the west of the kingdom.
Elora	Pronounced El-Ora. Visok and K'raal[1]
M'rika	Pronounced Ma-Rik-ah. Visok and K'raal
D'ukastille	Pronounced Du-car-stil. Visok and K'raal. Warden of the Rohelinewaald
Ruith	Pronounced Roo-ith. Healer
R'ell	Pronounced Ray-ell
Bezal	Pronounced Bez-al. R'ells bonded Crow

Urak

Bartuk	Pronounced Bar-Tuck. Clan White Hand – Scout
Gromma	Pronounced Grow-ma. Called the Gutsplitter. Kin to Mar-Dur – warrior of the White Hand.
No-nose	Clan White Hand – Scout
Mar-Dur	Pronounced Mar-duur. Clan Chief of the White Hand
Rimtaug	Pronounced Rim-Taag. Raid chief for the White Hand
Krol	Clan Chief of the Red Skull
Tar-Tukh	Pronounced Tar-Tuck. Hurak-Hin (bodyguard) to Krol Clan chief.
Nartak	Pronounced Nar-Tack. Hurak-Hin (bodyguard) to Krol Clan chief.
Grimpok	War Chief in the White Hand.
Muw-Tukh	Pronounced Mow-Tuck. Hurak-Hin (bodyguard) to Mar-Dur Clan Chief.
Baq-Dur	Bortaug tribe chief. White Hand Clan.

[1] See Ilf Dictionary that follows for pronunciation guide and meaning.

Ilf dictionary

Ilf	Means child/children
Ilfanum	Means child of
Nu'Rakauma	Pronounced Nu-racka-uma means in literal terms giant tree mother
K'raal	A type of Lord/Lady
Visok	the term for a High Ilf
Anum	Means several things of/from
Umphathi	Means warden
Roheline	East/eastern
Ka'harthi	Means, gatherer's, gardeners.
Fassarunewadaick	The name for the Fossa River near the Torns mountains.
Fassa	Means fast/quick
Rune	Means running/flowing/moving
Wada	Means water
Ick	Means ice/cold/frozen
Rohelinewaald	Means guardian of the eastern forest
Waald	means forest

Look out for

Shadows Fall

Book Two of the Morhudrim Cycle

Available now on Amazon

Congratulations, you've made it this far. I really hope you enjoyed Rivers Run Red as much I did writing it. If so, please leave a rating and/or review. It would mean a lot and help my books gain visibility so that others may find and enjoy them.

Being an Indie author, I have worked hard to bring a fresh experience to the fantasy genre. Fantasy tropes are common throughout most fantasy books, I guess that is why they are tropes, but I believe I have brought enough imagination to my story to make them feel fresh. A lot is going on that is yet to play out and will be revealed over future books. It is my hope that you will join me on this journey.

Shadows Fall, Book Two of the Morhudrim Cycle is out now. Book Three, Darkness Resides is currently being written.

If you want updates on book three and beyond, or to give me honest feedback and suggestions, or want to be added to my mailing list, then please check out my website https://adgreenauthor.com/ it is packed with information on my books, maps, lore and you can sign up for newsletters with promotions, free books, reviews and a little witty banter (no spam – I promise).

You can also find me on:
Facebook @adgreentheauthor
Twitter @adgreenauthor

Thanks for reading.

A D Green

Printed in Great Britain
by Amazon